MAY   2021

CRY DARKNESS

Also by Hilary Bonner

The David Vogel mysteries

DEADLY DANCE *
WHEEL OF FIRE *
DREAMS OF FEAR *

Other titles

THE CRUELLEST GAME
FRIENDS TO DIE FOR
DEATH COMES FIRST

* *available from Severn House*

CRY DARKNESS

Hilary Bonner

severn House

This first world edition published 2020
in Great Britain and 2021 in the USA by
SEVERN HOUSE PUBLISHERS LTD of
Eardley House, 4 Uxbridge Street, London W8 7SY.
Trade paperback edition first published
in Great Britain and the USA 2021 by
SEVERN HOUSE PUBLISHERS LTD.

British Library Cataloguing in Publication Data
A CIP catalogue record for this title is available from the British Library.

ISBN-13: 978-0-7278-9051-1 (cased)
ISBN-13: 978-1-78029-748-4 (trade paper)
ISBN-13: 978-1-4483-0486-8 (e-book)

This is a work of fiction. Names, characters, places and incidents are
either the product of the author's imagination or are used fictitiously.
Except where actual historical events and characters are being described
for the storyline of this novel, all situations in this publication are
fictitious and any resemblance to actual persons, living or dead, business
establishments, events or locales is purely coincidental.

All Severn House titles are printed on acid-free paper.

Severn House Publishers support the Forest Stewardship Council™ [FSC™],
the leading international forest certification organisation.
All our titles that are printed on FSC certified paper carry the FSC logo.

Typeset by Palimpsest Book Production Ltd.,
Falkirk, Stirlingshire, Scotland.
Printed and bound in Great Britain by
TJ Books Limited, Padstow, Cornwall.

For Maggie Forwood
Fifty years of friendship and still counting . . .

All the powers of the universe are already ours. It is we who put our hands before our eyes and cry that it is dark.

Swami Vivekananda

THE FACTS

An American paraplegic, Matthew Nagle, known as the first real bionic man, was fitted at Rhode Island Hospital in 2004 with an electrode implant designed to assist him to channel and focus his thoughts in order to send out brainwaves powerful enough to operate mechanical devices. He successfully learned how to use a computer, operate a TV, and draw on screen.

In 2013, a quadriplegic American woman, fitted with a brain implant developed by a US government research agency, flew an F-35 fighter-jet simulator using only her thoughts.

Clinical trials, bankrolled lavishly by governments convinced that the brain is the next battlefield, look set to continue indefinitely. In 2013 the US launched its Brain Initiative, with an estimated budget of 4.5 million dollars, spread over a twelve-year period, and in the same year the European Union announced that it planned to devote 1.34 million dollars (almost 1.25 million euros) to a ten-year Human Brain project.

Meanwhile, over the last thirty years laboratory-controlled experiments conducted throughout the world, known collectively as the Global Consciousness Project, and linked to a database at America's prestigious Princeton University, have indicated repeatedly that it is possible for the human mind to predict and therefore potentially influence outside events, both mechanical and physical.

The scientists running these experiments claim that this involves appearing to predict events of global significance like 9/11, the massive Boxing Day tsunami of 2004, and the death of Princess Diana.

They believe that if the power of consciousness could be channelled and controlled the human race would have within its grasp a force of infinite magnitude quite beyond present comprehension.

PROLOGUE

They waited until the moon had passed behind a cloud. Then, cloaked by darkness, they made their approach, running hard across the lawn until they reached the protection of the building itself. Pressing their bodies against its walls, they moved stealthily sideways, almost crab-like, towards their chosen point of entry.

Breaking in was not a problem to them. They were experts in the art. Even the most sophisticated of security systems presented little difficulty. They had the knowledge, they had the equipment, and they had already studied the target.

It took only a few minutes to gain entry to the building, and a couple of minutes more to reach the designated room within.

Once there, the younger man removed the black rucksack he was carrying on his back and passed it to his older companion, who took from it what appeared to be a quite unremarkable piece of office equipment. A cardboard box file, mottled grey in colour.

The older man flipped up the lid of the box file, and focused the narrow beam of his pencil torch on its contents. Inside lay a cylindrical object, apparently constructed primarily of metal, but more innocent looking and perhaps smaller than might be expected of a weapon with a quite terrifying capacity for destruction. It was a pipe bomb, an explosive device used primarily by terrorist organizations worldwide, all the components of which are legal and easily obtained. On detonation a shock wave passing through the device causes every particle to break down simultaneously, and a major explosion is therefore completed in just a few millionths of a second.

The man studied the pipe bomb for a moment before flicking down a switch at one end of it, thus completing its lethal circuit.

He then carefully closed the lid of the box file, and placed his torch on a convenient shelf so that its beam focused on a nearby filing cabinet, the bottom drawer of which had already been opened by his younger colleague, who had also removed most of the contents of the drawer.

Even more carefully, he carried the grey box file across the room, using both hands, and lowered it into the cabinet drawer, pushing it to the very back. Then he replaced the various other files and papers, which had previously been removed, and shut the drawer. Slowly and silently.

It was unlikely that anyone would even notice the file before the explosive device it contained had fulfilled its dreadful purpose, activated at exactly the optimum time by mobile telephone. But if they did, the chances were that the grey file, so ordinary, and so like several others used in the filing system into which it had been integrated, would not give any particular cause for alarm.

The two men exchanged a fleeting smile of satisfaction at a job well done before making their way, quickly and quietly, out of the building, using the same route by which they had entered. They took pride in completing any task that they undertook with total efficiency.

And as they slipped outside, waiting again, on a night of changeable weather conditions, for the moon to pass behind a cloud, before heading for the cover of the tall trees conveniently grouped at the far side of the lawn, neither of the men gave a thought to the havoc they were about to wreak.

The horror of death by explosion, or indeed almost any other means, was nothing new nor even mildly disturbing to them. They had no qualms at all about deliberately setting out to kill and destroy.

The device they had planted was capable of reducing most of the building in which they had left it to a pile of rubble, and blowing to pieces anyone who might be inside at the time. This did not concern them one jot.

They considered themselves to be professionals. They believed that their cause was the only right and proper one, and that any means, however foul, would be ultimately justified by the end that they sought.

PART ONE

PART ONE

ONE

The phone call that would change everything came out of the blue one Monday afternoon, as Dr Sandy Jones was sitting at her desk feeling dangerously pleased with life.

Sandy Jones was a TV boffin, every bit as much a media figure as an academic. Thanks to a succession of series for the BBC presenting science to the people in what was generally regarded as a remarkably accessible way, she had, without really intending to, become something of a celebrity.

She was Professor of Astrophysics at Devon's Exeter University, but it was her media success which had brought her a degree of material wealth and a certain standing in society.

She'd just enjoyed rather a good lunch, a treat she rarely indulged in, but earlier that day she'd received a letter offering her the chancellorship of Oxford University, her old alma mater. And she still couldn't quite believe it.

Sandy Jones had been brought up in a sink housing estate on the outskirts of Birmingham, and attended a far from adequate inner-city comprehensive, which nonetheless had successfully fast-tracked her through her early education.

By the time she was seventeen, brilliant and precocious, she had a string of GCSEs to her name and had won her Oxford place. At barely twenty she achieved a double first in physics and found herself – almost, it had felt, without being actively involved in the process – studying for her MSc and then her doctorate at Princeton, USA, having gained a much-coveted post-graduate research position.

She was internationally regarded as a leading force in her chosen area of expertise, and in the UK had become as famous outside the scientific establishment as she was acclaimed within.

The vast majority of her contemporaries at the top of their fields in British academia still came from highly privileged backgrounds.

Jones did not. She fingered the battered gold Longine watch

which had been her father's most treasured possession. He had acquired it in Berlin during the last days of World War Two. It was about the only thing of any value Jack Jones ever owned, and when he died, far too early at fifty-three, the watch passed to his only child. Sandy Jones had been eight, a bright little girl who spent the rest of her childhood watching her mother struggle horribly to provide even the barest essentials of life.

The Longine was a big watch for a woman of slim build and slightly less than average height but Jones didn't care. She wore it always.

Now she was going to become the Chancellor of Oxford, having been elected by the university's Convocation from an imposing list of nominees.

Jones glanced out of the window of her office in the heart of the Exeter campus. It was a green and leafy academic oasis, the kind of environment which, in her early life, she could only have dreamed of.

She picked up the Oxford letter lying open in front of her on her desk and, with some reluctance, folded it in its envelope and popped it into a drawer.

It was at that moment that the phone rang. Jones reached out with one hand and almost absent-mindedly lifted the receiver to her ear.

'Yes,' she said, rather more curtly than she'd intended, her thoughts still far away.

'Don't you "yes" me, you arrogant English upstart,' responded a voice she instantly recognized. It had been a long time. That made no difference. For a start nobody else in the world would speak to her like that.

'Connie, how the devil are you?'

Jones felt her face split into a grin as she spoke.

Constance Pike, psychologist, philosopher, and innovator, a woman who, when Jones had met her at Princeton, had displayed an intent rather more extreme than Jones's comparatively modest aim of seeking to better understand the universe. Connie had wanted to turn it upside down, inside out, and totally restructure it, and had never given up trying to do so.

She'd had a profound effect on the young Sandy Jones, and although the path Jones had chosen could not have taken her much further away from Connie, within the confines of science anyway, Jones probably still admired her more than anyone she'd ever met.

'Better than I deserve, I expect. And how are you, Sandy? Still taking charge of the world?'

'I thought that was what you always wanted to do.'

'No damned fear. Just change it a bit, that's all.'

Sandy Jones laughed. Connie always had made her laugh, even when she wasn't trying to be funny.

'And how's the rest of the team? Paul OK?'

'Right enough. He's got a new puppy. Brings it to the lab, as usual. And does it ever stop pissing? Does it hell!'

Jones laughed again.

'Nothing changes then.'

'Nope. The lab stinks worse than ever before.'

'Which is saying something.'

'Sure is.'

'Anyway, you still keeping on trucking out there?'

Jones fell easily into the American vernacular. It was something that she did. One of her communicating tricks was to almost automatically try to speak the same language as anyone she was trying to connect to. It wasn't a trick with Connie though. Just the way things had always been between them.

'Doing our best not to let the bastards get to us, anyway. Do you know they put sprinklers in here last week? Health and safety. Fire regulations, they say. Bullshit! More than forty years since Paul started it all, and suddenly the dorks can't leave us alone.'

'Did you think they'd forgotten you?'

'Only when it suits 'em. There's a sprinkler right above my computer, would you believe. Don't dare even light up a cig. It goes off, I'm sunk.'

'Literally.'

'Yeah, literally.'

They both chuckled. Smoking had already been banned inside most of the university buildings even when Jones had been at Princeton, but Connie, Paul, and their team had been then, and obviously remained, a law unto themselves.

There was a silence. Jones waited for Connie to speak again. After all, it was she who had called her, and it had been a long time since the days when they'd made regular phone calls across the

Atlantic to each other just for a chat. It must have been the best part of a year since they'd been in contact at all, and that had been just an email exchange. She suspected Connie must have a specific reason for calling her now.

She heard Connie cough, clear her throat.

'You all right?'

'Right as I'll ever be.'

There was another silence. Jones surrendered.

'Is the great pleasure of this phone call down to anything in particular?' she asked, keeping her voice light.

'Oh, I don't know. The last time we were in touch you said you'd be coming to see us. I'm still waiting, you jerk.'

'Yeah, I know. I was going to take the train over when I was in New York giving the Triple A last year.'

Jones paused, remembering. It had been a great honour to be asked to give the keynote address to the American Academy for the Advancement of Science, and she had to admit that she had made the most of every moment of it.

'I just didn't get time in the end,' she finished lamely.

'Any chance in the near future?'

'Well, not for a bit. I'm kind of busy right now.'

That much was true enough. The BBC now liked her to produce a major series annually, and they'd rushed her current one, *The Big Bang and You*, onto the screen with such haste that there was still footage to be shot for the final episode. She was also soon to begin filming a major sequel, *After the Big Bang*.

In addition she always took pains not to neglect her duties at Exeter, which was why she frequently filmed at weekends.

And later that month she was to attend a dinner at Oxford, being given in her honour, prior to the ceremony inaugurating her as chancellor early the following year.

'I'm going to be up to my eyes for the next few months,' she continued.

'Oh, I see.'

She had expected an instant tirade from Connie, whom she knew had remained every bit as idealistic as she'd been twenty years earlier, in spite of now being over sixty, Jones reckoned. While her contemporaries strove for glory, or at least for tangible reward for their efforts, Connie seemed to stay exactly the same. She was dedicated,

evangelical about her work, and of course poor. She was also inclined
to be brutally scathing of those who had chosen other more materi-
ally rewarding paths, and could be particularly cutting in her dealings
with Jones, who didn't mind because she was well aware that was
how Connie treated those she was especially fond of. So when Connie
didn't react in the expected way, Jones was puzzled.

'You sure you're OK, Connie?'

Another pause, followed by an indirect response.

'There was something I wanted to talk to you about, that's all.'

Connie sounded flat. And there was an inflection in her voice
that Jones couldn't make out. But she didn't have the time to worry
about it.

'Well, go on then, shoot.'

She checked her watch. Fond as she was of Connie Pike she
really was going to have to end this conversation. She'd actually
hoped to make a couple of important telephone calls before leaving
her office to attend a crucial faculty meeting in the administration
block. But time was running out. She had little more than ten minutes
to get to the other side of the campus if she didn't want to be late.
And Sandy Jones was never late.

'It's not that easy . . .' Connie's voice tailed off.

'What?'

'. . . You'll probably just think I've really gone mad,' Connie
continued. 'I'm not even sure I should be talking on the phone.'

Jones was in a big hurry now, and barely took in the meaning
that might lie behind her words.

'Spit it out, Connie, I really do have to go.'

'I'm sorry, I don't know quite where to begin . . .'

There was another pause. Would she never get on with it?

'Well, you know what it's like here. We're not exactly flavour of
the month at RECAP.'

'No. But that's nothing new, is it?'

RECAP – REsearch into Consciousness At Princeton, Connie
Pike's life's work – was a project which had always hovered on
the questionable fringes of established science.

'Of course not,' Connie agreed. 'It's just that, well, things have
happened. You're in a hurry. I won't go into detail. But things
have happened that have made Paul and I think that people in high
places want to close us down altogether.'

Jones wasn't surprised. In fact it had always been something of a mystery to her that RECAP had survived as long as it had in its own wonderful crazy backwater at the famous Ivy League university.

'I'd be very sorry about that,' she responded truthfully enough.

'Well, it's a lengthy old story, and maybe I don't really know what I'm talking about . . . but I just thought you might be able to help. You were always the one who could do what others couldn't . . .'

Her voice tailed off. Jones would indeed be deeply sorry to see the end of RECAP, but Connie Pike was taking her into territory she had no wish to re-enter. Nor was she keen on using whatever influence she might have to help save RECAP. The project wasn't something that any ambitious academic would wish to be too closely associated with. And Sandy Jones had always been rather more ambitious than she liked to admit.

'That was many years ago, Connie,' she said.

'Well I thought maybe you could do something . . . have a word . . .'

'A word where, exactly?'

'Well I don't know, Sandy, but I was hoping you might.'

'I can't just go around sticking my nose into areas that no longer concern me, Connie, not even for you.'

She mentally kicked herself. She hadn't meant that to come out the way it did, but the damage was already done.

'I'm sorry, Sandy,' Connie responded at once, her voice unusually small. 'I know you're busy, this is obviously a bad moment.'

Connie Pike was tough, but not always as tough as she talked. Jones knew she'd hurt her feelings, and she did adore the bloody woman after all.

'Look, why don't I call you back.'

'I'd appreciate that, Sandy.'

Connie sounded curiously formal. Quite unlike herself. Jones felt a small pang of guilt, sparked by a half-forgotten legacy of long ago.

But all she said was: 'OK. Fine. I really do have to go now, though. But I'll call you, tomorrow at the latest.'

'Thanks, Sandy.'

Connie hung up at once. No banter. No more insults. Jones

reflected that she hadn't even said goodbye properly. There was something wrong, something definitely wrong. Damn. She'd call Connie back tomorrow, for sure. Just as soon as America was awake.

TWO

F our days later Jones was at her home just outside the little East Devon seaside town of Sidmouth. Northdown House had been built in the 1920s on a site chosen for its spectacular views over the Jurassic coast and out to sea.

This was the place where she had brought up her twin sons, now twenty-year-old students, largely on her own. She was really on her own nowadays, except when either of the boys descended for a weekend, and the house was far too big for her. However, she loved it, had never quite been able to get over the fact that it was hers, and had as yet proved unable to make the intelligent decision to downsize.

It was early evening. She was sitting at her kitchen table with a sandwich and a glass of wine, having just returned from a day in London at the BBC. Through the rest of the week her university duties had consumed virtually every waking moment. She remembered suddenly that she hadn't returned Connie Pike's call, and cursed her tardiness. She would do it straight away. As soon as she'd finished her sandwich.

She'd switched on the TV as a matter of habit. It was tuned to Sky News, as usual. Jones was a news junkie. But the volume was low, and her mind was elsewhere. Suddenly though, something the newsreader was saying both alerted and alarmed her. It couldn't be, could it? She turned up the volume.

'. . . police are still unclear of the cause of the explosion at Princeton. It is hoped that the laboratory at the heart of the blast will provide enough forensic evidence to ascertain exactly what occurred. Early reports suggest that the university may have been targeted by an unknown terrorist group. New Jersey police refuse to confirm whether or not they suspect foul play, but the entire area is now a designated crime scene. The explosion occurred just after eight thirty this morning, and the two scientists known to be already working in the RECAP laboratory at the time of the explosion, Professor Paul Ruders, and project manager Constance Pike, are missing, presumed dead.'

Jones felt a numbness spread through her body. She stared at the TV screen, willing it to tell her more, or best of all, tell her the item was just one big mistake.

There was a roaring and a screaming inside her head. A part of her that she valued perhaps more than anything else, a part of her half-forgotten, totally neglected, and probably more important and more significant than anything else in her life, except her sons, had been suddenly ripped apart.

Paul and Connie were dead. It couldn't be true. And yet it was. She switched to CNN, which carried an almost identical report. She checked online, and quickly found the same item. Just a few paragraphs, so far. Those special people, their hopes and dreams, their work, their extraordinary special work, to all intents and purposes destroyed, and it only merited a few paragraphs.

Jones felt a stab of pain in her heart.

Connie's phone call had been a cry for help. Jones had known that at the time, of course, which only made matters worse. There remained a bond between them, between all of them, really, who had been involved with RECAP during those heady pioneering days towards the end of the previous century.

Connie had been trying to tell Sandy something, something that had been worrying her, something about the project. And Jones hadn't even bothered to call back. Now it was too late. Connie was dead. Jones vowed that she would at least try to find out what it was that had clearly been so important to Connie Pike. She had to. For Connie. For Paul. For all of them.

Her first call was to Thomas Jessop, the Dean of Princeton University. Thomas was the second in his family to achieve the elevated post. As a leading academic of international renown Jones was in touch with Jessop, as she was with a number of university chiefs worldwide. In addition she remembered Thomas as a post-graduate student at Princeton, when his late father Bernard had been dean. It had all seemed a little cosy to Jones when Thomas was appointed to the top job, but now she was rather glad of the link.

She didn't have his mobile number, so dialled his direct line at the university, which switched immediately to message service. She left a brief message but did not expect a reply, not in the near future at any rate, even though it was early afternoon in Princeton on a working day. She guessed that the entire university would have been cleared. After all, she'd already learned from the news bulletin that at least part of the campus was now a designated crime scene.

She then tried the university switchboard number, just in case. It rang and rang. Again no surprise.

Finally she sent Thomas Jessop an email, then went into the Princeton website in order to call up and print out the staff list which she knew included email addresses as well as, in most cases, direct line phone numbers. She copied a message, asking for information about the blast, to everyone on the list.

Not only were they all likely to recognize her name, but Americans, Jones knew, were inclined to be permanently logged in to their email and usually replied swiftly. Indeed she received two messages almost by return, but neither sender seemed able to add anything to what she had already learned on TV and online.

She cursed herself for knowing so little about Connie and Paul's personal lives. Everything to do with them had always seemed to revolve around RECAP. Indeed Jones had never been aware of Connie having any personal life at all. She had lived alone ever since Jones had first met her, as far as she knew. Paul, on the other hand, had been married for many years, and his wife, a frequent visitor to the lab during Jones's days at Princeton, had been almost one of the team. But Jones knew that Gilda Ruders had died a couple of years previously after a short illness, and Connie's recent remarks about Paul, during the brief phone conversation she had so thoughtlessly curtailed, appeared to indicate that he, too, had lived alone.

In spite of that, bizarrely perhaps, she repeatedly called both Connie Pike and Paul Ruders' home numbers.

The sound of Connie's voice on her answer service cut like a knife.

'It's Connie. Talk to me.'

Talk to me. That is what she had wanted Jones to do four days earlier. If only Jones had done so.

The first time she phoned she left a message.

'Anyone who picks this up, will you please call me. I'm an old friend of Connie and Paul's. I'm devastated by the terrible news and just want to find out exactly what happened at RECAP, and to see if there's anything I can do to help.'

As if, she thought to herself. She kept the TV on, channel-hopping the news stations. There was a succession of further reports. Jones learned that the cause of the blast remained uncertain. One report suggested that the explosion may have been accidental and caused by a gas leak. But terrorist action, unsurprisingly in the modern climate, remained the most frequently mentioned possibility.

She also learned that there had been other casualties. A research scientist working in the biology laboratory on the floor above RECAP was believed to have been killed and two students injured, one seriously. Both CNN and Sky News explained that the list of casualties would have been much greater had the explosion not occurred early in the morning, before most staff and students had arrived in the building devoted to scientific research.

Jones leaned back in her chair and struggled to think clearly. Was it likely that Princeton had been attacked by terrorists? And, if so, could RECAP really have been the target? It was well known that Connie and Paul were early starters, who treated their lab more like a second home than a workplace. Anyone wishing to destroy both them and virtually all trace of their project, without causing a significant number of other deaths, might well have chosen to arrange an early morning explosion. Indeed, it was quite probably bad luck that anyone else had been hurt at that hour, let alone killed. And Connie had certainly been ill at ease. Perhaps more than that. Had she been afraid? Jones wasn't sure.

Her mind was racing. She called Princeton police. On the umpteenth attempt she managed to get through to an officer who gave her the number of a helpline that had been set up for concerned relatives and friends. Again she had to redial the number several times before getting through. And, in spite of allegedly operating a help line, the young woman who eventually responded seemed unwilling at first to give any help at all.

'I am afraid there's a security clampdown on all information at the moment, ma'am, until we get a clearer picture of what has happened,' she said.

'Look, I'm Connie Pike's cousin, from the Irish branch of the family,' Jones lied. 'The family over here are quite devastated, of course, and I'm just trying to find out exactly what happened.'

The woman's attitude to her changed very slightly.

'I'm sorry for the situation you and your family find yourselves in, ma'am,' she responded. 'But I'm afraid there's really very little more information we can give you than has already been released to the media. Over the phone anyway . . .'

'Well, where are Connie and Paul? Presumably there is no doubt that they are dead. Have their bodies been removed from the scene yet?'

As she spoke Jones realized what stupid questions those were. More than likely, Connie and Paul would have been blown to bits.

She winced. That was not a prospect she wished to dwell on.

There was a brief pause before the young woman spoke again.

'Nothing at all has been removed from the scene yet,' she eventually replied diplomatically. 'The site of the explosion is still sealed off as part of the investigations by the various authorities involved. The entire campus has been evacuated and resident staff and students temporarily accommodated well away from the area, primarily at the Jadwin Gymnasium. There really is no more I can tell you, ma'am.'

Jones's head hurt. She had hunched herself so tensely over her phone and her computer that the muscles of her neck and shoulders seemed to have seized up.

She needed to take a break. She made coffee, with which she washed down a couple of paracetamol, swallowing quickly before the heat of the liquid began to melt the pills.

She glanced up at the clock on the kitchen wall. She couldn't believe how the time had raced by. It was now almost one a.m. Eight o'clock the previous evening in New York and Princeton.

She couldn't rest, and she certainly couldn't sleep. She had to do something. The weekend lay ahead, and Jones had few commitments over the early part of the subsequent week, apart from routine lectures which could be delayed.

She logged onto the British Airways website and booked herself on the lunchtime flight from Heathrow to JFK. Her visit need only

be a fleeting one, she told herself. She would return in good time
for both her Oxford dinner and her next filming commitment the
following weekend.

In any case it was as if forces from another, until now, half-
forgotten time were driving her to do it. As if she had no choice.

She left home soon after seven in the morning, driving herself
northwards along the M5 and then east on the M4 to the UK's
premier airport, where she'd booked valet parking.

Her sporty Lexus SUV was a fine motor car, and it rarely failed
to give her pleasure to drive it. But not on this occasion.

She'd had far too little sleep, but she didn't feel tired, just spaced
out, as if she were not quite conscious of, or certainly not in total
control of, what was happening. As if she had been somehow taken
over by her own past.

On the aircraft Jones found her thoughts drifting back to that
special time in her life when she was at Princeton, and to her first
meeting with the two extraordinary academics whose lives had been
so brutally ended.

She remembered her first visit to the RECAP laboratory as if it
were yesterday. She could see it clearly in her mind's eyes. And
she doubted that the place had changed much until its terrible
destruction.

REsearch into Consciousness At Princeton. A wonderful, crazy,
innovative venture which had never been more than tolerated by
the powers that be. A scientific study of the power of the mind.
The forgotten art, Connie had always called it. A series of laboratory-controlled experiments aimed at proving once and for all, in
accordance with the accepted rules of mathematics and physics,
whether or not the human mind really could exert control over
matter. Whether the process of thought, conscious or even uncon-
scious, could control the performance of machines.

And beyond that, of course, an examination of mankind's greatest
secret, the meaning of consciousness.

It had begun in the 1970s, when a small group of trailblazers
had launched themselves on what they had believed to be the ultimate scientific journey: an ongoing exploration of the human mind,
conducted under strict laboratory conditions, and hopefully leading
towards not only a fuller knowledge of the mind's powers but also,

maybe one day, to at least some level of understanding of the final mystery. What is consciousness? And what, if we surrender to it, is consciousness capable of?

It had always been something of a dream. But Sandy Jones, the girl from the wrong side of town, also knew that dreams could come true. And, rather to her surprise, she had become enthralled by RECAP, and those who had made it their life's work.

PART TWO

The most beautiful experience we can have is the mysterious. It is the fundamental emotion which stands at the cradle of true art and true science. She to whom this emotion is a stranger, who can no longer wonder and stand rapt in awe, is as good as dead.

Albert Einstein

THREE

J ones had not even heard of RECAP when she arrived at Princeton in 1994. But her, at first reluctant, association with the charismatic underworld of the project and its people began by accident just a few weeks later.

Princeton itself had been a culture shock. And Jones was still getting used to the air of unreality about the place, from its perfectly manicured lawns and immaculately sited sculptures to its curiously out of place architecture.

Mock Tudor mansions dominated the campus, most serving as dining halls for students. To Jones, accustomed as she had quickly become to the famous dreamy spires of Oxford, arguably the grandest old university in existence, it all looked totally false. The buildings didn't really belong. Jones thought they were like a cross between the more pretentious examples of English suburbia and the set of *Stepford Wives*. Everything about the place created an atmosphere of some kind of alternative world. Students and staff wafted about in a bubble of their own superiority, a state not uncommon in great universities internationally. But at Princeton this seemed to be taken to extremes, without a hint, of course, of what Jones considered to be the saving grace of good old British cynicism and self-deprecation. Princeton and its people, she learned, took themselves and their reproduction architecture very seriously indeed.

When Jones had excitedly told her favourite Oxford lecturer that she had landed a place to study for her doctorate in America, at the famous Ivy League university, the man, a somewhat grizzly and very English don of the old school, replied sagely, 'America? Princeton isn't in America.' Jones soon learned exactly what the lecturer had meant. Moreover, she quickly concluded that not only was Princeton most certainly not in America, it probably wasn't even on planet Earth. But that didn't concern Sandy Jones at all.

Whatever she felt about the curious unreality of Princeton, Jones knew she had been given a wonderful opportunity to complete her studies there. Princeton was at the cutting edge of her area of science.

And it was where probably the greatest physicist of all, Albert Einstein, had sought his ultimate refuge from Nazi Germany and completed so many of his great works.

However, to begin with, she thought she was never going to fit into the place. She was a blue stocking with few social graces. The air of casual sophistication she acquired later in life was still a long way off. She hadn't known how to dress then, and in any case had yet to acquire any interest in clothes. And she hadn't a clue about make-up. She reckoned, in those days, that she was skinny rather than slim. Her breasts had barely developed since adolescence, which embarrassed her – particularly after the doctor who carried out her Princeton medical told her she was the nearest thing he'd ever seen to a hermaphrodite. However she had good skin, intelligent hazel eyes, and unusually glossy black hair, shaped into a sharp bob. She did know she was not entirely unattractive, and there had been one boyfriend – or very nearly – at Oxford, who had relieved her of the burden of her virginity. But after three rather fraught months he ended it, telling her that he couldn't cope with being treated as a biological experiment. And Sandy Jones was honest enough to accept that he'd probably assessed her attitude to sex rather accurately.

She became something of a loner at Oxford, and felt destined to become even more of one at Princeton. She was, in fact, painfully lonely – and therefore receptive to, and even grateful for, the attentions of fellow student Ed MacEntee.

Ed was a brilliant mathematician, a child prodigy, but, not unlike Sandy, something of a lost soul away from his own rarefied world. He was, however, clearly smitten with Sandy Jones from the moment they met.

They became friends, at first no more than that, very quickly studying together in the evenings at the Firestone Library, and often sharing a table at the dining club at mealtimes. They walked around campus together. They pooled their resources to occasionally visit the town's hippest bar – not that Jones considered anything Princeton, town or university, could offer to be remotely hip really. They went swimming together in the campus pools, and at weekends they would sometimes go to the movies, or a nearby bowling alley.

Ed was tall, thin, and more than presentable, even though he was already losing his wispy blonde hair. He was also the kindest and gentlest of men. Best of all, because of him, she was no longer lonely.

When the friendship ultimately moved on, and they became lovers, Sandy Jones was glad, if only because this surely made her like everybody else. The earth most certainly did not move for her. Ed, in the second year of his BSc was a year or so younger than Jones, and possibly even less experienced. But the sex was pleasant enough, and she at least tried not to give the impression that she was treating it as a scientific experiment.

Perhaps surprisingly for a mathematician, Ed, it turned out, was heavily into RECAP. He frequently talked to her about the project, but most of the time she didn't even listen properly. After all, he was inclined to tell the same thing over and over again.

One warm summer's evening when they were sitting in the shade of Nixon's Nose – the irreverent name given by the students to Princeton's massive Henry Moore sculpture which from a certain angle is considered to resemble the profile of the disgraced former president – Ed was particularly persistent.

'I mean, people think it's weird, but it's not,' he told her. 'Connie says it's all about studying powers of the human mind which have always been there. We've lost the use of them, that's all, just like you'd lose the use of your legs or arms if you didn't exercise them. That's partly why Paul came up with the name, RECAP, because at least part of the purpose of the project is to look way back in time over the way the mind has developed and changed, in order to move forwards . . .'

Jones nodded sagely. *Connie this . . . Paul that.* She really wasn't that interested.

'The thing is nobody can explain why it happens, but laboratory condition experiments across the world are proving that it does happen.'

'Uh huh,' Jones responded. *Why what happens?* She couldn't even be bothered to ask. In any case he had probably told her already. Repeatedly. She just hadn't taken any of it in properly. She had her own work to think about.

'You know, you should come along and meet Connie and Paul, see what they're doing first hand,' Ed continued.

'Of course I should, I'd love to,' Jones replied resignedly. She wasn't keen, but she'd known this was going to happen sooner or

later. And she'd grown fond of Ed. She valued their easy relationship. She didn't want to offend him.

Ed duly arranged a visit a couple of days later. He led her to the
Science Research Building and through a network of corridors before
pausing outside a stained wooden door. 'Room 38' was scribbled
in faded biro on a piece of yellowing white card held in place by
a rusted drawing pin. It was RECAP's only announcement of itself.

'This is it,' he said, his voice a mix of awe and pride.

'Great,' she said. 'Shall we go in?'

What she had meant, of course, was, shall we get it over with.

They were greeted by a tall angular woman with a mane of wild
red hair, standing in the centre of the most extraordinary laboratory
Jones had ever seen.

Several smaller rooms, doors all wide open, led off one central
one in which place of honour was given to a low squashy sofa
housing a host of cuddly toy animals. A young man sat in the
middle, almost submerged in a heap of fluffy rabbits and bears.
Green plastic frogs were balanced on the back and arms and
gathered in occasional piles on a desk in the corner and elsewhere
throughout the room. There were other toys too, and assorted
mobiles dangled from the ceiling.

The young man on the sofa broke off briefly from staring at a
giant pinball machine on the wall opposite him, and waved cheerily.

Clutter was everywhere. The walls were covered in the kind of
plastic wood cladding that at the time was a favourite of mass-market
DIY stores worldwide, and further adorned with an extraordinary
selection of pictures and slogans.

Jones realized she had stopped dead in the middle of the doorway.
Whatever she'd expected it wasn't this.

'Come on guys, don't be shy.'

The red-haired woman beckoned them forwards. Jones guessed
she was probably in her late thirties or early forties. Her smile
transformed a long, narrow, and otherwise quite plain face. It radi-
ated warmth, caused her eyes to sparkle with life and mischief, and
instantly made her look not only years younger than she probably
was, but almost beautiful. She had a great smile. She had great eyes
too. They were a vivid green and perfectly oval.

Yet Jones quickly realized that this was that rare human being who genuinely had no personal vanity. Her face showed no trace of even a dash of make-up, and her clothes were truly awful. Indeed, by comparison, she made Jones, in her habitual jeans and nondescript shirt, look rather well turned out. The woman was wearing a baggy tunic top in a particularly startling shade of orange, and ill-fitting murky grey trousers that might or might not have begun their life black.

A button badge pinned to her T-shirt proclaimed: 'Subvert the dominant paradigm'.

Jones smiled in spite of herself. She couldn't imagine ever being any kind of rebel. She was a thoroughly logical, extremely ordered, and ambitious young woman blessed with a brain like a bacon slicer. But all she wanted to do was fit in to the academic world, not radically challenge it.

None the less she appreciated the message on the badge, maybe even envied slightly the spirit that lay behind it. And as an analytical scientist she understood the message absolutely.

Subvert the dominant paradigm. Subvert meant change, turn upside down, forcefully. Dominant paradigm was the accepted pattern. It was a call to rip aside parameters. And it was, of course, what scientists were supposed to do.

Jones stepped forwards. As she did so, she felt her right foot slip and very nearly lost her balance entirely. Grabbing the door jamb for support she only narrowly avoided falling to the ground. Looking down she saw that she had stepped directly onto one of several pieces of newspaper spread across the tiled floor of the lab.

The piece of paper was still beneath her right shoe. She lifted her foot. The paper was stuck to it. She noticed that it was wet and stained a rather suspect yellow colour, with one or two even more suspect brown patches. She shook her foot but only managed to detach the unsavoury looking paper by scraping her shoe against the edge of the door.

'Sorry,' said the woman. 'It's Paul's new puppy. She hasn't learned the ground rules yet.'

'Right.' Jones moved further into the room, this time looking carefully where she put her feet. Ed followed, closing the door behind them.

'I'm Connie Pike,' said the woman. 'You must be Ed's new friend.'

'Yes, Sandy Jones,' said Jones.

And if it wasn't for being Ed's friend, there was absolutely no way she would ever visit a place like this. It was clearly a madhouse. Jones was mainstream. She already knew exactly what she wanted to do with her life. Did these people really believe that mind power could alter the pattern of machines, for God's sake? It was lunacy.

'Good to meet you,' said Connie Pike.

'And you,' responded Jones disingenuously.

Not that I have any desire to meet you, she thought, and not that I have any interest in this project which I reckoned was completely off the wall even before I saw this room, and now I am even more convinced of it.

'We never try to convert anyone here, but if you're prepared to suspend your disbelief I will gladly show you round.'

Jones blinked rapidly. She was momentarily startled by the insight Connie Pike had displayed with this remark. Could the woman read her mind, or what?

Fortunately Ed stepped in whilst she was still searching for the right response.

'But Connie, Sandy doesn't have disbelief,' he said. 'She's fascinated by what you're doing here. I've told her so much about it all. She's already convinced. That's why she wanted to come here and meet you, and Paul, and maybe take part in the experiments.'

'Really?' Connie Pike raised one eyebrow quizzically in Jones's direction.

By then Jones had found her voice again.

'I would absolutely love to look around the lab, Connie,' she said, surreptitiously checking her watch.

FOUR

Sandy Jones would never forget that first day in the RECAP lab. She sceptical, bordering on cynical. Ed so eager. And Connie just being Connie. Getting on with it. Prepared to talk, to share her ideas with anyone who would listen. Jones had assumed that she was used to being dismissed as a nutter, accustomed to mockery.

'This is our pinball machine, giant size, five thousand marbles. And this is Stephen, one of our volunteer operators.'

Connie gestured towards the young man sitting on the sofa, who again waved a hand while keeping his eyes riveted on the machine.

'Simply put, the question is, can Stephen's mind power alter the pinball's accepted function?'

'I see.'

Jones tried to keep her voice non-committal. She was actually wondering why the university even allowed this lab to operate on campus.

Connie led her into one of the smaller rooms off the main reception area.

'That's our REG,' she said, pointing at a box-like structure with dials which could, Jones thought, have come straight out of a very early episode of *Doctor Who*.

REG. Random Event Generator. Jones knew vaguely what it was and what it was supposed to do, and she also knew it was Professor Paul Ruders, director of the RECAP project, who had invented the curious machine.

'It's fascinating seeing something I've heard so much about,' Jones said. The remark was half true, and not entirely down to Ed, but misleading in that the handful of mentions she had spotted in scientific journals had almost all been disparaging.

Connie smiled that small enigmatic smile Jones was to become so familiar with.

'"Any sufficiently advanced technology is indistinguishable from magic," Arthur C. Clarke, Clarke's third law,' she said suddenly.

Jones did a double take. She had suddenly realized that whilst Ed might accept her bogus interest in RECAP at face value, Connie Pike was not the tiniest bit taken in by her. She knew Jones thought the whole thing was hocus-pocus. She damned well knew.

'I'm sorry,' said Jones.

Connie smiled and shrugged. Unfazed. Jones glanced towards Ed who looked puzzled.

'I really would like you to tell me about the REG,' she told Connie. After all there wasn't much point in making the effort to come to the lab and meet the team if she didn't try to at least appear open-minded.

'Really?'

'Really,' said Jones.

Connie Pike stared at her for a few seconds, almost as if considering whether or not she was worth the bother, Jones thought. Then Connie nodded, and placed one hand on the REG, a rectangular box about a foot high and deep and eighteen inches across.

'This machine repeatedly generates at random numbers one and zero,' she told Jones. 'As I'm sure you know very well, the laws of physics dictate that these numbers, over a sufficient period of time, will be produced equally. We, however, are in the process of proving that under certain circumstances random events can alter the results.'

'Events or people's minds?' asked Jones.

Connie smiled.

'Both,' she said. 'Our experiments with meditation seem to prove that the machine's sequence can be affected by the power of the human mind. Yet we cannot explain why. Now, you are a scientist and a sceptic . . .'

Jones opened her mouth to interrupt.

Connie waved a dismissive hand at her.

'No, you are, and that's fine. We like sceptics here. Keeps us on our toes, and it's the only way to spread the word, isn't it? What's the point in preaching to the converted?'

Jones nodded her head in meek acceptance. To her surprise, she was beginning to rather enjoy this visit.

'As I was saying,' Connie continued. 'You are a scientist and a sceptic, so let me give you some data. Some indisputable data, we think. To date, forty-seven different operators have generated two hundred and ninety complete REG experimental series, all under strict laboratory-controlled conditions. That's a total of over two and a half million trials. We make a graph of the results, a cumulative deviation graph.

'Now, we accept that the laws of physics dictate that over extended periods of time the line of the graph will be level, because pure chance will ultimately produce exactly the same number of zeros and ones, or heads and tails, if you prefer. Right?'

She paused, studying Jones as if to see if she was listening. Jones was concentrating hard.

'Right,' she said.

'OK,' Connie continued. 'If at any time you want to study these graphs you are welcome, but in overall terms of a fifty per cent hit rate, i.e. fifty per cent zeros and fifty per cent ones, which is what would be expected if left entirely to chance, our experiments with operators showed an overall deviation of one per cent. In other words, varying between fifty-one per cent zeros, forty-nine per cent ones, and conversely.'

She paused again.

'Doesn't sound like much does it?'

Jones shook her head.

'Statistically the odds on that level of deviation happening by chance are a trillion to one,' Connie said quietly.

Jones did another double take. She had no idea that this kind of data even existed, and there was something about Connie's calm and considered approach that left her in little doubt of its accuracy.

'Are you sure?' she asked none the less.

Connie nodded.

'Absolutely. Look, I'm just giving you the results. The data is all here.'

She gestured towards a row of battered filing cabinets.

'I told you, take a look any time. Help yourself.'

Jones responded thoughtfully.

'Let's take it that your results, as they stand, are unimpeachable. But how can you guarantee the integrity of the REG? If it is possible that the machine might at any stage cease to function perfectly, then your entire database loses all scientific value.'

'We don't allow that to happen,' said Connie. 'A Random Event Generator is based on a source of electronic white noise generated by a random microscopic physical process. That's how it gets its name. Several other research establishments now have them. Ours utilizes as its random source a commercial microelectronic noise diode unit commonly incorporated in a variety of communications, control, and data-processing equipment circuitry, rendering this noise into an output distribution of binary counts, and entailing extensive fail-safe and calibration components which guarantee its integrity—'

'Hold on,' interrupted Jones. 'You've totally lost me.'

It was clear that, beyond the cuddly toys, this project was considerably more hard-nosed than she had expected it to be. It was also a world away from her field of scientific expertise.

'All right,' said Connie. 'Just think of it as a sophisticated electronic coin-flipping machine with loads of built-in safeguards. Instead of heads and tails it flips numbers.'

'Ah,' said Jones. 'Why didn't you say that in the first place?'

'I kinda thought I had,' responded Connie, grinning easily.

'So, have you recorded any deviation in the results attributable to individual operators?' Jones continued.

'Yes, we have discovered operator patterns. We have also found that the effect is on average generally greater if more than one person is using the same mental intention on the same REG. We experimented with co-operating couples, and we have even found that the composition of the pairs is a factor. It is not just a case of two people automatically getting results that are twice as large as one person's results.

'Same sex pairs, men or women, tend if anything to produce more negative results, in other words they often influence the REG less than one individual. But opposite sex couples have consistently produced an effect that is indeed approximately twice that of individuals, and, beyond that, emotionally linked pairs – lovers, close family members, spouses – have consistently produced an effect more than four times that of individuals.'

Jones cocked her head to one side, intrigued in spite of herself.

'So what you are establishing here is not only the power of consciousness, in these instances, and in the most simplistic terms, the possible power of mind over matter, but also how much greater that power is if two minds are linked together and dedicate themselves to one purpose?'

'Exactly.' Connie beamed at her.

'So, leading on from that, how much greater is the effect if a large number of minds are concentrated together in this way?'

'Ah, the power of global consciousness,' Connie said quietly. 'Now that is the most exciting prospect of all.'

Global consciousness. It wasn't the first time Jones had heard the term, but there was something in Connie Pike's voice when she spoke of it which made the hairs on the back of Sandy Jones's neck stand up.

'We have considerable evidence of the REGs being affected by the mind power of the masses,' Connie continued. 'And also by monumental and emotionally charged events.

'We have recently developed a field version of the REG which we have taken to places where something enormous, something tragic perhaps, or something wonderful, has happened – a natural disaster, a murder, a huge rock concert – and the graph has been significantly affected. But if the event is big enough you don't have to take the REG anywhere. Live Aid in 1985, which was almost a celebration of global consciousness, resulted in a marked deviation on this REG right here.'

Jones glanced involuntarily towards the unlikely looking box. Her gaze travelled again around the equally unlikely and curiously homely decor of the lab, the panelled walls, the carpet, the squashy sofa and the cuddly toys. It was like a room in a home that was properly lived-in, and almost certainly by a happy family. The lighting was low, and came mostly from various small table lamps. The aroma of fresh coffee filled the lab. Music was playing softly, so softly that she could barely discern its nature. It was something classical, something gentle, something dominantly piano. Mozart perhaps?

'The decor is deliberate, you know,' said Connie, breaking into her thoughts.

'I assumed so.'

'Yes. We encourage relaxation coupled with an almost playful approach, and the lab staff interfere as little as possible. Our operators take part in the experiments as and when they are in the mood, and sometimes if they are in a particular mood or emotional state, if they are aware that their attitude at a certain moment is particularly negative or positive for example, then they may wish to explore the effect on their performance.'

'Can I have a go?' Jones startled herself with the request.

Connie, however, did not look even mildly surprised. Jones considered it likely that most visitors to the lab found it impossible to resist wanting to take part. You might think the whole thing was a load of baloney, but there was still an almost irresistible urge to see if you, personally, could upset the accepted laws of physics.

'What, now?' Connie asked.

'Why not?' Jones shrugged. 'I've nothing else to do except complete a thesis on super conductivity by tomorrow night.'

Connie grinned.

'Perfect attitude,' she said.

Jones found herself grinning back.

'But weren't you coming with me to the library?' asked Ed, who had been almost entirely silent until then. Reverential, Jones thought.

'Sod it, I'll do what I have to do first thing tomorrow, get up at dawn,' responded Jones.

'Well, I'm going to have to go now,' said Ed. 'I've got hours of work to do before the morning.'

'OK. You go on. Maybe I'll catch up with you later.'

'Right. I'll be off then . . .'

Ed hesitated at the door, glancing back over his shoulder. Sandy didn't notice.

She gestured to the armchair in front of the REG.

'Is this where I sit?'

Connie nodded, and pointed at a piece of paper, upon which was a typed chart titled 'REG Experimental Options'.

'You can choose the number of bits, coin flips if you like, per second, and the number of trials you wish to undertake by turning these switches.'

She indicated four raised knobs on the front of the REG next to a round dial.

The whole thing was more than a touch Heath Robinson, Jones thought. None the less she was now intent on seeing for herself what it was all about.

'I would suggest a counting rate of a thousand bits per second and five hundred trials. That will probably take about an hour.'

Connie glanced at her quizzically.

'Can you spare an hour, Miss Jones?'

Sandy held out her arms in a gesture of submission.

Connie opened the top drawer of a filing cabinet which stood beneath the table carrying the REG, removed a ledger and passed it to her.

'Our log book,' she said 'Now, first you must record the choice of programme you have selected in the book, then set the REG controls accordingly.'

Jones did so dutifully, passing the ledger back to Connie, before focusing her full attention on the REG. The controls were fairly self-explanatory, the purpose of each ridged knob clearly labelled. She needed only a very little additional prompting from Connie in order to complete the task.

'OK, now what?' she asked.

'You need to decide what direction you are going to take,' replied Connie. 'In other words, whether you want more ones than zeroes or the other way around – and then record that in the log.'

She passed her the big ledger again. Jones was aware that Connie had not looked at what she had written. She once more did as she was told and, when she passed the ledger back, Connie again did not look at it. She passed Jones a small handheld remote-control device, not unlike a television remote, but simpler, containing only an on and off switch.

'When you are ready, activate the REG with that remote, and do your best, with the power of your mind, in any way you wish, to influence the output of the machine so that it conforms with your intentions, the intentions you have already recorded in the log,' Connie instructed.

Jones nodded. Connie held up a hand, her body language telling Jones not to flip the switch yet.

'It's usually best not to concentrate too much,' she advised. 'This is about your inner consciousness, an area of our being most of us barely acknowledge. We are rediscovering a forgotten art here.'

A forgotten art. This was the first time Jones heard Connie use that phrase. She did it in such a way that Jones, an arch cynic, found herself meekly accepting what was being said as fact. For that moment, at any rate. And in the surroundings of that laboratory.

'It's not about will power,' Connie went on. 'It's much more than that. You have decided on your intentions, so just relax. Let your inner consciousness take over.'

Jones smiled, a little of her natural scepticism resurfacing.

'You sure I have one?' she asked.

Connie smiled back. 'Sure I'm sure,' she said. 'Whether it's still operating after the neglect you have no doubt shown it throughout your life is another matter.'

'Touché,' Jones responded, as she flicked the switch.

*   *   *

Almost exactly an hour later the REG shut down. It had completed the programme she had set for it.

Connie, who had retreated into her little office and left Jones alone, re-emerged by her side.

Jones watched expectantly as she began to check the dials on the machine.

'So, was it ones or noughts that you went for, young lady?'

'Ones,' Jones replied.

'Umm. And what sort of result do you think you've had?'

'I have absolutely no idea.'

'In the way that I explained it to you – the REG flipped fifty-two per cent ones during your hour of operation.'

'One per cent more than the average, yeah?'

'Yeah.'

'Is that good?'

'It's not supposed to be good or bad, Sandy. But the odds against that two per cent swing being chance could be a trillion trillion to one.'

'I don't understand "could be". Surely, with your knowledge of this phenomenon and the data you have already accumulated, the odds of probability are not a moveable feast, are they?'

'Damned right they're not. But you have completed just one experiment, you need to complete a full series in order for your results to have any real significance.'

'Right, but just say that it stays at fifty-two per cent. What would that mean?'

'It would mean you are more receptive than most of our operators, that's all. Just a fraction more actually, but highly significant, in fact, phenomenally significant, in terms of the odds involved.'

Jones felt a quite idiotic surge of pride. There was something extraordinarily seductive about the RECAP project, she realized. She supposed that was why there were always so many willing participants for experiments like these, however time-consuming they were. Most people liked to think that they were particularly perceptive, blessed with greater depths and a deeper sensitivity than those around them. Most human beings liked to think themselves special. You could call it what you liked, but in Jones's experience people often got a huge buzz out of thinking they were psychic.

Rather to her surprise, even at Oxford, where a certain degree of intellect was supposed to be taken for granted, there had been a Psi Society made up entirely of students who believed that they were psychic. Jones had previously been inclined to regard such tendencies as the prerogative of the less cerebrally gifted. Indeed, she'd always avoided the term psychic in almost any context, and had considered the bad press levelled at psi over the years to be totally justified. Obviously Connie Pike and Paul Ruders were having to fight against that. Jones's own initial attitude to the project was proof enough. And yet, in spite of her innate prejudice against everything RECAP and the REG experiment was about, she felt herself being drawn in.

'But why?' she asked suddenly. 'That's the question, isn't it? Why did I get these results? Why, if I were in this room with my mother, or my husband, if I had one, would I probably get even more significant results, according to what you have told me today? Why?'

Jones raised her arms and placed the fingertips of both hands against her temples, as if willing her brain to tell her what was going on inside her head. Inside her mind.

'We don't know why, Sandy.'

Connie produced a packet of cigarettes. Jones watched silently as she removed one and lit up. As an afterthought she held the packet out towards Jones inquiringly.

Jones declined. Apart from the obvious more serious consequences, cigarettes made your breath smell and discoloured your teeth.

'If we knew why, then we would have solved the secret of consciousness. And that, Sandy, as I am sure you know, is arguably the last great mystery of mankind.'

Jones nodded.

'Thing is,' she responded, 'you are compiling evidence put together under laboratory conditions. That's valid and inspiring scientific exploration, Connie. But it is just so hard for someone like me, for most people, I think, to accept that the power of the mind could possibly affect a machine like this. I mean, I'm a person who has never accepted psi at all . . .'

Connie took a long pull on her cigarette. The little room was filling with smoke. Jones was not surprised that she so blatantly ignored the university's no smoking rule – she assumed that Connie Pike would ignore any rules that didn't suit her.

'Sometimes I think the terminology is wrong,' Connie replied. 'Certainly the way we look at things, the way we see what's around us, is highly suspect. The lay person, but probably most of all the scientist, has an attitude all too often governed by the times we live in, by a pragmatic materialistic society, and by the dictates of a regimented kind of thinking that is imposed upon us from birth. Let me turn it around for you.

'Do you really think that man is on this earth merely as a visitor whose presence has absolutely no effect on the world he meanders through?'

'Well no, of course not,' responded Jones. 'Most of us leave a mark of some kind, good or bad, and many of us, particularly scientists, medical practitioners, creative people too, architects, designers, writers, artists, can change the world significantly.'

'Yes, but you are still looking through eyes with limited sight. You are seeing only the material, the tangible. Only what you can reach out and touch. Take that a stage further, Sandy. Move on to what you can feel. Take our traditional way of thinking to the other extreme. Turn it around, a full one hundred and eighty degrees. Embrace ancient and traditional concepts, cultures and beliefs from other eras. Recognize that within you, somewhere, the memories of lost skills remain, skills which it might not be impossible for you to retrieve by the simple inexplicable power of your own mind.

'Try to imagine that it is possible for every single experience that you have in your life time to be created by your own consciousness. Can you even begin to get your head around that, Sandy?'

'Probably not. It's a quantum leap, isn't it, Connie.'

'It certainly is. But most of us can probably cope with the in-between ground. "We are both onlookers and actors in the great drama of existence."'

'Neils Bohr,' said Jones.

'You've read him?'

'Of course. I am a physicist. Read a bit of Shakespeare too. "All the world's a stage, and all the men and women merely players."'

'If you like. But Sandy, do you see that if you take those two diverse perspectives and explore the ground in between, if you accept that consciousness involves at least some mixture of the passive and the active, and if you then do what we are doing here, which is to record and collate all of this in an approved mathematical manner, then at the very least, Sandy Jones, we are embarking on probably the most thrilling, and most significant scientific journey of discovery of our age.'

Connie's eyes were not shining any more. They were blazing. Jones had the feeling she had said all this before many times. It did not make her outburst any less genuine nor any less passionate.

'Wow!' she said.

Connie laughed abruptly.

'Sorry. I get a bit carried away at times.'

'You're allowed,' said Jones.

She was going to say more when the door to the lab opened and in walked a big, bumbling sort of man, probably not a lot older than Connie but with thinning white hair. He had a straggly white beard, and was wearing an untidy tweed jacket and baggy grey flannels. He was surely everybody's idea of an absent-minded professor. Under one arm he carried a Yorkshire terrier puppy, with which he seemed to be engaged in conversation.

'Now, you're going to sit in your basket like a good girl, Lulu, aren't you? Aren't you, honey? And when you want a wee you're going to tell me, Lulu. Like I've taught you.'

With that the big man placed the small dog in a basket, surrounded by more newspaper, which stood in one corner of the room.

He then turned towards Connie and Jones as if noticing their presence for the first time.

'Good afternoon, Connie, and who's your new friend?'

Connie introduced Jones.

'And this, Sandy, is Professor Paul Ruders, the director of RECAP,' she said.

'I'm very pleased to meet you, sir,' said Jones.

'Good show. Good show.'

'Sandy's been operating the REG today,' continued Connie.

'Good show. Good show.'

Paul Ruders smiled benignly and disappeared into an office next to Connie's. The Yorkshire terrier puppy followed at once. Ruders either didn't notice or was used to being disobeyed by the creature. He simply closed the door, shutting himself in with the little dog.

'Don't be misled by appearances,' Connie instructed. 'Paul is the brains behind RECAP. He's quite brilliant.'

Brilliant or deluded? Jones wasn't sure. But against her better judgement she found that she wanted to know more. She turned again to study the REG, that Heath Robinson wooden box with its range of dials and switches. Maybe it did hold the key to man's most extraordinary secret. She had no intention of allowing herself to become too fanciful – but she realized suddenly that she did want to continue to explore the possibilities. To take a further part in Connie's scientific journey, and at least discover just how much the parameters of her own mind could be expanded.

'So how many more sessions would I need to do here before my data became valid?' Jones asked.

'We'd need to complete a series, and the length of the series should be set now, at the start of the experiment,' replied Connie. 'A series typically consists of 2500 or 5000 trials in blocks of fifty or one hundred runs. And a full series usually takes an operator anything between two and six weeks. I'm afraid it does call for quite a major commitment, particularly when you consider that almost all of our operators, like you, have their own heavy workloads away from RECAP. But we have found that only series on this scale produce the absolute minimum base of data from which consequential systematic trends can be reliably extracted.'

'I see.'

Jones turned away from the REG to directly face Connie.

'Right, then. See you tomorrow? Same time, same place? And let's go for the full series of 5000 trials in a block of one hundred runs, shall we?'

Connie Pike raised her eyebrows in surprise, but this time Jones wasn't so sure that her behaviour was genuine. She must be well accustomed to the affect she, her project, and her unlikely laboratory had on people, Jones reckoned. Converting sceptics was probably her house speciality.

'Abso-damned-lutely!' said Connie.

She showed Jones to the door, then put a restraining hand on her arm.

'Wait.'

Connie turned on her heel, disappeared into her office for just a few seconds, and returned carrying a blue button badge, just like the one she was wearing.

Smiling she pinned it to one of the lapels of Jones's denim jacket.

'Have a good evening,' she said.

'You too,' Jones replied, touching the badge with the fingers of one hand. 'And thanks for this.'

Once outside she remembered the time, the all too pressing thesis she had to complete, and the fact that she'd only visited RECAP to keep Ed happy.

'I must be going barking mad,' she muttered to herself as she hurried along the corridor and out into the grounds en route to the main building. When she reached the entrance hall, she unpinned the little blue badge Connie had given her, held it in the palm of her hand and looked at it.

'Subvert the Dominant Paradigm.'

She muttered the words aloud, wondering what it was about Connie Pike, and the whole RECAP project, that was sucking her in so quickly.

Nonetheless, she then tucked the little button badge into her jeans' pocket. She might be turning into a psi freak, but she had no intention of advertising the fact.

FIVE

From that very first visit to the RECAP lab, flattered by the possibility of being a particularly receptive operator, captivated by Connie Pike, in awe of Paul Ruders, whom she came to believe really was a genius, Jones was hooked.

Until nearly the end of her four-year stint at Princeton she spent much of her spare time at the RECAP lab, endlessly operating trials on the REG, correlating results, making up graphs. And always working in the dark, with little idea really either of what was likely to be achieved or even of what it may be possible to achieve, yet nonetheless enthralled by the prospect of what might be.

The secret of consciousness, the last great mystery of the human race. Most people, Jones realized, had a story to tell of sensing something strange, or of an awareness of a situation or an event which contemporary science could not explain. Being aware of eyes staring at you, even from behind your back, was perhaps the most common experience, followed closely by having some kind of knowledge of the death or injury of a loved one in another place. But all these stories, at the end of the day, were merely the kind of anecdote that had been related and passed on throughout the ages.

The trials being conducted at Princeton and elsewhere, as initiated by Paul Ruders, were something different. This was valid correlated scientific exploration. At the beginning Jones, always a sceptic at heart, looked everywhere for flaws in the way the various tests were conducted. She could find none. Just as Connie had told her in the beginning, all RECAP experiments were governed by the strictest of laboratory conditions.

She therefore came to the conclusion that the results of the RECAP trials were inarguable.

Yet they remained inexplicable. Paul Ruders never seemed to doubt that one day the mystery of consciousness would be solved, but he didn't say a lot. Connie, on the other hand, talked enough for both of them. And always colourfully.

'Chasing the rainbow,' was how she usually referred to the ultimate aims of RECAP.

'Do you realize we could find what we are looking for and not even know it?' she remarked one night when she and Jones were alone together in the lab in the early hours, Professor Ruders, the by-then at least partially house-trained Lulu trotting along behind him, having finally gone home to his wife.

'I'll know,' Jones replied at once.

Connie raised both eyebrows.

'Not short of confidence are you, Sandy?'

'Maybe not,' Jones replied. 'Mind you, I was absolutely confident that I would never in my life get involved in anything like RECAP.'

'Well, we're all very glad you did,' Connie told her.

And Jones felt a warm glow in her belly.

The glittering academic career to which Sandy Jones aspired, was a world away from the psi experimentation of RECAP, and she was aware that her association with the programme might be regarded by the academic establishment as the only blot on an otherwise exemplary residency at Princeton. But she continued to risk it, ignoring the odd puzzled frown from the hierarchy. The REG programme fascinated her. She couldn't leave it alone.

However, ultimately the natural conflict between the hard fact of her ambition and the seductive vagary of RECAP led to Jones having to make a choice. A choice, deep inside, that she had probably always known, was inevitable.

During her final year at Princeton, she began to think seriously about her immediate future. The American university was rich, both in material wealth and in opportunity. She had been left in little doubt that there were openings within its diverse employment structure which were hers for the taking. And she and Ed had somehow drifted into discussions about their joint future, almost as if that were inevitable. Nobody proposed marriage, but Ed did mention casually more than once that if she married him, the resulting American citizenship would remove any obstacles there might be to her enjoying a high-flying career in the States. Then, towards the end of her last semester, when her final thesis had been completed and her doctorate was about to be bestowed, she learned that she was being considered for a particularly sought-after research fellowship back in the UK, at London's Goldsmith College. It was a position considerably more senior than would usually be offered to a newly qualified doctor, and one which she knew would open the door to the most elevated areas of British and international academia.

She told Ed that she wasn't sure if she wanted it, which was a lie, and that she didn't think she would get it anyway, which was true. And she reminded him that acquiring nationality by marriage worked both ways round, which she really shouldn't have done because she had absolutely no intention of marrying Ed MacEntee.

She flew back to London to meet the Goldsmith hierarchy, and it was there that Professor Michael O'Grady came into her life. He was probably Britain's top biologist, not only was he brilliant, and a TV star with his own BBC Two series, *The World Around Us*, but he was also handsome, and oozed Irish charm. He was known as Dr Darling. And Sandy was later to wonder how she had failed to realize immediately that he had to be too good to be true.

Instead, she fell under his spell from the beginning, and, even though he had made no secret of being a married man, allowed herself to be seduced by him that very first night. O'Grady was everything Ed wasn't. He was an accomplished and passionate lover, and the sex was by far the best Sandy Jones had ever experienced.

She hadn't realized that she could care about it that much. But during those few days in London, O'Grady overwhelmed her, physically and in every way. When they weren't in bed, he whisked her off to the best restaurants in town, to a reception at 10 Downing Street, and to a garden party at Buckingham Palace.

It was all totally seductive for the girl from the wrong side of the track. In just a brief few days she fell head over heels in love, for the first time in her young life. And her head was totally turned. She realized also that what O'Grady had could possibly also be hers, that maybe she could be a part of that world. Indeed, amongst the high-flying media people he introduced her to was the TV executive who would one day offer Sandy Jones her first opportunity in broadcasting.

She quickly learned that O'Grady, who was fourteen years her senior, had a reputation for being an inveterate womanizer, but she didn't care. It would be different with her. She would change him.

On the day before she was due to return to Princeton she was formally offered the Goldsmith research fellowship and accepted it on the spot. She travelled back to Princeton merely to collect her belongings and formally receive her doctorate.

She told Ed as little as possible, indicating disingenuously that the Goldsmith position was not a permanent one, and she had made no long-term decision.

She certainly did not mention that she'd fallen heavily in love with another man.

Ed appeared to take the news well enough, even congratulating her on her appointment, but she could only suspect what he was really feeling, this quiet, genuine man who had been her very best friend for four years, and whom she knew loved her in a manner she had never quite been able to reciprocate.

'Just say the word and I'll come and join you,' he'd remarked lightly.

'Oh, I'll be back before you know it,' she'd replied, knowing full well that was another lie, and that she was almost certainly about to break Ed's heart.

She realized that she was being cowardly, but she couldn't face telling him that their relationship was over.

Ultimately she only remained in Princeton for a few days, during which she avoided Connie, and all concerned with the RECAP project, as much as possible, merely letting them know casually that she would not be staying in Princeton after all. She was vaguely aware that Connie and Paul, Connie in particular, were deeply disappointed. But, at that moment in time, Jones didn't care.

Back in England, she at once became so immersed in her new life that Princeton and most of what had happened there slipped swiftly into a compartment at the very back of her mind. She and Connie kept in touch, but she very soon broke off all communication with Ed. Without a word of explanation. Not least because she had no idea what to say to him. She knew how shabbily she was behaving, but didn't seem able to stop herself. She was already pregnant. Unlike with Ed, she and O'Grady had never taken any precautions. She didn't even remember the subject being mentioned. The whole thing was crazy. But quite wonderfully so. At first.

O'Grady divorced his wife, not only with unseemly haste, but also with apparent ease. Jones eagerly agreed to marry him as soon as he was free. The birth of their twin sons, Lee and Matt, led her new husband to commend her on her efficiency in producing an instant family. For a brief period she took a break from her academic work, and was blissfully happy caring for her new babies, and basking in the love of her charismatic husband. Or that's how she saw things. But in what seemed like no time at all, O'Grady's perennially roving eye reasserted itself, and alighted upon a research assistant even younger, and certainly prettier, than his wife. History repeated itself. Within three years Sandy found herself divorced and bringing up her sons largely on her own.

Only then, not infrequently besieged by a terrible sense of emptiness, did her thoughts turn to Princeton again, and she would experience the dull ache of regret, and an overwhelming longing for what might have been.

Two decades later, flying across the Atlantic in the aftermath of tragedy, the memories were suddenly startlingly vivid, including her shameful behaviour when she had so carelessly cast it all aside.

And it caused Sandy Jones more pain than she would ever have believed to know that Connie and Paul were dead. That she would never see either of them again.

Their work had mushroomed, of course, beyond Paul and Connie's original dreams. The computer age and the Internet had seen to that.

Jones knew there were now more than a hundred Random Events Generators throughout the world, more than a million series of laboratory condition tests had been completed, producing literally billions of trials, all with similar results to those achieved at RECAP from the beginning.

These REGs, sometimes known as RNGs, or Random Number Generators, were installed at various accepted academic and scientific establishments not only across America but in all five continents, in cities as diverse as Beijing and Edinburgh, Tokyo and Sydney, Amsterdam and Moscow. All of them were linked to a database at RECAP, the home and the heart of the Global Consciousness Project, under Paul's directorship. Or rather, they had been until the lab had been destroyed and Paul killed.

They weren't Heath Robinson boxes any more. Nowadays a REG was a USB device, not much bigger than a standard memory stick, which merely plugged into the appropriate computer outlet. And many of those who had installed them worldwide – often postgraduate students yet to be pressurized into moving away from such a controversial area of science – were initially sceptics, just as Jones had been to begin with. Often, they barely believed the results of their own experiments. Yet they were united in being convinced of the accuracy, and also in believing that the Global Consciousness Project was at the very least nipping at the ankles of something quite extraordinary and revolutionary.

In spite of that, RECAP had remained ever under pressure, always under some sort of threat, usually financial. Jones was acutely aware of how much she could have helped the project over the years, had she wished to do so. But they'd never asked for her help – not until Connie's call of a few days ago, that is – and she had never offered it.

Yet now, when it was probably too late, certainly too late for Connie and Paul, she was jetting off to the rescue. And a good half of her didn't know what the hell she thought she was doing, nor indeed who the hell she thought she was. A cross, perhaps, between Wonder Woman and her near namesake, Indiana Jones?

At times during the journey she tried to sleep but largely failed, her brain racing as she began to consider the task ahead. Whatever exactly that might prove to be.

She didn't even know if her dead friends had any relatives. Paul had been a widower, and Jones was aware that his only child had died very young. As for Connie, well, to her shame, Jones realized that she'd never known anything much about Connie Pike's personal life, beyond the fact that she had been married as a young woman and quite swiftly divorced. She had no idea what relationships Connie may or may not have had since then. It had always seemed to her that Connie's whole existence revolved around RECAP and those who were involved with the project. She'd always been there for Sandy Jones, and for the others. But, looking back, it had all been rather one sided. Which, perhaps led to the real reason why Sandy Jones was on this aircraft. She felt so guilty about so much.

The instructions were given to fasten seat belts for landing. Jones decided that all she could do now was to take things step by step.

At JFK she would grab a yellow cab to New York's Penn Station and then catch a train on to that so familiar other-worldly university town. Newark would have been a more convenient airport to fly into en route to Princeton, but there had been no suitable flight available.

She checked her watch. The flight was due to arrive at four thirty p.m. and appeared to be on time. If she was lucky she could be at Penn by around six. The train journey to Princeton Junction would take just over an hour, the trains were frequent, and Jones was travelling light with only hand luggage, just the one capacious shoulder bag.

Suddenly she knew exactly what she was going to do first when she reached Princeton, whom she would visit straight away. She doubted she'd be welcome, but she didn't care. And she certainly did not intend to give any warning.

PART THREE

Most people . . . make use of a very small portion of their possible consciousness, and of their soul's resources in general, much like a man who, out of his whole bodily organism, should get into a habit of using and moving only his little finger. Great emergencies and crises show us how much greater our vital resources are than we had supposed.

William James

SIX

S he rang the bell on the intercom system. He didn't answer, instead buzzing the front door open. Maybe he was expecting someone else? She entered anyway, and made her way upstairs to his apartment.

She could hear a dog barking.

It was another minute or two before he came to the door, a little black terrier bouncing around his feet. His face was pale and drawn, etched with shock and grief. He was wearing a grubby grey tracksuit which hung from his bony frame. His eyes opened wide with surprise when he saw her.

'It's been a long time,' Jones heard herself say, immediately thinking what a terrible opening remark that was.

'Sandy?'

He appeared to be asking her to confirm her identity.

'Yes, it's me.'

She managed a tentative smile.

Ed just stared at her.

'Aren't you going to invite me in?'

For a split second she thought he was going to refuse. Send her away. And she wouldn't have blamed him if he did. Also, it occurred to her suddenly that he may not be alone. Connie had told her that Ed had married, only a couple of years after she did, that there had been a daughter, and that he and his wife had later divorced. But that was all she knew.

Eventually Ed stepped back into the hallway and gestured for her to enter. It was a small but cosy apartment. He led her to a bright blue and yellow kitchen at the rear.

The weather was unusually warm and muggy for New Jersey in mid-September, but Ed's air-conditioning was so powerfully cold that Jones felt herself involuntarily shiver.

Ed's shoulders were slumped low, his walk a shuffle. He moved the way Jones felt, on that dreadfully sad day. He sat down at a little scrubbed wooden table, bearing an overflowing ashtray and an empty coffee cup, and gestured for her to join him.

'I didn't think you'd ever take up smoking,' she said, more for something to say than anything else.

He looked at her with something bordering distaste, and she didn't like it at all.

'How the hell would you know anything about me?' he enquired sharply.

She winced.

'In any case, I don't smoke,' he continued. 'Not usually.'

'Well, this is certainly not a usual day,' Jones ventured.

'No.'

His voice was just a little softer.

'I'm sorry, I feel a bit raw,' he continued.

'Of course.'

It was weird. So awkward. As if she were a stranger. But then, she supposed that's exactly what she now was.

'I'm sorry to spring myself on you, Ed. I just, well, I just booked myself onto a flight and came here. Straight away, almost, after I heard the news.'

Ed stared at her levelly.

'Why?' he asked.

She was startled.

'W-why?' she repeated uncertainly.

He was clearly irritated. He made a little clicking noise with his tongue.

'Why have you come here?'

The irritation was in his voice too.

She sought the words to explain. They didn't come. she gave the only answer she could.

'I had to, Ed, I just had to.'

'After all this time . . .'

There was an inflection in Ed's voice that Jones could not quite identify. She looked down at her hands on the table.

'They would have been glad, though, that you came,' he said suddenly.

Jones was touched. This was the first moment of comfort of any kind that she had experienced since the shock of seeing that first news item about the explosion.

And Ed had been closer to Paul and Connie than anyone. He and his younger brother Michael had been brought up by their maternal grandparents after their mother and father were killed in a car crash. Ed, aged three at the time, and Michael, just a baby, had been in the car, strapped in on the back seat. Their survival was considered a miracle. The much-loved grandparents had both died while Ed was at Princeton. So the boys were orphaned all over again, more or less, and Connie and Paul had become even more important to Ed.

'Thank you,' said Jones.

Ed shrugged.

'I'm sorry,' Jones blurted out impulsively. 'Sorry I've never been in touch . . .'

Ed shrugged again.

'That's life,' he said, his voice expressionless.

'I know, but I should have . . .'

She paused, not knowing quite what to say next, which, of course, had been the problem twenty-one years earlier.

'You should have said goodbye,' he finished for her, raising his voice. 'That, at least, would have been nice. You didn't even tell me it was over. You let me think you were coming back. You didn't tell me anything. You just walked out on me. I read about you and Dr damned Darling online, for God's sake.'

'I-uh, I'm sorry,' she said again.

And she was too. Probably far sorrier than Ed would ever know.

He lit another cigarette, puffing on it in the slightly desperate way of someone not used to the habit.

'So, how can I help you, then?' he asked, his voice quiet again, polite and distant.

'Do you know what happened to Paul and Connie, exactly what happened?' she asked abruptly.

'There was an explosion, Sandy. I'm sure you know that as well as I do.'

'Yes. But was it an act of terrorism? Was it a bomb? And was RECAP the target?'

'They're saying that it might have been a gas leak.'

'I know. And I don't believe that. Do you?'

'I don't know what I believe. Why would terrorists attack Princeton? We're a university, a seat of learning.'

'And not the first innocent place to be torn apart that way. Think of Bali. The Twin Towers, the London Underground, Paris, that concert in Manchester. Not exactly military targets.'

'No.'

'Thank God you weren't in the lab, too.'

'I teach more or less full time, now.' Ed laughed without humour. 'At the high school. It was either that or skid row. So I have a price too. Ironic really.'

'Yes, I suppose so.'

She knew what he meant. Whilst Jones had taken the career path, Ed had stuck to his vocation, to following his dream. And now he was teaching school, because it had been that or the street.

'So you haven't been working with Paul and Connie lately, then?'

'Oh I have. Unofficially. That's always been the euphemism round here for not getting paid. RECAP's budget had been slashed to a fraction of what it used to be. And God knows, it was never great. But I couldn't really stop. I've been monitoring things . . .' His voice tailed off. 'You know, the usual.'

'I've got a fair idea.' She paused. 'Look. Connie called me a few days ago. She sounded . . . troubled. Something was wrong. Very wrong. I'm sure of it. She wanted to talk, only . . .'

She didn't want to tell Ed how she had failed so dismally to respond to Connie's plea for help, though she reckoned he'd probably already guessed.

'I was going to call back,' she finished lamely. 'But . . . but then it was too late . . . So I wondered if you knew what was bothering her. She mentioned something about the lab being put under pressure. She was afraid there were plans to close it down.'

'Close it down?' Ed sounded genuinely puzzled. 'There've always been plans to get rid of RECAP. Nobody has ever succeeded though . . .'

The sentence tailed off as he realized what he'd said.

'Did Connie talk to you about it at all?' Jones asked.

'No. Not really. Well, she was always grumbling about lack of resources, that sort of thing. That's all.'

'What about Paul?'

'Oh you know Paul. If the lab were going to close he wouldn't have noticed until he was actually physically thrown out of the place. All he was ever aware of was his work, particularly after Gilda died.'

Jones tried again.

'Ed, have you really no idea at all what may have been troubling Connie?'

'Absolutely not,' he responded immediately.

'Well, she was troubled. I'm sure of it.'

'OK, but even if she was, what has that necessarily got to do with the explosion?'

'I have no idea,' Jones replied. 'But I sure as hell would like to find out. I'm convinced there's a connection.'

'Really?'

'Really. What do you think?'

He shrugged. 'Knowing Paul and Connie, the explosion could well have been some kind of accident. Not connected with anything. For a start she still smokes . . .' Ed paused, remembering. 'She still smoked in the lab. She and Paul weren't exactly hot on health and safety, were they?'

'The health and safety people had just been in, Connie told me. Fitted sprinklers.'

'So what?'

'Ed, it really could have been a bomb, you know.'

Ed shrugged again. 'Or a gas leak. You can choose whatever you like to believe at this stage, can't you?'

'Yes, so can you think of any reason why RECAP would be a target for a terrorist attack?' Jones persisted.

'I don't think it was. Even if some terrorist group was responsible for the blast, then surely it would have been just a matter of hitting another high-profile target. Princeton is a major Ivy League university, after all.'

'Yes. And RECAP was an obscure half-forgotten research lab tucked away deep in the bowels of the campus.'

'Sandy, what are you trying to prove?'

'I haven't the faintest idea. But, look, Ed, I let Connie down. And it wasn't for the first time.'

'So that's what this is all about. Your fucking guilt. Well, you damned well should feel guilty, that's for sure.'

He spat the words at her. Angry again. She was startled, and recoiled at once.

'I'm sorry,' she said.

'Me too,' he responded quickly. 'I'm just, so, so on edge—'

'It's all right. I understand,' she interrupted. 'I don't suppose either of us is thinking straight. I'll go now. Maybe I'll phone tomorrow, if that's OK?'

'OK.'

They both stood up. The dog started to bark again, demanding attention.

'No, Jasper, it's not time,' said Ed, scratching the dog's head affectionately.

'Does he want to go out?' asked Jones, in an effort to make normal conversation.

'I take him around the block every night, but not yet, or he'll only want to go again.'

Jones attempted a smile. Ed just looked at her. No smile. No comment.

'I'll call tomorrow,' she repeated.

He nodded curtly. She deserved it, but it still hurt. She felt not only bereft, but a little surprised. She suspected Ed's anger was rather more because of the way she had treated him, than because of her neglect of Connie and Paul. And that had been twenty-one years ago.

Either way, on that awful day, it was irrelevant. And Ed had said nothing at all to shake her growing conviction that the explosion at RECAP had been neither accident nor random.

Outside a man wearing a hooded anorak, quite unnecessary on such a balmy evening, was walking up the path towards Ed's apartment block when the front door opened. Ed had escorted Sandy downstairs, possibly to make sure she left the premises, she had thought wryly. He opened the door for her, stepping momentarily outside as she departed. Intent on dodging the shaft of light emitting from the building, the man dived for cover in the shrubbery to one side of the picket-fenced garden area.

Crouching there, he watched Sandy Jones walk down the path, open the white-painted gate and step out into the street.

Jones was at first silhouetted against the lights of the building as she headed almost directly towards the man in the anorak, and then had her back towards him as she proceeded down the street.

The man had been unable to see her face. And he had no idea whether or not he would have recognized her even had he been able to do so.

Once Jones was out of sight the man emerged from the shrubbery, approached the apartment block again, and without hesitation pressed one of the row of doorbells set in a panel on the wall. Very soon the man would know who Ed MacEntee's mystery caller had been. He would make it his business to do so.

Jones had no idea that anyone had observed her leave Ed's home. She strolled slowly into what passed for the centre of Princeton. It seemed extraordinary that she had never returned to the place. Not once since 1998. Yet it was still so familiar. Little seemed to have changed, visually at any rate. Nassau Street, the main drag on the edge of campus, continued to house a number of bars and cafes. But as it was now after nine o'clock at night the place seemed pretty much deserted, and Jones didn't think that necessarily had anything to do with the explosion. Princeton had never been hot on nightlife.

She walked across Palmer Square, past the life-size bronze of a boy sitting reading, until she reached the Nassau Inn, where she had already reserved a room. She checked in, then went straight to her room where she immediately showered and washed her hair, which her boys insisted on calling her 'Claudia Winkleman'. She still wore it in a long bob, and it was still an exceptionally glossy black. Keeping it that way was probably her biggest vanity. Although she had also developed a liking for designer clothes, albeit favouring a casual look. And she had retained her penchant for jeans and unfussy shirts.

After her shower she ordered wine and sandwiches on room service, and channel-hopped the television for a couple of hours before trying to sleep. However, although she felt bone weary, sleep did not come. She was besieged by unwelcome thoughts, and disorientated by jetlag.

Somewhere around four a.m. local time, and God knows when by her body clock, she gave up trying. She couldn't lie there any longer. She just had to do something. She dressed swiftly in the black jeans she had worn on her journey, and her black DKNY hoodie, let herself out of the front door of the Inn, as quietly possible, and started to walk towards the campus.

It was a dark night. No moon and no stars. In the dim glow of the streetlights and the occasional lit-up shop window Princeton looked even more unreal than ever. At one point a lone police patrol car drove slowly by, drawing almost to a halt alongside Jones, who became acutely aware of being closely scrutinized. One of the few examples of the power of human consciousness experienced on a regular basis by almost all of us, she reflected. As Connie had always pointed out to her critics, we often know when the eyes of another creature, human or animal, are fixed upon us, even when we cannot see them. How can that be, Connie would ask, if there is no link between our minds?

Jones continued steadily on her way, deliberately letting her arms hang loosely at her sides. Apparently she did not look suspicious because, even though it was so early in the morning and she had yet to see another pedestrian, after a few seconds the police car proceeded on its way, accelerating past her up Nassau Street.

She had half expected to be stopped, walking through the town in the early hours, and less than two days after a fatal explosion. Being a woman had probably helped, she thought, even in this age of almost obsessively applied gender equality.

As she turned right into the Princeton campus, past Nassau Hall, she was further surprised that, apart from the lone patrol car, there appeared to be no visible police presence. This was Princeton though, she reminded herself. The campus blended seamlessly with the town. She knew the authorities had evacuated the university buildings, but it would be virtually impossible to physically shut them off from the town. And the university itself had never been too hot on security, not in her day anyway.

That had been before 9/11, of course, and the various international terrorist attacks which had followed. But only a few weeks after the tragedy of the Twin Towers, Jones had chatted to a colleague, who had just returned from a trip to Princeton, and expressed surprise at the continued lack of security there.

The famous Orange Key Tours still ran several times daily, when not only prospective students but any casual visitor to the town, and indeed any would-be terrorist, could join a small group and be shown around the campus by an eagerly informative student.

Dormitories and lecture rooms were all on the itinerary for a visit as well as the main university libraries, including the cavernous

Firestone, the Art Museum, Nassau Hall, and other hallowed places. Those joining the hour-long campus tours underwent no security checks whatsoever. There were no electronic gates to pass through, no bag searches, certainly no body searches, and not even a routine identity check. Indeed visitors weren't even asked to give their names, let alone show proof of identity.

Jones continued to walk along shadowy paths, which she did not have to be able to see clearly in order to know were immaculate, the buildings around her bringing back even more memories. She crossed the lawn at Nixon's Nose, and scuffed at the ground with the toe of a shoe. It had been a favourite place for her and Ed. She was reminded again of how badly she had treated him.

The Science Research Building was just around the corner now, but the RECAP lab was at the far end. She assumed the main entrance to the building would be a protected crime scene, and she was right. She stood very still in the shadows by the corner of the block, hoping to see without being seen.

The front of the science building was lit by arc lights, as, being an aficionado of TV detective shows, she had expected. Yellow tape stretched around the building cordoning it off. Four armed men in dark uniforms, flak jackets, and helmets, were standing by the door silhouetted against the stark light of the arc lamps, casting elongated angular shadows across the paved forecourt. She could see quite clearly the bulk of their body armour and the angular shape of their automatic rifles as well as the bulge of their pistol holsters. Jones had no idea whether they were police or military. Either way she didn't intend to allow herself to be confronted by them.

Instead she backed slowly and quietly off and began to make her way in a big loop around to the right of the affected building in order, she hoped, to arrive unnoticed at the site of the lab at the rear. It was no accident that she had chosen to wear black.

Another set of arc lights illuminated the building which housed the RECAP lab – or rather, she realized with a sudden flash of unpleasant reality, the place where the RECAP lab had once been.

Jones had known what to expect. Or she'd thought she had. The TV news items on the explosion had shown the scene only from a safe, almost discreet, distance; a television reporter standing in the foreground. But, like most people, Jones had over the years seen enough television footage of bombings to feel that such a scenario, however horrific, would hold no surprises for her. However, she'd never before actually been present at the scene of a major explosion, nor indeed of any similar incident involving huge devastation, and she found that she was completely unprepared.

Once again this area of campus was cordoned off and guarded. Once again Jones held back, reluctant to confront those patrolling the site. After all, what would American security forces make of a lone Englishwoman wandering around a designated crime scene at this hour? Particularly when the possibility of an attack by unknown terrorists was still being investigated. American security services, rightly or wrongly, had a reputation for being rather quicker on the trigger than their British counterparts. And even the British police, in the widespread near-panic which had followed the 7/7 London Underground bombings in 2005, had at one point killed an innocent man by mistake.

Jones positioned herself behind a conveniently placed tree, and stood as still as possible while she surveyed the scene. The lab area was partially concealed by a large tarpaulin construction. Nonetheless Jones could see clearly the level of devastation. And even if the presence of security forces had not halted her, she would have been totally stopped in her tracks.

It seemed that a large chunk of the ground floor of the building, and of the first storey above, had been totally demolished. Metal-reinforced concrete girders hung, broken and twisted, at crazy angles. The Science Research Block was four storeys high, and the rest of the structure too had been severely affected to such a degree that it leaned sideways at an angle, giving the curiously shocking impression of being a brick and concrete jaw, gaping wide open.

Jones could only imagine what it must have been like to have been inside the building when the explosion occurred. She realized now, looking at such devastation, just how remarkable it was that so few had been killed and injured, even taking into account the time of the blast.

The three people who had died, including her two old friends, would, she thought, have known absolutely nothing about what had happened. But she couldn't help thinking about the injured students, at least one of whom, according to news bulletins, had been very seriously hurt. They may well have been aware of the full horror.

Jones shuddered.

Pulling her hood over her head, she took a cautious step forward, trying to guess exactly where a bomb might have been placed in order to cause the devastation she saw before her. It was hard to tell exactly, but there seemed little doubt, she felt, that its location would have been within the RECAP lab.

Jones could feel her brain beginning to work properly again, but, as certain unwelcome thoughts began to race through her mind, she reckoned she would probably prefer to be still wandering around in a jet-lagged fog.

Her vision of the lab the way it had been before was still extraordinarily vivid. She wondered if the bomb had been given to the lab by someone, disguised within one of those famous cuddly toys Connie had always welcomed, or maybe just hidden behind the old sofa. Nobody would have checked. Nobody would have dreamed of it.

Jones moved slightly to her right, trying not to make a noise. She was grateful for the various trees and undergrowth which surrounded this corner of the building, and which, thankfully, were somewhat less manicured than in other areas of the campus.

She noticed that a large piece of tarpaulin had come loose from the building, and that the only two guards she could see were standing together some distance away. Their heads came close, almost touching, brought into sharp relief by a small flash of light. It looked like they were having a smoking break. It was more than likely that they were not the only security operatives present, of course, but Jones still decided to take the opportunity to make her way a little nearer to the building.

She inched further forward. Conveniently the arc light was shining directly through the area from which the tarpaulin had fallen away, so she could see clearly into what remained of the interior.

There was nothing inside at all. Nothing except a pile of ash and twisted rubble. It was horrible. Eerie. Jones might have expected little else. But she was shocked to the core. She could smell the acrid stench of burning. And she thought she could smell the stench of burned flesh. She knew she was probably imagining it, but it still made her want to retch.

As she fought against the urge, she heard a sound directly behind her. The sound of movement. A crunching noise, possibly from gravel or loose soil, or maybe rubble from the blast, beneath an approaching foot. Startled, she turned right around, 180 degrees, and found herself staring almost directly into the glare of the arc lights. For a few seconds she could see nothing. Then she became aware of an approaching human shadow. She could see no features, just a dark shape.

Overcome by fear, she swung around in the other direction, away from where she felt the immediate danger lay, and began to run.

She didn't get far. The front of her right shin hit an immobile object, a piece of debris from the blast. The pain shot through her leg as her upper body carried on moving whilst the lower part remained locked solid. She catapulted over whatever it was that had tripped her up and crashed heavily to the ground, falling flat on her face.

If her presence had gone unnoticed before, there was no longer any chance of that.

A man's voice shouted something. Then a second voice joined in. She thought she heard the word 'stop', but beyond that had no idea what they were saying.

Heavy footsteps approached. She had fallen just outside the area illuminated by the arc lights. She was aware of being caught in the beam of a torch. She struggled to rise to her feet. Then she heard a gunshot. For a second she froze. There was a second gun shot. Was she being fired at? She had no idea. She reacted instinctively. She tried to run again.

A heavy body cannoned into her. Jones fell to the ground once more, with a bone-crunching thud. The heavy body descended upon her, pinioning her down. Jones kept struggling. But it was hopeless.

She heard swearing, then a burst of some kind of liquid hit her full in the face. The pain was instant. As if her eyes were on fire. Instantly they began to stream water. And it hurt like hell. She realized she must have been sprayed with something highly unpleasant and injurious, possibly toxic. Oh my God, she thought, involuntarily squeezing her eyes shut. Could it have been acid? She continued to struggle and was rewarded with another face-full of noxious spray. She collapsed in agony, desperately trying to get her hands to her face, to wipe her burning eyes.

But a second assailant had now joined the first. Jones's arms were pulled roughly behind her back and handcuffed together at the wrist. Probing fingers were all over her body, rough and intrusive, presumably searching for a weapon. Then a torch was shone right into her damaged face, and her hood pulled back.

'It's a goddammed woman,' she heard a gruff male voice mutter.

However, the revelation of her gender did not appear to make things any easier for her. Not this time. A knee was pressed into the small of her back, and an arm wrapped around her neck almost choking her. There was no longer a chance of Jones moving or resisting in any way, even if she'd had the slightest intention of so doing. Which she didn't. Not anymore. Her entire face felt as if it was burning, and the wind had been knocked out of her. She couldn't see. She could barely breathe. She had been afraid before. Now she was plain terrified.

Then the pressure was abruptly released. Strong hands grabbed her upper body and strong arms hauled her upright.

She felt so weak she could hardly stand. She seemed to have no control over her body at all. She feared that she was about to wet herself.

'Stand still with your legs apart!'

The order was barked at her. Jones, her breath coming in short sharp gasps, obeyed at once to the best of her ability. Squinting through swollen eyelids, she tried to get a glimpse of the faces of the men holding her. They wore shiny black helmets and goggles, which concealed most of their features, a bit like the headgear she'd seen riot police wear in England. Jones wondered what on earth they were expecting to confront on the campus.

Their appearance alone was quite terrifying. So much so that Jones wondered again if they really were police – or indeed any other security force. Perhaps they were terrorists. She just couldn't think straight.

Suddenly, and none too gently, a pair of leg irons were fastened around her ankles.

'Right. Walk. Now. Straight ahead!'

She did her best to comply. But the hard unforgiving metal of the irons bit into the already bruised flesh of her ankles and lower legs, grating against the bone.

Involuntarily she cried out. The only response from her captors was a rough push forwards. She could only shuffle awkwardly in the irons, and would have fallen again were she not still being more or less held upright.

Jones was frightened out of her wits. She had absolutely no idea what she'd thought she was doing wandering around the scene of a major crime at such an hour in the morning. And, as, coughing and spluttering, she was half dragged along the ground by what appeared to be a small regiment of black-clad men, armed to the teeth, she could only hope that she would be allowed to live to regret it.

SEVEN

They manhandled her towards a parked van and told her to climb in the back. Even without the leg irons she wouldn't have had the strength, so they more or less picked her up and threw her in.

The doors slammed shut, and the van set off almost at once at considerable speed.

With her hands still cuffed behind her back and her legs still in irons, she lay spread-eagled on the bare metal floor unable to use her arms to raise herself into a sitting or even a kneeling position.

Every time the van swung around a corner, or its speed increased or decreased, she was flung from one extreme of the rear compartment to the other, causing her already bruised and battered body even more damage. To make matters worse her eyes, nose and mouth still burned. And she couldn't stop coughing.

There were bench seats along each side of the van's otherwise empty rear compartment. During one particularly violent movement Jones found herself lifted in the air. She smashed into one of the benches with considerable force, the side of her face colliding with the edge.

It felt as if her cheekbone had been crushed. She could taste a salty wetness on her skin. Blood. She was bleeding.

What the hell had she got herself into?

The van suddenly lurched to a halt. Jones gratefully released the tension in her legs. Then she heard the handle which fastened the van's double doors turn.

She still didn't know who her captors were. They could well be the people who had caused the dreadful explosion.

The van doors swung open. Jones could feel her bladder involuntarily opening again, and only just managed to restrain it.

Outside the van two of the men, still with their balaclavas pulled down over their faces, were standing to one side. And, framed in the rear doorway, illuminated by bright lights from the building behind them, were two more men, each wearing, without any doubt at all, the uniform of the New Jersey State Police.

Big double gates closed with a loud metallic clunk. Jones looked around. At first she had no idea where she was, except that she, and the vehicle she had travelled in, had now been shut in some kind of enclosed yard. Then she spotted a sign by the door leading into the building. 'Booking Office Entrance. Princeton Borough Police Station'.

And if chemically-induced tears had not already been tumbling from her eyes, Sandy Jones would probably have wept with relief.

She was led straight into what she assumed must be the booking office, known in the UK, she was aware from that predilection for TV detective shows, as a custody suite. Her head was immediately and unceremoniously dunked into a small washbasin to one side where a kind of customized fountain gushed water upwards into her burning face. At first she wondered what the heck was going on, and was further unnerved. But the relief the water instantly brought made her realize that this must be what the washbasin was for, and that spraying a noxious substance into the face of a suspect was probably common practice in these parts – or certainly when the suspect was dumb enough to appear to be putting up a fight.

Jones's cuffs and leg irons were removed by the two officers who had arrested her, and she was asked to empty her pockets. All she had on her was a few dollars and her mobile phone, which were duly placed in a brown envelope. She had left everything else in her hotel room. She hadn't planned to be gone long. Her father's watch was also removed and bagged. She hated being without it.

She was then told to stand with her legs apart and arms akimbo while she was searched by a third, female, officer.

'Look, there's been a dreadful mistake,' she said, eventually gathering courage. 'I'm Dr Sandy Jones from Exeter University in

England. I just came to see the damage for myself. Two great friends of mine have died. I realize I behaved stupidly, but I wasn't doing anything wrong . . .'

Jones wished she hadn't left her shoulder bag containing her passport, credit cards and all the rest of her documentation in her room at the Nassau Inn. Glumly she realized that she couldn't even prove her identity. Not immediately anyway. But it seemed to make little difference. Nobody was listening.

'I want to see the British consul,' she demanded.

Even as she said the words she was struck by how silly the request sounded. The officers didn't exactly smile – it was hard to imagine them smiling, actually – but they definitely looked mildly amused.

'I must speak to someone. I'm entitled to representation. Surely I'm entitled to representation?' Jones continued.

'You will be interviewed in due course, ma'am,' said one of the officers eventually, as he replaced, in spite of her protests, Jones's cuffs, but mercifully not the leg irons. 'Meanwhile, please cooperate and you will come to no harm.'

It sounded like a threat. Jones stopped protesting and did as she was told. She had no choice, it seemed.

She was led to a cell by the two officers. One of them, a short skinny man who somehow gave the impression that he was acting extra tough in order to compensate for his lack of height and bulk, pushed her ahead with what Jones felt was unnecessary force. The second officer removed her handcuffs.

The cell was a surprise. Jones had never been in a police cell before, but doubted if many were as smart and clean as this one. A stainless-steel lavatory and wash basin ensemble had been installed behind a slotted wooden bench which ran along one immaculately white wall, and neither would have looked entirely out of place in some kind of ultra-modern, minimalist-designed apartment. Jones was reminded that this was Princeton. And Princeton was not only smarter and richer, but also totally different from anywhere else on earth. There was even a phone on the wall. She glanced enquiringly at the officer.

'Collect calls only,' growled the short skinny officer. 'But it's out of order, anyway.'

The officer seemed to derive a certain amount of pleasure from that. And it occurred to Jones that the phone being out of order might well be no accident. Even in Princeton, cops will be cops, she thought.

Her arms still ached. She flexed and stretched them, seeking relief. The two officers backed watchfully away, as if she really was some sort of violent criminal. She made one last futile attempt to explain herself.

'This is a mistake, a complete mistake,' she began. 'I'm Dr Sandy Jones, ask anyone. I'm always on TV back home. I'm very well known.'

She couldn't quite believe she'd said that. It was such a crass remark. But these were desperate circumstances. And it made no difference anyway. Nobody was listening. Nobody cared. The officers retreated into the corridor. The cell door slammed shut.

Without either her phone or her treasured watch, she had little idea of the time. And there was no window.

Jones wasn't normally claustrophobic, and this cell was far less unpleasant in every way than she might have expected. All the same, she couldn't quite conquer the feeling that the walls were gradually closing in on her. She felt as if she was suffocating. It took a great effort of will not to panic.

There were actually two cells side by side – their doors iron-barred gates and the division between them also made of iron bars – within one bigger outer room. The second cell was unoccupied. Jones didn't know whether that was good or bad. Periodically an officer opened the solid door of the outer room and looked in. At first Jones called out every time, demanding to speak to someone in authority, to be allowed to make a phone call from a phone that worked, to be given the chance to explain herself.

After a while she realized she was wasting her time. At some stage a packet of fat cheese sandwiches, wrapped in paper bearing the legend Wa Wa, and a paper carton of luke-warm milky coffee, were pushed through the bars. Princeton Borough Police Station did not, apparently, run to a canteen. But it still fed its prisoners. Jones recognized the Wa Wa logo from her Princeton days, and assumed the food and drink must have come from the store over by the Dinky Train station. She couldn't eat anything. However, she drank the insipid coffee gratefully.

Soon afterwards the outer door opened again, and two different police officers entered. Jones had absolutely no idea how long she had been in the cell. It seemed like days, but she knew it must only be a few hours at the most.

The officers, in what she regarded as normal uniform, were both reassuringly ordinary looking, one tall and very young, the other shorter, plumpish, and middle-aged. Jones was rather glad not to see the skinny aggressive man she had encountered earlier in the day.

'Right, let's go then,' said the middle-aged officer, unlocking the barred gate to Jones's cell.

'Go where?' asked Jones.

'There's somebody wants to talk to you.'

Jones relaxed slightly. She welcomed the opportunity of speaking to almost anybody.

''Fraid we've got to cuff you again first.'

Jones flinched. She knew well enough this was the way American police did business. Those under suspicion of almost any sort of crime were cuffed all the time when they were not actually under lock and key.

Meekly, she held her hands out.

'Behind your back, ma'am.'

Resignedly, she thrust her arms behind her back as directed, and the cuffs were locked into place.

They took her to what she assumed was an interview room and directed her to sit at a small table. The room was not equipped with any visible recording equipment. Jones guessed there would be a video system. She glanced upwards. Sure enough, there was a tiny camera in one corner of the ceiling.

The door opened again. A large man of indeterminate years, probably nearing retirement, Jones thought, advanced into the room in a business-like manner. He was wearing a cream jacket rather cleverly tailored so that he looked big rather than fat. and stood with a hand on each hip looking Jones up and down.

Jones began to get up out of her chair. The man gestured for her to stay sitting.

'I am Detective Ronald Grant of the New Jersey State Police Force, and you, ma'am, are in a great deal of trouble,' he announced.

Jones opened her mouth to again plead her innocence. Detective Grant, straightening with one hand a tasteful cream-and-brown striped silk tie which did not need to be straightened, didn't give her the chance.

'Right. I would like to know who you are, and what you were doing lurking around at a major crime scene?'

Almost gratefully Jones answered the first question, but found she had no proper answer to the second.

'I just wanted to see it,' she finished lamely.

'Any particular reason?'

'I worked with Constance Pike and Paul Ruders years ago. I . . . uh . . . I wanted to see for myself what had happened to them, what had happened to the lab.'

'You came over from the UK specially?'

Jones considered lying. But she knew she wasn't thinking clearly enough to successful maintain a lie.

'Yes, I did.'

'You were arrested just before five a.m.,' Grant continued. 'Funny time to be visiting a crime scene, wasn't it?'

'I couldn't sleep,' Jones replied, acutely aware of just how lame that sounded.

'I see. So if your attentions were so innocent why did you resist arrest?'

'I didn't. Well, I didn't mean to. I was just frightened. I wasn't even sure it was police out there.'

'You weren't? But the officers identified themselves as police, did they not?'

'No. I mean, I don't know. They shouted "stop". I couldn't hear properly. Anyway, they weren't regular cops, were they?'

Detective Grant did not answer that question.

'Were you alone at the scene, ma'am?' he asked instead.

'Yes, I was.'

'Our boys reported seeing someone else with you. Someone who ran away from the scene, in spite of warning shots being fired over their head.'

'What?' Jones was momentarily puzzled. 'I don't understand. I was alone.' She fought to clear her head. 'I heard the shots. I thought I was being fired at.'

Detective Grant's ample chins wobbled. He was well over six feet tall and probably weighed getting on for twenty stone, Jones thought obliquely.

'This is Princeton and we are the New Jersey State Police. It is part of our legislation that we do not shoot suspects, except in self-defence.' Grant paused. A small smile played around his lips. 'In any case, if our boys had been shooting at you, ma'am, you would not be sitting here with me. You would be dead.'

Jones's throat, still sore from the spray, felt dry as dust. She gulped some air down. She was once more on the verge of panic. Her eyes continued to sting.

'What did they do to me?' she asked suddenly. 'What was that stuff they sprayed in my face? I thought I was going to go blind.'

'Oleoresin Capsicum, ma'am. Pepper spray. That's all. Standard procedure when a suspect resists arrest. No danger of your sight being permanently harmed.'

Jones grunted. She wondered how Detective Grant would like to have the stuff thrown in his face.

'Right,' continued the detective. 'Let's get some answers, shall we? How exactly did you come to trip and fall this morning, ma'am? You tried to run, didn't you? Just like whoever else was out there with you.'

'No. I mean, yes. I started to run, but nobody was with me. I was startled. No, frightened. I heard footsteps close by, saw a shape. I didn't know who it was. I didn't realize it was a police officer.' She paused. 'Was it a police officer?'

Detective Grant looked down at his hands, two huge plates of pale pink meat clasped together on the table before him. Again he made no attempt to answer Jones's question.

'Ma'am, I have already informed you that it has been reported that someone else was with you when you were confronted. So please will you tell me who that was?'

'Nobody was with me. I keep telling you. I mean, there was someone there, but I don't know who the hell it was. Like I said, I was scared. I tried to get away. Only I fell, and the next thing I knew there was a knee in my back.'

'So you couldn't identify this other person?'

'No. Absolutely not. I couldn't see. I knew there was someone there, but I've no idea whether it was a man or a woman, even. Then, after I was arrested, I just assumed it had been another police officer, or somebody from whatever security forces were out there. But you're telling me you don't know who that person was either, isn't that so?'

Jones felt shakier than ever. This interview seemed to be going in all the wrong directions. Detective Grant leaned back in his chair. The cream jacket strained against its central button. Grant undid the button and the jacket fell open, revealing his rotund belly. The chair creaked. Jones wondered if it might collapse under the strain. Grant frowned.

'I'm not saying anything, ma'am. Just answer the questions please. Did you know anybody else at all who was involved in the explosion?'

'No. I don't think so. Not the other scientist who was named, anyway, and almost certainly not either of the injured students. It was a long time ago that I was at Princeton.'

'So how exactly would you describe your relationship with Connie Pike and Paul Ruders?'

'We are old friends.'

'Are old friends?'

Dear God, these people were going to pick her up on everything.

'Were old friends, I suppose. I haven't got my head around that yet.'

'And is that all?'

What on earth was the man getting at? Jones realized she really was going to have to get her act together, shake off her shock at what had happened to her. It was time she asserted herself.

'Look, I'm a British National and I am also a leading academic and a television personality.'

She felt so stupid taking this line of approach, but she really didn't know what else to do.

'I am internationally known,' she heard herself continue. 'I really feel—'

'Unfortunately, ma'am, you appear to have no proof of any of this, do you?' Detective Grant interrupted. 'You do not have your passport on you, nor any other identification.'

'It's all at the Nassau Inn. I checked in there last night. Nobody's given me a chance to explain, for God's sake. Why don't you just let me go and fetch my stuff?'

'I'm sorry, ma'am, I'm afraid you're not going anywhere until your presence in Princeton has been fully investigated. I'll send an officer round to the Nassau. Meanwhile would you please tell me when you arrived at Princeton?'

'I got here yesterday evening. I only arrived in the States yesterday afternoon. I was on the other side of the Atlantic when the lab exploded, if that's what you're getting at. You can check airline records, can't you? And I can give you the names of all kinds of people in the UK who will vouch for me, at my university and so on. Even the BBC for God's sake. Surely you can contact them?'

'We are in the process of making enquiries in the United Kingdom. These things take time. Meanwhile, I would like to know if there is anyone in Princeton who can confirm your identity.'

Jones thought first of all of Thomas Jessop, and straight away suggested him. There couldn't, surely, be anyone much better to speak for her than the dean of the university.

'I am afraid the dean isn't here, ma'am. He was in hospital in New York having a minor operation at the time of the explosion, and I understand will not be discharged until tomorrow.'

Jones groaned. That only left Ed. And Jones was not at all sure she wanted to involve Ed in this, or even if he would allow himself to become involved.

She tried asserting herself again.

'Now look, it would take only the most elementary of checks to establish who I am, and that the information I have given you is correct. Can't you check online? I present a television programme back home. My presence here is completely innocent. And I'm not prepared to cooperate with you further until I'm allowed some sort of representation. I should like to contact the British Consulate in New York . . .'

Suddenly the door of the interview room swung open yet again. A younger man, of average height and build swept into the room. His dark blonde hair was slicked back, and he was wearing a neat black suit, white shirt, black tie, and heavily tinted spectacles. In different circumstance Jones would have found it difficult to take him seriously. He must surely have been sent round directly from Central Casting. He wasn't just the complete stereotype of some kind of special agent. He was straight out of *Men in Black*.

Jones stopped speaking. The Man in Black slammed the door shut behind him and advanced swiftly towards her. His walk was a strut, his head jutting forwards and his shoulders pushed back. He smashed his fist down on the table with tremendous force. The noise it made reverberated around the room. His hand must hurt like hell, Jones thought – but the man did not flinch.

He leaned closer to Jones. The tinted glasses made it impossible to see his eyes properly. His breath smelt of garlic.

Jones instinctively backed away.

'I would advise you to continue to cooperate fully, Miss Jones.'

The Man in Black's voice was low and full of menace. Jones had little doubt that his use of the prefix 'miss' instead of 'doctor' was deliberate. It seemed clear that he had been observing the interview through the video system.

'We are investigating three deaths here, Miss Jones. Several more people have serious injuries. And I don't give a fuck who you are. You can be a four-times fucking Nobel prize winner for all I care. You will answer all questions put to you, and you should know that we have every damned right to detain you here for as long as we damned well please.'

Jones asked herself for the umpteenth time how she had got herself into such a situation. She knew that the American police force lived by vastly different rules to the police back home, but this was surely especially heavy. And she didn't even know whether the Man in Black was a police officer or something more sinister. He certainly liked to give the impression of being something more sinister, Jones reckoned.

'Would you please tell me who you are?' she plucked up the courage to ask. 'Are you FBI? Who are you?'

The man's face was still only inches away from Jones's. She had never before met an American who smelt so strongly of garlic, as if, almost, he'd been pickled in the stuff rather than had merely eaten it.

'None of your goddamned business,' he snarled.

He stared at Jones for several seconds before straightening up and backing off, nodding slightly towards Detective Grant.

'I will ask you again,' said Detective Grant, sounding exaggeratedly patient. 'Apart from the dean, is there anyone in Princeton who can vouch for you?'

Sighing, Jones gave Ed's name and address.

'Right then, ma'am. I am now going to arrange for everything you have told us to be checked out. Meanwhile you must remain in custody.'

He turned to the uniformed officer standing by the door.

'All yours, Dave.'

Dave stepped forward.

'Stand up and put your hands behind your back,' he ordered.

Oh God, thought Jones. She was going to be handcuffed again. But she made no further attempt to protest.

The officer called Dave, this time unaccompanied – which made Jones absurdly hopeful that maybe Princeton Plod was finally realizing she presented no threat to anybody – marched her back to her cell.

Once her cuffs had been removed, Jones sat on the wooden bench bed and reflected again on her predicament. How could she have been so stupid as to go alone to a designated crime scene at such a crazy time of day. And in America too, the home of the trigger happy.

She groaned out loud. She hoped the worst might be over, but if the American authorities did start checking her out back home before releasing her, eyebrows were sure to be raised among the hierarchy of both the university which currently employed her and the more exalted one which was about to appoint her chancellor. Not to mention the BBC. And her sons didn't even know she had left the country. They would be worried sick.

There was what seemed like another interminable wait before they came for her again.

Once more it was Detective Grant, and Dave, carrying Jones's bag, and the black leather jacket she had worn on her journey over.

'Your story has checked out and you are free to go now,' said Grant.

'I should hope so,' Jones snapped, in a vague attempt at some kind of bravado. She was relieved, nervous, and angry all at the same time.

Detective Grant and Dave both ignored her. Grant handed her a brown envelope.

'Your watch and everything that was in your pockets are in there,' he said. 'Just sign here for it.'

He held out a clipboard and passed Jones a pen.

Jones signed, tore open the envelope and straight away slipped on the old Longine. Somehow it made her feel less like a victim.

She checked the time. It was nearly two o'clock in the afternoon. She had been in police custody for almost seven hours.

'We've looked through your papers and replaced them in your bag,' Detective Grant continued.

Jones took her bag from Dave, lifted it on to the wooden bench, and quickly made sure that both her laptop and her documents were inside, along with the few clothes she had brought with her for what she had always planned would be a short stay.

'We've checked you out of the Nassau, and your credit card will be debited,' said Detective Grant. 'We assume you will have no wish to stay on now.'

He made that sound like an order. Jones picked up her bag, slung it over her shoulder, and wordlessly followed the two police officers out of the cell, along the corridor and up the stairs to the main foyer.

'So where do you suggest I go?' she inquired, a certain irony in her voice.

'That, of course, is entirely up to you, Miss Jones.'

The reply came from behind Jones and slightly to her right. She glanced quickly over her shoulder. The Man in Black was leaning against the wall by the glass box which enclosed the reception area.

'Dr Jones,' she corrected.

'Indeed. I understand you are leaving Princeton now, Dr Jones.'

It was another order. Jones felt an overwhelming urge to protest, to argue. She was being more or less run out of town, it seemed, a bit like a character in a Western B-movie.

On the other hand, if she refused to leave, what exactly would she achieve apart from making her life even more difficult? She still had little real idea why she'd travelled to Princeton in the first place. Except that she had felt compelled. Maybe it was one of those bonds of consciousness which RECAP had been set up to study, she thought wryly.

'You're right, I don't think I do have a reason to remain here,' she responded.

'Good.'

The Man in Black straightened up, turned on his heel and disappeared behind reception back into the interior of the station.

Jones was suddenly struck by the feeling that there was something vaguely familiar about him, but she just couldn't place it. In any

case, she couldn't think when she would ever have been likely to
have met him, or indeed, anyone like him.

'Perhaps we can provide you with transport to Princeton Junction,
Dr Jones?' Detective Grant suggested. 'As it happens I need to go
that way myself, so why don't you let me give you a ride?'

Jones had no doubt about what lay behind the offer. The police
wanted to make sure she really did leave town, even going to the
extent of providing an escort, it seemed. Under the circumstances
she didn't feel at all inclined to cooperate.

'No thank you, detective,' she replied. 'I think I have endured
quite enough New Jersey police hospitality for one day.'

She also had another reason for declining. She wanted to see Ed
again, and not just for old times' sake. She still felt there had to be
something he could tell her that would shed some light on all that
had happened, even if he didn't know it.

Detective Grant seemed about to push the point. Then, as if on
cue, into the foyer from the direction of the station interior
came Ed. He spotted Jones at once, and a look she could not quite
decipher spread across his face.

Was it concern? Or exasperation? Or a bit of both? She
wasn't sure.

'What are you doing here?' she blurted out without thinking.

'What would you think I'm doing here, Sandy?' He glowered
at her. 'I was brought here, whether I liked it or not, to convince
the New Jersey police that you are who you say you are and not
some crazy terrorist.'

'Ah.'

'What have you done to your face?'

Jones raised a hand to her injured cheek. She assumed that her
eyes still looked red and puffy too.

'I had an argument with a van.'

'Oh.'

Ed couldn't have sounded much less concerned. She wondered
why he even bothered to make the enquiry.

'Look,' she began, 'I was hoping to have another chat before
I leave—'

'Sandy, my two best friends in all the world have just died in
the most horrible violent way. I feel as if my whole life is in ruins.
And you want to drop by for a chat?'

'Well, I just thought we could talk things through . . .'

'Talk things through? No, Sandy. Everything those of us who believed in RECAP have worked for all those long years is finished. You left over twenty years ago, and you never looked back. Connie and Paul are dead. It's over, for God's sake. I don't have anything more to say to you. To tell the truth, Sandy, I haven't had anything to say to you since you walked out on me the way you did.'

He took off then, powering his way through the police station's big swing doors, his back stiff with anger.

She watched him go with sorrow. She had wondered, when she'd visited him the previous evening, if there might be a chance of at least rebuilding their friendship. It now seemed clear that was out of the question.

Detective Grant stood silently alongside her, his broad fleshy face giving little away.

'Maybe I'll take that lift to Princeton Junction after all,' Jones muttered.

EIGHT

At Princeton Junction, Detective Grant carried Jones's bag onto the platform, in spite of her protests, and stayed with her until she was able to board an Amtrak train bound for Penn Station.

Jones really did feel as if she were being drummed out of town. She accepted, however, that it was largely her own fault. She had an IQ of 150. That meant that she was officially a genius, for Christ's sake. But she had behaved stupidly.

She considered what she would do next. She supposed it lurked in the back of her mind that she wanted to pay her respects to Connie and Paul. Although she didn't quite know how. There weren't going to be any funerals. Not yet, anyway. There were, after all, no bodies to bury.

The Man in Black had made no secret of his desire that Jones should not only leave town, but also, preferably, the country.

Indeed, she would have been more likely to accept that the explosion might well have been a tragic accident were it not for the treatment she'd received at the hands of the Princeton police, and in particular the threatening demeanour of the mysterious Man in Black. Nonetheless that possibility remained, and in any case, what more could she do?

She switched on her mobile, for the first time that day. A string of messages awaited. She checked them in cursory fashion. Almost all of them were from various colleagues puzzled by her peremptory absence and the brief notes of vague explanation she had emailed to them. They could wait. Clearly neither her sons nor anybody else back home had been contacted by the American police, which was a relief. And if she were to take the obvious sensible course of action, she would be back in the UK the following morning.

She checked the time. It was three twenty p.m. She should be able to catch the evening's BA flight to Heathrow easily enough. She called up the phone number for reservations, and then paused.

She hadn't slept for the best part of forty-eight hours. She was bone tired. Her right shin was still very sore from the bashing it had received outside the RECAP lab. Her eyes were no longer inflamed, and the worst effects of the capsicum spray had worn off, but none the less her entire face felt sore. Her injured cheek was throbbing. She didn't feel at all like a seven-hour flight.

When Jones had been in New York the previous year, giving the Triple A address, she had stayed for the first time at Soho House, the city's hotel version of the famous London club.

Stretching her back and shoulders in a vain attempt to ease the tension, Jones found her thoughts focusing on the House's superior plumbing. Most of the rooms had baths right in the middle of them, so that you could soak yourself while enjoying the state-of-the-art entertainment facilities, including a huge TV screen.

She shut her eyes and dreamed a little. The very idea of one of those baths was quite seductive. And after all, she thought, what was the hurry? She wasn't being deported, even though the Man in Black probably wished that she was. She would book into the House, indulge herself thoroughly, and hopefully manage a good night's sleep, before flying home the following evening. She would still be back in time to fulfil her BBC filming obligations and attend that Oxford dinner engagement.

She called the House. There was a room available. She confirmed it at once with her credit card.

The following morning Jones felt considerably better. She had slept like a baby. She felt almost like a human being again, and hoped she looked like one too. There was a mirror on the wall to the right of her big double bed. She turned towards it. Her face had thankfully returned pretty much to normal after the capsicum assault, just as Detective Grant had promised. There was no longer any soreness or swelling. And the injury to her left cheek, although not pretty, had not become as unsightly as she had feared.

Lazily she stretched her long legs beneath the covers, reached out a languid arm, dialled room service, and ordered tea.

It was barely six a.m. In spite of her total weariness, jet lag had caused her to wake early again. At least that meant she would have a full day to enjoy her favourite city after London. But first she switched on the TV, and tuned in to CNN to check the latest on the Princeton explosion, which turned out to have been relegated to fourth on the news list. And the item was certainly not revelatory.

New Jersey Police this morning refused to confirm or deny a report in today's *New York Post* that the explosion at Princeton University earlier this week was caused by a gas leak. 'Our investigations are continuing, and a full statement will be released as soon as possible,' said a police spokesman.

So the police were still hedging their bets. Well, they would, wouldn't they, thought Jones. Room service had brought two newspapers along with the tea she'd ordered. The *New York Times* and the tabloid *New York Post*. She unfolded the *Post* first. The splash headline jumped off the page at her.

PRINCETON BLAST MYSTERY. WAS IT NEGLIGENCE?

The deadly explosion at the Ivy League university earlier this week was caused by a gas leak, it was claimed last night. According to an FBI source, New Jersey Police are about to announce they have found no traces of a bomb at the scene of the explosion. Instead, the source has revealed exclusively to the *Post*, it is believed that a technical malfunction led to a leak which caused the devastating blast, and that routine maintenance on the university's gas system may have been neglected . . .

Was that it then? Jones didn't know what to think. However, since becoming a media personality she had endured considerable attention from the tabloid press, and had learned that, contrary to a widely held belief, they were more often right than wrong when they splashed on an exclusive story.

She had promised herself the previous day that she would move on. And that was what she was going to do. She dressed in the jeans she had worn the day before, which along with her black hoodie, she'd sent to be laundered upon arriving at the House. Like her, she hoped, they appeared to have made a good recovery from any damage suffered at the Princeton crime scene.

It was a pleasantly sunny morning, so she wandered up to the roof terrace for a leisurely breakfast. Afterwards, at around nine a.m., she took the lift to the ground floor and stepped out on to the cobbled street outside the House's discreet front door on the corner of Ninth Avenue and 13th Street.

The sun was already surprisingly hot again for mid-September. She squinted into the line of approaching traffic. She had yet to properly work out which cabs were for hire and which weren't on the streets of New York, and her dilemma was not helped by bright sunshine which made it impossible to tell whether the cabs had their lights on or not.

She'd learned to do what New Yorkers do – just stand on the pavement with your arm held out high in the air in front of you. She knew from her previous visit that the area right outside the House, in the heart of the Meatpacking District, although it didn't look promising, was a pretty good place for picking up cabs.

All the same, she was mildly surprised that morning by the alacrity with which a yellow cab pulled up right alongside, causing her to take a step backwards in order to avoid being knocked over.

She opened the door of the rear compartment and, having decided to start the day with a little shopping, gave the address of one of her favourite fashion stores.

The driver made no verbal response but took off with an unnerving squeal of tyres. This was, Jones knew, par for the course in New York. She'd long ago discovered that cabbies in the Big Apple were nothing like their London contemporaries, who were inclined to treat their passengers to their views on the weather, the traffic, the cost of living, the latest sporting event, the state of the country if not the world and indeed all aspects of life, at the drop of a hat. They were also obliged to learn The Knowledge, to know every detail of the layout of their city, in order to gain a licence to operate. In New York no such regulations were enforced. Taxi drivers' Medallions were bought rather than earned.

Jones made herself settle back in the seat and try to enjoy the ride. Vaguely she wondered why the driver was taking the route he was. It seemed obtuse even by the standards of New York cabbies.

She repeated the address of the store.

There was no response at all. The glass panel between the driver's compartment and the passenger seat was closed. Jones tapped on it and raised her voice.

'Driver! Hey driver! This isn't right. We're going the wrong way.'

Still no response. Jones tapped even louder and then pushed her fingers against the glass panel in an attempt to make it slide open. The panel was either locked or jammed. She tapped yet again, more forcefully.

'Hey driver!'

'Just relax, ma'am, I know exactly where I'm taking you.'

Jones was taken by surprise. The voice, pure New York, deep and resonant, was projected through a speaker just above the back seat. She hadn't known that New York cabs had that sort of sophistication.

'But we're going in the wrong direction,' Jones shouted back.

'You don't need to shout, ma'am, I can hear you just fine.'

The glass panel remained closed. Jones glanced around her. There must be a microphone somewhere, she assumed.

'Then for God's sake listen to what I'm saying,' she countered irritably, before repeating the address once more, complete with the obligatory cross street.

'We're heading the other way, surely?'

'I know where I'm taking you, ma'am.'

Jones opened her mouth to say it damned well didn't look like it to her. Then closed it again. There was something disconcerting about the way the driver had delivered the last remark. Jones was beginning to suspect that if this man was taking her the wrong way, it was not by mistake.

The bile rose in her throat. She fought to remain calm. Perhaps the events of the previous day had been too much for her and she was just being paranoid. She decided to have one last attempt at normal behaviour.

'Just pull over,' she commanded. 'I'll get out here.'

Jones delivered the remark as if it was an order she expected to be obeyed. But she wasn't at all surprised when the driver ignored her. Stifling a growing sense of panic, she began to formulate a plan. She was sitting on the left of the cab directly behind the driver. She shuffled along the seat to the right until she could see clearly ahead. There was a set of traffic lights just a couple of hundred yards ahead. To her irritation they remained on green. So did the next three sets. In American cities traffic lights often seemed better synchronized than at home. She waited impatiently, her fingers tight around the door handle, until finally a set of lights turned red as the taxi approached.

The driver braked. And as the cab drew to a halt Jones wrenched at the door, preparing to hit the street at a run. The door didn't budge. She twisted the handle frantically, pushing and shoving with all her might. It made no difference. The door was locked.

'Driver,' she yelled. 'Driver, will you please unlock the doors. I told you, I want to get out.'

There was again no response. The lights changed. The cab moved forwards, unhurriedly.

'Driver, will you damned well pull over and unlock these fucking doors!' Jones shouted even louder, aware that her voice had turned into a kind of shriek.

The driver made no attempt to slow the cab down, but at least he responded.

'Just calm down, ma'am. You're not going to come to any harm.'

As he spoke he reached behind his head with one arm, and an enormous black hand adorned with assorted bling appeared directly in Jones's line of sight. Bracelets around the wrist jangled as ring-laden fingers flicked some kind of switch and slid the glass panel to one side. Then the driver glanced briefly over his shoulder, and Jones was confronted by a smiling face, big and broad-boned. She did not find the smile reassuring. In fact just the opposite.

The man's domed head was entirely without hair except for a Mohican stripe along the centre. Earrings dangled from both his ears and more bling hung in layers around his neck. His appearance was surreal. For just a fleeting hopeful moment Jones wondered if she might be dreaming.

'I'm only taking you to someone who wants to spend a little time with you, that's all.'

The driver's voice was loud, clear and resonant. This was no dream.

'My name is Dom, I'm mighty pleased to meet you, Dr Jones, and I want you to know you are absolutely safe with me.'

Jones couldn't believe what she was hearing. 'Dom' had introduced himself as if he were someone Jones had met socially in a bar rather than the driver of a motor vehicle taking her God knows where against her will. And, chillingly, he knew who she was.

Jones reckoned she had never felt less safe in her life, not even the previous day when she'd been clamped in irons by New Jersey's finest. She made no attempt to reply to 'Dom'. Instead she slumped back into the seat of the cab feeling as if she'd been hit in the face. Again.

Oh shit, she thought. Oh shit. Oh shit. Not a repeat performance. This really couldn't be happening. Not for the second time in twenty-four hours. Was she being arrested? Was she being kidnapped? She had absolutely no idea. She just knew that once more she was locked inside a strange vehicle being taken against her will to an unknown destination by someone she'd never seen before in her life. If only she'd flown back to the UK the previous night as she'd originally planned.

She covered her face with her hands. Ultimately she could not stop herself breaking down. And in the back of that yellow cab wending its relentless way through the streets of New York to an unknown and quite probably highly dangerous destination, Sandy Jones wept tears of fear.

NINE

Minutes later the cab turned abruptly off the main drag into what was little more than an alleyway between two tall buildings. They had been driving for almost twenty minutes, but Jones was pretty certain they were still in the Meatpacking District, and had actually travelled in a kind of circle.

Jones became aware that the driver was talking into his mobile phone. Then the man slowed down and swung the cab sharply left, heading straight for a set of big metal doors, their scant coat of pale blue paint peeling away in strips, which opened as if by magic as they approached. The vehicle coasted into a double garage alongside another already parked there.

Jones had regained control and was no longer crying. But she remained in shock. It was a good thing she didn't have a heart condition – as far as she knew anyway – or she would already probably be dead. She asked herself yet again what the hell she had thought she was doing, flying into the US of A to play amateur detective?

For a few seconds the driver sat unmoving in front of Jones, who was still locked in, and was by then far too afraid to say or do anything. Then she heard a rumbling sound behind the cab, and turned around to see the double doors slowly closing and ultimately shutting with a bang.

There was another noise to the front of the cab. Jones turned to face forwards and saw that a smaller door at the rear of the garage, the sort that normally leads into a house or an apartment, was opening. A figure stepped through the doorway. The lighting at that end of the garage was not very bright. Jones squinted into the dimness. But it was only when the figure approached the cab, moving into the more brightly lit central part of the garage, that Jones could see that it was a woman. A woman in her late fifties or early sixties, Jones guessed, spreading just a little around the waist. She had pretty pale hair, a pleasant-featured face lightly made-up, and was wearing extremely clean pale-blue jeans with sharp creases down the front, a pink silk shirt, and a multi-coloured silk scarf knotted around her neck.

Jesus Christ, thought Jones, who and what was this? The woman was the very epitome of Mrs Middle America. She should have been out the back somewhere making apple pie, taking her grandchildren to school in a four-wheel drive, or attending a suburban cocktail party on the arm of a be-suited, be-spectacled and ever-so-respectable husband.

Jones was completely taken aback. She could not believe that this person was either a terrorist, a police officer, or any kind of security agent. But then, what the hell did she know?

Mrs Middle America approached the cab, stopped adjacent to the driver's door, and looked in the back at Jones, studying her carefully. There was something about the woman that was vaguely familiar to Jones. She remembered that she had felt much the same about the Man in Black. Perhaps she was now so knocked off kilter by events that every other person she came in contact with looked familiar in some way.

'Hi,' said Mrs Middle America, speaking through the glass.

Jones was dumbfounded. She heard herself say 'Hi' back. This is absurd, she thought, truly absurd.

There was an electronic whirr as Dom lowered the window on the driver's side. Once it was fully open Mrs Middle America stuck her head through, and took an even longer look at Jones. Dom raised a bling-laden hand and passed her a piece of paper which seemed to be a page torn from a magazine.

'I'm pretty sure I've got the right gal, but I can always drop her back off,' remarked Dom conversationally.

Mrs Middle America grinned at him, and glanced down at the piece of paper.

'No need, this is her for sure,' she said. 'Thanks, Norman.'

Norman, thought Jones. What about Dom? This great hulking creature, dripping bling, surely could not be called Norman?

Jones guessed that the piece of paper probably carried a photograph of her. Even in America, where she was not a widely recognized face, she appeared occasionally in specialist science magazines. But who was this woman?

The front door of the cab opened and out stepped Dom. Or was it Norman? It seemed to take him quite some time to stand up. He appeared to be somewhere around six-and-a-half feet tall, Jones reckoned, and built like a brick shit house, as her father would have said. If he really was called Norman it was possible, she thought, that nobody on earth had ever been more inappropriately named. Norman was a giant. Jones was glad she had not had the opportunity to even attempt to quarrel first hand with her hijacker.

'Any time, Aunt M.'

Aunt M? Things were becoming increasingly bizarre.

'Just always glad to be of service, Aunt M, honey.'

The big driver's voice was pure Willard White.

'Well, you'd better let the lady out then, Norman dear.'

This really was surreal, thought Jones. And for reasons she couldn't explain, even though she remained locked in a cab within a locked garage somewhere in the bowels of one of the toughest cities in the world, she did not feel quite as frightened as she had only a few minutes earlier.

Norman/Dom leaned into the driver's compartment and pressed a button on the cab's central consul. There was a click, and Jones guessed that the rear doors had been unlocked. She turned the handle of the door nearest to her. It opened.

Dom, who had moved alongside, reached out with one mighty arm, placed a huge hand under one of Jones's elbows, and with surprising gentleness, helped her out of the cab. Jones was quite grateful for the assistance. Her legs still felt as if they were made of jelly.

'Sorry for the rough ride, lady. You've nothing to fear here, I promise you.'

Jones was not entirely reassured. She leaned against the cab, still needing support.

'You can go, Norman,' she heard Mrs America tell the driver. 'I know you've places to be today. I'll take it from here.'

'You sure Aunt M, sweetheart?' he replied.

'Sure I'm sure, Norman. Look at the poor woman. She's no danger to anyone, is she?'

Norman/Dom turned to look at Jones, who eased herself away from the support of the cab and tried very hard to stand up straight. Cautiously she flexed her legs, which, rather to her surprise, appeared able to hold her upright after all. But only just.

The big cabby laughed. It came from his belly. Quite friendly laughter, but mocking at the same time.

'Guess you're right, Aunt M, honey. But I'll be in the neighbourhood all day, OK? You have any problems, you just holler, all right?'

He turned to face Jones.

'And you, ma'am. I'm going to open these doors and get my ass out of here, while you just stand quietly over there. I don't want you even thinking 'bout running off or nothing. Do you hear?'

Jones nodded. Norman/Dom pointed to the far end of the garage. Jones meekly walked to the exact spot.

'Right on. So you just stay there, ma'am, or you'll be hellish sorry. Got it?'

'Got it,' said Jones, being careful to stand very still.

'Now Norman, there's no need for that,' said Mrs Middle America reproachfully.

'Mebbe not,' responded the big driver. 'But I ain't taking no chances. Not with you, Aunt M, sweetheart.'

He glowered at Jones one last time before pointing a hand-held remote control at the garage doors which once again opened obligingly. He then climbed back into his cab, and set off into the street. But he stopped outside, and Jones could see that he was still watching as the doors closed again.

Jones stood so motionless she might have been rooted to the ground.

Only when the doors were firmly shut, and Dom/Norman safely locked outside, did she allow herself the luxury of lifting a hand to her head in order to wipe away some of the sweat that had gathered on her forehead.

'I really must apologize for all of this,' began Mrs Middle America. 'But we couldn't think of an alternative.'

'We? We?' Jones found she was suddenly angry. Her relief at the departure of Dom, or Norman, or whatever he was damned well called, appeared to have given her some temporary bravado.

'Who the fuck is "we"?' she yelled. 'Who the fucking fuck is "we"? And what fucking right do you think you have kidnapping a British citizen in broad daylight on the streets of New York. Eh? Eh?'

She spat the words out.

Mrs Middle America took a step backwards. Emboldened, Jones took a step forwards.

'Well?' she shouted. 'Well? Are you going to answer me, woman, or what?'

As she spoke she was aware of the smaller door at the far end of the garage opening yet again.

A second figure stepped into the dimness there. Again all Jones could make out was a shape. But when that shape spoke Jones felt her already extremely wobbly knees buckle.

'Stop making such a goddamned fuss, you Limey lamebrain.'

Jones peered into the gloom, straining her eyes. It couldn't be. Yet it had to be. It could not possibly be anyone else. Not only had nobody else ever spoken to her like that, but she would recognize that voice always. Any time. Any place. And under any circumstances.

Even when the person it belonged to was supposed to be dead.

'Connie,' she whispered, half under her breath.

Then louder: 'Connie?'

'Who the hell else do you think it is, chowderhead?'

The figure moved further into the garage. It was Connie Pike, all right. An older, slightly broader Connie, but, by and large, a remarkably unchanged Connie, standing there looking as if nothing much had happened, and still with her trademark mane of unruly red hair.

'I don't believe it,' said Jones. 'I just don't believe it. What the fuck is going on? You're supposed to be dead.'

Connie smiled, and her face lit up just the way it had the very first time Sandy Jones had seen her. She still had a great face. Never beautiful, but strong boned, sharply defined, and kind.

'You're not wrong there, Sandy,' she said. 'I sure am supposed to be dead, and the longer I can remain so, the safer I am.'

'Jesus Christ, what's going on, Connie?' Jones asked. 'What on earth is going on?'

'Now that's one hell of a long story,' Connie replied. 'One hell of a long story.'

She was dressed in a vivid orange shirt and baggy purple trousers. She clearly still had the same penchant for bright colours which fought each other. And she still appeared to have the same absence of any awareness at all of the impact she had on those around her, with her startling clothes, her big red hair, her flashing green eyes, and her way of looking right into your soul. This was the same wonderful old Connie. And this time she really was a miracle on legs.

Jones was probably in an even greater state of shock than she had been at any stage over the previous couple of days. And that was saying something. She was also totally confused. She began to fire questions at Connie.

'Why all the cloak-and-dagger stuff? How did you escape that explosion? I've seen the mess the lab's in. Nobody could have survived. Why the fuck aren't you dead, Connie?'

The smile faded.

'Now that would be funny, really funny, if only . . .' She paused. 'If only Paul were here.'

Jones didn't say anything. Connie's eyes were full of pain. Jones stepped forwards. Connie held out her arms. They hugged. Jones felt close to tears again. Her nerves were in bits. But Connie Pike was clearly not going to allow herself to break down. So neither must Sandy Jones.

'I'm so very sorry, Connie,' she said as calmly as she could manage.

'I know.'

'But you're alive. I can't believe it. Connie, you're alive!'

'Yup. And I can't believe you're here. That you came.'

'Of course I came. Too little too late. I can't explain why I stayed away so long, but—'

'It's all right,' Connie interrupted. 'You don't have to explain.'

Jones glanced around.

'But you have to,' she said, after a pause.

She gestured at Mrs Middle America.

'Who's she? Who's Norman, or is it Dom? And why did you hijack me off the streets? I nearly died of shock. I've been in America less than forty-eight hours, and I seem to have spent most of the time being terrified out of my wits.'

Connie smiled. 'I'm sorry, we couldn't think of another way.'

Jones gestured towards Mrs Middle America again, pointing an extended thumb at her.

'That's what she said.'

'That's Marion,' said Connie.

Marion smiled. Jones waited to be told who Marion was. Instead Connie ushered her towards the door at the back of the garage.

'Right. Well, come on in. We'll have coffee and talk properly.'

She led the way up several flights of rickety stairs to a huge loft style apartment. They entered directly into a vast open-plan living area, which included a kitchen at one end and a huge oblong wooden table surrounded by a set of quite formal dining chairs.

The floor was of polished dark oak and most of the furniture was made of tubular steel, the soft furnishings black leather. A couple of in-your-face abstract paintings, one predominantly green and the other mainly pillar box red, were the only adornment on bare brick walls. The grey painted ceiling was criss-crossed with huge wooden beams. Big arched windows gave a magnificent view across the rooftops of Lower Manhattan towards the famous high-rise buildings around Fifth and Sixth Avenue and Madison.

The whole place was minimalist and scrupulously tidy – apart from a messy pile of newspapers and magazines scattered across the big glass-topped coffee table which stood between two black leather sofas. Jones could not imagine that the apartment had anything at all to do with Connie, and the accumulated clutter which had always been so much a part of her.

'Wow,' she said, at the same time glancing questioningly at the two women.

'Norman's place,' said Marion. 'He's staying with his girlfriend, given us the run of it.'

'Norman's place?' Jones echoed. 'A New York cabby with a Mohican haircut owns this?'

'Norman is not quite what he seems,' responded Marion.

'I think I've gathered that. He seems to have more than one name for a start.'

'He's only Norman to Marion,' explained Connie. 'No one else dares call him anything other than Dom.' She grinned. 'It's short for the Dominator.'

'It's short for what?'

'The Dominator. Dom used to be a World Series wrestler. Had to give it up because of a back injury, but unlike most of 'em he invested the money he made wisely – in property.'

'Good God.'

Connie gestured towards the two sofas. Jones obediently sat on the nearest one.

'I'll make the coffee,' Marion offered.

Connie murmured her thanks as she sat down next to Jones. She rummaged beneath the pile of papers on the table before her and unearthed a packet of cigarettes. Jones watched in silence while she removed one and lit up. No health campaign in the world was ever going to stop Connie Pike destroying her lungs if she so wished.

'Right then,' said Connie calmly. 'I expect you'd like a few answers, Sandy?'

Jones looked at her in disbelief. Upon closer examination the voluminous head of hair was almost certainly dyed red now. The roots were grey. Maybe Connie did have some personal vanity after all. Her hair was also slightly singed around the ends, and there were scratches on her hands, the only visible signs of any damage the explosion, and her miraculous escape, may have caused her.

'I think that's something of an understatement, Connie,' she said.

TEN

There was one question Sandy Jones wanted the answer to which overshadowed all others.

'So, Connie Pike, how the hell are you still alive?' she asked.

'Ah yes. I lay awake most of last night listening to my heart beating. Strange how comforting that sound is when you know it has no right to be beating at all. I should be dead, like Paul . . .'

She paused, the anguish of loss all too apparent.

'Well, you know how we've always managed at RECAP to keep ourselves apart from the rules of Princeton,' she continued eventually.

'Don't I just.'

'Yes, in every way really, how the lab looked, how we worked, what we did. We were always a law unto ourselves. The toys, the cards on the wall, even the design of our equipment, and, of course, Paul's various dogs . . .'

Her voice tailed off. The memories came flooding back to Jones again. For just a moment she almost half forgot the terrible tragedy which had struck in such a final and irrevocable fashion.

'Paul's dogs,' she murmured. 'Have they all been incontinent?'

'Only at the beginning and the end of their lives. It's just that the house-training phase went on forever with Paul. He had his own views on dog training, if you remember, and they weren't always immediately successful. I reckon Gilda was a saint.'

Jones chuckled. Then she had a thought.

'I wondered . . . did Paul have a dog with him in the lab when . . .'

She didn't bother to finish. She knew.

'I told you on the phone he had a new puppy,' said Connie. 'Well, she died with her master.'

'Ah,' said Jones.

The thought of that made her sadder than ever.

Connie looked away.

'Anyway, I was telling you how I escaped,' she continued. 'You'll remember that we always allowed smoking in the lab, even though it was against the rules. Not least because we were both smokers. And I still am, but Paul had given up, of course.'

She paused, as if she had said something profound.

Jones was puzzled.

'Yes?' she queried.

'I'm sorry, I thought I told you. On the phone?'

'Told me? Told me what?'

'The sprinklers. Health and Safety suddenly remembered we existed and put in sprinklers. One right above my desk. Well, I was deep into something really fascinating one morning, the morning after you and I spoke on the phone, I think, and forgot all about the damned stupid things. I dropped a match in my ashtray which carried on burning for a moment. Next thing it's raining. Place got drenched. Miraculously the computer system survived, not that it was to matter much . . .'

'But obviously even I knew better than to attempt to smoke in the lab again. So, well, thankfully we were on the ground floor, with those big low windows, remember? I started the habit of climbing out of a window and walking around the quadrangle when I wanted a smoke. And that's where I was, outside having my breakfast-time nicotine fix, when, just four days after the sprinklers had done their stuff, the lab was blown up.'

'Jesus Christ.'

It was, thought Jones, so wonderfully simple, so ordinary, so human.

'And so, if it was a bomb, whoever planted it still thinks that you were in the lab?'

'It was a bomb all right, I'm sure of it.' Connie leaned back and stretched her legs. 'And yes, of course, whoever planted it almost certainly still thinks I was inside when the explosion happened. The university authorities too. Everybody involved believes I was there. And that I was blown to pieces, like Paul. Everybody who ever knew me – except Marion and Dom, and now you. No reason to think otherwise. Nobody knew I left the lab at all that morning. I certainly didn't leave through the only door, did I?'

She turned her back to Jones and pulled the orange shirt down off one shoulder. There were several angry looking lacerations clearly visible on the skin of her upper back.

'I think some fragments of glass got me, but I was extraordinarily lucky. I'd walked over to that little pond in the far corner of the quad. It's full of some quite interesting fish now.' She paused again. 'Or it was, anyway. I was just standing on the path looking at the fish, when the entire place blew. The force of the blast sent me catapulting forwards, right into the scrubby bushes around the pond. Picked up a few scratches too, but I sure got off lightly.'

'I don't suppose you've been back there since, have you?' Jones enquired conversationally.

'Uh, yes. I went back.'

'I see.'

It was suddenly all becoming clear.

'And did you by any chance happen to go back there very early yesterday morning?' Jones queried carefully. 'And did you just happen, perhaps, to be there when I was there?'

'Well, yes—'

'Yes,' Jones interrupted. 'And so it was you, was it, who half frightened the wits out of me, thus leading to me being thrown in a police cell, given the third degree, and generally having the worst day of my entire life?'

Connie's smile was the broadest so far. Almost up to the standard Sandy Jones remembered.

'C'mon,' said Connie. 'You took off like a startled rabbit before I had a chance to make myself known to you, fell over with a great crash, attracted the attention of every policeman or security guard within a ten-mile radius I shouldn't wonder, and nearly blew my cover completely.'

'Well, I suppose that's one way of looking at it,' Jones responded wryly.

'Sure is. What the hell were you doing there, anyway?'

'Much the same as you I expect.'

'Me? I just had to go and look. I needed to see what was left of the place, if there was anything that could be salvaged. Maybe see if I could spot any clues too . . .'

She stopped, lowered her face briefly into her hands, then looked up again at Jones.

'Any clues? You saw the place. Modern forensics may discover something, but what the hell I thought I was going to find out just by taking a look, I have no idea. I left in such a hurry after the blast I didn't take any real notice of anything. I realized at once that nobody inside could possibly have survived. I knew Paul must be dead, and I knew I had to get away fast or I would be too. I was quite sure straight away that the explosion was deliberate, and that Paul and I had been the targets. I told you on the phone, didn't I, that I was already concerned about a campaign to get rid of RECAP. I hadn't imagined anything like that explosion though. I never thought anyone would go that far. Anyway, I remembered the steam tunnels. You knew about them, didn't you, in your time?'

Jones nodded. 'Of course. The CHP system, cooling, heating and power supplied throughout the campus within a network of pipes housed underground in tunnels. Like here in New York, yes?'

'Yes,' Connie agreed. 'And the tunnels criss-cross the entire campus. I knew there was a manhole cover at the far side of the quad from the lab. I went straight to it. The cover opened easily. The manholes are in regular use for maintenance, of course. I pulled it down behind me and felt my way along the tunnel until I reckoned I had put enough distance between myself and the explosion. I could see strips of light around the edges of manhole covers all the way along. Eventually I chose one to come up at. It was right on the edge of campus, as I'd hoped, and, as luck would have it, right by a public phone. I'd left my cell in the lab, and in any case it wouldn't have been safe to use it if I'd still had it. Not if I was supposed to be dead. I called Marion. The one person I knew I could trust. She came to get me as soon as she could. She even remembered to bring me some fresh clothes. I hid in someone's back yard till she arrived. But actually all attention was focused on the scene of the blast. And if anyone had thought they'd seen me, then they more than likely wouldn't have believed their eyes, would they?'

Jones looked at her in amazement. 'Jesus Connie, I'm amazed. How did you have the presence of mind to do all that? You must have been terrified, groping your way along a dark tunnel, and after what you'd been through?'

She shrugged. 'I think I was beyond terror. The tunnel didn't really worry me, though. Don't forget I'm an old Princeton graduate myself, and I'd been involved in my share of student games in those tunnels. Races. Mock battles. I knew the tunnels like the back of my hand once upon a time. You never went down them then, Sandy?'

Jones shook her head.

'Not even for a dare?'

Jones was momentarily puzzled. 'No. Nobody ever dared me.'

'That figures.' Connie smiled at her. 'Anyway, I guess I was operating on auto pilot.'

'Some auto pilot,' said Jones. 'So Marion came to get you and brought you here.'

'Yes.'

Marion had re-joined them, carrying a tray containing a cafetière of coffee, three mugs, and a plate of biscuits, which she put on the table.

'I thought of Norman at once. I knew he'd let us stay at his place, and that he wouldn't ask too many questions. He's very resourceful too, a man of many parts is Norman.'

'I don't doubt it,' said Jones wryly.

Marion passed her a mug of coffee, and then handed one to Connie. Jones was puzzled by the look that passed between them. She glanced towards Connie enquiringly.

'Dom is one of the few people who have known about Marion and me for a long time,' said Connie suddenly. 'She's my partner.'

'Right.' Jones realized she was allowing her surprise to show and tried, too late, to check it.

'You seem a tad taken aback, Sandy. What is it? Can't believe I'm a dyke or can't believe that I have a partner of either sex?'

Jones pulled a face.

'You know me too well, Connie, just like you always did,' she said. 'I realized when I thought you'd died that I'd never known anything about you, really. About your life. I'm ashamed of myself, but, back in the day, I never even thought about you having a personal life. Away from RECAP.'

Jones turned towards Marion, who still looked vaguely familiar.

'And yet, I can't help thinking I've maybe met you before, Marion,' she said.

The woman nodded.

'Marion Jessop,' she said quietly. 'I don't think we ever met, but you may have seen me around with my husband . . .'

Jessop. Of course. Mother of Thomas, the current dean of Princeton, and wife of Bernard, who had been Princeton's dean when Jones had been there. Bernard Jessop, who had once privately advised Jones to have nothing more to do with RECAP if she wanted anything like the level of success in the academic world that she'd already seemed destined for.

If this relationship dated back to Jones's time in Princeton, then Marion would have been very much married to the dean of that most conservative of academic establishments. No wonder she and the others had not been allowed to know anything about it.

'My goodness,' Jones remarked lamely.

Connie smiled almost apologetically at her.

'Poor Sandy, you've had an awful lot of shocks haven't you, old friend?'

'Yes I have, rather.'

Marion sat down next to Connie and another look passed between them. In just a glance it spoke volumes about their shared history, and left Jones in no doubt, somehow, that theirs was an abiding love.

To her surprise Jones felt a fleeting stab of jealousy. She ignored it. She still had a lot of questions to ask, and could not allow herself to be diverted by the news of Connie and Marion's relationship.

'So were you also there yesterday morning, Marion?' she asked.

'Sort of. I drove Connie to Princeton from here. That's my car you saw in the garage. I was parked just around the corner, waiting for her. I didn't see what happened, but I heard the shots, of course, and the commotion when you fell and the police, or whatever they were, jumped on you. That was a bad bad moment. I thought it was Connie they'd got, at first. Then she came rushing out from behind those trees just outside the quad, badly shaken but OK, and told me about you. We decided that she shouldn't take any more risks of being seen. I got her to take the car and said I'd try to find you, and follow you.

'I went straight to the borough police station, found a secluded corner, and waited outside. You could have been taken elsewhere, but I chose the most obvious option and hoped for the best. It was a long wait but there was nothing else to do, and eventually I realized I'd got lucky when you came out. Then you got into a cop car, and I thought at first my luck had run out. I was on foot. I had no way of following you. But of course, Ed MacEntee was there, and he spoke to me as he was leaving. I asked him, as casually as I could, if I'd just spotted who I thought I had from so long ago. He told me, more or less, that you'd come to pay your respects, you'd had a misunderstanding with the police, and you were off to the station on your way back to New York.

'I got a quick cab to the Junction and just managed to jump aboard the same train as you. I followed you to Soho House. Then Connie and I hatched the plot to get you here, and called in Norman to pick you up.'

'I never noticed you at all,' remarked Jones.

'I think you had other things on your mind,' said Marion. 'Doubt you were noticing much.'

'A pretty impressive piece of surveillance, none the less,' Jones persisted.

Marion smiled. Her eyes shone much the way Connie's always had.

'I actually got to ask a taxi driver to follow the cab in front,' she said. 'Extraordinary thing was, he didn't bat an eyelid.'

'Yeah, well, that meant he didn't have to find his way anywhere, didn't it?' Jones remarked a touch acidly.

Marion's smile broadened.

'Fair comment,' she said.

Jones thought for a second. 'So you recognized me straight away then, by the lab, Connie? Even in the dark.'

'Of course I did. There were lights all over the place, and you

weren't nearly as good at dodging them as you probably thought
you were. How you weren't seen at once by the police or whoever
it was out there—'

'Who did you think was out there, Connie?' Jones interrupted.
'Those guys didn't look like normal state police to me. And they
sure as hell didn't behave like it either.'

'God knows. Special forces? Since 9/11 we've had a thing called
The Joint Terrorism Task Force, made up of Feds, secret services,
police too, and all kinds of unmentionables, I should imagine. Maybe
it was those boys. Anyway, I don't think you're cut out for surveillance work, Sandy. At one point you succeeded in positioning
yourself in the full glare of an arc lamp. I couldn't believe it. The
armed-to-the-teeth alleged defenders of our liberty, however,
managed to be all looking the other way. I was trying to get close
enough to speak to you, then you did your startled rabbit act and
fell over.'

'Um. Not one of my finer moments, I must confess.'

'Well, I somehow or other escaped unseen again, in spite of you.
But I'm quite convinced that if it got out that I was still alive, I
would be in grave danger again.'

'You would? The *New York Post* splashed on a story this morning
that the explosion was caused by a gas leak. Surely that would be
one heck of a big fib?'

'Goddamn it, Sandy. If what I believe is halfways right then there
would have been an immediate cover-up operation, orchestrated at
the highest level.'

Connie gestured towards the assorted pile of newspapers on the
table before them.

'Have you seen the *Post*? They've got no confirmation from
anyone. An anonymous FBI source, for Christ's sake? Story's been
planted if you ask me. RECAP was deliberately blown up, Sandy.
Someone put a bomb in the lab. Gas leak, my ass. We'd just had
Health and Safety crawling over the place like nits. There was no
gas leak. Trust me, somebody out there wanted to destroy our
project and get rid of me and Paul at the same time. Thing is they
haven't entirely succeeded, and the trump card we have is that
they don't know that.'

'But why? I know RECAP has never been the most popular
project in certain quarters, we've discussed that often enough. But

to blow the place up? To deliberately kill and maim? Who on earth would do that?'

'Now that, Dr Sandy Jones, is the million-dollar question.'

'And you have no more idea than I do?'

'I could speculate. There are plenty of candidates. But no, I haven't a clue.'

'OK, so we don't know who. What about why?'

'Ah, that's a different one. I think I may know why.'

'Yes?'

'Paul thought he'd cracked it.'

'What?'

'Paul told me he'd worked out a scientific formula which explained at last what lay behind our work at RECAP. Our REG results, in the lab, and the field tests. And internationally, of course. All the data we have so patiently correlated. The dice. The pinball. The meditation sessions. Every experiment we've ever conducted. Paul believed he had found his way to our journey's end, or to the beginning of our journey's end, anyway. He believed he'd discovered what the world has been looking for since the beginning of time. And you know what that is, Sandy, don't you?'

Jones could barely believe what she was hearing. But she certainly knew the answer to Connie's question. And she understood at once the enormity of it.

'The mystery of consciousness,' she murmured, her voice only just above a whisper. 'Paul believed he'd solved the mystery of consciousness?'

'Yep.'

'But that's huge. Massive.'

'Yes, massive.'

Connie's voice was flat.

'Do you know exactly what Paul had found out? Do you have his formulae?'

'No.'

'He didn't share his discovery with you? But you two always worked together. You conducted your experiments together, shared your results, correlated your data together. That's how you've always worked.'

'Not this time. I knew he'd been using nanotechnology almost obsessively recently. He'd believed for some time that was how the next step forwards would be achieved.'

Jones nodded. Nanotechnology. Atom-sized mechanics.

'I remember that Paul was just introducing the concept of nano-technology into RECAP in my day,' she said. 'RECAP and the GCP have always focused primarily on how mind power can change the physical, haven't they? The level at which the mind can control and operate machines. And if you work in the area of nanotechnology everything is microscopic and any mental intention required is therefore much smaller. That's the theory, anyway. Paul always said we needed to imagine a microscopic coffee pot, and how little physical effort would be required to induce it to pour.'

Connie smiled.

'But he didn't go into any more detail with you?' Jones persisted.

'No.'

'I wonder why not.'

'He told me he wanted to dot every "i" and cross every "t". Even before letting me see. He stumbled across it initially, you see, whatever it was . . .'

Connie's voice trailed off. Jones suspected she had momentarily moved away from the horrific events of the last couple of days. She'd gone to another place, a place of discovery, of inspired scientific exploration, a place where, to bastardize the words of Arthur C. Clarke, what seemed at first to be magic ultimately became explained as fact, and successive mysteries of the world were systematically explored and sometimes, just sometimes, revealed for what they really were.

'Is that all Paul said?' Jones asked.

Connie seemed to almost physically shake herself back to the present.

'Well, yes. I know he had long since come to the conclusion, as indeed had I, from the work we have done over the years, that the power of human consciousness is much greater than even we had thought initially, and that it is just waiting inside us to be properly developed. Our experiments with REGs all over the world have surely proved irrefutably that global consciousness does exist, that the human race is capable of at least a certain level of shared understanding between minds, not to mention shared communication. You came to believe in that too, Sandy, didn't you? Even if you have been trying to deny it, or at least ignore it, for the last twenty years and more.'

She paused. Sandy smiled wryly and nodded.

'But it was the means of explaining it, the proof, the inarguable proof, that Paul claimed he had finally discovered,' Connie continued.

She sighed and took another cigarette from the packet on the table in front of her.

'Paul's thinking, and mine, of course, was that in the early twenty-first century we were working towards discovering something which would seem just as extraordinary, and indeed as shocking, as when it was learned at the dawn of the twentieth century that matter and energy were essentially the same. The laws of quantum physics. The step forwards that we were heading towards, was that mind and matter are also essentially the same.'

'But you've always talked about it just as a remarkable journey, Connie,' said Jones. 'You've never thought you were even close to that end, have you?'

'Well, not really. And, as you know, I've always been happy with just continuing the journey. Paul wanted an end result. He wanted to prove to the world that we weren't all barmy at RECAP. Me? I accepted my barmy label long ago. Anyway, I'd noticed that Paul had been behaving differently for several weeks. Out of character. He seemed tense and wound-up all the time. Excited too. I kept pestering him. Finally he told me he believed he'd found the answer, that he was on the verge of explaining what consciousness is, and how it functions. But he asked me to be patient.'

'Well, if you had such trouble getting him to share that much, it's not very likely that he told anyone else, is it?'

'I suppose not. Not before me, anyway. He was planning to go public, of course, in due course . . .'

'So again, why would anyone deliberately sabotage the lab?'

'Maybe somebody else did know. There are other ways of finding out things. Computers, the Internet, email contact, have led to the biggest leakages of information in the history of the world.'

'Perhaps.' Jones paused to think for a few seconds. 'This does seem far-fetched, Connie, I have to say that. But even if the news of Paul's alleged discovery had fallen into the wrong hands, come to the attention of somebody powerful who also grasped the practical implications, I still don't necessarily see the connection between that and RECAP being sabotaged. I mean, the lab was destroyed and everything in it. I can understand all sorts of powerful people wanting to get their hands on such a ground-breaking discovery, but not wanting to destroy it.'

'Ah, but what if they'd managed to get hold of Paul's data already? What if they just didn't want anyone else to have the chance to study it and learn from it?'

'Christ, Connie, you really are going into outlandish territory, you know?'

'Sandy, Paul and I thought the lab had been broken into the night before the explosion.'

'Oh my God. Presumably that's on record then? I mean, you must have reported it to security, if not to the police.'

'No. We weren't sure. When we arrived in the morning we couldn't unlock the door at first. Then something seemed to snap, and it opened. It turned out the lock was broken. Paul studied engineering as a young man. He was very good with anything mechanical, as you know. He built the first REG himself. He was convinced the lock had been tampered with. However, we checked out the lab and nothing seemed to be touched. Certainly nothing was missing. So we didn't report it. We barely had time actually. We arrived about eight as usual and the bomb went off half an hour later. In any case, the powers that be have always thought us quite dotty enough without our reporting non-existent burglaries.'

'OK, so that's when a bomb could have been planted. With a timer set for early the next morning, or perhaps radio activated.'

'Indeed, yes.'

'And you think that your computer system could have been hacked? Paul's theory copied?'

'Well, it wouldn't have been easy. The one thing we did have at RECAP was sophisticated user protection software, and everything was password protected. We've always been meticulous about that in order to be able to guarantee the integrity of our experiments. But I suppose some hot shot IT geek could have done it.'

'Ummm.'

'In any case, Sandy, don't forget Paul's reputation. He believed he'd made an extraordinary breakthrough, and he was a quite brilliant scientist. It's possible that the wrong people simply found that out, and knew enough to want us stopped. It could all be that simple.'

'Even without having possession of his paper?'

'You know what I've always believed, Sandy. I believe the world is run by people who don't want it changed. And nothing, absolutely nothing would change the world more than an explanation of global consciousness. Imagine the international importance of people from different nations being intrinsically linked, through the power of their consciousness and nothing more. For a start the control of national governments over their own people could shrink to insignificance.'

Jones was thoughtful.

'Paul used to liken the power of consciousness to having possession of an exotic spy satellite which is capable of miracles, like seeing through buildings. It doesn't always work, but it works enough to be useful.'

'More than useful,' said Connie. 'Powerful beyond our dreams.'

'That's why I still think any government would rather have that power than destroy it. It's a riddle, Connie. And, by the way, you still haven't explained why you got in touch with me before the explosion. I knew you wanted help, but RECAP had always muddled along all right without any help from anyone.'

'Well, I wanted your influence more than anything. Your power, I suppose. You are a figure of some acclaim not only in the academic world, but also in the media, in the UK anyway. We thought if we had you on our side, if you were prepared to publicly support us, we might look a bit better to the outside world. Not so much like nutters' corner. As I told you on the phone, we believed we were under threat, that there were people in high places who wanted us closed down once and for all. Lots of things, apparently unconnected, had started to happen, long before the break-in and the explosion. Both Paul and I, quite out of the blue, were being investigated by the Internal Revenue, for a start.'

'You two? For God's sake.'

'I know. And my finances are, or rather were, totally tied up with RECAP. Any kind of threat to me was a direct threat to our work. I wasn't all that worried by it, not really, because I couldn't think they had anything on me. I mean, do I have a fortune salted away?'

'No. But your bookkeeping's never been all that, has it, Con? Nor Paul's, as far as I remember. Couldn't the Revenue's attentions just have been attracted by bad accounting?'

'Not for them to come in as heavy as they did. Anyway, there were other things. All niggles really. Paul and I suddenly kept getting tickets for speeding offences allegedly picked up on cameras. And of course the university authorities started bugging us, laying down the law about stuff, introducing rules and regulations, and that in itself was odd. After all they'd spent the best part of the previous forty-something years more or less trying to pretend RECAP didn't exist. Suddenly we were being asked to log in and log out, told we couldn't use the lab in the evenings after standard office hours, asked for an inventory of our fixtures and fittings . . .'

Jones couldn't stop himself laughing at that. 'Hope you gave them a list of the cuddly toys, names, manufacturers, descriptions . . .'

'That's what Paul said. Well, we were both cool about it to begin with. But they kept coming at us all ways. We were told we were going to have to move out of the lab we'd been in for so long, and into a smaller work space.' She paused. 'There were also rumours that we were going to be the subject of a major FBI investigation.'

Jones knew enough not to react too strongly to that.

'Well, they've investigated before, haven't they? And other government bodies. Way back in the 1980s, the US army initiated a report on psi. And there have been a succession of government sponsored scientific review committees set up to examine the evidence for psi effects, and the implications for national security, right?'

'Yes. But nobody at that kind of level has contacted us recently. Actually, we've had no official contact with the CIA, the FBI or any government body whatsoever for years.'

'We're heading towards a conspiracy theory, aren't we, Connie? I can feel it coming.'

'Of course. That explosion wasn't an accident, nor a random terror attack. Our location was too obscure, for a start.'

'So again who?'

Connie shrugged.

'The possibilities are endless. The US establishment has always been suspicious of us. It's hard to believe the government blew us up, although you never know, but I reckon some maverick government agency might well have done. Governments throughout the world are confused by us. Military and intelligence organizations here in the US, and in many other countries, have used psi consistently over the years, as have various police forces internationally, even though they almost always deny it. Think of the effect on crime and policing if we could take what we do a step forwards, and not only enhance our abilities to use psychic forces in such work, but also be able to explain exactly what these forces are and how they function. Just imagine, Sandy?'

'I first thought about that twenty-five years ago, Connie.'

She nodded. 'Of course you did. You were always the one with the practical bent. Well, we've moved on since then. And that is frightening for so many. There's a widespread belief, amongst those who hold the balance of power in this world, that there are some things we shouldn't be allowed to find out about. All forms of organized religion, including the extremists, obviously, hate RECAP. Then there's international business chiefs, media moguls, and so on. Almost anyone who relies on the furtherance of the status quo. Man's mind interconnecting across the world, and governing the machines we use just by the power of thought, a scary concept for all of these. Political leaders and those in charge of security across the world, remain the major threat, in my opinion. But, I wonder how far any of these might go to stop the secret of global consciousness being discovered?'

'Or if it was, they would want it just for themselves, wouldn't they?'

Connie nodded again. 'It could make the atom bomb look like a pretty pathetic weapon, by comparison. And just consider the scientists who invented the atom bomb. Robert Oppenheimer was a genius, but he never came close to realizing the full extent of the effect splitting the atom would have until it was too late. Then he said, "I am become death. The shatterer of worlds."'

'I remember. It's a quote from the *Bhagavad Gita*, the words of Krishna, actually. And, as a matter of fact, the closest Indian philosophy ever gets to the nature of consciousness.'

'Whatever, you annoyingly clever person. It's the cross Oppenheimer had to bear. And the discovery Paul believed he had made could shatter worlds, no doubt about it . . . Look, I need your help more than ever, Sandy. I need your brain. You do have the gift you know, far more than any of the rest of us, Paul, Ed, or me.'

Jones looked down at the floor.

'It's all right,' continued Connie. 'I know it was never a gift that you wanted. From the beginning, you were intrigued, captivated even, but I think a half of you always wished that wasn't so.'

'Oh, come on,' Jones protested mildly.

Connie smiled.

'If anyone has a chance of getting to the bottom of this mystery, and of making it possible for me to return to Princeton and somehow rebuild RECAP, and continue with what must surely have been Paul's greatest work, it's you, Sandy,' she said.

'I'm flattered,' replied Jones.

Connie raised her eyebrows in feigned surprise. 'You shouldn't attempt modesty, Sandy. You never did do it well.'

'Fair comment,' said Jones mildly.

ELEVEN

J ones concentrated hard on working out a plan.

'Look Connie, surely Paul would have kept records, not just at the lab, but elsewhere, wouldn't he?'

'Yes, undoubtedly. On his laptop, and possibly his computer at home. That's partly why I went back to Princeton the night you were arrested. I went to Paul's house first, but it was guarded by armed police. There were people in those white suits all over the place like flies. Forensics officers, I assumed. Every so often they'd come out carrying something wrapped in polythene. I saw someone bringing Paul's desktop computer out. And that's what I'd wanted to get at.'

'So if the police, the security forces, whoever, already have the computer from Paul's house, they'll already have gone through it with a toothcomb I should imagine.'

'Presumably.'

'Connie, did Paul have his laptop with him on the day of the explosion? Can you remember?'

'No, Sandy. I don't remember. He usually did. I can picture him carrying it. But I can't be sure. I've wracked my brains.'

'Is there anyone else Paul might have talked to, given a copy to even?'

'If he'd trusted anyone with a copy, I feel pretty sure it would have been me. After Gilda died Paul cut himself off from the world, even more than ever. There was nothing and nobody in his life anymore, apart from his work. Except, well, there was always Ed, of course.'

'So could he know more than you?'

'I doubt it. But he might know something different to me, I suppose. He might have a piece of the jigsaw that I don't.'

'Well then, we should seek Ed out again, shouldn't we?'

'Whaddya mean we? I'm dead, remember?'

Sandy grinned. 'Of course. You're dead and I've been as near as dammit deported.'

'Only as near as dammit. The police and whoever the hell else it was who gave you a hard time in Princeton had no power to deport you. You've not committed a crime. America is still a free country. Loosely speaking.'

'Yeah, very loosely speaking. They can still scare the pants off me though. That's why I was planning to go home tonight. I'm booked on a flight—'

'You can't go, Sandy,' Connie interrupted. 'You really can't walk away from this. I need you. RECAP needs you. The legacy of Paul's work needs you.'

Jones sighed.

'You could at least call Ed,' Connie encouraged.

'What if his call records are being checked? Or the phone bugged, even?'   ·

'And you accused me of getting carried away with conspiracy theories?'

'Yeah, yeah. Look, we seem to have an enemy. We do not know for certain who that enemy is, but we believe there are at least some people involved who are part of the very fabric of this country, and quite possibly at the highest level. We don't know what information they have access to, but we suspect it may be extensive.'

Connie smiled. 'I like it that you're saying "we", Sandy. You're not going home then?'

Jones grunted. 'I suppose not. Not today anyway. I must be mad.'

'You and me both then, but I'm more used to the label. They don't have CCTV in private cars yet. Marion could drive you back to Princeton.'

'Simple as that, eh? Well, if Marion's going to drive me why doesn't she do the entire thing? Go and see Ed. Talk to him. Pick his brains.'

'Because she's not a scientist. It has to be you, you're the only person who might be able to recognize that missing piece of the jigsaw. Apart from me, of course. And I'm dead. In any case, you're one of the few people Ed would trust.'

'Really? You mightn't say that if you'd witnessed his recent reaction to me.'

'Ah. He would still trust you, though. With something as important as this anyway.'

'Maybe. Maybe not. But what if his flat is being watched?'

'How about this. Marion calls on him and sets up a meeting with you. Somewhere anonymous. Marion's the widow of a former university dean, for goodness sake. No reason why she shouldn't call on Ed.'

Jones thought for a minute.

'I'm British and high profile,' she said. 'They'll bully me, but I don't think they'll harm me. You know what, if Marion gets involved, apart from her maybe being put in danger too, her involvement could more easily lead to you, I reckon. Then you could really die.'

Connie curled her legs up onto the sofa and narrowed her eyes.

'I'm a cat,' she said. 'I've got nine lives.'

'Yeah, and you've just used eight of them, all in one go.'

Jones glanced towards Marion.

'Look, can I borrow your car?' she asked.

'Of course you can. But don't you think you might be underestimating how dangerous this could be for you, too? If you got picked up again, it mightn't be as simple as you think.'

'Everything seems dangerous right now,' Jones responded. 'I have one small advantage – I know Princeton like the back of my hand. I think I can contact Ed without being spotted.'

'Really?' Marion sounded doubtful.

Connie touched her hand.

'How long have you two been together, anyway?' Jones asked suddenly.

'It depends upon what you mean by together. In our eyes it's coming up twenty-three years.'

'Jesus,' said Jones. 'So you were an item back when I was at Princeton. How the devil did you manage to keep it a secret?'

'The way to keep a secret is to tell no one, and that really means no one.'

Connie was still looking at Marion.

'It hasn't always been easy,' she said. 'But it's sure been worth it.'

'Didn't you ever want to say to hell with it? You of all people, Connie. When have you ever cared a jot about convention, about what other people think?'

'That wasn't it, Sandy. You don't find happiness by walking over other people's souls, you know.'

'What?'

Marion interrupted them.

'Do you remember my husband, Sandy?'

'Yes, of course I do.'

'And how well would you say you knew him?'

'I didn't know him at all.'

'Yet you met him many times? Socialized with him sometimes?'

'Yes.'

'Yes. Well that's pretty much how it was for me, really. Bernard lived and breathed Princeton. I never doubted that he loved me, and loved our children. He was never unkind. He provided and cared for his family. But well, he was twenty years older than me, of course, and he had different values. He had his job, as dean, and mine was to look after the children and our home. In a funny sort of way, we were never really that close.

'Then, when I started to get to know Connie, well there was so much more. I don't think I realized what was happening at first. I had never been with a woman before. But in any case, that was irrelevant. Connie's gender was irrelevant. I just knew she was the person I wanted to spend the rest of my life with . . .'

Marion leaned over and refilled Jones's mug with more coffee.

'But neither Connie nor I had any wish to hurt Bernard,' she continued. 'He didn't deserve that, really he didn't. There were young children to consider, and also his position as dean which meant so much to him. So Connie and I decided that our commitment to each other would be a private thing, that we would have our own secret life.'

'But now? I mean, Bernard died years ago. Your relationship isn't still a secret, is it?'

'An open one,' said Connie. 'We have friends who know, of course, the remains of what family I have certainly know, and Marion's children must know now, but—'

'But they're like their father – or rather the oldest one is,' interrupted Marion. 'Sometimes I think Thomas is more conservative than Bernard ever was. Even in this day and age he couldn't cope at all with having a mother who is a dyke. Or, rather, a mother who is publicly known to be a dyke. I think he just pretends it isn't happening. He prefers to think of Connie and me as friends. We're old ladies, Sandy. I'm sixty-one, and Connie hits sixty-five next year. Well, in the eyes of the world we are pretty old, even if we don't feel it. But we never expected what the younger generation expects. We still don't expect to get everything that we want. And we're not on a crusade. As long as we can be together that's all we care about.'

'Two more questions,' said Jones, changing the subject only slightly. 'Why does the Dominator call Marion Aunt M? And if he's so rich why does he drive a yellow cab round New York?'

Connie shrugged. 'He's not that rich. Bought his Medallion when he started wrestling so he had a day job. Got himself his own cab. Nowadays he just likes to keep his hand in, I guess. And he calls Marion Aunt M because she took him on as a foster kid when he was a mad bad fifteen-year-old from the Bronx and nobody else would have him. She sorted him out like you wouldn't believe. Dom was never going to be a college kid, but he sure as hell got his life together thanks to Marion.'

'Yeah, now he's a mad bad thirty-five-year-old,' said Marion, the pride in her voice belying her words.

'I noticed,' responded Jones.

'Right, so now you have our story, Sandy,' said Connie, smiling. 'Shall we get back to the matter in hand.'

* * *

Jones called Soho House, authorized them to take payment from her credit card, and told them a friend would be along to pick up her bag. Marion had agreed to run the errand. Nobody knew who she was, and if they used Dom it was just remotely possible that someone might be watching, and he might be recognized from his wrestling days, or even just as the cabby who'd picked up Jones outside the House that morning.

Jones left the apartment shortly after six p.m. She preferred to arrive in Princeton under cover of darkness, and in any case the timing suited her plan. First she sought out a cashpoint in central Manhattan. She then took out the maximum cash she could. Even if her bank records were checked all that could be learned was that she was still in Manhattan. That wouldn't get anyone anywhere much. And she would be able to avoid leaving a trail to Princeton by not using credit cards at gas stations and so on.

Marion's choice of car was one of the most common in America. The unassuming saloon coasted along comfortably enough but appeared to have absolutely no acceleration. Pulling sharply onto Route One, the main freeway heading for the university town, Jones actually thought the box-like vehicle was going to tip over.

The journey, sticking strictly to all speed limits, took almost two hours, including a stop for fuel and a visit to an electronics store, where Jones bought three untraceable pre-paid phones. Burners. One for her, one for Connie, and one for Marion. She ultimately coasted into Princeton just before eight thirty p.m.

She drove straight to Ed's apartment block, and parked a little way down the street, tucking in behind another vehicle. She hoped not to be noticed by anyone else who might be watching the building, whilst at the same time having a reasonable view of any comings and goings.

Her intent was to approach Ed without being seen. And her plan was a simple one.

Ed had been a creature of habit, already a man of routine, when she had known him. He'd told her, when she had so spontaneously paid him that not entirely successful visit, that he walked his dog every evening. She didn't know when exactly, except that it would be some time after nine – he had said nine was too early – and almost certainly well before midnight. Ed had never been a night owl. She just hoped he was still the same person, and that, sooner or later, he would step out into the street with Jasper the little black terrier.

She hunkered down to wait. It was a lovely starlit night. And quiet. Several vehicles passed, two or three turning off the main drag into driveways and parking areas, just one pulling out. A woman strolled by walking a Labrador. That was all.

Then just before ten p.m. her patience was rewarded. Out stepped Ed, with Jasper on a lead. He turned right, walking away from Jones. She waited until he disappeared from sight after turning right at the next junction, then she started her engine and followed, drawing the car to a halt once she was alongside him, and opening the window.

'Get in, please,' she instructed.

'What the fuck?' said Ed.

'Please, we need to talk. But not here. It's possible you may be under surveillance. Please get in.'

For a moment she thought he was going to walk away. But he didn't. He obediently climbed into the passenger seat, with Jasper jumping swiftly onto his lap.

Jones pulled away at once.

'Where the fuck are we going?' asked Ed.

'Somewhere away from here, with no CCTV,' replied Jones.

'Why?'

'I told you, we have to talk.'

'Yes? So what is wrong with the telephone, may I ask? Followed by a normal house call perhaps?'

'I just said. You may be under surveillance. Your phone could be bugged.'

'Sandy, for Chrissake. What on earth makes you think anyone is likely to be following me?'

'Look, I don't think there's much doubt that the RECAP lab was blown up, deliberately—'

'You don't think?' Ed interrupted. 'Since when were you any sort of forensics expert? You've been interviewed by the police, for a very good reason, and released, like any other suspects there may have been. You've seen the news reports, haven't you? They say it's a gas explosion.'

Jones spotted an unlit lay-by ahead and pulled in. She stopped the car and turned to face Ed.

'No they don't,' she replied. 'The *New York Post* said the explosion was caused by a gas leak, and the authorities have yet to confirm or deny it. But I don't believe the blast was caused by gas, and, you know what, I don't think you do, either. I think you've got the same gut instinct about this thing that I have.'

'Do you really have any idea what I think about anything?'

'I used to have.'

'That was a very long time ago.'

'I know. I'm sorry.'

Jones paused. She had to pick her words carefully. She mustn't tell Ed that Connie was still alive. The pair of them and Marion had agreed that would be far too risky.

'Look, I actually talked enough to Connie on the phone, when she called me a few days before the explosion, to realize how worried she was,' Jones improvised. 'She said that she thought the lab, and she and Paul in particular, were being targeted in some way.'

She told Ed then about the Internal Revenue checks, the speeding tickets, the threats to the financial future of RECAP, and all the other things Connie had related to her. Including the sudden and intrusive attentions of the state Health and Safety department.

While she was speaking she became aware of Ed's attitude changing, just a little.

'You didn't know about any of that?' she ventured.

'No, I didn't. Why didn't you tell me the other night?'

'You didn't give me much chance,' said Jones. She actually hadn't known it all then, of course.

Ed didn't respond.

'What are you thinking?' Jones ventured.

'Look Sandy, it's been no secret for years that half the academic establishment, what am I saying, more like ninety-nine per cent of the academic establishment, would like to have seen RECAP closed down,' Ed said eventually. 'That doesn't mean that anyone was going to actually blow the place up, for God's sake.'

'No. But, and this is what I wanted to see you about, is it possible after all these years, all these series of experiments, that the RECAP team was on the brink of discovering something the establishment couldn't cope with. Wanted to destroy?'

'For God's sake, Sandy. Conspiracy theories are one thing but—'

'People have died, Ed,' she interrupted. 'Including those you and I loved . . .'

She was taking poetic licence there, knowing as she did that Connie was still alive. Ed was quickly on to her anyway.

'People you and I loved? You've got a damned cheek, Sandy. You've barely been near any of us for more than two decades.'

'I didn't think you wanted me near,' she said, keeping her voice calm. Ed's comment was fair enough, after all.

'Maybe not,' he replied. 'But they did. Paul and Connie. Particularly Connie.'

'Yes, well perhaps what I'm trying to do here is honour a debt of love. I'm trying to repay something.'

He sighed. Short, sharp, impatient.

'What do you want from me, Sandy?'

'I want to find out if you know anything which could throw light on all of this . . .'

'Don't you think I would have told you straight away.'

Jones repeated Connie's words.

'You may have a piece of the jigsaw in your possession, and because it's just one piece of many, not even realize it.'

'I don't think so.'

'Look Ed, you and Paul were close, weren't you?'

He turned away.

'Yes.'

'Well, Connie told me in our phone conversation that Paul had indicated that he'd made progress, real progress' – she paused for dramatic effect – 'that he may have brought all those years of work to a final conclusion.'

'So?' muttered Ed.

Jones did a double take.

'You knew that?' she queried.

'Yes. That's what he thought, anyway. He told me that much. He wasn't sure though, he was still working on his theory, finalizing it, and that is why he didn't want to go public, or even to tell me or Connie exactly what his findings were.'

So Connie had been right. Ed at least knew something – and quite probably more than anyone except Connie.

'Did you believe him?'

He turned back to face her, but she couldn't see his features, just the dark shape of him.

'Did I believe Paul? Do you remember who you are talking about, Sandy? Of course I believed Paul. He was at the top of his field. Had been for decades. He didn't make mistakes. Not in his work. And he didn't make statements he couldn't back up.'

Jones nodded. That was true enough. And it was pretty much the way the entire academic world, and anyone else who had knowledge of Paul Ruders, would regard the man.

'But you'd no idea exactly what he'd discovered?' she persisted.

'He believed he may have found out why all the sometimes quite inexplicable data we had correlated over the years had occurred. Why REGs behaved the way they did, why the behaviour of machines, according to the results of detailed scientific experimentation, really could be affected and sometimes controlled by the power of the human mind.'

For a few seconds Ed sounded just like Connie: evangelical.

'The secret of consciousness?' Jones prompted.

'Maybe. All those years of the GCP, had surely proved beyond any reasonable doubt, to anyone with a mind that wasn't totally closed, that global consciousness does exist. And yes, Paul finally believed that he had discovered what it really is. How it works. I don't know how you put that exactly, but . . .'

His voice tailed off.

'But, if he'd succeeded, dammit, if he'd halfways succeeded, then in the early part of this millennium we would have the most important scientific discovery since the beginning of the last, since Einstein's theory of relativity, and since the development of quantum physics,' said Jones, paraphrasing the way Connie had explained it to her. 'Maybe greater. I think greater, don't you?'

'Maybe.'

Jones was aware that Ed was sitting very still.

'And now we'll never know,' he said quietly. 'Paul is dead. He won't be able to tell us. He won't be able to offer the world what could have been its greatest ever gift. And Connie, oh Connie . . .'

Ed seemed unable to finish what he was trying to say. Jones thought she could just see his shoulders begin to heave. She reached out a hand and touched his cheek.

'Don't be upset, dear Ed,' she murmured.

Ed knocked her hand away at once.

'Don't be upset? You stupid woman. Don't you realize my whole world has just exploded – literally? I've lost the only people left who really cared for me. Apart from my brother, I suppose . . .'

'I'm sorry . . .'

'You're always sorry.'

'I know.'

Ed was audibly sobbing now.

'You know what, I'm not sure how much I care about RECAP any more. Connie is the greatest loss, the most awful loss to me. I loved her best. You see. From the beginning . . . After you . . .'

Jones hadn't expected that. She hadn't expected Ed to break down. She certainly hadn't expected him to mention his feelings for her. She didn't know quite what to do. His sobbing seemed out of control. Maybe he'd been holding it all in until now. Cautiously she reached out to him again. This time he did not pull away from her, instead moving closer and continuing to sob into her shoulder. It was heartbreaking. She couldn't let it go on. She had to tell him. She just had to.

'Ed listen, Connie's alive,' she blurted out. 'She escaped.'

He stopped sobbing at once and immediately pulled away from her.

'She's a-alive?' he stumbled. 'Oh my God, she's alive!'

She told him all of it then, everything that she had promised Connie and Marion she wouldn't tell him or anyone else. And as she spoke she told herself that if she couldn't trust Ed MacEntee, she couldn't trust anyone.

When she had finished Ed had just one question.

'When can I see her, when can I see Connie?'

'I don't know. I wasn't supposed to tell you she'd survived. For your sake as well as hers. I'll have to pick my moment to confess—'

'You really think she's still in danger, don't you?' Ed interrupted suddenly.

'Yes. We all do. And we think if we had possession of Paul's thesis we could put a stop to it all. Actually, Connie and I both hoped that he may even have given you a copy of his work, hard copy, USB memory stick, whatever . . .'

'Why would he? He had all the normal backup. He would have kept copies himself, on different devices. He wasn't expecting to be blown up, for Christ's sake.'

'I suppose you're right.' Jones paused. 'Paul was a meticulous man. In his work, that is. Though you wouldn't think it from the way he looked – nor the behaviour he allowed from his dogs.'

She smiled. She thought Ed might be smiling too, but she couldn't see.

'Thing is,' Jones continued, 'Connie saw the police take Paul's home computer away. So they, the FBI, the CIA, people in government, any of those could well have a copy now of all his work.'

'I doubt they'd understand it.'

'Maybe not. But maybe they don't need to understand. They just don't want anybody else to. After all, to understand the meaning of consciousness, for people to be able to communicate in that way, would upset the status quo more than anything else discovered in the name of progress that you could possibly imagine.'

'Isn't that a bit fanciful, Sandy?'

'Is it? Well, the whole concept of RECAP is fanciful, isn't it. But do you really think it is likely to have been a coincidence that the RECAP lab exploded and Paul was killed just as he was on the brink of going public with a literally earth-shattering discovery?'

'I don't know.'

Jones took from her bag a piece of paper, on which she had written the number of her new burner phone, and handed it to Ed.

'Look, call me tomorrow, on this phone, it's safe,' she said. 'Or any time if you can think of anything that might help. We need to protect Connie as well as Paul's thesis.'

'OK,' said Ed. 'I certainly can't think of anything right now. Oh, except . . . I do have a pal in the police. I could sound him out, if you like. He might at least tell me if the cops really believe the gas explosion theory.'

'Well, that would be something.'

'I'll call you then.'

'Good, but please don't use your cell or your home line. Call from a pay phone, and not one too near your apartment, either. Or get yourself a pay-as-you-go. Promise?'

'Are you sure all this subterfuge is really necessary, Sandy?'

'I'm sure we shouldn't take unnecessary risks.'

'OK. OK. I promise,' Ed replied.

Jones dropped him off where she had picked him up. Ed walked slowly home around the corner, allowing Jasper some more time for a sniff around and a wee or two.

The man sitting in a black sedan with tinted windows, parked across the street from Ed's apartment building, watched their arrival. He'd seen them leave about thirty-five minutes previously, on what he knew to be their regular nightly walk. They had been a little longer than usual, but it was a beautiful night.

As Sandy Jones had hoped, the man had taken no notice of her in her commonplace saloon car.

Indeed, as soon as Ed and Jasper had disappeared around the corner he'd taken off down the road in the opposite direction heading for a nearby Mexican takeaway. He didn't even see Jones pull out. This was not the first time he'd kept watch on Ed MacEntee, mainly to monitor any visitors he might have. And the man was already in the habit of fetching himself some supper during the habitual dog walk. After all, Ed couldn't receive any visitors if he were out with the dog, could he, the man reasoned. He was perhaps not the cleverest or most diligent of surveillance personnel.

He kept an eye on Ed and Jasper until they'd entered the building, but was actually concentrating rather more on the beef and bean burrito with chilli sauce he had acquired.

Then his cell phone rang. He answered at once.

'Of course, Mr Johnson,' he said. 'I'll do it straight away.'

He took a final enormous bite of his spicy Mexican sandwich before reaching into the back of the car for an anorak which he pulled on over the black suit, white shirt and black tie he always wore. Glancing longingly at the juicy burrito, now abandoned on the passenger seat, he climbed out of the car, tugging up the hood of his anorak as he crossed the road.

Chilli and garlic sauce dribbled from the corners of his mouth down over his chin. He wiped the stuff away with the back of one hand, as he opened the white painted gate to the apartment block and made his way up the path to the front door.

TWELVE

I t was well after midnight when Jones arrived back at Dom's loft. She used the remote control Marion and Connie had given her to operate the doors of the garage. As she switched off the car engine the small door at the back opened and there stood Connie.

'I thought you'd be in bed by now,' said Jones.

'You have to be joking,' said Connie, as she led the way upstairs.

Marion was sitting on one of the big leather sofas. She gestured for Jones to sit next to her, and poured her a glass of wine from the bottle on the low table in front of them.

'Right, Sandy, tell us all,' commanded Connie, as she sat on the other sofa.

'I'm afraid there's not a great deal to tell,' Jones began, nonetheless proceeding to give a fairly full account of her meeting with Ed, without dwelling too much on how upset the man had been. Neither did she mention her indiscretion regarding Connie, which she was already beginning to regret.

'So unfortunately it seems Ed has little to offer, apart from the vague promise of approaching his police department chum,' she concluded. 'Paul had indeed told him about his final thesis, and the remarkable conclusions he had drawn, but Ed certainly doesn't have a copy of any of Paul's work. I suppose it was always a long shot . . .'

Connie and Marion were clearly disappointed – as indeed Jones had been.

There seemed to be little more to say or do that night. The three women finished the open bottle of wine and then retired to bed. The sofa had already been made up for Jones, and her shoulder bag, collected from Soho House by Marion, as promised, stood on the

floor alongside. Jones still felt jet lagged and tired, unusually so for
her. She supposed stress probably had a lot to do with that. She
climbed gratefully beneath the covers, and in spite of her abiding
anxiety, fell asleep almost at once.

However, all too soon she was woken by the sound of a spirited
rendition of the cancan. She opened her eyes, lying bewildered for
just a moment, while struggling to remember where the heck she
was and what the heck was going on. She felt as if she'd only been
asleep for five minutes. Eventually she realized that the cancan
music was the somewhat inappropriate ringing tone plumbed into
her burner phone. She struggled onto an elbow, registering as she
did so that daylight had arrived, and glanced at the clock on the
wall. It was just after seven thirty a.m.

She picked up the phone and squinted at it, bleary eyed. She
couldn't even read the number which had appeared in the display
panel. Was it safe to answer? Surely it had to be safe. Nobody
could have traced the phone to her that quickly, if indeed
they ever could. And only Ed had the number. It must be him
calling. It was him.

'Hi Sandy, how are you?' he began.

'Oh, never better,' she responded ironically. 'Not quite awake,
actually . . .'

'Sorry if I woke you. I just wanted to make sure you'd got
back to New York OK, and to check that you and Connie were
all right.'

Ed sounded cheery. Surprisingly cheery, Jones thought, considering the state he'd been in the previous evening.

'All's well,' she responded obliquely. 'Don't know quite what
to do next, though.'

'Maybe you don't need to do anything.'

'What do you mean?'

'Have you seen the news yet this morning?'

'No.'

Instinctively Jones looked about her for the remote control to
the TV.

'The police have confirmed that the explosion was caused by
a bomb, but they're blaming animal rights protestors.'

'They're doing what?'

Jones tried to clear her head. She wasn't fully functioning yet.

'It's a long story,' Ed continued. 'Tune in to a news channel and then you'll know exactly what I'm talking about. Point is, RECAP wasn't the target. That seems almost certain.'

'Well, maybe . . .'

'This is an official police statement released to the media, Sandy. Not a tabloid exclusive. And it makes sense. I did think last night that you and Connie were getting a bit carried away with your conspiracy theory, you know.'

'Perhaps,' Jones muttered vaguely, aware that her voice sounded hoarse.

'I also think Connie should tell the authorities exactly what happened and come home to Princeton, I really do. Look, can I speak to her?'

'Uh no, not yet.'

Jones really wished she'd kept her mouth shut about Connie. Meanwhile she decided to lie. She didn't have a lot of choice.

'She was asleep when I got back. I haven't had a chance yet to tell her you know she's alive.'

'Ummm.'

She thought Ed was about to challenge her. He didn't. Instead he continued with another near instruction.

'All right. But you can fly home to England now.'

Jones was confused. She felt uneasy. Why was Ed saying this?

'I, uh, I'm not sure—' she began hesitantly.

'There's no reason for you not to,' Ed interrupted. 'I really believe that. After all, you've never had any evidence to back up any of what you said last night, have you? Just all that stuff from Connie about the Internal Revenue and the sprinklers, and strangers lurking in shadows. Connie can be a bit fanciful, you know. I mean, you probably have to be a bit fanciful to have run the RECAP project for all those years.'

She knew Ed was right about Connie. Perhaps he was right about the other stuff too. It probably was all getting to be a bit James Bond, in her head at any rate.

Not for the first time since it had all begun she considered the sheer unreality of events since her arrival in America. Everything had happened so fast, she'd just been swept along on the wave. She'd been running around playing spy games. In the cool light of a New York morning, it suddenly seemed all too likely that Ed was right and the whole thing had been nothing more than a misguided fantasy.

As she yawned and stretched her way to complete wakefulness, Jones also realized suddenly just how much she wanted that to be the case.

She remembered what her mother always said about things looking different in the morning. Yesterday had been a crazy, emotional, roller coaster of a day, beginning with what she had assumed to be a kidnapping through being confronted with a still alive Connie, and ending with her thoroughly unsatisfactory meeting with Ed.

Yesterday, Connie's conspiracy theory had seemed absolutely real. Today, lying in that quiet double-glazed loft, a peaceful hidden-away space in the heart of one of the busiest and noisiest metropolises in the world, Jones found it hard to believe any of it was real.

There had been crazy moments yesterday when she had almost enjoyed playing spy games, buying burner phones, stalking Ed and surreptitiously meeting up with him. Today she just wanted to go back to being plain old Dr Sandy Jones.

'Look, I'll talk it all through with Connie again,' she said. 'But she seems so sure . . .'

'Of course she's sure. Have you ever known her be uncertain about anything? Even Paul had moments of doubt about RECAP over the years. Not Connie. She doesn't do doubt.'

Jones laughed.

'Look,' Ed continued. 'You know I told you about my cop pal? Well, I called him after watching the news. He confirmed the reports absolutely. Says the animal rights angle is rock solid. The police have no doubt now that the bomb was planted by extremists protesting against animal experiments at Princeton . . .'

'I didn't know there were animal experiments going on at Princeton.'

'No. It's not widely known, and that's deliberate, apparently. Hardly surprising when you see what happened once certain people did get to know about it.'

'I'll talk to Connie,' said Jones. 'Ring me again later. And don't forget to use a call box.'

'Yes, sure,' Ed replied.

Just a little absently, Jones thought.

'Oh, and Ed,' she added. 'The rules haven't changed. I know it must be tempting, but you really mustn't tell anyone about Connie yet. OK?'

'Of course not.'

'Speak later then.'

She ended the call and switched on the TV.

The new revelations about the explosion had made the lead item on every news channel. The ABC breakfast news report seemed unequivocal.

It is now confirmed that the massive explosion at Princeton University four days ago was caused by a bomb. Forensics and fire service experts have found evidence that an explosive device had been concealed in a laboratory on the first floor of the university's Science Research Block. However it is believed the target was almost certainly the Ivy League school's little-known animal research department on the floor above, and the bomb was placed in a room on the lower floor simply because it was more easily accessible.

New Jersey State Police have revealed that they have information indicating that an as yet unnamed breakaway animal rights group was responsible. PETA (People for the Ethical Treatment of Animals) and SHAC (Stop Huntingdon Animal Cruelty), the two major animal rights organizations which campaign internationally against vivisection, have both denied direct involvement, but refuse to condemn the bombing.

'Princeton has been secretly conducting horrific experiments on live animals for many years, and the more we have learned about these experiments, the more we have come to regard them as unacceptable,' said a PETA spokesman.

It is not known exactly what experiments animals are used for at Princeton. However, university sources report that research into pesticides and food additives is involved as well as medical research, and that live animals – mostly rats and guinea pigs, but occasionally other animals more likely to provoke an emotive response, including cats and rabbits – are also used for teaching purposes.

According to the police statement the university had received threats in the past from various animal rights groups, and it is likely that whoever planted the bomb had detailed knowledge of the layout of the building and had deliberately targeted those who worked in the department while avoiding as much as possible harm to animals. Most of the animals currently being kept at Princeton survived the explosion unhurt, as they are housed in a designated area at the far end of the Science Research Building, some distance from the laboratory where experiments are conducted.

The explosion occurred just before eight thirty a.m. and, according to our Princeton sources, the head of the animal research department, George Kadinsky, who died in the blast, was known to start work early, often with research students alongside him. It is believed that the deaths of two other scientists, Professor Paul Ruders and psychologist Connie Pike, uninvolved in the animal research project, were almost certainly unintentional.

Well, thought Jones, so that was it. Or was it? asked a small voice buried somewhere in her head. Wasn't it strange that the RECAP lab, where the bomb had unquestionably been planted, had not been named? But perhaps not, if the bomb's location really had no significance other than its proximity to the animal research department. Jones reminded herself that conspiracy theories had become almost a mainstay of modern life.

The police statement made perfect sense. Jones knew well enough some of the outrages which had occurred in the UK in the name of animal rights. The body of an elderly woman, whose family bred animals for experimentation, had been stolen from her grave. The destruction of property was common place. Violence directed at those involved was certainly not unknown. And this would be far from the first time that explosives had been used. Most animal activists were uncomfortable with the use of violence leading to loss of human lives. But as with any such movement, there were plenty of extremists prepared to go to almost any lengths for their beliefs.

'Animal rights activists, eh?' The voice came from behind Jones. 'Well, I doubt Connie will be convinced.'

Jones turned to see Marion had come into the living room, and had clearly picked up the gist of the news bulletin.

'I don't suppose she will, but I may have to try to make her be convinced,' said Jones thoughtfully. 'Ed just called. He's quite certain now that we, I mean I . . .' She stopped herself in mid-sentence. She had nearly let slip that she had told Ed about Connie, and she was still not ready to confess her indiscretion.

'. . . That I got it all wrong,' she continued. 'That there is no conspiracy. It's not just the news bulletin. He's talked to his police contact, who confirmed that the cops are absolutely sure about the animal rights thing.'

'Really?' Marion's voice was quizzical. 'All the same, I hope he didn't call on your usual cell phone.'

'No. Absolutely not. It was the new burner.'

Marion headed for the kitchen area without any further comment. There was suddenly the crash of shattering crockery.

'Goddamn it to hell,' said Marion loudly.

'Problem?' called Jones.

'Smashed a mug and a plate, that's all. Norman will not be pleased. He's terribly house-proud you know.'

In spite of everything Jones felt the corners of her mouth twitch. The very thought of that muscle-bound man-mountain fussing about his crockery was just too much.

'And that's not the worst news,' continued Marion. 'I can't find any coffee. Think we must have drunk it all yesterday. No juice either. And no more food. We finished that for supper last night. Or rather I did.'

Jones was just beginning to realize that she'd woken feeling very hungry indeed, in spite of the burger she'd picked up on her drive back from Princeton. The events of the past few days did not appear to have impeded her appetite.

She also knew how serious the lack of coffee would be for Connie, a caffeine addict, and from the tone of her voice suspected it was much the same for Marion. Given a choice, Jones was not a coffee drinker in the morning.

She walked across the room to join Marion.

'Norman got any tea?' she enquired hopefully.

'Never touches the stuff.'

Jones ran her tongue around her fuzzy mouth. At least she had re-acquired her toothbrush and toilet kit, but only tea would ultimately clear that fuzziness. Let alone clear her head.

'Right, well why don't we all go out to breakfast?'

'Why don't we all do what?' enquired Connie, as she emerged from the bedroom.

She was wearing a towelling dressing gown which presumably belonged to their host as it was about five sizes too big. Her abundant red hair formed a kind of fuzzy halo around her face.

'Go out to breakfast,' Jones repeated. 'Why don't we?'

'How can I go out to breakfast?' Connie asked. 'My face has been plastered over every newspaper and every television news bulletin. I'm not exactly indistinctive. I'd be recognized.'

'Do you think so?' responded Jones. 'I never think people take these things in. In any case you're supposed to be dead. People only see what they expect to see. You said that yourself yesterday.'

'It would be an unnecessary risk, Sandy. I'm not hungry, anyway. I feel vaguely sick if you must know. I have done ever since the explosion. All I want is coffee.'

'There isn't any,' said Jones.

'Look Connie, you should know that Ed just called Sandy, and there's been a development,' interjected Marion. 'It was on the news.'

'Really?'

Connie glanced questioningly at Jones, who gave a quick summary of both Ed's phone call and the news bulletin she had just watched.

'Ed has also spoken to his police contact, who confirmed everything,' Jones continued. 'He believes the authorities are being totally straight.'

'That will be the day,' countered Connie defiantly. 'This is America you know. Think Watergate. Think Irangate. Think Bill Clinton. We had a president who even tried to reinvent the definition of the sex act, for God's sake. And I don't know where to damned well begin with what's happening in the present day. The powers that be in this country don't know how to be straight, Sandy. It isn't in their genetic make-up.'

Jones smiled in spite of everything.

'I'm not totally convinced yet either, but I'm not entirely convinced by you either, Connie—'

'Just look back at the long history of lies the people of this country have been fed, for fuck's sake,' interrupted Connie.

Jones held up both hands in a soothing motion.

'Whoa Connie,' she said. 'OK. We should go through it all again. Treat it like lab data. Apply some physics. But you don't function properly in the mornings without your coffee, and I certainly need my tea. So why don't Marion and I go out for a quick breakfast, and bring some coffee back, and maybe some other provisions? Then we'll talk. Huh?'

The sense of urgency Jones had felt yesterday had diminished somewhat overnight, particularly following Ed's phone call. She just wanted to calm Connie down.

Connie looked at Marion. Marion nodded almost imperceptibly.

'All right,' she said. 'Off you go to breakfast. But have you seen the weather?'

Jones glanced out of the window. Autumn had suddenly arrived with a vengeance. The sky, which had been so bright and clear the previous day, was leaden. It was raining heavily, and a small gale appeared to be blowing.

'Have you got a coat, Sandy?' asked Connie.

She nodded.

'Of sorts,' she said, thinking of the thin grey plastic waterproof she carried with her everywhere, which she had stuffed into a corner of her bag. She fetched it, and her newly acquired burner phone, and her wallet. She left her usual mobile in her bag. In spite of what Ed had said, and her own comments to Connie, she wasn't quite ready to use it yet. Just in case.

Meanwhile Connie produced an oilskin cape, and helped Marion into it.

'I don't want you getting wet through,' she said solicitously. 'You know how prone you are to bronchitis. This is my best waterproof, I'm so glad I asked you to get it. When it rains in New York, boy, does it pour. Now fasten the zip to the neck, and pull the hood up before you dare take a step outside.'

Marion obediently zipped up. Then she and Jones made their way down the stairs and into the garage. Marion opened the big door at the front, and the two women peered unenthusiastically out onto the wet grey street. The rain was almost horizontal. New York was in the grip of one of the not-infrequent near-tropical rainstorms which Connie had been referring to.

'Who's idea was this anyway?' Marion asked.

'Just think about eggs and crispy bacon,' responded Jones.

Cursing loudly, Marion pulled up the hood of the oilskin, as Connie had directed, and, with one hand, tugged it forwards at the front as far as it would go, while reaching with the other for a big black umbrella leaning against the wall.

She studied the flimsy plastic of Jones's raincoat without enthusiasm.

'Well that's not going to do much to protect you, is it? You'd better cuddle up to me, Sandy, it's your only hope of keeping dry.'

Jones smiled. She could see why Marion had become Connie's long-time partner. She put her right arm around Marion's waist. Marion flipped up the umbrella and they stepped out into the street huddled together. Wind and rain instantly whipped around Jones's legs, and streams of water began almost at once to run down over the inadequate plastic raincoat further drenching her feet and legs.

'There's a diner a couple of blocks away,' said Marion, raising her voice above the noise of rain and wind. 'We may have to swim there though.'

Jones found herself laughing easily. She no longer felt so tense. She really was coming around to the notion that Paul's death and the destruction of the RECAP lab had been nothing more than the tragic accidental consequence of an attack on an unconnected target.

Marion positioned the umbrella in front of them, aiming it at the driving rain, so that it gave their faces and upper bodies at least some protection.

'I hope you can see where you're going,' Jones shouted. 'Because I can't see a damned thing.'

'What about your inner consciousness, Sandy?' Marion asked. 'You were a RECAP kid. Can't you use your extra sensory perception in order to guide us?'

Sandy laughed.

'I think I prefer to hang on to you,' she said. 'You're the New Yorker.'

'Princetonian,' Marion corrected. 'I'm one of the few who was actually born and bred there.'

They were approaching a road junction and were almost at the curb edge.

'Be careful,' Marion warned. 'We need to cross here.'

Jones looked down at her feet and tried to adjust her step to avoid stumbling. But a small river was running in the gutter, rendering the shiny surface of the cobbles, which still formed many of the Meatpacking District's roads, quite treacherous. Jones was caught off balance. As her left foot landed in the gutter with a squelch, it almost slipped from under her. She fell backwards, the momentum of her body pulling her arm away from Marion, who was already stepping into the road.

Marion looked back over her shoulder in time to see Jones, whose limbs seemed to have turned to jelly, land on her bottom on the pavement.

'Are you all right, Sandy?' she asked.

There was a crazy sense of release about Jones that morning. She started to laugh again.

'I think only my pride is hurt,' she said.

Marion beamed at her.

Jones was still laughing when the black Chevy pick-up truck appeared out of nowhere.

First she heard the noise, a powerful engine roaring loud and angry above the sound of the weather. Then she saw the front of the vehicle, its metal radiator grid and fender resembling the mouth and teeth of some terrible monster, stretched into a hideous threatening grin. The truck was heading straight for Marion. At speed. And Marion was looking at Sandy Jones, still smiling, still unaware of any danger.

Jones screamed her name at the top of her voice, whilst struggling to scramble to her feet.

'Marion! Marion! Look out!'

She pointed towards the fast approaching vehicle. Marion's smile faded. Her eyes followed the line of Jones's outstretched arm. She tried to leap out of the way, half throwing herself further into the road.

It was hopeless. Marion didn't stand a chance. The black truck hammered into her, sending her flying into the air like a rag doll.

She was propelled forwards several feet, then crashed to the ground directly beneath the truck's front wheels. She didn't utter a sound. At first it seemed that all Jones could hear was a dull sickening thud as a couple of tons of hard metal slammed into the soft compliant flesh of Marion's body.

It happened so quickly, and yet, to Jones, as if in slow motion. Marion's arms and legs stretched and curved almost balletically. Her head bounced as it met the road's unyielding resistance, and then Jones heard the crunching sound of breaking bone.

The black truck had run right over Marion's lower body. Jones could see that her left leg now protruded at an impossible angle, and blood was seeping through her jeans, trickling into the river of water in the gutter, turning it pink. Jones could hear the screech of the pick-up's tyres on the wet cobbles as it continued, at speed, in her direction. With what felt like the last vestige of her strength, she hurled herself sideways, rolling across the pavement. The truck roared past, missing her extended feet by a whisker.

Jones turned to look at Marion again. A dreadful realization hit her. Marion's left leg looked to have been almost completely severed above the knee. She could see bits of white bone sticking through the blue denim of her jeans, those same jeans that had had such neat creases down the front, and the blood oozing from her terrible wounds had turned almost black in colour.

Jones felt perilously nauseous. Yet she was curiously mesmerized. For a moment she lay still on the pavement, staring at the dreadful tableau which had unfolded itself before her.

Meanwhile the red brake lights of the Chevy flashed as the truck squealed to a halt just fifty yards or so up the road, then began to reverse, accelerating towards Jones, each wheel kicking up a fine spray of rain water.

She realized that she was the target now, but she was totally unable to do anything about it. She certainly couldn't move. Both her brain and her body had ceased to function.

She could smell the truck's diesel fumes. She fancied she could feel the heat from its engine. She prepared herself for the inevitable.

But the blow, when it came, was not at all what she had expected. Her upper body was lifted off the ground and she was propelled into the air so that she almost completed a somersault, landing face down, sprawled in the doorway of the liquor store on the corner. Her entire being felt like one huge bruise. There was a crushing weight on top of her. But it sure as heck wasn't a Chevy truck. And she was still alive.

'Right, let's get the hell out of here, lady,' said a low growling voice in her ear. The weight lifted from her body. One strong hand grabbed her under one arm, another slotted itself beneath the other arm. She was hauled to her feet, and found herself looking into the eyes of a man-mountain with a Mohican haircut. It was Dom.

'Can you walk?' he asked.

Jones was hurting all over. Her left leg, the knee already damaged at Princeton, was sending shooting pains through her whole body. But she could stand on it, just about. At least nothing was broken, it seemed.

'Yes,' she said, although she wasn't entirely sure. 'I-I think so . . .'

'Come on then, the cab's round the corner.'

Jones grabbed Dom's arm.

'But Marion?' she queried. 'What about Marion?'

'There's nothing we can do for her.'

Dom's voice was strangely calm. Jones glanced up at him. An isolated tear rolled down the big man's cheek, but his mouth was set in a hard line and his eyes were expressionless.

Jones looked back. Marion still lay in a crumpled heap in the road. She couldn't tell whether or not the wheels of the truck had passed over her a second time. But Marion seemed to be in a different place. Jones glanced at Dom again, in amazement. She suddenly realized what must have happened. The big man had either pulled or pushed poor Marion, as much as he could, out of the truck's path, while, at virtually the same time, cannoning into Jones and almost certainly saving her life. Only someone with rare strength and speed could have achieved it.

'Come on, before the goddamn cops arrive,' said Dom.

A small crowd was gathering around Marion. People were speaking into their mobile phones. Probably calling the emergency services.

Jones hesitated. Suddenly a concerned young woman appeared at her side.

'Weren't you hurt too?' she asked in the nasal twang of the Bronx. 'Are you all right?'

'She's fine,' said Dom.

'I'm fine,' Jones repeated, surprised she could even get the words out. The shock was setting in now. Her whole body was trembling. She was controlling her nausea only with great difficulty. And she knew she must look far from fine.

However, the young woman's attention had been diverted by the wail of the siren of an approaching police car.

'C'mon,' said Dom again. 'You're still in danger, Dr Jones. And Connie. I'm gonna find a way to keep you both safe, that's what Marion would want.'

Dom hooked an arm around the small of Jones's back, propelling her forwards. She leaned against him. He half-carried her along the street. By the time they reached the cab Jones could contain her nausea no longer. She bent over and emptied the contents of her stomach, partly in the gutter and partly down the side of the vehicle.

'Oh shit!' said Dom. 'Just get in.'

He unceremoniously pushed her into the back of the cab before virtually jumping into the driver's seat.

The tyres screeched on the wet cobbles, just as the tyres of the fearsome Chevy had done, and the cab catapulted forwards as Dom slammed his foot on the accelerator. Jones, still barely in control of her limbs, nearly bounced off the rear seat and was then flung backwards so that her head rocked on her shoulders.

'Where are we going?' she asked.

'Anywhere that's the fuck out of here,' replied Dom.

The cab swung from side to side as they hurtled through the Meatpacking District as if it were Monte Carlo and Dom was determined to win the annual rally.

Jones's stomach seemed to have transported itself upwards to somewhere around chest level. She feared she was going to be sick again. And this time she would have little choice except to throw up inside the cab.

But thankfully, after just a few minutes, Dom slowed down to a more or less normal speed, presumably confident that he had put enough distance between them and the scene of the incident, and

Jones's stomach descended to very nearly its normal position within her abdomen.

With the release from extreme discomfort, came the full awful realization of what had just occurred. If Dom had not arrived on the scene and manhandled her so dramatically out of the way of the charging truck she would be dead. She had no doubt of it. And she had no idea whether he had managed to save Marion, who, at the very least, had been dreadfully mutilated.

Christ, she thought. How was she going to tell Connie?

Suddenly Dom's deep voice filled the rear of the cab, the speaker system amplifying its Willard White resonance.

'Right Dr Jones, what we gotta do first is get Connie to safety. But we can't just go back to my place and get her. Not if we want to live. Have you got a safe way of contacting her?'

Jones slipped her hand inside her raincoat pocket. Miraculously the burner phone was still there, and, even more miraculously, it did not appear to be damaged.

She opened her mouth to tell Dom. Then shut it again. Her head was beginning to clear. And she didn't like the thoughts that were filling it. Jones put the phone back in her pocket, and pressed her hands tightly together in a bid to stop them trembling.

'Did you hear me, lady?' Dom's voice boomed.

'How could I not?'

'Well, we gotta move. We gotta get Connie outta my place. She's the target. She gotta be the target. Do you see?'

Jones saw. Connie had almost certainly been right all along. The RECAP lab had been deliberately blown up, just as she'd always believed. And Connie had indeed been the target back there on that street corner. The driver of the Chevy had made a mistake. He'd mown down the wrong woman.

The would-be assassin must have been waiting and watching outside Dom's apartment. And when Jones had emerged with Marion wearing Connie's cover-all oilskin, the assumption had been instantly made that she was Connie. Marion was slightly shorter than Connie, but about the same build. She had been bent into the weather, and had pulled the hood of her cape up and forwards over her forehead. The little of her face that could have been seen had been further concealed by the umbrella she'd been holding in front of them both. In addition, the assassin may not even have known that there was a second woman in the apartment along with Connie and Jones.

So persons unknown must already have been aware that Connie had not been killed in the Princeton blast, that she was alive and in hiding in New York. They had then tracked her down and attempted, yet again, to kill her. Or so they had thought.

And who the hell were they, anyway, these murderous bastards? Connie suspected the establishment. The government even. Or at least a government affiliated body. But did the American government really go around arranging for its citizens to be mown down on the streets of New York?

The sequence of events had been such that the attack had to have been orchestrated by someone in a position of considerable authority and power, that was for sure.

Jones studied the back of Dom's head. Dom, as Marion had said, was a man capable of summoning all manner of unknown resources, and Jones had just seen him act in a way that would have been far beyond the capabilities of most human beings. It seemed bizarre that she was so suspicious of a man who had almost certainly saved her life. And it was highly unlikely that Dom would ever be involved in anything that might harm Marion, whom he adored. But Marion had not been the target. Dom himself had said that. Certainly Jones considered Dom to be too much of an unknown quantity to unreservedly trust. For a start, how exactly had he contrived to arrive so conveniently on the scene right after Marion had been mown down?

No way was she going to hand over her burner phone to him, nor use it herself to contact Connie. Not for as long as she was with him.

'Come on, ma'am, I need your help,' boomed Dom from the front.

'Sure, sure,' muttered Jones.

Dom eased the cab to a halt at a set of lights. The traffic was a little heavier now. There were vehicles queued in front of them, and behind.

'I'm just trying to think, that's all . . .' Jones continued.

The lights changed. The line of traffic approaching from the other side of the road junction began to move slowly forwards.

The vehicles in front of Dom's cab also began to move. Jones

yanked at the handle on the roadside door of the cab. She wrenched
it open, and leapt, as best her battered body could manage, out into
the street. Thankfully Dom had not locked her in this time.
Presumably he had either not considered it necessary. or merely
been in too much of a hurry to even think about it.

Somehow or other, Jones managed to land on her feet. Or very
nearly. She took off at a run, ignoring the shooting pains in her
leg. She heard the cab squealing to a halt again, and the big man
yelling after her. She didn't look back. She'd noticed an empty
yellow cab in the line of slowly approaching traffic. She hailed
it as she ran across the road, and somehow or other managed to
open a door and throw herself inside while the cab was still
crawling along. Dom moved fast. He came running across the
road, still yelling, right on Jones's heels. There was a lot of
hooting going on from the line of vehicles trapped behind his
abandoned vehicle.

Jones slammed the cab door shut and flipped down the lock.

'Grand Central Station,' she told the driver, not because she
wanted to go there but because it was the first place that came into
her head, and one of the few that even a New York cabby could
find without a full address including cross streets.

Suddenly Dom's face loomed alarmingly at the window, just
as Jones's new driver accelerated away. Mercifully the traffic
had begun to flow quite freely. Equally suddenly the face was
gone.

Jones looked back over her shoulder as an irate Dom disappeared
into the distance.

The best news was that there was absolutely no chance of Dom
getting back into his cab and swinging it around in time to follow
Jones and her driver, who thankfully seemed quite oblivious to
the fact that anything untoward was happening. He had barely
even looked at Jones, which was all for the best, or he might not
be driving her anywhere. She breathed a huge sigh of relief and
leaned back in her seat.

But she couldn't believe what she had just done, and her heart
was racing. She had to contact Connie. And fast. She had to get
her to safety. And if she was right in her suspicions of Dom, then
the former wrestler could well be already on his way to the loft
apartment.

Jones used her burner to dial the one she'd already given Connie, who answered quite cheerily. Jones steeled herself.

'It's me,' she began lamely, keeping her voice low so that the driver wouldn't hear.

'I know it's you, woman, who else has this number anyway . . .' Connie stopped.

Jones's voice had sounded strange even to her. Connie had picked up on that. As she would.

'What's wrong?' Connie asked sharply.

'There's been an accident—'

'Marion,' Connie interrupted at once. 'Oh my God. It's Marion, isn't it?'

'Yes.'

Jones could still see that broken and bloodied body lying in the street. And she didn't know how to tell Connie what had happened to the woman she clearly loved so much. But Connie didn't even give her a chance to start to explain before firing questions at her.

'What happened? Where is she? What have they done to her? Tell me where Marion is? I must go to her—'

'No, Connie, no—'

'What do you mean, no? Is she dead? Is Marion dead? Is that what you're trying to tell me?'

'I don't know, Connie. The truth is I don't know whether she's dead or alive. I really don't. I had to get away. I was going to be next. Marion's injured. But I don't know how badly.'

The last sentence was a total lie, of course. If Marion had survived, if she was alive, Jones knew only too well that she had suffered the most terrible injuries. But she didn't want Connie to totally fall apart.

'You've left her?' Connie barked.

'No. Well . . . yes. It w-wasn't like that . . .'

'Never mind, just tell me where she,' Connie repeated, still shouting. 'I must go to her. What happened? What the hell happened?'

'Look Connie, you have to listen. And do as I say. Marion was hit by a truck. It wasn't an accident. T-the thing is, I think she was mistaken for you . . .'

'Oh my God.'

Connie spoke flatly, not shouting any more.

'Somebody knew you were alive, Connie, and that somebody wanted you dead, really dead,' Jones continued. 'Right now they may still think they've got you, and they may not be watching Dom's place. But they'll know they failed soon enough. Leave the loft, straight away. Get out. Just get out . . .'

'Yes, yes. But I must go to Marion. Where've they taken her? Which hospital?'

'I don't know. And even if I did you mustn't go to her. Not yet. That would be suicide.'

'Dom could fix it. Dom would know what to do—'

'No,' Jones interrupted sharply. 'I think he might be involved. He was there. When it happened.'

'Dom would never hurt Marion.'

'Connie, it was you they were after. Not Marion. Look, will you just go along with me on this for now. Put on a scarf or a hat or something, hide that hair of yours, and get a cab to Grand Central. I'll meet you by the gate to platform one. OK? Platform one.'

'OK.'

The shock was strong in Connie's voice, but Jones also detected resignation. Thankfully, it seemed that she was going to do what Jones said.

'Good. Now, I need you to bring my bag with you. I wouldn't ask if it wasn't important. It's got my laptop in it, my personal mobile, and another burner phone. Can you do that?'

'Yes.'

'And Connie, remember what I said, avoid Dom, do you hear me? He may even be on his way to you. I reckon you could have . . .'

She checked her watch, trying to visualize the place where she had abandoned Dom's cab and its proximity to the loft apartment.

'Ten minutes max before he could be there . . .'

'But Sandy, Dom is Marion's closest, dearest friend, her surrogate son. He'd never hurt either of us, I just can't believe . . .'

'Connie!'

Jones realized she had shouted at her. Aware of the presence
of the cab driver, albeit behind a glass screen, she lowered her
voice to a kind of urgent hiss.

'Connie, you're wasting time. Please, do as I tell you. Get the
fuck out of there and come to me. I'll explain then.'

Connie murmured something indecipherable, which Jones
hoped to God was agreement, and ended the call. Jones leaned
wearily back in her seat and closed her eyes. She was living a
nightmare.

The taxi pulled to a halt with a jolt outside the Vanderbilt Avenue
entrance to Grand Central. Jones opened her eyes again. This was
a nightmare from which there was no waking up. A bleak terrifying
reality the like of which Sandy Jones had never experienced before.

Meanwhile, in the bowels of a warehouse in Chelsea, only a half a
mile or so away from Dom's loft apartment, the man who always
wore a black suit, white shirt and black tie, paced anxiously up and
down. As usual he was wearing shades, even though he was inside
a big cavernous basement which was only poorly lit.

He was, of course, the nameless interrogator at Princeton police
station whom Jones had dubbed the Man in Black. Ed MacEntee's
not entirely effective tail. And while he continued to try desperately
to look the part of a tough, cool super-agent, the Man in Black was
extremely uneasy.

As far as he was concerned the whole operation was spiralling
out of control. He'd only begun it as a way of increasing his standing
in the organization. He'd wanted to draw attention to himself. Well,
he'd certainly done that. He'd wanted to impress. He'd particularly
wanted to impress Mr Johnson.

But the man had not thought things through properly. And now
it was too late, far too late, to even attempt to put a stop to it all. He
liked to project an image of himself to those around him which
he could not always live up to. He was inclined to let his imagination run away with him. Yet never in his wildest imaginings had
it occurred to him that a situation like this might develop.

The Man in Black was waiting for the Enforcer. The Enforcer
and his Apprentice. He didn't really want anything to do with them.
They frightened the life out of him. But he had to be there. He had
to know.

He heard them before he saw them, the low rumble of the engine of the Chevy pick-up truck, and the rhythmic squeal of its tyres as it swung round and round the winding ramp which snaked its way down from street level.

The truck coasted to a halt in its allotted parking space. Both the front doors opened. The Enforcer had been driving. He had sandy hair thinning at the front and a small neat moustache. He was wearing a tweed jacket over corduroy trousers bagging slightly at the knee. He looked like a schoolmaster, until you saw his eyes. There was no life in those eyes. The man in the black suit thought they were the most frightening eyes he had ever seen.

The Apprentice was very young and very cocky. He had orange hair and freckles, and he walked with a swagger. He was swaggering now, but the Man in Black could see that he was sweating and his hands, hanging loosely at his sides as if he were John Wayne, were trembling.

The Enforcer strolled casually to the front of the truck and bent down to examine its big chrome over-bumper. He leaned close until his face was just inches away, reaching into the pocket of his trousers to remove a white handkerchief with which he thoroughly wiped the protective metal bars.

Then he straightened up and, still holding the handkerchief in one hand, walked slowly towards the Man in Black. The handkerchief had turned pink, in places bright red.

It was blood, for sure. Blood thick enough to have been still clinging to the undersides of those bars, in spite of the heavy rain.

The Man in Black gulped. His throat was made of sandpaper. He felt sick. He struggled not to let it show, not to let his so carefully orchestrated act drop.

The Chelsea warehouse was the new secret headquarters of the FBI's anti-terrorism unit, set up after 9/11. And the special agents employed there were a breed apart. They had much in common with their brothers and sisters who represented the public face of the Bureau and who worked out of the FBI's famous New York headquarters at 26, Federal Plaza, and other openly declared addresses throughout the country. But the Chelsea Feds were there to perform tasks and pursue courses of action that took them much further along an extremely rocky road, in a country still purporting to be a benevolent democracy. They had carte blanche to do whatever was necessary to protect an America which had never quite recovered from the blind panic which followed the deadliest terror attack in human history. They had never played by the rules. They weren't supposed to.

But word was, that under the auspices of arguably the most maverick and unpredictable president of all time, they had been given an autonomy and a level of operational freedom way beyond anything that had originally been intended.

The Enforcer and his Apprentice were considered to be two of the Chelsea Feds' finest sons. They did what others neither would nor could do.

The Man in Black sucked his dry lips. He was totally out of his depth. And he knew it.

PART FOUR

Our consciousness rarely registers the beginning of growth within us any more than without us; there have been many circulations of the sap before we detect the smallest sign of the bud.

George Eliot

THIRTEEN

I t was all Jones could do to muster the strength to climb out of
the cab. She paid the driver from her stash of dollar bills, then
stood still for a moment trying to be sure that she had control
of her body.

The rain, thankfully, had eased, because Jones's grey plastic
raincoat, now badly torn, was likely to provide even less protection
than before. She still felt extremely shaky and her left leg almost
gave way when she tried to put her full weight on it. She took a
step sideways and reached out to hold on to a water hydrant to
steady herself.

Passers-by were glancing at her curiously, then quickly turning
away. She wasn't surprised. She was a mess. But even in her state
of shock she was aware that most of the blood that had been
splashed on her had landed on her torn raincoat. She shrugged
herself out of it, scrunched it up, and tucked it under one arm.

Moving as quickly as her injured leg would allow, while also
trying to be inconspicuous, she made her way up the station steps,
past the line of pavement cafes, and into the cavernous central hall,
where she stood at the top of the steps overlooking the concourse
and glanced anxiously around for the nearest public convenience.

There was a pronounced police presence. Two machine-gun-
toting soldiers, wearing fatigues and flak jackets, stood just to Jones's
left, fortunately facing away from her.

Involuntarily Jones took a step backwards, but reminded
herself that this was, of course, normal in America. And had been
since 9/11.

Nonetheless, she retreated through the imposing gateway
from which she had just entered. Then, standing outside, she remembered The Campbell Apartment, an unlikely cocktail bar to which
she had been introduced on her last visit to New York, and headed
for the heavy wooden doors which she knew led to it. The Apartment
had been leased in the 1920s and 30s by a businessman and alleged
bootlegger called John W. Campbell who transformed the thirty- by

sixty-foot room into a reproduction Florentine palace which he used both as an office and for entertaining. Or actually, some said, for storing and selling his illegal hooch.

Jones knew the bar would be closed that early in the day, but hoped that the exterior doors would be open. They were. She hurried across the tiled ground floor lobby, from which a short flight of steps led to The Apartment itself, and ran up them as fast as her battered legs could carry her. At the top was a ladies' lavatory. To her relief, that was open too. And it was deserted.

Once inside, she studied her reflection in the wall mirror. No wonder people had been looking at her curiously. There were splashes of blood on her face. Her right cheek still bore the signs of the damage it had incurred the previous day, and her chin was now swollen on one side and seemed to be turning a bluish yellow colour almost as she watched. It was also seeping liquid from an unpleasant looking graze. Obliquely she wondered which of the blood splashes were her own and which might be poor Marion's.

She shivered. Her body felt icy cold and yet her face was burning. Her heart was still racing.

She dumped her destroyed raincoat in the trash can fastened to one wall, reached for some paper towels, ran the cold tap in the washbasin, soaked the towels and dabbed them against her damaged face. The cold water felt wonderful, cooling and restorative. She realized then how thirsty she was. She dropped the paper towels on the floor, cupped her hands underneath the tap, raised them to her mouth and drank the water gratefully. She wiped her face dry with more paper towels, then paused to look in the mirror again. She still didn't look good. Her face was clean enough now and pretty much free of blood. It was also a pale whitish grey. Her features were drawn. It was almost as if she had aged twenty years in as many minutes.

Obliquely, she wished she had her make-up with her, but that was in the bag she had left in Dom's apartment. Hopefully it and Connie would arrive soon.

The graze on her chin continued to ooze a little, but seemed to be actually only a shallow wound. Most of the blood she had wiped away must have come from Marion. She was surprised to find that she could think about that in such a detached way. She was operating on a kind of auto pilot.

She ran her tongue over her teeth. Somewhat to her surprise they all seemed to be there and apparently undamaged, although her gums were sore.

She turned her attention to her clothes. She was wearing the same jeans and hoody she'd had laundered at the Soho House. Both were dirty and torn. The rip in the left sleeve of the hoody was so bad that the lower half had become almost detached from the upper, and was hanging from just a few threads of wool. She rolled both sleeves up, which improved things very slightly.

She rubbed ineffectually at the dirty marks and the few spots of blood which her raincoat had not protected her from. There was nothing at all she could do about the rip in the knee of her jeans. In any case, she only needed to make herself presentable enough to meet Connie at the appointed spot. Fortunately both her jeans and her tracksuit top were black. And this was New York. Hopefully nobody would even notice. She glanced at her watch again. If Connie had followed her instructions and left the loft apartment immediately, she would arrive soon.

She made her way back to the station concourse, keeping her head down, and limping as little as possible.

Remembering something from all those bad movies she'd watched, she paused at a news stand to buy a paper. At the entrance to platform one she propped herself against a conveniently positioned wall and held the newspaper up in front of her face. She didn't really know what she was playing at, but it seemed like a good idea at the time. She still had a famous face – barely known in America, outside of scientific circles, it was true, but Britons did travel – and she had just left the scene of a terrible crime.

With one eye she peeped around the edge of the paper.

Connie arrived only a couple of minutes later, hurrying across the concourse. She had at least followed the first of Jones's instructions and was wearing a baseball cap which she had presumably found among Dom's belongings. Unfortunately, however, she hadn't managed to tuck in all of her expansive red hair. And the cap was a strident yellow colour. The result was that she was probably likely to attract attention to herself even more than usual, particularly as she was wearing a green coat.

Oh my God, thought Jones. She had tried so hard to make herself inconspicuous, and now this multi-coloured vision, hair sticking out like a clown's around the skull cap effect of the baseball cap, was tearing across the station, attracting a certain amount of attention even in this city.

A passing cop glanced first at the approaching Connie, and then at Jones. Jones buried herself deeper in her newspaper. The cop walked on by. Jones peeped around the newspaper again.

To her relief she saw that Connie had her bag over one shoulder, and the smaller cloth bag she always carried over the other. Both were being wielded almost like weapons. The station was far from crowded, nonetheless Connie scattered people in all directions as she rocketed through them like a multi-coloured windmill.

Jones would have laughed out loud at the sight of her, were it not for the tragic nature of the occasion. And as Connie approached she could see that tears were streaming down her face. Her anguish was all too apparent. She was oblivious to everything, looking but not seeing. She rushed right past Jones, who lowered her newspaper.

'Connie,' she called after her, sotto voce.

Connie turned, saw Jones, and threw herself at her, grabbing her shoulders, knocking the newspaper out of her hands.

'Sandy, Sandy. Tell me everything that's happened. I have to go to Marion. I have to!' she shouted.

People began to stare. Jones had to stop her behaving like this. She pushed her away as gently as possible, then grabbed both her hands.

'Connie, shush, shush,' she said. 'You must calm down. You are in terrible danger. And people are staring . . .'

'Do you think I care?' Connie's green eyes blazed. 'Do you think I care about myself? I have to find Marion. I have to go to her . . .'

'Connie, for God's sake . . .'

Jones looked anxiously around. Connie was behaving crazily. They could not afford the attentions of a curious police officer.

'We can't stay here,' Jones continued. 'We need to go somewhere we can talk. Please.'

Perhaps surprisingly, Connie stopped shouting and nodded her agreement. She didn't seem able to stop crying, though.

Jones coaxed her across the concourse to the Vanderbilt entrance and the Campbell Apartment. The place was still deserted. It was the nearest to private she could come up with at the moment.

Once inside she wrapped her arms around Connie and drew her close. Connie's body felt so tense, it was almost as if she were made of some substance much less malleable than flesh and blood.

'It's my fault, it's all my fault,' she wailed into Jones's shoulder.

'No, Connie, no,' Jones soothed. 'Of course it's not your fault.'

'Yes, it is. I should never have involved Marion. None of this has anything to do with her. But I did involve her. I got her into it. And now she might be dead . . .'

Jones didn't know what to say, so she didn't speak. It seemed like for ever but was probably only a minute or two before Connie's sobs eased. Jones continued to hold on to her. The almost comical baseball hat had fallen from her head. Jones stroked her hair gently.

'Listen, Connie, it's not just you who is in danger, it's me too,' she said. 'We have to work out what to do next. We both have to at least try to be calm and rational.'

Jones reckoned that Connie Pike was just about the most unselfish person she had ever met. She knew that if anything could get through to her it was the suggestion that somebody else dear to her might also be in danger, because, in her mind at any rate, of her actions.

After a few seconds Connie stopped sobbing and looked at Jones as if seeing her, and the state she was in, for the first time.

'You're hurt too,' she said. 'Are you all right?'

'I'm fine,' Jones replied, for the second time that morning. It was a considerable exaggeration.

Connie nodded. She was clearly making a huge effort to pull herself together.

'All right, let's talk,' she said. 'And first I have to know everything about Marion.'

Jones gestured towards the flight of steps leading up to the locked and bolted Campbell Apartment itself.

'It's not a Chesterfield, but why don't we sit down,' she suggested.

Connie did so at once. Jones joined her gratefully, stretching out her injured leg before her, and proceeded to tell the other woman everything, just as she had demanded, even about her fears that one of Marion's legs had been severed. Connie reacted with only the faintest flicker of an eyelid. Jones told her about the truck reversing back at both of them, and how it was possible that its far-side wheels may have run over Marion's head.

Connie then let out a little gasp, and her eyes filled with tears again. Almost impatiently she brushed them away with the back of one hand.

'Possible?' she queried.

'Well, I really don't know,' Jones continued honestly. 'Dom pushed us both out of the way. He knocked all the breath from my body. By the time I'd recovered enough to get up on my feet again, and I tried to see what had happened to Marion, she was just lying there, with a crowd gathering around her. Oh God, that sounds awful.'

Connie put a hand lightly on Jones's right arm.

'Did you think she was dead, Sandy?' she asked, even more quietly. 'Was that what you thought?'

'I couldn't be sure,' Jones answered truthfully. 'But if she is alive, then she has certainly suffered the most dreadful injuries.'

'That I can live with,' said Connie almost absently, adding almost conversationally, 'but I don't think I could live without her, not without Marion.'

'Oh, Connie,' Jones murmured.

'Thing is,' Connie continued, 'before we do anything else, I have to find out about Marion. You must see that.'

'I do. But I don't see how without putting both of us at risk.'

'That's the sort of thing Dom would sort out . . .'

'Connie. I don't see how we can trust him. He had the information to set that incident up. And don't you think he'd have the means? He moves in nefarious ways . . .'

'But he saved your life, Sandy. And he may have saved Marion's life. He's probably put himself in danger . . .'

Jones opened her mouth to try to explain further.

She was interrupted by a loud bang and a crash as the big double doors to The Campbell Apartment foyer burst open. In strode the Dominator, his huge form filling the door frame. Jones was astonished. She could not imagine how the big man had found her, and Connie, so quickly. And Dom looked even bigger and more menacing than ever.

'So here you are, you dumb fucking bitch,' he yelled at Jones. 'What the hell did you jump out of ma cab for?'

For what seemed like the umpteenth time since she'd arrived in America, Jones was overwhelmed by panic. She quite surprised herself by managing to speak. And at volume.

'Because I don't trust you,' she yelled back. 'Because everything you do makes me suspicious of you. How did you know where to find us, for a start?'

'I didn't. But it was the only place at Grand Central left to look. You took a cab here, didn't you, chowderhead? And you actually stayed at the place where the driver dropped you off. There's a brotherhood among New York cabbies, lady. I took the guy's number when you did your damned fool suicide dash into his cab. Took me ten minutes to get his name and phone number, and another fifteen to get my ass here. I hoped you might contact Connie. I didn't dare go back to my place. I'm just so glad you're here, honey.'

He reached out and touched Connie on one shoulder.

'And I'm just so goddamned sorry,' he added.

'I know you are, Dom,' Connie responded quietly.

Jones slumped forwards, resting her face in her hands. She wasn't cut out for any of this. Everything she'd attempted to do so far had gone wrong: visiting the RECAP lab and getting arrested; trying to extract information from Ed and then ending up telling him about Connie; running away from Dom. James Bond? Indiana Jones? Eve and Villanelle? Their worlds were not hers. She didn't fit at all. She was a disaster.

'You think any of that makes me trust you any more, Dom?' she asked eventually. 'You knew Connie was alive, and you're just the sort of man who would have the contacts to set up a hit . . .'

'A hit on Marion? Me? Are you out of your mind. I'd never hurt a hair on her head.'

'No, but maybe you'd hurt Connie. She was the target. You told me that. Maybe someone got to you, bribed you, blackmailed you. How the hell do I know? But what I do know is, I can't think of anyone else who would have been able to set up that hit. Only you.'

Dom made a low growling sound and took a step towards Jones who just froze, still sitting on the step, looking up at him. Not again, she thought. Not more violence.

Connie stood up quickly and positioned herself between the two of them.

'That won't help, Dom,' she said sternly, placing her hands on his huge chest. The big man stopped in his tracks at once, lowered his clenched fists, and took a step backwards.

'I sure am sorry, Connie, and, you know what, I've never beat up a woman in my whole goddamned life. But this one sure is trying my patience. I wouldn't do nothing to hurt you, any more than I would Marion, and I cannot believe she's dumb enough to think I would.'

Connie sighed. 'Look Dom, nobody but you, and poor Marion, even knows I'm alive. Sandy does have a point you know . . .'

'Does she hell as like! Don't say that, Connie. Anyway, Dr fucking Sandy Jones knows you are still alive. Maybe she set it up.'

'You don't believe that for a second, Dom, any more than I do.'

'Maybe I don't. But if it wasn't her and it wasn't me, who the hell could it have been? Somebody else must have known, Connie. I'm dead sure you and Marion haven't told anyone else. And I sure haven't. What about you, lady?'

Dom pointed a beefy finger at Jones, who shifted awkwardly on the step.

'Sandy?' queried Connie.

'Well . . .'

'Oh, Sandy. What have you done? Who have you told?'

'OK. I told Ed. I sort of couldn't help it. He was so dreadfully upset about you and Paul. He started to cry, and couldn't stop. I just wanted to cheer him up.'

'You just wanted to cheer him up? You put all of us at risk, to cheer Ed up?'

Connie sounded stunned and bewildered.

'Yeah.' Jones looked down at her feet. 'But it didn't occur to me that Ed wouldn't be absolutely trustworthy . . .'

'Oh, Sandy,' said Connie again.

'Ed would never do anything to harm you or Marion, Connie,' Jones continued. 'And he wouldn't have a clue how to go about it even if he wanted to, for God's sake.'

'Ed mightn't ever do anything knowingly to hurt us, but who knows what he may already have unwittingly done,' Connie responded, her voice still low. 'My darling Marion is at best terribly injured, at worst she could be dead. And the chances are it's your fault, Sandy. All your fault.'

She yelled the last sentence at Jones, who knew she deserved it. If she could only put the clock back she wouldn't have left the United Kingdom at all, that was for certain. She really had made everything worse.

'I'm sorry,' she muttered.

'Well now,' said Dom, 'so I'm not the only one in the frame after all.' He glowered at Jones. 'Know what, I'm beginning to wish I hadn't gone and saved your goddamned arse.'

Jones winced. She still didn't entirely trust the big man though.

Dom turned to address Connie directly.

'I intend to look after you, Con,' he said. 'Because that's what Aunt M would want.'

He paused, raised one huge paw, and rubbed at his face and eyes. The Dominator was wiping away tears.

'Goddamn it, Connie,' he continued. 'I should have been able to protect Marion. I was too slow. I saw that pickup truck coming at her. I saw it, but I couldn't get to her in time . . .'

Connie reached with one hand and touched his tear-stained cheek.

'I'm sure Marion knows you tried your best, Dom,' she told him gently. 'I know that too.'

The Dominator took a big spotted handkerchief from the pocket of his leather jacket and blew his nose loudly. The bling on his wrists and fingers jangled.

'Well, I'm just gonna have to make sure I do a better job for you, Connie darlin',' he said, looking down at her with affection and concern.

Then he glanced towards Jones and his expression changed.

'But I'm not so sure I want anything more to do with your crazy friend,' he scowled. 'I done my best for her already, and look how she's repaid me?'

Connie glanced towards Jones.

'Yep, Sandy's not covered herself in glory these last coupla days,' she began. 'But we go back a long way, and she did come here to try to help as soon as she heard about the explosion . . .'

Dom held up a massive hand. 'OK. For you, Connie, we'll keep the lady on board. We need to get you both off the streets. Go somewhere safe.'

He turned toward Jones.

'But, just you try one more of your tricks and that's it, Dr Dim. You're on your own. Yeah?'

Jones nodded. She felt defeated. She was certainly totally unqualified to protect either Connie or herself. She had little choice but to go along with the Dominator.

'Right,' said Dom aggressively, pointing a finger at Jones. 'You do exactly what I say, lady. Yeah?'

'Yeah,' repeated Jones meekly.

'Then let's get this show on the road.'

Dom was wearing a long black scarf around his neck. He whipped it off and handed it to Connie.

'First of all, let's not advertise who you are, Connie darlin',' he said. 'Wrap this scarf round your head and hide that damned red hair of yours. Will you?'

Connie obeyed. Her hair disappeared. She no longer looked nearly so conspicuous. Dom's scarf worked a hell of a lot better than the unfortunate yellow baseball cap.

Then Dom turned his attention to Jones, looking her up and down.

'That your bag?'

He gestured to the hold-all by Jones's feet. Jones nodded.

'Good. You gonna need to change your clothes. It will have to wait, though. I'd rather get you both away from here without wasting any more time. OK?'

'OK,' said Jones.

She felt anything but OK. Two days ago she had been sitting at her desk in Exeter indulging in a certain amount of self-congratulation. Since then she'd embarked on a crazy wild goose chase, been arrested, more or less kidnapped, and, finally, caught up in an attempted murder that had nearly led to her own death. Worse still, there was a possibility, although she could hardly believe it, that her own indiscretion may have precipitated that murder attempt.

And now she was a fugitive, on the run from an unknown enemy, and left with no choice but to accept the protection of a man whom she still half believed could be the enemy.

FOURTEEN

Dom hurried them outside, a big protective arm around Connie's shoulders. Jones followed as best she could.

His cab was parked on the rank just around the corner in 42nd Street. He hustled them towards it.

'Don't you think this might be a target too now?' Jones asked, pointing at the yellow vehicle.

Dom turned to look at her. 'Who do you think is after you and Connie?' he asked. 'Every security force in America?'

Jones shrugged. Dom seemed to think she was being paranoid. Well there was a pretty good reason for it. A reason they'd left lying on a New York street.

'No lady,' continued Dom, once they were all in the cab. 'Somebody's after Connie, there's no damned doubt about that, and somebody with resources. Of course they can get to me because of the apartment, and once they've traced me it's on record that I work as a cabby. And of course my medallion number's listed. But they gotta work their way through all of that. And I've kept the cab out of the way too, remember. Even when the truck hit you guys I was parked out of sight, and I'd been following you on foot.'

Jones mumbled assent. The Dominator was probably right. He was certainly capable, there was no doubt about that. He also seemed able to keep his head while all around were losing theirs.

Connie, meanwhile, was very quiet.

'You all right?' Jones asked, realizing as she spoke what a darned silly question that was.

'What do you think?' Connie snapped the words out.

'Sorry,' said Jones.

Connie's face was red and blotchy from her tears, her eyes red-rimmed and full of pain.

'And I'm so so sorry about Marion. I can't believe it could have been Ed though—'

'What? No. Of course it wasn't Ed. I mean . . . not deliberately anyway.'

'All the same, I shouldn't have told him.'

'No, but like you said, we all go back a long way.'

Connie sounded reasonable again. Understanding. It made Jones feel even worse.

'Yes, we do.'

Jones felt her own tears pricking.

'It's OK, Sandy. Really it is.'

'Thank you for not blaming me,' said Jones. 'Or not entirely, anyway . . .'

'You are not responsible for any of this. You came to help. No other reason. And there's so much . . . so much . . .'

Connie stopped suddenly, as if she'd been about to say something and had thought better of it.

'Anyway, this is where we're at,' she continued. 'And I have to find out about Marion. Dom, why can't I phone from a pay phone? Will you pull over?'

'Hey Connie, no way, girl.'

The big man's voice sounded rather more highly pitched than usual.

'Who you gonna phone, eh? The police? All the hospitals in New York? You gonna try it anonymous, you gonna get nowhere. You tell them who you are and you're asking for big trouble.'

'I'd be quick. This is the middle of Manhattan. We could be twenty blocks away before anyone could trace the call.'

'You reckon? Connie darlin', it takes exactly fifteen seconds to pinpoint a call in this city. No. Trust me, Con, for Christ's sake, trust me. I know a safe place. I'm gonna take you there. And then I'll find out about Marion for you. I promise you, darlin'.'

'You will?' Jones interjected. 'If you're not a target yet, Dom, you surely will be soon. How can it be any safer for you to start asking questions about Marion than it is for Connie?'

'Yeah, well maybe I won't do it personally.'

'Please don't talk in riddles.'

'I'm going to introduce you guys to my girlfriend.'

'To your girlfriend?' If the situation hadn't been so tragic Jones would probably have burst out laughing. 'Are we off to the theatre and supper at Sardi's or something? Are you serious? You really want to get your girlfriend into this? Or were you lying just now? Have you told her already about Connie? And are we just supposed to trust her . . .'

There were traffic lights ahead. The cab screeched to a sudden halt. Dom turned around, twisting his body so that he was able to thrust most of his head into the rear compartment. He reached a long, bling-jangling arm through the gap and grabbed Jones by the shoulder.

'Will you shut the fuck up, you crazy Englishwoman,' he growled. 'We don't have any goddamned choice. I haven't told her yet, but I'm about to. Everything's different now. In any case . . .'

He paused in mid-sentence, as if he too were about to say something but had changed his mind.

'My girl's special,' he continued obliquely.

Jones was not impressed. All that indicated to her was that Dom was probably in love. And she'd had reason enough in her life to believe that love really is blind.

Dom drove them into the heart of Harlem, further north than Jones had ever been before, to an area the property speculators had yet to launch themselves on, a place where you still didn't see a white face in the street. Jones hunkered down in the back, still in shock, her hands clasped to stop them shaking.

Eventually Dom turned off Harlem's main drag, swung the cab into a narrow alley between two tall rundown-looking buildings and pulled to a halt in a yard at the back.

'It's a flop house, owned by a pal of mine who owes me big time,' he told Jones and Connie, as he opened the driver's door and stepped out of the cab.

'You two just wait here.'

It was both a command and a warning.

Jones and Connie obediently muttered their assent. They were entirely in Dom's hands now, and even Jones knew she just had to accept that.

The big man was back in less than five minutes.

'Right, all they have is one big room, with a kitchen and a bathroom,' he said. 'And it's not the Waldorf, that's for damned sure, but I reckon we'll be safe enough, for a while anyway. Now just follow me and keep quiet. We should be able to go in the back way without you two being seen.'

The back entrance to the flop house, through a narrow door beneath the fire escape, was damp and dark and smelt of something Jones did not particularly care to identify. The room was no better. It was more like a small dormitory. There were four iron-framed beds covered in dubious looking blankets. There was a kitchen area at one end, comprising a sink, a fridge, a microwave and an electric hob, none of which looked excessively clean. The door stood open to an uninviting shower room and toilet.

Jones wrinkled her nose in distaste, an involuntary gesture spotted at once by Dom.

'I say, so sorry it's not what you're used to, Your Ladyship,' he said, in what he presumably assumed was an impression of an upper-class English accent.

'I don't give a toss as long as a bunch of thugs with crowbars or worse don't come bursting through the door,' responded Jones, who was tempted to tell the big man what she thought of his panto-mime of an impersonation, but didn't have the energy.

'OK. I'll go find my girl,' said Dom. 'I'll call her on her cell from a public phone. I doubt they've got to me yet, my cell phone could still be safe, but we shouldn't take no more risks. Not after what's happened to Marion.'

'You can use my burner.'

Jones held out the phone.

Dom looked at it for a moment.

'You didn't tell me you had that,' he said accusingly.

'No, sorry,' muttered Jones, who wasn't actually sure she was sorry, or that she should even be giving Dom the phone now. But she and Connie had put themselves in his hands. There was no point in holding back.

Dom grunted. And reached out to take the burner. Then he stopped.

'Was that the phone Ed called you on this morning?' he asked.

Jones nodded.

'That could be how they traced you to my place.'

'I told him only to call from a call box.'

'Yeah, well maybe he didna do what he was told. Don't you see? Phone's almost certainly no good any more. Too dangerous to use. And the one you gave Connie.'

Jones wondered who was getting paranoid now.

'Whatever you say,' she muttered. 'I bought a third phone though.'

'You did?'

'Not been used. It's in my bag. I'll get it for you.'

'Right. But I should go out anyway. We need some food. Anyone hungry?'

Jones never got her morning tea. She and Marion hadn't made it to breakfast. However, food and drink were the last things on her mind. And she still felt nauseous. She shook her head.

Connie looked at Dom as if he was crazy.

'I haven't been able to eat properly since Paul died,' she said. 'I feel even less like it now.'

'I'll bring something back anyway. We gotta be strong, and if you don't eat you don't stay strong.'

'I could do with some coffee,' said Connie.

'Sure,' responded Dom. 'Maybe there's some here . . .'

He opened the fridge door, rummaged for a moment or two amongst goodness knew what, and then stood up clutching a foil pack of coffee that had been opened but was held together at the top by a clip.

'There you are. Coffee. And there's the thing to make it with, too.'

He pointed to a filter coffee machine standing on the worktop. Jones hadn't seen one of those in a long time.

'Right, I'll get off, then. Just don't do anything stupid?'

Again neither Jones nor Connie responded. Instead they watched in silence as the big man left.

Jones took the opportunity to finally remove her dirty, torn, and blood-spattered clothing, then shower and, as ever, wash her hair. The shower turned out to be much more effective than it looked, sending out a restoratively powerful stream of piping hot water. Afterwards she dressed in a clean shirt, her Stella McCartney grey trousers, the only spare pair she had brought with her, and her leather jacket, and applied her make-up rather more heavily than usual in an attempt to at least partially disguise the damage to her face.

There was a hairdryer plumbed into the wall by the basin. Jones used it to swiftly blow-dry her hair into the sharp glossy bob she was so fussy about, which immediately made her feel considerably better.

When she stepped out into the main room Connie was fiddling with the coffee maker.

'Well, it boils the water, doesn't it?' she muttered unenthusiastically. 'Don't suppose we'll come to much harm. Anyway . . . seems like there's a lot more danger lurking for us than a few germs.'

She turned to face Jones.

'You look better.'

Jones managed a weak smile.

Connie rinsed the coffee machine then filled it with water and added the coffee. Jones watched for a few seconds as she produced a couple of mugs which she swilled under the tap.

There was a television in one corner. Jones hadn't seen the news since early that morning. She wanted to check if there were any further reports on the RECAP explosion, and to see if there was any mention of the incident with Marion and her. She switched on the TV just in time to catch a regional news bulletin.

The fourth item featured their hit-and-run.

'Passers-by report that the vehicle appeared to deliberately mow down the injured woman, and that it then reversed for a second attempt.'

A shiver ran down Jones's spine. Connie had turned away from her coffee-making activities, and was also watching.

'Police are withholding the name of the victim, whose condition is said to be critical, until next of kin have been informed. A second pedestrian, another Caucasian woman, who left the scene of the incident, was believed to have been involved, and police are appealing for her and any other witnesses to contact them.'

Connie uttered a big, deep sigh.

'Critical,' she murmured. 'That means Marion's alive, doesn't it, Sandy? She's alive.'

Jones nodded her agreement. She was also hugely relieved, not least because of the sense of responsibility she felt for what had happened. But her thoughts swiftly turned to what else had been revealed in the bulletin.

Police were withholding the victim's name until next of kin had been informed. That meant they already knew who Marion was. Of course, Marion had been carrying her handbag which had presumably been found in the road alongside her. No doubt it contained her credit cards, her ID, her phone, and all the usual paraphernalia of modern life. But did whoever had attempted to kill her in mistake for Connie now know that they had targeted the wrong woman? That was the million-dollar question.

In addition the police were appealing for the second pedestrian involved to come forwards. Did that mean they knew who Jones was too? She thought that was still unlikely, but couldn't be sure. She so hoped her boys didn't get to hear of any of this before she could safely speak to them.

Neither Dom, nor his intervention, were mentioned. What did that indicate? Or did it not indicate anything at all?

Jones glanced at Connie. She could tell that all she was thinking about was Marion's welfare. Almost certainly she had yet to consider the wider significance of the report.

The aroma of coffee was beginning to fill the room. It smelt wonderful, promising somehow to be even better than the tea she had earlier yearned for, and had more or less drowned all traces of the vaguely unpleasant odour that had previously lurked. Jones hadn't thought it possible that her body could, at this time, display any desire for food or drink, but her saliva buds had automatically kicked into action.

'Coffee smells done,' she said gently to Connie, who nodded absently.

Jones left her to her thoughts, made her way to the machine, and poured steaming liquid into the two mugs Connie had prepared.

She raised a mug to her lips. The coffee was very hot and very strong. Just how she liked it. There was no milk, but she always drank coffee black. She could feel herself being jolted back to some semblance of life.

She passed Connie the second mug just as Dom returned, carrying a large brown paper bag.

'Gee, that smells good,' he said.

Jones found another mug.

Meanwhile Dom emptied out the contents of his paper bag onto the worktop, alongside the coffee machine.

'Hot pastrami sandwiches, and red velvet cake, a Harlem speciality, just in case you two honkies don't know it,' he said. 'The best cake you ever gonna eat.'

Connie ignored him and the food.

'Do you have any news? Have you managed to find out anything about Marion? We know she's alive—'

'You do?' Dom interrupted anxiously 'How?'

'It was on the TV news,' said Jones. 'They said her condition was critical.'

'Did they identify her?' Dom spoke sharply.

'No. But I guess they know who she is already. The bulletin said that her identity was being withheld until her family could be contacted.'

Dom nodded, looking grim. Connie put down her coffee and moved swiftly and suddenly towards him. She grabbed one of his arms with both hands. Jones could see that her knuckles were white, and her fingertips were digging into the sleeve of Dom's jacket.

'So, Marion must be in hospital somewhere, we've got to find her, Dom. I have to know . . .'

Connie's voice had turned slightly hysterical again.

'Hey, Con, hey,' said Dom, raising a big fleshy hand in what Jones presumed was supposed to be a calming gesture. 'My girl's on the case.'

'Well, how's she going to find anything out? They'll only give information to family, won't they? It's not going to be easy . . .'

'It won't be too hard for my girl,' said Dom. 'I told you, she's special.'

Jones wondered what the hell the big man was talking about. Connie looked as if she was going to interrupt again, then turned away, beaten, and slumped onto a chair.

'Have some more coffee, Connie,' said Jones, holding out the other woman's abandoned mug. 'It'll make you feel better.'

Connie turned a jaundiced eye on her. Jones realized she must have sounded particularly trite.

'Nothing will make me feel better,' she responded sharply. 'Except knowing that Marion is going to be all right.'

Nonetheless she took the coffee and raised it to her lips.

Dom picked up two packets of pastrami sandwiches, handing one to Connie and one to Jones.

'So will food,' he said. 'And anyway, even if it don't make you feel better, you gotta eat, Connie babe. We gotta keep functioning. All of us. People ain't no different to machines. You, with all your fancy notions, Con, you ought to know that, girl. Gotta have fuel to keep going.'

He opened a packet of sandwiches himself and took a big bite out of one.

'Seriously goddamned good,' he said.

The smell of hot salted meat and mustard mingled with the aroma of the coffee. Once again, to her surprise, Jones's felt her saliva buds react.

She removed a sandwich from the packet Dom had handed her. And once she started eating she couldn't get the food into her mouth fast enough. Her nausea had evaporated. She found that she was absolutely ravenous. When she'd finished the sandwich she started on the red velvet cake. It was the colour of new brick and melted on her tongue like butter, every bit as fine as Dom had said it would be.

She was aware of Connie's eyes on her.

'It's good grub,' said Jones by way of encouragement.

Connie narrowed her gaze.

'If I ate a mouthful I would be sick as a hog,' she said.

The Dominator's girlfriend arrived about an hour later. It had seemed much longer to Jones, and she suspected that to Connie it had probably seemed like a lifetime.

She was not at all what Jones had expected. She hadn't realized she'd been expecting any particular kind of woman to be Dom's girl, but she must have been. This one took her totally by surprise.

She was tall, blonde and elegant, with good strong features and intelligent eyes. Her mouth was wide and generous. She wore her long hair swept loosely back in a ponytail. She was well dressed in a stylish, navy-blue, pin-striped trouser suit, and when she spoke her voice had a musical ring to it.

'Hi, I'm Gaynor,' she said, smiling easily. Her teeth were perfect, her manner relaxed and confident.

She was clearly a class act.

Jones realized it had been not only patronizing of her to have rather different expectations of the big brash wrestler upon whom her entire survival now seemed to depend, but also quite probably racist. It hadn't occurred to Jones that Dom's girl would be anything other than a woman of colour.

Dom beamed with pride as soon as Gaynor entered the room.

'Whaddya think of my babe, then?' he enquired.

Connie clearly took the attitude that the question was rhetorical, if she considered it at all. Before Jones had time to think of an appropriate reply, Connie Pike began firing questions at the young woman.

'What have you found out? Do you know where they've taken Marion? Is she going to pull through?'

Dom's girl was unfazed. She walked across the room to Connie and took both her hands in hers.

'Marion is at St Vincent's Hospital,' she said. 'She's very poorly, but they say she has a good fighting chance. She's just come out of surgery and she's in intensive care. I've been told the next few hours are critical. Then we'll know for sure if she's going to pull through.'

'Is she conscious?'

'Well, she's still under anaesthetic. She was knocked out, but apparently her head wounds are not believed to be that serious.'

Jones realized that meant the truck could not have run over Marion's head, after all. Relief washed over her.

'Thank God,' said Connie. 'But what about her other injuries?'

The younger woman did not attempt to avoid eye contact. It was almost as if she and Connie had formed an instant bond which demanded that there be no bullshit.

'She has four broken ribs, a dislocated shoulder and severe injuries to her legs,' said Gaynor.

'You said she'd just come out of surgery?'

'Yes.' Gaynor's voice was calm and matter of fact. 'Her right leg was virtually severed by the truck. The surgeons had to amputate what was left, above the knee.'

The line of Connie's mouth was very thin. Her voice sounded strange when she spoke. Almost as if it wasn't her voice at all.

'And the other leg?'

'They're trying to save it. It's broken in several places, and the ligaments are torn.'

'Do they think they can save it?'

'They don't know yet.'

'So what exactly are her chances of pulling through, with or without her remaining leg?'

Gaynor shrugged. 'They don't know that either.'

'Fifty-fifty then?'

'Thereabouts.'

'Only thereabouts?'

Gaynor nodded. 'Yes. I think that's the best prognosis. A good fighting chance, that's all they told me.'

'I see.'

'I need to go to her,' Connie said, for the umpteenth time.

'The hospital and the police know her identity,' Gaynor replied with quiet authority. 'That means that the people who made the hit on her, thinking she was you, Connie, probably now know you are still alive and well. And if they don't, they will soon. Marion's next of kin, her son in Princeton, has been informed of the incident and her identity will be released to the media shortly. Someone has tried to kill you twice, Connie. They'll try again. They'll be waiting for you . . .'

'That makes no difference. I'll take my chances. My life is no damned good to me without Marion.'

'Your life means so much in so many ways, Connie,' Jones reminded her gently. 'You are more likely than anyone else in the world to hold the key to whatever it is that Paul discovered. You have a duty to survive.'

'Fuck duty,' yelled Connie. 'Fuck duty and fuck RECAP!'

'Connie, there's a good chance Marion will recover,' Gaynor continued. 'You haven't lost her yet, remember? And how would she feel if she came through all this, and she'd lost you? If you'd done something foolhardy, something plain darned stupid, whether you thought you were doing it for her or not. If you'd put yourself in unnecessary danger. How would she feel about that?'

Connie sniffed loudly. She looked as if she was fighting back tears again.

'She'd be pretty angry,' she replied, in a normal tone of voice again.

'Yes,' responded Gaynor. 'She'd be angry. Like I'd be angry if it was that great lump of meat over there.' She gestured with one thumb at Dom. 'I love him like you love Marion, you see. Hard to believe as it may be.'

She shot Dom a piercing look. He wriggled a bit, trying not to smile too much, Jones thought.

'So,' Gaynor continued, 'I do understand, Connie. And I wonder, would you let me help?'

'How can you help?'

'Well, I could go to see Marion for you. It's not the same, I know. But I will report back absolutely honestly, I promise you. And, if she's conscious, I could give her a message.'

Connie walked to the window and appeared to be looking out. Jones guessed she was seeing nothing at all.

After a few seconds she turned around, and addressed Gaynor again.

'Deal,' she said.

'Right.'

'Just tell Marion she's to hang on in there. She's got to. For me. For us.'

'I will.'

Gaynor headed for the door.

'Thank you,' Connie called after her.

Gaynor turned again to smile and incline her head, very slightly, in recognition.

'There you go,' said Dom, after she had left. 'Told you guys she was special, didn't I?'

Jones nodded. Dom grinned at her over his shoulder as he headed for the bathroom.

This was all very fine, thought Jones, but all they seemed to have discussed so far was Marion. Connie was in danger whether or not she attempted to see Marion. And Jones herself was probably still in danger too. Then there was the small matter of Paul's discovery. A mighty step forwards in modern science which was apparently important enough, and presumably threatening enough, to lead people in high places to murder.

One half of Jones wanted more than anything to find out exactly what Paul had discovered. Maybe she even wanted to help Connie continue Paul's work, though she wasn't sure about that. The climate had changed, but RECAP and everything it stood for still hovered on the dubious fringes of the scientific world. And Jones had a pretty amazing career. She didn't want to jeopardize it any more than she almost certainly already had.

How much of a target was she, she wondered? If she decided to go home, perhaps whoever was behind all this would just be glad to see the back of her? Or would they?

Jones was tired. She was frightened. And she was bewildered. Nonetheless, the inquisitive, enquiring half of her, the half that had got involved with RECAP in the first place, didn't want to even attempt to walk away quite yet.

Her thoughts were interrupted by a series of bleeps from her burner phone. She'd been sent a text. It could only really be from Ed. She thought for a second. Dom had said she shouldn't use the phone, although she still couldn't believe that Ed was any kind of danger to them. But this was a text. Surely that was safe enough. In any case, she reckoned the importance of knowing what Ed had to say probably outweighed any small risk that might be involved.

She'd just called up the message when Dom came back into the room.

'What the fuck are you doing, lady?' he yelled. 'Haven't I told you not to use that goddamned phone?'

'It's only a text, Dom,' said Jones mildly. 'Surely there's no harm in picking that up.'

'It's the same. And you're a doctor? What kind of brain you got? You've sent out a signal to the nearest mast.'

'Oh.'

Jones was sure she'd read somewhere that text messages were not easily traced. Maybe she'd seen it on the web, that worldwide home of misinformation. People forget that you can only get out of the web what some other prat has put in it. Jones usually did not forget. However, her thought processes were still not working at one hundred per cent.

Anyway, the damage, it seemed, had been done. The message was now displayed. It was indeed from Ed.

'Meet me at the cornfield. Ten tonight. E.'

'Let's have a look at that.'

Dom snatched the phone from her.

'E?' he queried. 'Ed?'

Jones nodded.

'The cornfield? What the hell does he mean by that? You know what that is?'

'I certainly do.'

'Sure as hell ain't a real field of corn. Not anywhere round here.'

'No.'

'Anybody else know?'

'I very much doubt it.'

'Right. I guess you're gonna want to meet him whatever I say 'bout it?'

'Of course I bloody well do. Maybe he's found something out. Maybe he knows something he didn't tell me before.'

'And maybe he's setting a trap for you.'

'No way. Ed wouldn't do that.'

'But what if he's followed to this cornfield?'

'Well that, Dom, is a chance I'm going to have to take.'

FIFTEEN

Jones was suddenly very determined. She felt it was up to her to get to the bottom of this mess, to make it safe for Connie to return to a semblance of normal life again, and to begin to rebuild RECAP, if she so wished. As she knew Paul would want. Although she suspected that the murderous forces responsible for the Princeton explosion would have found Connie in New York sooner or later, her own involvement had so far almost certainly done more harm than good. She resolved to at least attempt to redress that.

Ultimately the Dominator seemed to accept that Jones's mind was made up, and that she was going to meet Ed with or without his help.

He even arranged a car for Jones to drive to the rendezvous. A big old Ford. Yet another favour called in, apparently.

Jones took the last remaining uncompromised burner with her.

'Just take care, d'ya hear?' instructed Dom. 'And I'll call you. From a pay phone. There's no way I'm gonna be able to get another safe cell till tomorrow. So I'll call at eleven p.m. sharp. Right?'

'Right,' responded Jones.

She drove slowly through Manhattan to the Bronx, to the place she'd known Ed was referring to as soon as she'd seen his text. Deliberately, she got there an hour early, and parked the Ford a couple of streets away, so she could walk – or rather limp – the last couple of hundred yards.

The earlier heavy rain had stopped, but this was a dark September evening. No moon or stars. There were few people about, and the place was so different from how it had been on her one previous visit. Somewhere inside her head Jones could still hear the noise from the last time. She could still feel the sense of anticipation, and the way the excitement had built inside her.

Now the legendary Yankee Stadium was about as quiet as it was possible for anywhere in New York to be. There was virtually no noise at all. And certainly no happy anticipation. Just a certain sense of foreboding, as far as Jones was concerned.

She would never forget going there with Ed to see a game between the Yankees and the Red Sox – her very first experience of baseball – and Ed would have known that. They had just watched a video of the movie *Field of Dreams* featuring Kevin Costner as an Iowa farmer who built a baseball diamond in his cornfield. In Costner's dreams games were played by the ghosts of baseballing legends. Jones had, somewhat to her embarrassment, enjoyed this ultimate feel-good movie rather more than she'd expected, but had shocked Ed, a native New Yorker whose love of the Yankees had been instilled in him by his grandfather at an early age, with her total lack of knowledge about baseball. And by admitting that she had never watched a game. Not even on TV.

He had insisted on taking her to see his team at their famous stadium. And as they'd stood in line to enter, with the thunder of the crowd and the band and the cheerleaders inside already roaring in their ears, she had looked up at the towering 50,000-seater ballpark looming above them, its lights blazing, and remarked, 'Some cornfield!'

From then on the two of them had always referred to the Yankee stadium as The Cornfield.

On this night, however, the mighty baseball palace was shrouded in darkness, and its sheer size seemed threatening to Jones. But then almost everything, right then, seemed threatening to Jones.

She made her way towards the main entrance, keeping close to the walls, and finally came to a halt in a particularly shadowy spot, avoiding the occasional security lights. She wanted to see him before he saw her, to make sure that he was alone and hadn't been followed. Or indeed, that he hadn't brought anyone with him. She knew she must keep alert. For her own preservation. And Connie's. In any case, she wasn't sure right then that she trusted anyone in the world.

The minutes ticked slowly by. Ten o clock came and went. She stood, pressed against the stadium's stone facade, making the most of its protection, watching and waiting. She tried to convince herself that she was calm and in control, but in reality her nerves were standing on end.

A sound to her left caused her to almost jump out of her skin. It was a loud high-pitched howling noise, not unlike the scream of a distressed baby. She turned quickly on her heel, twisting her damaged leg in her haste, but was unable at first to see anything. Then two creatures appeared, as if from nowhere, silhouetted against the street lights, the angle of their shadows making them seem twice the size they really were. Jones breathed a big deep sigh of relief. A pair of alley cats, their backs arched, teeth bared, tails wagging furiously, were facing up to each other in a combat every bit as fierce as any which had ever taken place within the historic ballpark.

Jones relaxed, just a little. She checked the time. Ten twenty-five. Perhaps Ed wasn't coming. Perhaps something had happened to him. Perhaps he had just changed his mind. The possibilities were endless. Perhaps the Dominator was right. Perhaps Ed was, at that very moment, in the process of arranging some sort of a trap.

She wondered how long she should wait. Indeed how long she could wait without being overwhelmed by weariness and dropping to the ground. She was bone tired again. It had been a long day. Her injured leg was hurting quite badly. Her face hurt too. And her brain was in turmoil.

Minutes later a vehicle finally pulled off the main drag and onto the paved forecourt in front of the stadium, its headlights illuminating almost the entire area. She pushed herself flat against the wall. Was it Ed? And was he alone?

The vehicle drew to a halt straight in front of the main entrance, its headlamps still full on. Jones strained her eyes but was staring directly into the lights and could make out next to nothing. Then suddenly the lights went out. Almost simultaneously she heard the sound of a car door opening and shutting.

Her eyes began to focus again. The vehicle was a small dark saloon car of some kind. There was a figure walking from it towards the gates of the baseball park. She narrowed her eyes, staring into the gloom. It was Ed all right, he'd walked straight into a shaft of light. And he seemed to be alone.

She decided to wait a while to make sure. The traffic on the road beyond continued as normal. No other vehicle had chosen to follow Ed's onto the stadium forecourt.

Jones took a cautious step forwards, into a better lit area.

Ed appeared to hear her move, and turned quickly.

'It's all right, it's me,' Jones called softly, remembering her own nerves earlier when she'd heard the cats fighting. She limped her way closer to him.

'My God, you really are hurt now,' said Ed. 'Your face. Your legs . . .'

'What is it, Ed?' Jones asked at once, ignoring his concern. 'Why did you want to see me?'

'Well, I was wrong, wasn't I?'

'What?'

'RECAP was the target,' Ed continued. 'It had to have been . . .'

'Well yes . . .'

'And now whoever planted the bomb is after Connie. I heard about Marion . . .'

'How? When?' Jones spoke sharply. Even if Marion's identity had by now been made public, it certainly hadn't been earlier that day when Ed had texted her.

'It's the talk of Princeton. The police came to see Thomas Jessop, to tell him about his mother. He'd only just got out of hospital himself . . .'

'Right. But how did you make the connection? I mean, did you know about . . . about . . .?'

'About Marion and Connie? Yes, I knew. Paul knew too. Although not in the very beginning. You've worked in the RECAP lab. Hard place to keep a secret for long. But it certainly wasn't common knowledge. Paul and I respected their privacy. We never talked about it. But we knew. So, it wasn't difficult to put two and two together. I heard on the news that there was another woman involved, and I guessed it was you. I also guessed that Marion had probably been attacked by mistake. Am I right?'

'Yes. Almost certainly.'

'There are things I have to tell you, Sandy.'

'Let's move away from the light.'

She led him into a darker part of the forecourt, and glanced nervously around for the umpteenth time. She presumed Ed had chosen this meeting place because he could give it to her in code, confident that she would know exactly where she meant, and others wouldn't. But Jones wasn't sure it was necessarily a safe place to meet.

'Are you sure you weren't followed?' she asked, yet again feeling like a second-rate secret agent in a very second-rate spy film.

Ed nodded and smiled slightly.

'I borrowed my neighbour's car, and he agreed to look after Jasper too. I told him my vehicle was off the road. I'm now as paranoid as you. What happened to Marion changed everything. We have an underground garage. My car is still at home, and I didn't leave on foot. If anyone was watching my place they would think I was still inside. Nobody followed me, Sandy.'

'You sent me a text.'

'I know. I'm sorry. I had to get in touch with you. Had to see you. I copied your trick though. I bought a pre-paid phone.'

'Perhaps too late. We think the one I was using was blown. Don't know how else they traced us so fast.'

'That might be my fault,' Ed admitted. 'I called you this morning from my home phone. I half forgot that you'd told me not to. Half didn't see the need to do anything other. I believed, then, what the authorities said. That the explosion was directed at the animal research people. It made sense. And I certainly didn't believe that my phone was bugged . . .'

'We did wonder,' said Jones. 'But, oh Ed . . .'

Her voice was a mix of reproach and regret.

'I know. That call probably led them to you. To you and to Connie. Until then they would have thought she was dead. It was all my fault. I can't believe I was so stupid.'

Jones just stared at him.

'I will regret it for the rest of my life.'

Ed's head was bowed. His voice had a quiver in it.

'I will never get over the guilt.'

'We've all been stupid,' Jones responded quietly. 'Me big time. The likes of you and I are not equipped for stuff like this, Ed. We do it all wrong. I should never have told you that Connie was alive. You didn't need to know. I put you in danger, and I put her in even more danger. We've seen just how much now. Marion may not pull through, and if she does she's going to be maimed for life. You and I share responsibility. But we couldn't believe any of it was really happening, could we? We're not professional spooks. We didn't know what to do. Still don't.'

'I should have listened.'

'Maybe.' Jones felt numb. 'You didn't want to meet me just to tell me that, did you?'

Ed shook his head.

'Do you remember my brother?' he asked. 'My younger brother Mikey? He was living with our aunt in New York when you and I were at Princeton together. Used to visit at weekends sometimes.'

Jones was puzzled. 'I remember him vaguely. I only met him once or twice, I think. He was just a boy.'

Ed smiled. 'Only a couple of years younger than me, actually. But he took a long time growing up, did Mikey. If he ever made it, at all.'

'Funny kid, wasn't he? Always making up stories. Seemed to live in a fantasy world. Didn't you used to call him Walter, after Walter Mitty?'

'Yes. And he was a funny kid. But not so funny now. He's in the FBI.'

'Oh fuck.' Jones dreaded to think what that might mean. But in spite of everything she managed a strangled laugh. 'Mikey in the FBI? I don't believe it.'

'I know. I've never been able to take him seriously either. That's been part of the problem . . .'

'What do you mean?' Jones prompted.

'Well, for a long time I really didn't believe he was in the FBI. After he left college he had a string of jobs, in real estate, working for a finance firm, in security. But there was always more to everything than there seemed, or according to Mikey there was, anyway. His stories got more and more outlandish. It was just Mikey, or so I thought. Same thing when he told me the FBI had its eye on RECAP. I never took any notice. I never told him anything. I didn't have anything to tell anyway. Well, nothing much . . .'

He glanced anxiously at Jones, as if seeking her acceptance of that.

'You knew that Paul thought he had made a breakthrough,' she said.

'Yes. I did. But that was all I knew.'

A thought suddenly struck Jones. The Man in Black. Her anonymous interrogator at Princeton police station. He'd seemed vaguely familiar at the time. Of course, that had to have been Mikey.

'I think I met him,' Jones said suddenly. 'Was he at Princeton when I was arrested there?'

Ed nodded.

'And does he have a penchant for shades and black suits?'
Ed nodded again.

'My God,' Jones blurted out. 'The man's a parody. He looked like some sort of a joke.'

'I know. I certainly could never take him seriously, not until . . .' His voice broke off.

'Until what, Ed?'

'Until after the explosion. It was Mikey who assured me that there was no link between any government body and the explosion, and that RECAP wasn't a target of any sort. The FBI supported RECAP. Those were his words. He came around right after the explosion to reassure me that all the speculation about RECAP having been deliberately destroyed was nonsense. He said then, straight away, that it was probably a gas explosion. A tragic accident. But he warned me not to talk to anyone about Paul. Said it might still be possible to salvage something from RECAP.'

'He warned you not to talk about Paul? So did he know about Paul's breakthrough? Did you tell him about it?'

'No. Well, not exactly. But he asked so many questions. Was I privy to Paul's work? It was nonsense, of course. I was just an occasional RECAP operator. I didn't even have anything like the involvement I'd had when you were at Princeton.'

'You had a special relationship with Paul, though, everybody knew that.'

'So it seems. Anyway, Mikey came round again the night you just showed up at my place, and also after you came back and hijacked me walking Jasper. That time he was quite aggressive. He wanted to know exactly what you were after. I'd never seen him be aggressive before. He kept going on about Paul's work. Even asked me if I had copies of it. As if I would. Like I told you.'

Suddenly the relative quiet of the night was shattered by the sound of a police siren. Both Jones and Ed jumped, quite literally. A police patrol car came into view, travelling fast, carving a path through the light traffic. Its headlights illuminated Ed's vehicle as it approached. But it didn't even slow, instead roaring straight past the Yankee Stadium, the wail of its siren fading into the night.

'Nerves,' said Jones.

Ed nodded, and continued. 'Anyway, Mikey was very persistent. And he was on edge. Just like us now. He was obviously wound up about something, but, as usual, he wouldn't talk to me properly. He kept checking text messages on his cell, and pacing around the place. He was sweating a lot. He took off his jacket and hung it around a chair. Then at one point he went out of the room with his cell phone, said he needed to take a private call. Well, I don't know quite what made me do it, what gave me the idea, but, well, I knew he kept a USB data store on his key ring. I looked in his jacket pockets. I found the key ring. My laptop was on the kitchen table as usual. I plugged the USB in and downloaded everything that was on it. Then I just put the USB back in his pocket.'

Jones had a feeling she knew where this might be leading.

'And?' she prompted.

'Well, after Mikey left I went through his files. There was one labelled Ruders. I went into it. It was Paul's work. His data. His breakthrough paper. I'm sure of it.'

'Jesus. Did you study it?'

'I tried to. I couldn't make any sense of it, though. But I didn't expect to. I'm not a scientist, Sandy. I'm a mathematician.'

'So, where is it? My God, this could be the key to everything. Have you got your laptop with you?'

'Yes, but . . . but I wiped the file off. Irrevocably.'

'You did what? Why? Just tell me you made a copy,'

'I did.'

'So you still have the file, Ed?'

'No. Well, not exactly . . . Mikey frightened me that night. He had assured me from the start that RECAP hadn't been the target of the explosion, but at that moment I didn't believe it anymore. And why was he so interested in whether or not I had a copy of Paul's theory when he already had one himself? What lengths might his people go to to silence me? I was scared. So I copied the file onto another USB, and wiped it off my computer. I didn't want to trust email. Plus Mikey is still my brother, and I didn't want to leave a trail that might lead to him. I put the USB in a jiffy bag, and first thing this morning I took it round to the post office and sent it off, anonymously, to you at your university in England—'

'You did what?' Jones interrupted.

'I posted it to you. Express. It should only take two or three working days.'

'I don't believe it.'

'I know. At least it's safe. But that, of course, was before I saw the news this morning. The authorities officially blamed animal rights activists for the explosion, and Mikey called me, backing that up. I believed it. I phoned you and told you that. For a while I was quite sure I'd got it all wrong, that you and Connie had got it all wrong, that I'd let my imagination run away with me, and RECAP had nothing to do with—'

'And the "pal in the police" you referred to, was actually your mad brother, the FBI agent, I presume,' Jones interrupted again.

'Yes.'

'For God's sake, Ed! Did you tell Mikey that Connie was still alive?'

'No. I didn't. I promise you I didn't.'

'Do you really expect me to believe that?'

'I didn't. I swear. I suppose I still had niggling doubts at the back of my mind. I'm not sure. But, well, if my phone is bugged . . .'

Ed didn't finish the sentence. He didn't need to. If the FBI, or anyone else, had been monitoring Ed's calls they would have learned from his conversation with Jones that Connie Pike was alive and well. And it wouldn't have taken them long to get a trace – fifteen seconds, Dom had said. Neither would it have taken them long to position someone outside Dom's apartment. Someone murderous.

'I can't believe Mikey would hurt Connie, though,' Ed continued. 'Jesus. I can't believe Mikey would hurt anyone.'

Jones sighed. 'I don't suppose he did. Not personally, that is. It really does look like Connie's conspiracy theory is right, Ed. All sorts of persons in high places could be involved. And they would have on their payroll, and in their control, the kind of people most of us don't even want to know exist. People whose life's work it is to perform little jobs like mowing down an innocent woman in the street.

'If your dumb brother has passed on his suspicions about you being privy to Paul's work, then I don't reckon you're much safer than Connie. I don't like to think about what they would do and how quickly they would do it if they suspected that you had stolen Paul's paper from Mikey. I need to see that paper, Ed. It really could be the key. I'll get the first flight home I can. And you should come with me. I really don't think you're safe here anymore.'

Jones paused.

'But I don't suppose you've even got your passport with you, have you?'

'Well, actually, yes I have. My passport. And my laptop. Like I said, I wiped the file right off my hard drive, but I'm never sure about leaving footprints. Also I destroyed my mobile before I left, so nobody could follow me that way, and I transferred all its data to my laptop first. I've got various other personal papers with me too. I was afraid somebody might break into my flat – search the place . . .'

'But they think you're still there.'

'For the moment, I suppose. But, well, to tell the truth, Sandy, I already wasn't sure that it would be safe for me to go back, not for a bit, anyway. I can't leave Jasper for long, though, my neighbour's wonderful, but there is a limit.'

'You may have to, because you're right. It won't be long before they find out you've given them the slip, and goodness knows what else. You can't go back to Princeton, Ed. You really can't.'

SIXTEEN

D om called from a pay phone at eleven p.m. precisely, just as he had promised.

'You alone?' he asked.

'No,' replied Jones. 'I'm still with Ed. There's a lot to tell you. I'll be back to you and Connie in half an hour. And I'll have Ed with me.'

'Now just hang on, lady. For a start, we ain't where you left us.'

'What?'

'No. The place was compromised, right, by the text you took earlier from that dumb-ass. I've moved Connie out.'

'So tell me where you are,' said Jones. 'I'll come to you.'

'Not with Ed MacEntee, you won't. I don't trust him.'

Jones sighed. This was absurd. Dom didn't trust Ed. Jones trusted that Ed was telling the truth, but no longer trusted Ed's judgement. She certainly didn't trust Ed's brother, a boyhood Walter Mitty turned Fed. And she still didn't entirely trust Dom. She really wasn't up to these spy games.

She moved a little away from Ed to continue the call.

'Look, something's happened that means I need to get back to the UK,' she told Dom. 'And I want to take Ed and Connie with me. Nothing you can say to me will convince me that any of us will be really safe until we get out of this damned country.'

'You're running away, lady, ain't you?' said the Dominator accusatively.

'If that's how you want to look at it, fine.'

'So what's happened exactly to make it so danged important that you get outa here?' Dom asked. 'It's something MacEntee has said, ain't it? Has to be.'

Jones sighed, gave in, and treated Dom to an edited version of Ed's story. She particularly did not tell Dom about the copy of Paul Ruders' work which Ed had acquired and posted to England – the real reason she wanted to return home. She'd become so paranoid about being spied upon and tailed and phones being tapped and traced that she was not about to take any more risks. She would tell Connie when she next saw her.

Instead she simply told Dom that she needed to get back to her power base, to the place where she had access to and influence over people in high places because of who she was. It didn't sound very convincing, even to Jones, and it certainly didn't make much of an impression on the Dominator.

'Oh yeah, getting a fast cab to Downing Street as soon as you land, are you?' asked the big man.

Jones ignored that.

'Look Dom, I'm not doing any good here,' she said. 'I can't cope with all this. And I'm pretty damned sure I can do one hell of a lot more back home now. It's not just my safety we're talking about here, it's Ed's and Connie's. I told you. I want to take Connie with me. As soon as it can be arranged. I want to make sure she's safe. Can you help with that, Dom? Can you get hold of papers? You know. A passport in another name. Stuff like that?'

'What do you take me for, lady?'

'Connie and Marion say you can fix almost anything.'

'Oh yeah? When you planning to leave, anyway?'

'As soon as possible. Tomorrow, if I can.'

'And with a new passport for Connie already freshly minted? You gotta be kidding me. Connie won't go with you, anyway. No chance. She won't leave the country while Marion's in hospital on the critical list.'

Jones feared that Dom might be right. She knew she was beaten. For the moment, at any rate.

'All right,' she said. 'But look, you've still got my bag, I hope?'

'Yeah.'

'I need it.'

This time Jones had her passport and credit cards with her. But her personal cell phone, which she hadn't dared use for two days, her laptop, her house keys, and the keys to her car waiting at Heathrow Airport, were all in the hold-all.

'Too bad. If you're gonna quit, then why don't you just get your ass outta here? Leave me to look after Connie.'

'Dom, you have to trust me on this. There are things I can do in the UK. Things that might help. But I do need my bag. Look, if you don't want me to come to you, won't you please bring it to me?'

There was a pause.

The Dominator appeared to be convinced that he was all that was standing between Connie Pike and death, yet only hours earlier Jones had been equally convinced that Dom was the villain of the piece and had fled at speed halfway across Manhattan in order to get away from him. Now she didn't know what to believe. Not about anything.

'I'm sorry, I got Connie somewhere real safe, and I don't intend to leave her whilst I run errands for you, lady. I didn't even like leaving her to make this phone call, to tell the truth.'

'Look, Dom,' Jones persisted. 'Surely you can get my stuff to me somehow? You're a man of initiative, aren't you?'

Jones heard the Dominator give a derisory snort. That's what it sounded like, anyway.

'OK, I'll ask Gaynor,' he said. 'I'll have to call you back. Give me ten minutes.'

'Right. And Dom, you will tell Connie I want her to come with me, won't you? I want her to have the chance to get out of this country before she gets hurt again.'

'OK,' said the Dominator again. 'Although how the hell we'd ever do that thing, only the Lord God Almighty knows.'

Jones suspected the big man was probably right about that too. She ended the call and glanced at her watch. It was nearly twenty past eleven.

After almost exactly ten minutes Dom called again.

'Gaynor will meet you with your bag in an hour and a half,' Dom instructed. 'In the financial district, by the Stock Exchange, on Wall Street. Know it?'

Jones affirmed that she knew it. Dom gave a precise cross street.

Jones checked the time. 'That's about one o'clock then,' she said. 'Why Wall Street?'

'It's near where she works.'

'What does she do at that time of night, for Chrissake?'

'Just make sure you're there,' replied the big man. 'She can't hang about.'

He hadn't answered Jones's question. Jones didn't really care. She just wanted to get away. With or without Connie. Maybe Dom was right. Maybe she was running.

She returned to Ed, climbing into the borrowed car alongside him. She gave him a brief version of her conversation with Dom, and the details of the planned meeting with Gaynor, suggesting he follow her Ford in his car.

'I think we should stick together, but, if possible, not be seen together,' she said. 'There's no hurry though, we've got a bit of time to kill.'

They passed a few minutes discussing what might be the safest way to leave the States.

'I've got some cash, enough for us both to travel to the UK without using credit cards, I reckon,' said Jones. 'But anyway, nobody's looking for you yet, we hope. And I'm banking on the bastards just wanting to see the back of me.'

She reached into the pocket of her leather jacket and removed a business card.

'Just in case something happens, and we get separated, these are all my contact details at home and I'll write the number of the burner on the back. Emergency use only.'

Jones rummaged further in her pocket.

'You got a pen?' she enquired.

Ed nodded, and produced a smart black and gold customized

roller-ball, with his name inscribed along the side, which he handed to her. As she wrote Jones issued further instructions.

'Just don't let this card fall into the wrong hands. Also, I still don't know whether I absolutely trust Gaynor and Dom. Keep a fair ways behind me and park up so as she can't see you, yeah?'

'Yeah.'

Gaynor was already at the appointed meeting place when Jones arrived, with Ed following at a distance as directed. Parking wasn't difficult. The financial district was deserted. At night this part of New York, which was so busy during the day, was eerily empty. Like a ghost town. A column of steam fountained steadily from a nearby manhole. Ed drove past Jones when he pulled to a halt at the appointed spot, and, just as he'd suggested, continued slowly on, turning left into a side street at the next junction.

Gaynor got out of her car as soon as she saw Jones arrive, and began to walk towards her, already carrying Jones's bag which she held out with one hand.

'Here you are.'

'Thanks,' Jones said, reaching to take it.

Gaynor was wearing a tan jacket over jeans and tooled cowboy boots. She looked every bit as stylish as she had when Jones had first met her. She also looked remarkably alert for very nearly the middle of the night.

'I have a message from Connie,' she said. 'She says there is no way she can go with you, but she wishes you luck.'

'Is that all?'

'What are you looking for? Absolution? You're running out on her, aren't you?'

Jones said nothing. She had no intention of trying to explain herself to Gaynor. In any case she had her own doubts about her motivation. She turned to go. Gaynor called after her.

'Wait. She asked me to give you this.'

Jones swung round to face Gaynor again, and took from her the small flat circular object she was holding out between one thumb and forefinger. Jones laid it in the palm of her right hand. A host of half-forgotten memories returned again as she looked down at an enamelled button badge that had originally been predominantly blue. The edges were badly chipped and much of the enamel had worn off. The message was still clear enough though.

Jones re-read the familiar words. 'Subvert the Dominant Paradigm'. It was a badge just like the one Connie had given her on her first visit to RECAP. Jones hadn't seen her old badge for years, and had absolutely no idea where it was, or indeed if she still had it. Conversely it was just like Connie, twenty-five years later and under such extraordinary circumstances, to be able to produce one of the badges from nowhere. Or more likely from that cloth shoulder bag which was always with her.

Jones felt her eyes well up. This was not the time to be emotional. She had a journey to make which was not going to be easy. Then she had work to do. Important work. She owed that to Connie. Connie had sent her a message in the form of that badge. A message which she reckoned told her exactly what her job was now. To subvert the dominant paradigm. That had always been Connie Pike's predominate aim in life. Jones had never quite had the courage. Not so far, anyway.

She looked up at Gaynor.

'How's Marion?' she asked.

'The same. Still critical. Still alive though. And that's a result.'

Jones nodded. 'I know. I saw what happened to her. Remember?'

'I remember,' said Gaynor.

Jones was going to say more. The sound of the radio from Gaynor's car, the driver's door of which stood open, stopped her in her tracks. She registered at once that this was no ordinary radio.

It sounded like a police radio.

Gaynor looked over her shoulder, took a step back towards the car, then turned to Jones again. Jones felt as if she had been punched in the face. Stark realization flooded over her.

'Who the fuck are you?' she asked through clenched teeth.

'I'm Dom's girl, Connie's friend, and your friend too. That's all you have to know.'

'Oh no it's damned well not!' Jones took a step forwards, and rather to her own surprise, reached out and grabbed hold of Gaynor by both shoulders. Her hold-all fell to the ground with a thud. Jones ignored it. Instead she began to shake Gaynor backwards and forwards, the anger and fear pouring out of her.

'Who the fuck are you?' she yelled.

'All right. Take your hands off me or, so help me God, I'll break your fucking neck.'

Gaynor's eyes were hard and narrow. Even in her state of near hysteria Jones believed that Gaynor was quite capable of doing what she had promised. Jones didn't remove her hands from Gaynor's shoulders, however. Instead she froze. Not for the first time recently.

The next thing she was aware of was searing pain as Gaynor delivered a smart karate chop, smashing the edge of her hands against Jones's lower arms in order to bounce them away from her. In more or less one fluid movement, she freed herself from Jones's grasp and turned her around, holding on to her left arm which she then forced upwards at a quite impossible angle behind Jones's back.

All Sandy Jones's remaining strength seemed to seep from her. She slumped meekly in Gaynor's grasp, which the other woman slackened only slightly.

'Just tell me who you are, will you?' Jones asked hoarsely.

'I'm Detective Gaynor Jackson of the New York Police Department, and if you don't behave your goddamned self I'm gonna arrest you for assaulting a police officer, you over-educated sap. Whether Dom likes it or not.'

Jones felt completely beaten. Not for the first time in the last few days. What the hell did this mean? Dom's girl was a cop? No wonder she had been able to find out about Marion's condition with such apparent ease.

Abruptly Gaynor let go of Jones altogether. Jones had no feeling at all in her left arm, but when she found that she could move again, she began to back off towards her car. She just wanted to get away from Gaynor.

'Haven't you forgotten something?'

Gaynor was pointing to the hold-all, still lying on the pavement. Obscurely Jones found herself hoping her laptop hadn't been damaged when she'd dropped it. She took a few steps back towards Gaynor, watching her all the while, bent down and picked the bag up.

Her brain was beginning to work again, albeit sluggishly, and she didn't at all like the thoughts which were flooding it. Her fears for Connie's safety in the care of a former World Series wrestler and his girlfriend were growing greater by the second.

'I assume it was no accident that neither you nor Dom thought to mention before that you were a police detective,' she said.

'No accident at all.'

She was cool. Jones had to admit that.

'Some people are inclined to react negatively when they find out you're a cop,' Gaynor remarked.

'Yes. Particularly if those "some people" are on the run, and they're not even sure who they're running from, but almost certainly, at this stage any rate, it includes the police.'

Gaynor reached out and put a hand on Jones's shoulder. Involuntarily Jones flinched away.

'Look Sandy, Dom and I are a team. I trust him. He trusts me. That comes before my job.'

'Does it? How can it? I'm a fugitive.'

'Actually no. And neither is your friend Ed. Not from the law I stand for. I make my own decisions. It's simple. I dislike people who do bad things. That's why I became a cop. And if people doing bad things, planting bombs and mowing down innocent women in the street, if they operate from within the various forces that are actually supposed to be upholding the law, protecting innocent men and women, then I dislike them even more. OK?'

'I don't know. Maybe you tipped someone off about Connie. I can't believe Dom told you about her. A cop, for heaven's sake.'

'Yep. A cop Dom trusts as much as Marion and Connie trust him.'

'Well, I don't trust either of you. I want you to take me to Connie now. I don't want to leave her.'

'No, Sandy. Get yourself a flight back to London. Get the hell out of here. Take your friend. And do what you can to find out what lies behind this damned awful business. That's your strength, Sandy. You told Dom that, didn't you? You might be running, but I guess it's the right thing for you to do. Let's face it, you're not exactly action woman, are you?'

Jones looked away. She could just make out what she thought must be the tail lights of Ed's car parked around the corner facing down town. She felt defeated. As if whatever she decided to do next was bound to turn out wrong.

A lone black sedan cruised slowly down Wall Street towards them, its headlamps dimmed. Jones was vaguely aware of it, seeing it only out of the corner of her eye, her mind elsewhere. She really didn't want to leave Connie behind.

The black sedan coasted to a halt, just a few yards away, right behind Jones's own borrowed vehicle. Its lights dimmed further and then went out. Jones turned around to get a proper look. Even the windows seemed to be matt black. Jones strained her eyes but still could not see inside, even though the spot where the sedan was now parked was quite brightly lit. It dawned on her that the car's windows were tinted. Jones glanced towards Gaynor. She was looking at the sedan too. Jones followed her gaze as the driver's door slowly opened. At first nobody emerged. Jones swung round to look at Gaynor again. She watched as Gaynor slipped her hand inside her jacket. With an increasing sense of horror, it dawned on Jones that Gaynor was probably reaching for a gun.

A noise behind her attracted Jones's attention back to the sedan. A dark-clothed figure flew out of the car in a kind of somersault and landed flat out on the pavement. Jones thought that only happened in the movies. She hadn't realized real people did it.

'Freeze,' yelled a male voice.

The dark-clothed figure was holding a pistol in both hands, in the regulation police grip, and the pistol was aimed at Jones.

Jones froze. For the second time in just a few minutes. Her gaze was locked on the man on the ground. There was quite enough light for her to be able to clearly see the man's face. Jones recognized him at once.

She managed to swivel her eyes towards Gaynor without moving her head.

'You bitch,' she said, as she watched Gaynor draw her handgun and level it. 'You've set me up.'

'Don't be a dork,' said Gaynor.

Jones realized then that Gaynor was aiming her weapon directly at the man lying on the pavement.

'Do not even think about it, asshole,' Gaynor yelled. 'Pull that trigger, and you're dead too.'

The man swung his pistol so that it was pointing at Gaynor.

Jones retreated cautiously into a shadow. This was a stalemate, she realized. Gaynor and the man lying on the pavement were now aiming their weapons at each other. Neither of them was looking at Jones any more.

This was her chance to escape, but she couldn't get to her own vehicle without moving directly into the line of fire. She began to shuffle slowly backwards towards the cross street where Ed was waiting in his neighbour's car.

'I'm NYPD,' she heard Gaynor yell at the top of her voice. 'Drop your weapon, asshole. Now!'

'I'm FBI. Drop yours.'

'Yeah? How do I know you're FBI? And why would I trust you anyway?'

'Oh shit,' said the man lying on the ground.

Jones had backed away almost to the street corner. Hoping that the two adversaries were too engrossed in their battle of nerves to notice, she turned, and began to run full out.

Almost at once she heard a gunshot. Quickly followed by a second shot. Then she thought she heard a scream. She glanced back over her shoulder, but she couldn't see what was going on. In any case she was in too big a hurry to care much.

She reached Ed and his car within seconds, wrenching open the passenger door and throwing herself and her bag in.

'Drive,' she shouted. 'Just drive.'

Ed stared at her, slack jawed. He looked terrified.

'I heard shooting,' he said. 'What happened back there?'

'I'll tell you later.' Jones shouted even louder, 'Drive! Now!'

The vehemence with which she delivered the instruction seemed to do the trick. Ed switched on the engine and slammed his right foot on the accelerator. The little car took off with a screech of rubber, hitting the pavement and then bouncing into the middle of the road.

'Oh fuck, oh fuck,' said Ed.

Jones glanced back over her shoulder.

'It's all right,' she said, as calmly as she could manage. 'Just take it steady. There's nobody on our tail.'

Ed slowed a little.

'Where am I going?' he asked suddenly.

'Anywhere for now, as long as it's away from here,' Jones replied, unconsciously echoing what Dom had said after she and Marion had been targeted by the Chevy truck.

'It's O.K. Corral back there. A gun fight's going on.'

'Was someone shooting at you, Sandy? You're not hurt, are you?'

'No. But never mind the questions. Drive, for fuck's sake.'

'Why don't we go to the police? I can't take much more of this. I can't protect Mikey any more. And I don't see how any of us can protect Connie. I'm frightened, Sandy. I really am . . .'

'Protect Mikey? Listen Ed, one of those raving lunatics waving a gun around back there is the effing police, I've just discovered. Oh, and the other one is your dangerous half-wit of a brother!'

'No. No. It can't be.'

'I'm afraid so. And I want to know how the hell he found us.'

'Oh my God.'

Ed turned to look directly at Jones as she spoke, and seemed to lose concentration. The car hit the curb again.

Jones grabbed the steering wheel and straightened the vehicle up.

'Is it safe to stop?' asked Ed weakly.

Jones thought for a moment. They had been driving for more than ten minutes and had put a considerable distance between themselves and the Wall Street incident. They'd pulled out of the financial district into parts of New York where there was always traffic, day and night. They were no longer conspicuous.

'I reckon so,' she said.

Ed turned into a side road and drew the car to a halt, slumping over the steering wheel.

'Was Mikey shot back there?'

'How the hell do I know?' asked Jones, who was not feeling at all sympathetic concerning Mikey MacEntee. 'It was all I could do to save my own skin.'

'Oh my God! What's he doing? What's he playing at? Was he on his own?'

'He seemed to be. As far as I could make out. It's how he got to be there in the first place that I want to know.'

'That's nothing to do with me,' said Ed quickly. 'I haven't spoken to him since early this morning. I certainly didn't tell him I was meeting you, or where. You believe me, don't you?'

'I don't know what to believe.'

Jones studied Ed carefully. He looked a complete wreck. Could it really be possible that he had deliberately led his crazy brother to them?

'I thought at first that Gaynor had set us up,' Jones continued. 'But she didn't react like that.'

Jones raised her hands to her face, trying to concentrate, to apply logic to a desperate situation.

'Let's try and work this out, Ed. It goes without saying, I hope, that I didn't tell Mikey anything. When he questioned me at Princeton, I didn't even have anything to tell. You say it wasn't you. That leaves Gaynor, Dom or Connie. It's idiotic that it would be Connie. Apart from which Dom's got her under guard almost. He won't leave her for a minute. None of this makes any sense.'

Jones tried desperately to think how a professional would. How they did it in all those movies she'd watched. The idea of electronic surveillance sprung to mind. It was perhaps the only other alternative.

'Could Mikey have bugged your car in some way, like you think he did your phone at home?'

'Sandy, this isn't even my car.'

'Of course not.' Jones was angry with herself for forgetting. 'And, anyway, he homed in on me. We were a hundred yards or so apart when he turned up. Modern surveillance equipment is usually dead accurate. It would have led him straight to you. Not me.'

The interior of the car was cool. But Jones was sweating.

Suddenly she smashed one clenched fist into the dashboard, and with her other hand reached into her jacket pocket.

'Your pen, Ed,' she said. 'Your fucking pen. I didn't return it to you. Did Mikey give it to you by any chance?'

Ed nodded.

'Yes. Just a few weeks ago. For my birthday.'

Jones produced the pen and began to attack it. She unscrewed its shaft and inside found a tiny battery attached to an equally tiny cylindrical object.

'That's a transmitter,' she said.

At once she got out of the car and hurried around to the driver's side, at the same time throwing both the transmitter and its battery on the ground and crunching them beneath her feet.

'Move across, Ed,' she commanded. 'I'm driving, and we're getting out of here. Mikey, or some other bastard, could still be tracking us.'

She slammed the gear shift into drive and took off at speed, only slowing down when they had put several blocks between themselves and the abandoned surveillance gadget.

'I just can't believe it,' said Ed. 'I really liked that pen. I carried it with me all the time. Mikey knew that. It never occurred to me for a moment.'

He broke off and grabbed Jones's arm.

'Oh my God. Is it a voice transmitter? Does that mean he's heard all that we've been saying tonight?'

Jones shook her head. 'I don't think so,' she said. 'For a start he didn't behave back there like a man who knew what he was getting into. I think he just followed the signal when he picked it up. And you know what, I also think it could have been a chance thing. We recently did an item on modern surveillance on my TV show. Even the most powerful of these particular little babies will only work within a radius of a couple of miles or so. They're air-band, not satellite or anything like that. Now, we believe that Mikey had no idea you were in New York, right?'

'Right.'

'But this is where he works most of the time?'

'Yes, I think so.'

'So suddenly, I reckon, we come into range of him and his radio receiver, after we've taken off in our separate cars. The signal bleeps at him. He tunes in, but doesn't get any conversation because I'm on my own with your pen. He gives chase, and tracks the signal down straight to where I'm having my confrontation with Gaynor. Does that make sense to you?'

Ed nodded. 'I guess so. Mikey was obsessed with me knowing more than I was telling him about RECAP and Paul. And he was always into spy gadgets. Even as a boy.'

'This is the sort of gadget anybody can buy on the net, Ed. It's not very sophisticated. I very much doubt it's FBI issue.'

Ed gave a little snort.

'The FBI probably don't trust him with any of their stuff,' he said.

'Well, there are restrictions, you know,' Jones pointed out. 'More than likely the bastards encourage their people to do this kind of thing unofficially. They're not supposed to go round bugging people. Remember the row when it was revealed that George Bush had authorized the use of electronic surveillance equipment on private citizens after 9/11? All hell broke out in the UK too, when the boss of the Met was caught out secretly recording telephone conversations.'

'I'll bet Mikey's got in way out of his depth,' said Ed, with uncanny accuracy. But then, he was Mikey's brother.

'His whole life has been that way,' Ed continued. 'A series of games that eventually catch up with him. Some game this time.'

'I just wonder who he's reporting back to,' said Jones. 'There has to be somebody. And just how far up the chain of command in this crazy country? That's what I'd like to know.'

'It's all totally unreal, Sandy, isn't it?' Ed commented. 'My brother bugging me. Connie on the run. Paul dead. Marion dreadfully injured.'

Ed fell back in his seat. He looked worn out.

'Where are we going, anyway?' he asked.

'Round in circles at the moment,' Sandy replied. 'But I've just had an idea. We've really got to get out of this town and out of this country fast, Ed. It's even more dangerous than I realized. And our only bargaining tool, the only thing that might stop whatever is going on here, and save Connie, is the Ruders Theory. So it's more urgent than ever that we get to the UK—'

'But how?' Ed interrupted. 'Do we really dare risk trying to fly out of a New York airport after what's just happened?'

'No, we don't. In fact I don't think we can risk any US airport.'

'So what are we going to do then?'

Ed sounded beaten.

'We're going to drive to Canada,' said Sandy Jones.

Meanwhile, Mikey, still lying on the pavement just across the street from the stock exchange, was aware only of a terrible burning sensation in his left thigh. She'd shot him. The bitch had shot him.

'Throw your weapon to one side,' Gaynor shouted.

Mikey's eyes opened wide. This was for real. And it was all such a shock. Mikey had actually never fired a gun in anger before. And even now all he'd done was to fire a warning shot over Sandy Jones's head. The bitch who'd winged him had presumably done so because she'd thought he was firing at Jones. He'd never intended to do any such thing. He'd wanted to find Ed, that was all. He'd expected to find Ed. Instead he'd found that danged Dr Jones and a trigger-happy broad who said she was a police officer.

Mikey prepared to throw his gun away, just as Gaynor had commanded. Gaynor took a step forwards, her eyes and her gun levelled on him. She sure was one hell of a frightening woman, Mikey thought.

The wail of a police siren cut through the quiet of the night. A patrol car was hurtling down Wall Street towards them. Gaynor turned to look at it. The barrel of her pistol wavered slightly. A surge of adrenaline burst through Mikey. He twisted his body around and, ignoring the pain of his injured leg, more or less dived into his car, slamming the door behind him.

Gaynor focused her full attention on him again, and aimed her pistol at his head through the glass of the window.

'Stop, or I'll shoot!'

'No, you won't,' said Mikey, surprising himself. He switched on the engine and drove off, thankful that it was his left leg which had been injured.

In his mirror he saw the patrol car pull to a halt alongside Gaynor, who was still pointing her gun after his car. She didn't shoot. Mikey knew that New York cops rarely dared fire after fleeing suspects any more. Not unless lives were endangered. And if they got caught out breaking the rules they could end up in jail for longer than the villains.

Gaynor couldn't believe it when the cop car arrived. Nobody would have had time to call the police yet, even if there had been anyone about to witness the shooting. The patrol car must have been just cruising around, she reckoned, until its team had been alerted by the sound of gunfire. She had no idea of the odds of one turning up like that in the middle of the financial district in the early hours of the morning, but she reckoned they were pretty damned long.

She took her shield from her pocket and held it out in her left hand, while continuing to grasp her police issue revolver in her right hand.

'I'm NYPD, Detective Gaynor Jackson,' she called, as soon as the front doors of the cop car opened, and two uniformed officers emerged.

'Put your gun down,' came the reply. 'Throw your shield towards us. Then put your hands up.'

Gaynor obeyed at once, groaning in frustration. Sandy Jones was long gone, presumably with Ed MacEntee in tow. And now she was starkly aware of Mikey's car disappearing into the distance. Neither of the two cops now studying her shield seemed interested in giving chase. But then, the thought occurred to her suddenly, maybe that was a good thing. She didn't recognize either of the patrolmen. They weren't from her precinct. Maybe that was a good thing too.

She had no idea who Mikey was, but she did know she had to think fast if she was going to keep her job. And maybe even her life. After all, she was up to her ears in a highly dangerous situation which was beginning to show every sign of being part of a major conspiracy. It was time she started to think of herself rather than Dom's friends and a project that was at best idealistic.

She managed to fairly quickly contrive a story about appre-hending a suspect in an armed robbery case she was working on, whom she'd spotted by chance. He'd pulled a gun on her. She'd managed to wing him, however the patrol car had arrived and he'd escaped.

Her story didn't sound very plausible, even to her. And she'd shot a civilian. Or at least, that's what she'd let the two patrolmen believe, because she chose not to mention that her adversary had claimed to be FBI. But the patrolmen didn't show a great deal of interest. Gaynor reckoned they were probably nearing the end of their shift. She knew they'd file a report, though. And therefore, of course, so must she, albeit one which would be rather economical with the truth.

Gaynor wondered if she'd taken one risk too many. She was capable, clever and tough. But, just like Mikey, Gaynor realized that she could be getting out of her depth.

In spite of having been shot, Mikey felt vaguely pleased with himself as he hurtled down Wall Street in his big black sedan, leaving Gaynor and the police patrol car safely behind. He'd surely acted just like a proper special agent for once.

Then he remembered the mess he'd got himself into. And his brother. He wasn't entirely sure whether he'd wanted to find Ed in order to help him, or whether he was the one who wanted Ed's help. He hadn't really thought at all when he'd picked up the signal from the bugged pen on his tracking receiver. He'd just taken off in hot pursuit. His receiver hadn't picked up any speech until he'd arrived in Wall Street, and that had been too muffled to decipher.

Now he was almost certainly in bigger trouble than ever – the thought of which, coupled with the speedily increasing pain in his left leg, brought him swiftly back to cold reality.

Jones had been quite right. Mikey's bugging equipment had not been FBI issue. He had bought it from a distinctly dubious online supplier. It was no longer picking up any sort of signal. In any case he had no intention of even attempting to keep on the tail of the tracking device. Sandy Jones seemed to have somehow or other acquired the pen he'd given Ed. Mikey didn't even know for sure that Ed was in New York.

And he had to get himself some medical treatment. Fast. But he knew what happened when people with gunshot wounds turned up at a hospital. The police were notified at once.

Gingerly he touched his left leg with one hand. It was beginning to feel as if it were on fire, and his trouser was sodden with blood. He was sweating profusely. His vision had started to blur. There was a set of traffic lights just ahead, and Mikey didn't notice until almost too late that they were on red. The jolt of stopping suddenly sent a searing flash of pain from his injured upper leg right through his whole body.

Mikey felt ill. He had just displayed the kind of bravado he'd always aspired to. Now he was truly terrified again. He was at the heart of an operation which was going more and more pear-shaped every minute. His brother was almost certainly in danger. Maybe he was too.

He couldn't cope. Also, he might bleed to death, if he didn't act soon. There was only one person in the world he could think of who could help him now, who would make sure that he got medical treatment, who would understand his motives for trying to chase after Ed the way he had. Just one person who knew what a valuable servant he had been to the American government.

He grabbed his phone and made a call from the top of his favourites' list. After several rings a familiar voice answered.

'It's the middle of the night, Mikey.'

'I'm sorry, Mr Johnson,' replied Mikey trying desperately not to let either the pain or the panic he was experiencing show in his voice. 'I have an emergency situation here, sir.'

Mr Johnson had been in bed with his wife, at their home in a peaceful residential district of Washington D.C., when he took the call. His mobile phone was always with him and he was prepared to answer it at any time of the day or night. He had to be. Mr Johnson was unique. A one-off. He operated in areas almost everyone he came into contact with, including his superiors, preferred not to know about.

Mr Johnson could never be off duty. He didn't mind. He liked being in a position of almost absolute power. When even the senior echelons of government in your country prefer not to acknowledge your existence, then you can pretty much do what you like. As long as you don't get caught out.

The power Mr Johnson was able to exert on his sole authority was actually rather shocking. And he had never been caught out yet.

Mr Johnson was used to waking up quickly. He had to be. He climbed out of bed and carried his phone into the bathroom so that he could talk freely. Mr Johnson trusted nobody. Not even his wife.

He sat on the toilet seat and reached into the cabinet beneath the washbasin for the packet of black cheroots he kept there, tucked away at the back. It was not uncommon for him to find it necessary to retreat into the bathroom in this manner in the middle of the night, and he believed that the little cigars helped him think more clearly.

Holding the phone in one hand, he removed a cheroot with the other and lit up. Acrid smoke almost immediately filled the small room. With the cheroot still between his lips Mr Johnson leaned sideways to open the window as wide as possible, otherwise, in the morning, his wife would make his life a misery. All the while he murmured soothing noises into the phone. It was vital that he calmed Mikey MacEntee down, assured him he would be taken care of, indeed told him almost everything he wanted to hear. And Mr Johnson was good at that sort of thing.

But when he ended the call Mr Johnson felt unusually ill at ease. Mikey was not going to be any use at all from now on. That was patently obvious. In any case Mikey was a lightweight, a Bureau joke, who had only ever been of use because of his connections with areas of scientific innovation the US government had always liked to keep under close observation. Which, of course, the Bureau had known about when they'd hired him. And this operation was not turning out the way Mr Johnson had planned at all. It had originally seemed so simple, in his mind a perfectly straightforward case of confronting anything or anyone that might ultimately constitute a threat to America. Of putting a stop to the enemy within. But the initial mistake, of somehow allowing that mad woman scientist Connie Pike to escape the RECAP explosion, had led to a catalogue of disasters. Not least the continued interference of the troublesome Englishwoman.

Extreme measures were called for. Radical decisions must be made. Drastic action had to be taken. And quickly.

Mr Johnson was used to working alone. But sometimes he was confronted with matters of such international import that even he knew better than to even attempt to do so.

Mr Johnson stood up, flushed the end of his cheroot down the toilet, and sprayed the bathroom with air freshener. Then he sat down again on the toilet seat and lit another cheroot.

There were several phone calls, all overseas, which he had to make before giving the orders he hoped would end this affair once and for all.

Mr Johnson checked his watch. It was two a.m., outside normal office hours in Europe as well as in the US. That didn't matter. Mr Johnson first dialled a number in the United Kingdom of someone who could be regarded as his British equivalent, or as near as would ever be possible. A lone operator who believed the security of his nation rested squarely on his shoulders. A patriot of the old school. A man who also was never off duty.

SEVENTEEN

Meanwhile Jones and Ed headed northwards out of New York City towards the New Jersey Turnpike and the succession of freeways which would take them virtually all the way to the border and on to Montreal.

Jones had done most of the journey before, from Princeton, when as one of a group of impoverished post-graduate students she had driven to Montreal for a weekend convention. But that had been long ago. She knew, however, that the drive should take little more than six hours, particularly as they were travelling during the early hours of the morning, however, not daring to use satnav in case they were tracked, it was not out of the question that they might take a wrong turning. They were both bone tired too.

They set off from the centre of Manhattan around two a.m., at almost exactly the same time as Mikey made his call to Mr Johnson, and three hours later had not quite travelled halfway when Jones decided that she just had to turn into a rest area to sleep for a bit.

Ed seemed even more wiped out than she was, and although he offered to take a turn at the wheel Jones declined. Ed had never been much of a driver, and, judging from his earlier spell at the wheel, the stress of the night's events appeared to have turned him into a liability. In any case she saw no reason not to stop for a while, as she was pretty sure there wouldn't be any flights back to the UK from Montreal's Trudeau Airport until late afternoon or early evening.

They also needed fuel, and Jones congratulated herself on having drawn so much cash out of that Manhattan cashpoint two days earlier. It was more important than ever not to leave a credit card trail. She just hoped she had enough to also pay for their air tickets in cash.

Ultimately they arrived at Trudeau just after noon. Crossing into Canada from the United States had been as easy as Jones had remembered. Immigration and customs procedures between the two countries remained cursory. Border control on the freeway felt and looked much the same as passing through a toll road pay station. Jones and Ed had briefly shown their passports to the Canadian officials, confirmed they were not carrying illegal drugs or livestock, and been waved on their way.

Jones thought that the airport also felt much more relaxed than either US or British airports, since 9/11 certainly. There was little visible sign of armed security presence, and nobody took the slightest notice of her or Ed.

The street shoot-out involving Gaynor, and the revelation that she was a cop, had been the final straw for Jones. Her nerve had gone and she just couldn't wait to leave North America.

Ed desperately wanted to try to contact Mikey, and also his Princeton neighbour to explain, as best he could, about the car, and to ask him to keep Jasper a little longer. But Jones talked him out of it.

'No unnecessary risks, not at this stage, please,' she said. 'Let's not contact anyone until we're safely in the UK.'

To her relief, she did indeed have just enough cash left to buy the cheapest tickets for the next available flight to Heathrow, which she was told would arrive just after six a.m. the following morning. She waited until the last possible moment before booking, so that her and Ed's names would be on the Air Canada passenger list for only a short period of time before departure.

Nonetheless, they were both on tenterhooks going through security and passport control, but everything passed without incident.

Only when finally aboard, and the aircraft had begun taxying for take-off, did Jones breathe a huge sigh of relief. She really was going home.

The aircraft was packed, and Jones realized that she had become somewhat spoiled. She wasn't used to flying economy any more. In addition her entire body was still sore from the battering it had received over the last few days. Yet in spite of her discomfort, her exhaustion was such that she quickly fell asleep, and did not waken until shortly before arrival at Heathrow, when she was disturbed by the dubious antics of some of her fellow passengers who had learned that a certain Hollywood superstar and his new bride were travelling in first class. One young woman actually sank to her knees in the aisle, as she begged a flight attendant to acquire an autograph for her.

Jones couldn't wait to disembark, and being on British soil again almost magically restored at least a degree of her usual self-confidence. Her unfortunate experiences in Princeton and New York began to acquire a veneer of unreality. Suddenly she felt ready to deal with almost anything that needed dealing with. She was Dr Sandy Jones, celebrated academic and media personality, and this was her territory.

*   *   *

Ed walked silently by her side through UK immigration and customs. Jones noticed how white and drawn he still was. He'd always been such a gentle man. It was no surprise, really, that he'd proved to be even less able to deal with violent mayhem than she was. She felt a rush of concern and affection for him.

Impulsively she took his hand in hers and squeezed. He glanced at her in surprise, but did manage the ghost of a smile.

And it was at that moment that the two of them were engulfed in the blinding light of a host of camera flashes. A group of photographers gathered in the arrivals hall were rattling off shot after shot.

'Who's the new man, Dr Jones?' shouted one.

'What about a kiss for the cameras, Sandy?' called another.

'Oh fuck,' muttered Jones under her breath.

'What's happening, Sandy?' asked Ed, leaning to whisper in her ear, thus causing the photographers to snap away all the more furiously.

'Have the FBI put these guys onto us or something? Or MI5? Why are they photographing us?'

Ed's mind was, perhaps understandably, still back in the place they had come from, a place occupied by spooks, special agents, and unidentified hitmen. He appeared to have no awareness at all that the two of them had stepped unwittingly into a completely different world.

'Paparazzi,' muttered Jones through clenched teeth. 'Just keep walking. Fast as you can. My car should be outside by now. I called the valet service as soon as we landed.'

One snapper leapt in front of them then, thrusting his camera so aggressively close to Jones that she was nearly hit in the face by the protruding lens. Her nerves were still not in a good state. It was only with difficulty that she resisted the urge to lash out, but she knew perfectly well that a loss of control was what paparazzi photographers sought more than anything else. Jones was not only a public figure in the UK, but also a highly eligible single woman. She was used to any hint of romance in her life attracting attention. She had never before, however, faced a barrage on quite this scale – the Nikon choir, as a former Fleet Street picture editor of her acquaintance referred to it. And she'd had absolutely no reason to expect such a reception on her unannounced return to the UK. Then it dawned on her.

The assembled paparazzi were not there to meet her. They were after the Hollywood superstar and his new bride. To them Sandy Jones and a mystery male companion were merely a bonus.

But for her and Ed, this now almost certain imminent exposure in the tabloid press could spell potential disaster.

Once in the Lexus Jones explained to Ed what had been going on and why she thought it had happened.

'I didn't know you were such a big star,' he remarked.

'The power of television,' she replied. 'But only by default in this case. Same result though, unfortunately.'

'Will we be in the papers here tomorrow, then?'

'Almost certainly,' Jones muttered. 'And on line before that.'

'So it will be common knowledge that we're here. Won't we be in just as much danger as in America?'

'I don't think so,' replied Jones, hoping she was speaking the truth. 'We've no reason to think anyone followed us here, or even that whoever is trying to kill Connie is set up to hit on us here. This is Britain, Ed.'

'Yes,' he riposted. 'One of the world's greatest terrorist targets. The Russians even splashed a deadly poison around one of your great cities. Or do you still believe in an England where bobbies ride bicycles and criminals say, "It's a fair cop, guv"?'

Jones flashed a grim smile.

'Touché. We do have a secret weapon, though.'

'We do?'

'That lot back there,' she said, cocking a thumb in the direction of the terminal building they had just left. 'We're almost certainly going to have a press presence at my place soon. I put it to you that we might be slightly less likely to be murdered or kidnapped with Fleet Street's finest on watch outside our front door. And dodging the press sure beats running for your life.'

Ed looked startled.

'Is your love life of that much interest?' he asked.

'Apparently.'

'And you really believe there's no other reason for the paparazzi to mob us? And that it has nothing to do with Connie, and RECAP, and Marion, and all of that?'

'Absolutely.'

'I see,' said Ed, although Jones doubted that he did.

By the time they got to Reading, Ed was asleep. Jones switched on the radio and tuned in to BBC Radio Four in order to help keep herself alert. They had a clear run and, even though Jones stopped for half an hour so that they could stretch their legs and buy coffee and sandwiches, arrived at Northdown House well before midday. So far there appeared to be no press presence.

'Not a bad little place,' murmured Ed as they motored through the electric security gates. 'What views!'

Jones remembered Ed's unprepossessing Princeton apartment, and thought there might be a little edge in his voice, but ignored it.

As she pulled the car to a halt, she used the fob on her key ring to disengage the burglar alarm.

'I see you don't rely entirely on press protection,' Ed continued.

'You can't depend on them being around 24/7,' replied Jones wryly. 'And TV exposure does lead those with an inclination toward burglary to think your house must be Aladdin's cave.'

Once inside Ed asked straight away if he could use her computer to email Mikey. Jones saw no harm in that. Not now they were out of the USA. And, after all, their whereabouts was already in the process of being made public by the great British press.

'In spite of everything, I can't help still wanting to know if the little bastard is all right after the shooting,' said Ed. 'And I also want an explanation. I want him to tell me what is going on, and exactly what part he has played in it all.'

Jones didn't think that there was much chance of that, but none the less showed Ed to her office and switched on her desktop Mac. He said he'd better email his long-suffering neighbour too.

'Tell him I'll pay for a recovery service to get his car back to him,' said Jones. 'It's the least we can do.'

When Ed had finished his emailing she escorted him to her best guest room.

'You may like to have a shower and a rest,' she said. 'I'm going to the university to check if the package has arrived. Help yourself to anything you want from the kitchen. I'll make sure all the alarms are on. You will be safe here.'

Everything at the university seemed almost disconcertingly normal. Clearly nobody had any idea of what Jones had been involved in on the other side of the Atlantic. But she had known they wouldn't. Not yet. She'd tried again to camouflage the injuries to her face with make-up. Nonetheless one or two people commented on her bruised and battered appearance. She muttered something vague about being involved in a freeway pile-up. Other than that it was just like any other day. On the surface.

The package hadn't arrived. She supposed it had been overly optimistic to have thought it might have done. She was just going to have to be patient. She tried to deal with some of the messages and other mail awaiting her, but found it virtually impossible.

She decided to check if her and Ed's arrival at Heathrow had made it online yet. The *Mail* had indeed already posted a picture of the two of them, alongside a headline asking: 'Is this Dr Jones's new love?'

'Shit!' muttered Jones.

She knew that as 'the thinking man's crumpet' she was very much *Daily Mail* fodder. All the same, it must be a really poor news day, she reflected. There was also a close up of her battered and bruised face next to a strap-line asking: 'Whatever happened to Sandy?'

Her and Ed's whereabouts was certainly public knowledge now. Which was only as she had expected. But, in spite of her assurances to Ed, she could not imagine that they would be totally safe anywhere in the world.

However, within the next day or so Jones would hopefully be studying Paul Ruders' theory of the mystery of consciousness. She would have access to probably the greatest scientific work of her lifetime. Maybe, even, the greatest and most far-reaching scientific work there had ever been. In spite of everything she could not suppress a certain excitement rising within her.

But somewhere in America, Connie Pike was in hiding. Her safety, if indeed she was still safe, at least partially depended on Jones and what she did next. On how she handled the revelatory scientific discovery which might soon be in her grasp. And at that moment she had absolutely no idea what she was going to do.

She returned to Northdown not long after six. Ed was still in his room. He emerged about an hour later.

'Did it arrive?' he asked.

Jones shook her head. 'I'd have called you straight away.'

She asked if he had received a reply to either of his emails.

'Nothing from Mikey, unfortunately,' he said. 'Heard from my neighbour. I only told him the barest details, obviously, but I think his involvement, by default, in our dash to Canada and then back to the UK, might be the most exciting thing that's ever happened to him. He took it all rather well, and is happy to look after Jasper for as long as it takes.'

'Oh well, as long as Jasper's being well looked after, we don't have a thing to worry about, do we?' responded Jones, with a smile.

They sat in the kitchen together, picking at fruit and crackers and cheese, chewing over yet again the events of the last few days and what it all meant. Jones had opened a bottle of wine.

Being together was beginning to feel easy and natural again. Just as it had done all those years before.

'You know, much as I want to get my hands on your USB, I just can't stop thinking about Connie,' said Jones. 'Paul's work, whatever it proves, won't necessarily help protect Connie. Possibly just the opposite—'

'Nor us either, we must still be in danger, whatever you say,' interrupted Ed.

'Yes, to some degree at least we must all be in danger,' Jones admitted. 'I suppose we could go to the authorities here, but the police would just be bewildered, I reckon, and I don't know who else to trust—'

'I've had an idea,' Ed interrupted suddenly. 'You're a high-profile media figure. A celebrity. I saw that at the airport. Turn it to your advantage. Call a press conference. They'll come. If only to question you about your new love interest.'

Ed laughed briefly.

'Look, if you put it all out there: our belief that RECAP was the target of the Princeton explosion; all that happened in New York; the hit on Marion; everything, in the public domain, then surely that could put Connie and us out of danger,' he continued. 'You'd create an international storm. If anything happened to any of the three of us it would look just too suspicious, wouldn't it?'

Jones stared at him in silence for a few seconds.

'You could be right,' she said eventually. 'Why the heck didn't I think of that?'

Ed shrugged.

'Not such a genius after all. Obviously.'

'Obviously,' repeated Jones.

PART FIVE

A human being is part of the whole, called by us Universe, a part limited in time and space. He experiences himself, his thoughts and feelings, as something separated from the rest – a kind of optical delusion of his consciousness. This delusion is a prison, restricting us to our personal desires and to affection for a few persons nearest to us. Our task must be to free ourselves from this prison.

Albert Einstein

EIGHTEEN

The next morning Jones arrived at her Exeter University office just as her mail arrived. The package she was so eagerly awaiting was still not there. But she had decided the previous evening, that she would go ahead with a press conference without it. She couldn't afford to wait. Lives were at stake. Including, possibly, her own.

In any case, she reflected a little guiltily, regardless of that, it was about time she made a stand on behalf of RECAP.

If there was anything at all she could do to help keep Connie Pike safe, and herself and Ed, she needed to get on with it. She had witnessed first-hand just how fast those who were out to get Connie could move.

She picked up her desk phone and called Sally Brice. Sally had worked in admin at Exeter University for almost twenty years, and was something of a Jackie of all trades. One of her many jobs was to organize and, in as much as was ever possible, control any dealings the university and its staff had with the press. She had been doing it for years and was rather good at it.

'I want you to be a little vague about the exact reason for calling this gathering,' she told Sally in response to her obvious question. 'But feel free to drop some loud hints. Have you seen the *Mail*?'

'Yes I have,' responded the cheery voice at the other end of the phone. 'What did happen to your face, and who is the new man in your life?'

'Exactly,' responded Jones obliquely, not quite sure whether Sally was actually hoping for a proper response or merely repeating the headlines.

The press call brought about a healthy response, as predicted by Ed. It was, reflected Sandy Jones, disconcerting to consider how much depended on her celebrity, a dubious commodity at the best of times.

More than a dozen assorted journalists, both written and broadcasting, turned up. The tabloid representatives including reporters and photographers from the *Daily Mail*, the *Mirror*, and the *Sun*, were doubtless hoping for the opportunity to quiz Sandy Jones on her new love interest, and to acquire a posed snap of the happy couple.

For once, Jones thanked God for the media attention she attracted.

Sally had arranged for the conference to be held in one of the university meeting rooms. On the dot of three o'clock, and not a moment before, Jones made her entrance.

'Good afternoon, ladies and gentlemen,' she began, getting straight to the point. 'My real reason for bringing you here today may come as something of a surprise. My facial injuries are the result of an attempt on my life in New York, which I believe to be part of a major conspiracy, a conspiracy which might well involve American government agencies at the highest level, and which will almost certainly have far-reaching international consequences.'

There was a collective gasp in the room. Jones's television work had taught her the value of a good intro. She was also aware of the importance of placing herself at the heart of the story, if she was to get the level of coverage she hoped for from the ever-insular British press.

She looked around. She had them, and she knew it.

'I am sure you all know about the fatal explosion at Princeton University last week,' she went on. 'The authorities have told us the target was the animal research department. But I have reason to believe that is not the truth, ladies and gentlemen, and that the truth is being deliberately covered up. The bomb was planted in the RECAP lab, that's REsearch into Consciousness At Princeton, and I believe RECAP was the true target.

'While studying for my doctorate at Princeton many years ago I became involved with the work of RECAP. My ties remain deep, and I went to America in order to personally investigate that explosion and its aftermath – an explosion I believe to have been deliberately targeted at destroying RECAP and those involved in this extraordinary ground-breaking project.'

Jones paused. She was aware of a buzz around the room. She had spent most of the previous twenty-one years keeping very quiet about her involvement with RECAP, and her one-time closeness to

Paul and Connie. To publicly align herself now with the project and its people, was in some ways as disconcerting to her as facing all the dangers she had encountered in America. Fleetingly she wondered if that was why the idea had not presented itself to her before Ed suggested it.

Paul's paper might change everything. Meanwhile Jones could imagine only too vividly the reaction she was now likely to provoke in academic circles, particularly at Oxford, the university which had just chosen her to be their next chancellor.

'There is something else,' she continued. 'The psychologist Connie Pike, the RECAP lab manager allegedly killed in the blast, is in fact not dead. She survived, due to a freak chain of events, and has since also survived a second deliberate attempt on her life. This was the same incident in which another woman was grievously injured, and from which I only narrowly escaped.'

Jones paused again. You could have heard a pin drop in the room. All eyes were riveted on her.

'Connie Pike is currently in hiding,' Jones continued. 'She has told me that Professor Paul Ruders, the director of RECAP, who was killed, had recently made a sensational scientific discovery. Paul believed he was finally able to explain the secret of consciousness.'

The journalists gathered in the meeting room were general news men and women, area staff mostly, but they were still quite obviously aware of the significance of what she was telling them.

'Paul believed that he had solved the greatest single mystery of mankind's very existence,' Jones went on. 'And Connie Pike and I both believe that is why he was murdered. I have decided to go public with that, and with my conviction that RECAP and all associated with it have been the target of a deadly conspiracy, almost certainly executed by establishment figures quite probably in senior American government circles. My intention in telling you this, ladies and gentlemen, is that I hope to blow that conspiracy wide open.'

For just a few seconds the deathly hush in the room remained unbroken. Then a kind of humming noise began, as the realization of the magnitude of Jones's statement bounced from person to person, like a current of electricity whizzing along a row of pylons. The questions came thick and fast. Jones told no lies but withheld as much of the truth as suited her, giving only a very edited version

of Ed's involvement, and she allowed the assumption to be made
that Paul Ruders' work had either died with him or been stolen by
those responsible for the Princeton explosion. She certainly didn't
mention the imminent arrival of Ed's USB.

Sandy Jones knew just how to present a story in order to make
it irresistible. If she could do that with the theory of relativity, for
God's sake, then selling a tale of a deadly explosion, a fugitive
scientist, a killer truck, a series of life-threatening events, and the
possibility of a major conspiracy at US government level, was a
piece of cake.

Everybody wanted to know where they could find Connie. And
Jones was glad that she was genuinely unable to tell them.

'I'm sure Connie Pike will come forward now,' she said. 'The
whole purpose of this news conference, of revealing all that I
have today, is to make it safe for her to do so. And, indeed, also
to ensure my safety, and the safety of Ed MacEntee.'

Jones could tell from the way the gathered throng all took off at a
run as soon as the press call was over, that it had been a success.
She'd effectively dodged questions concerning her relationship
with Ed, but, in any case, for once even the tabloid press present
had allowed her dramatic revelations to overshadow their abiding
fascination with the love lives of the well-known.

She called Ed as soon as it was over and gave him a quick run-
down, so that he would know what to expect. She then called her
sons to provide them with a précised account of events, hopefully
before they learned of it from the media, and to assure them that
she was fine. She lied that she had exaggerated the danger a bit in
order to be sure of blanket coverage, but she knew they weren't
convinced. Matt threatened a visit at the weekend to see for himself
how she was, and Lee expressed outrage that she had taken off on
such a crazy mission without even telling him or his twin. Jones
ended up feeling rather more like the child than the parent.

The calls from the specialist science correspondents on the various
papers and broadcasting news services began minutes later. Soon
afterwards came calls from crime correspondents and political
editors.

Two national newspaper editors of Jones's acquaintance called
her directly. She could tell they were almost as amazed by her

embracing RECAP as they were by the rest of her revelations, including her allegations of an American government conspiracy concerning the Princeton explosion.

She stayed in her office until almost seven in order to watch the main national news broadcasts on the BBC and ITV. To her delight, and a tad to her surprise too, her story was the lead item on both.

She also channel-hopped on satellite and found it featured prominently on Sky News and CNN. That meant worldwide exposure. Most importantly, the allegations would soon be known all over America. The New Jersey State Police, the FBI, the whole of the American establishment including the doyens of science and academia, and every area of government, national and regional, would very soon be aware of the hornet's nest Dr Sandy Jones had stirred up. They surely would not dare attack Connie, or her and Ed, now.

Ed's USB had still not turned up when Jones left for home. But she was in considerably better spirits than she had been since she first heard of the Princeton explosion. However, her mood changed again, when, just as she was stepping out of the building, she received a phone call from Oxford University, postponing her dinner appointment the following week. Jones had actually half-forgotten about it, and in any case would be unlikely to attend – certainly if she had that USB in her hands by then. Nonetheless the significance of the postponement was not lost on her. She had no doubt at all that her endorsement of RECAP was the real reason. The Vice Chancellor was probably playing for time, giving himself and his cohorts opportunity to discuss and perhaps even reconsider Jones's appointment as Chancellor. Jones didn't think that the decision of the Convocation – the body of Oxford MAs and MScs who had cast their votes in the traditional election process – could be overturned. But she wasn't sure. She cursed under her breath, as she hurried to her car, but still remembered to smile for the assorted press gathered in the car park.

More press were outside the gates of Northdown, as she had rather expected, some of them, no doubt, still interested primarily in the possibility of a picture of her with Ed, but most of them now with bigger fish to fry. The narrow approach lane was lined by a string of assorted vehicles. Cameras flashed.

Jones had no further interest in them. She was looking forward to a bath and another evening with Ed, whose company she was beginning to enjoy so much more than she might have expected.

There was nothing else she could do now. Not until that USB arrived.

The anonymous looking man sitting alone in a vehicle parked just a small distance further back from the others, made no attempt to leave his equally anonymous silver grey saloon car as Jones drove by. Instead he merely watched the performance of the rest of those gathered there, some of whom actually ran after Jones's Lexus, stopping only when the big electric gates closed in their faces.

There was a camera on the passenger seat next to the anonymous man, but he didn't even pick it up. Instead he waited until Jones had disappeared into the grounds of Northdown House, before finally climbing out of his car, and walking around to the rear to remove from the boot a small leather case which he opened rather furtively, glancing from side to side to ensure no one was nearby. He seemed to be checking the contents of the case, in which nestled a very sophisticated looking sniper rifle, its stock and barrel in two separate sections, a silencer, and a box of ammunition.

He turned to study the press corps again, most of whom were now grouped together by the electric gates, looking as if they were discussing what to do next. Nobody was taking any notice whatsoever of the anonymous man. With one hand he smoothed down his already smooth mousey brown hair. With the other he turned up the collar of his raincoat, a garment, almost exactly the same shade of brown as his hair, which was perhaps not entirely necessary on a dry and relatively warm September evening. Then he removed the rifle parts from the case, and with practised ease, quickly assembled and loaded the weapon.

He replaced the case in the boot, slid the rifle beneath his raincoat, holding it close to his body beneath one arm, and began to walk casually towards a wooded area just to the right of the gates.

He went straight to a spot from which he had a particularly good view of the house, even though he was then quite well concealed by trees and shrubs. Anyone watching might have assumed he knew exactly where he was going, and that he had already checked out the vantage point. But there was nobody watching.

The light was fading fast. It was very nearly dark. The anonymous man liked that. Darkness surrounding illuminated windows. Silhouettes standing out clearly against brightly-lit backdrops. Even in properties where windows were hung with heavy curtaining, there were almost always moments of vulnerability at dusk. Moments when lights were switched on before the curtains were drawn.

Lights were being switched on now upstairs in the house. And he could already see a shadow moving around in what he knew to be Jones's bedroom. The shadow moved beneath the room's bright central light. It was her.

He grunted in satisfaction. His was the simplest of plans. And it was extraordinary how often such a plan could circumnavigate the most advanced of security systems. There was no need to even attempt to breach the well-protected perimeters of Northdown. The anonymous man was an expert at what he did. Swift and accurate. And he liked to attack from without.

The gathered press had unwittingly provided him with his cover. Sandy Jones had been wrong to think that a press presence would give additional protection to her and Ed, not when a would-be assassin of this man's calibre had been deployed. Depending on how quickly the waiting journalists became aware of the incident that would soon occur, they might yet also provide a displacement activity covering his escape from the scene.

The anonymous man lifted the rifle to his shoulder and took aim.

Meanwhile in New York, in a tall thin Brooklyn brownstone, Dom was trying not to nod off in an armchair while Connie slept surprisingly soundly on a bed in the same room. Sheer exhaustion had finally caught up with both of them.

The big man hadn't slept properly for a long time either. Gaynor had given him a full account of the Wall Street fracas, and that had made Dom all the more nervous and on edge. He no longer left Connie's side for a minute. Even when she used the bathroom he stood outside the door.

When she'd popped in with provisions earlier, Gaynor had offered to take her turn looking after Connie, but Dom had refused, sending her off back to work, telling her this was his problem and he'd sort it. The truth of course was, that, even though she was a cop, and she was smart and she was tough, Dom now wanted to involve Gaynor as little as possible. At best the incident in the financial district could destroy her career. At worst she could also now be targeted. Indeed, she may already have been targeted. They neither knew the identity of the mystery gunman nor his intent. Dom didn't want Gaynor put in any more danger.

The big man yawned deep and long. It was the middle of the day in New York, but that made no difference. Dom's eyelids felt like they were made of lead. They weighed more than he could bear. He just couldn't stop them closing.

He was snoring gently when the Enforcer and his Apprentice arrived, their mission having been assigned to them by Mr Johnson and various of his associates.

Mikey hadn't known who Gaynor was, of course, beyond her claiming to be a cop. But because an NYPD patrol car had been involved it had been easy enough for the Chelsea Feds to track down the patrolmen's report and identify her. Just a little more checking had revealed that she was the girlfriend of one Norman Bishop – otherwise known as the Dominator. All the Enforcer and his Apprentice had to do then was to tail her. They'd banked on her leading them to the Dominator and to Connie Pike, the woman they'd been entrusted to remove from the face of the earth. Ultimately Gaynor had done just that.

The Enforcer could break into almost any property almost anywhere without causing a disturbance. He knew as much about electronic security systems as the people who designed and manufactured them. Indeed he could probably have designed a system as well, if not better, than most of them, were it ever in his interests to do so.

It was the Enforcer who opened the door to the room where Connie and the Dominator slept. He was good at opening doors without making a sound. He moved silently towards Dom, sprawled in his armchair, snoring rhythmically, and gestured to the Apprentice, who, the sweat standing up on his brow, began to approach the bed where Connie slept.

The Enforcer reached into the inner folds of his grey overcoat and produced a butcher's knife. The Apprentice glanced across at him. He was already carrying a smaller, but equally lethal looking, knife in his right hand. Its long narrow blade gleamed in the shaft of afternoon sunshine shining through the room's one window. The Apprentice moved closer to the bed and aimed the point of the blade directly at the base of Connie Pike's throat.

Dom was still snoring softly, his chest moving up and down as he breathed in and out. The Enforcer leaned over the big man, drew his knife hand back a little, and tensed the muscles in his shoulder and arm ready to deliver a lethal stab to the heart. The Enforcer was a professional. It would only take one blow.

Connie Pike and her unlikely protector were about to die.

NINETEEN

B ack in the UK, in the thick undergrowth just beyond the iron railings which surrounded Northdown House, the anonymous man was ready for the kill. His first target was in his sights, clear as could be. He could not have asked for better.

He curled the index finger of his right hand around the trigger of his rifle. The man was able to hold his hands and arms almost unnaturally still. He was a professional. And to him, this was almost too easy. Sandy Jones had just seconds to live.

He began to squeeze. Gently. Steadily. Smoothly.

Within the inner pocket of his raincoat his mobile phone, set on silent mode, began to vibrate. The man paused, his finger now rigid on the trigger. He made himself relax his body. Then he lowered the rifle and reached inside his coat.

Only his employers contacted him on that phone. And he knew better than to ignore them. He was being sent a text. He called it up and read it through. The message was short and to the point. Just one word, repeated a second time.

'Abort abort'

The anonymous man slid the phone back into his pocket, flipped on the rifle's safety catch, once more tucked the gun inside his raincoat, and walked nonchalantly back to his car where he dismantled the weapon even more swiftly than he'd assembled it, replaced it in the case in the boot, and drove off.

*   *   *

In the Brooklyn brownstone the Enforcer, who rather enjoyed his work, was anticipating the moment when the cold steel blade of his butcher's knife would plunge into warm softly compliant flesh. His fingers were clenched tight as a vice around the knife's shaft, when he felt the cell phone in his trouser pocket vibrate.

Only his employers called him on that phone. The Enforcer knew better than to ignore them.

He reached for the phone and glanced at the text message he had just been sent. The Enforcer was disappointed, but it did not occur to him to do anything other than to obey the instruction he had been given. He relaxed his knife arm, and began to replace the weapon within the folds of his coat. With his other hand he made a kind of horizontal slashing motion. The Apprentice understood at once that the mission had been called off.

Once they'd left the building, the Enforcer held out the cell phone towards the Apprentice, so that the younger man could see the displayed message.

'Abort abort'

Meanwhile Dom jolted suddenly awake, blinking furiously, cursing his own weakness. Something had disturbed him. What was it? Had he heard a noise? Or was it his imagination? Could he have been dreaming?

He hauled himself to his feet, shaking off his bone weariness. No harm was going to come to Connie Pike while he had care of her, that was for certain, whatever that up-herself damned Englishwoman thought.

Dom looked across at Connie, who was still sleeping peacefully. It was the first time he'd seen her at peace since it all began.

He checked the locks on the window by Connie's bed, as he'd done a dozen times that day, and peered outside into the street. Everything seemed normal. But Dom's antennae were waggling. He slipped out of the bedroom, and began to make his way systematically through the house, checking each room, every window and door.

Everything was as it should be. In any case surely nobody could have found them there, could they? Not yet. The brownstone belonged to Gaynor's grandmother, who was in hospital. And Gaynor and Dom had agreed it was about as safe a house as they were going to get.

None the less Dom still felt uneasy. He still felt that something was not quite right, although he couldn't explain to himself what or why.

Then the house phone rang. It was Gaynor.

'Have you guys seen the news?' she asked.

Sandy Jones was totally unaware of just how close she had come to death. She had no idea that an armed assassin had been about to cold-bloodedly shoot her through her bedroom window. And, of course, she had no idea that, in New York, Connie Pike and her minder had also only narrowly escaped a violent death.

To her, everything at Northdown seemed peaceful.

She drew her bedroom curtains, undressed, showered in the en suite, then pulled on jeans and a clean shirt. Downstairs again, the aroma of frying bacon hit her as soon as she opened the kitchen door.

'I raided your deep freeze for the bacon, and I'm going to scramble some eggs I found in your fridge, if that's all right,' said Ed.

'More than all right,' said Jones, who had hardly eaten anything all day again, and now, smelling the bacon, realized just how hungry she was

As she opened a bottle of wine, she glanced sideways at Ed, busying himself over the frying pan. He was such a kind, thoughtful man; still quite attractive, too, in spite of having now lost most of his hair. But then, he'd not had much left when she'd last seen him twenty-one years earlier.

She gave Ed a fuller account of the press conference as they ate, and they were still discussing what they both hoped would be achieved when her phone rang.

'It's me, you fucking genius.'

Jones's face broke into a wide grin.

'I knew you'd see the light one of these days,' she responded.

'Connie,' she hissed in an aside to Ed, who let out a yelp of delight. Connie was alive.

Jones returned her attentions to the phone.

'Are you all right, Con?' she asked. 'It's just wonderful to hear from you.'

'I'm fine. One hundred per cent. Thanks to you.'

Jones's grin grew even wider. It was already clear that Connie not only knew that Jones had gone public, but that she approved.

'Where are you? Are you still with Dom? Are you still hiding away somewhere?'

'I'm with Gaynor. In her car. Along with two very large male detectives. She picked up the news first.'

There was a brief pause.

'I understand you found out what she does for a living, Sandy,' Connie continued.

'Uh huh.'

'Yes, well, Marion and I didn't know that either. Not when we went to Dom for help. But Dom's right. The only good cop is a tame one.'

She chuckled.

'So what are you doing now?' asked Jones. 'How are you handling this?'

'Well, straight away we reckoned you'd made me pretty much bullet proof. For a while anyway. You've also given credence to my conspiracy theory. I've already given a statement to the police. Put everything on record. Gaynor and her friends are taking me to CNN. I'm doing a TV interview. They're my police protection apparently, though I don't reckon I need it. Anyone in high places who's been after my tail is going to back right off now.'

'Uh huh. I didn't know the NYPD ran a chauffeur service for television stations.'

'Maybe it depends on whether or not they have a personal interest.'

'And Dom?'

'He's sleeping, I hope. He's been watching over me day and night. He's exhausted. None the less he still wasn't happy about letting me out of his sight. I think his nose might be a bit out of joint.'

Jones laughed.

'I guess I misjudged him.'

'I guess so. Anyway, Sandy. I think you've worked a miracle. I couldn't do any of this if you hadn't gone public in the way you did. I do understand what it took for you to speak out like that, you know.'

Jones was silent for a moment. Connie knew better than anyone what her career meant to her. She also knew what damage an acknowledged association with RECAP could still do to Sandy Jones. Connie was, more than likely, the only person in the world who did understand. Except perhaps Ed.

'Yes, well, not before time,' she said.

'Without you nobody would have given a shit,' Connie continued. 'Nobody would have listened. I would just have been that psi nut. More than that, if I'd come out of hiding without your backing I would almost certainly have had a fatal accident.'

'I think we all feared that.'

'Yep. I didn't know you had so much clout. You clever bitch.'

'Careful Connie, I'm not used to flattery from you. Even if it is wrapped up in your usual vernacular.'

'Yeah, well. You may just have given me my life back, Dr Sandy Jones.'

'I hope so.' Jones paused. 'How's Marion? Have you been to see her yet?'

'I have. Gaynor took me to the hospital on the way to the police station. It's awful to see her looking so ill. But she's conscious, she's stable, and they're planning to move her out of intensive care tomorrow. She can't really talk much yet, but she is on the mend. And it looks as if they've managed to save her other leg.'

'I'm so glad, Connie. You've been through a hell of a lot. Both of you.'

'I guess so. But we might be on the home straight now. You're all over the news here, with your allegations. Did you know that?'

'I've caught a couple of bulletins,' Jones murmured.

'Everyone's denying all knowledge, of course. The FBI knows absolutely nothing, as usual. Our national government knows even less, it seems. And our apology for a president has gone on holiday to Camp David. I can't wait to see the papers tomorrow. Fox TV are already calling it Connie-gate.'

Jones smiled. Connie sounded quite like her old self. Jones was delighted. She also felt she should counsel a little caution. Whoever had tried to kill Connie after she'd escaped the Princeton blast, and whoever had been responsible for that explosion, the death of two scientists and the injuries to the students, would probably want Connie dead more than ever. Even if they didn't actually dare do anything about it, for the time being.

'Take care, Connie,' she said. 'You may not be out of the woods yet. It's hard to second guess what will happen next. You're still a target you know, you have to be—'

'C'mon, you downbeat,' Connie interrupted cheerily. 'If an accident should befall me now there'd be an international outcry. I'm suddenly safe as houses. I'm not just bulletproof, I'm goddamned nuclear missile proof. Thanks to you.'

'Well, I guess so, but—'

'No buts, Sandy. Connie Pike is in business again. I reckon we'll get RECAP back up and running after this. The university won't have any choice. Not with all the publicity. I knew you were the one person who could put things right. RECAP could get a whole new lease of life, Sandy. It could be better than ever.'

'Well, yes maybe.'

Jones was a touch surprised. She hadn't expected Connie to react quite so effusively.

'But Paul is still dead,' she continued quietly. 'We can't bring him back.'

'No, none of us will ever get over Paul's death,' Connie responded. 'But he would have wanted his work to go on. And that's what's going to happen, Sandy. RECAP is going to go on and on, for another thirty years, forty years, for as long as it takes. The journey will continue.'

'But what about an end to that journey? Paul's final work, his paper—'

'If it's lost, it's lost,' Connie interrupted. 'That's been one of the big media lines here already, by the way. Has the secret of consciousness been lost for ever? But we won't stop. We will carry on Paul's work. That's what matters.'

Ed tugged at the sleeve of Sandy's sweater.

'Why don't you tell her? Tell her I copied Paul's paper.'

'Hold on a minute, Connie.' Jones put her hand over the receiver.

'I nearly did, just then,' she whispered. 'But she's got half the NYPD with her, for Christ's sake. She thinks we're all bulletproof now. I'd like to hold back the trump card until we're sure of that. Do you want to talk to her?'

Ed nodded furiously. Jones handed him the receiver.

'Just remember, don't mention that USB.'

She wondered if she was being overly cautious. But upon reflection she didn't think so. They still didn't know who had been responsible for the bombing, or the attack on Marion. Jones felt strongly that danger continued to lurk. The reasons why she'd withheld all mention of the existence of a USB containing Paul's work at the press call remained totally valid.

Ed broke off his conversation with Connie in order for Jones to say a quick goodbye. Apparently the car was just about to arrive at the TV station.

'Gotta go kick some ass,' Connie told her.

Not for the first time Jones wondered at the woman's strength and resilience. With all that she had been through and all that she had lost, it seemed that Connie Pike was already in the process of picking herself up and starting again.

She turned to Ed.

'How do you think Connie sounded?'

'Great.' Ed beamed at her. Then his smile faded.

'What's wrong?' asked Jones.

'I can't help thinking about Mikey. Still no response to my email. I switched on my cell phone again, after the press conference, there seemed no reason not to, and I called him a couple of times. No reply, and he's not called back. He's at the heart of all this craziness, after all. I know it's his own fault, but I can't help worrying about him. I mean, he might have been badly injured . . .'

'He'll be all right. I think your brother is a survivor.'

'I hope so.'

Jones reached out and touched his arm.

'And I hope he knows how lucky he is to have a brother like you.'

'Oh, come on.'

'No. I hope he does. I was too dumb to know how lucky I was, when I had you in my life.'

'You're embarrassing me, Sandy.'

'I'm sorry. It's just that, even with everything that's happened, it's been so very good to have you around these last few days, to be with you again . . .'

Abruptly Ed pulled away and turned his back on her. Jones kicked herself. She hadn't meant to say any of that.

Ed was silent for what seemed like for ever. Then he turned to face Jones again.

'I'm very proud of you, Sandy,' he said. 'Not because you're a big shot celebrity scientist. But because of what you've done for RECAP, for Connie, and for me. And I like being with you too.

But you should know, I've never really got over what happened between us, what you did to me. And I'm not sure I ever will.'

'I'm sorry,' said Jones. 'I know I behaved abominably. I'm really so sorry for the pain I caused you.'

'It was a long time ago . . .'

'Yes. And you know what? I think I've spent my life ever since looking for what we had back then. But, at the time, bloody fool that I was, I didn't even recognize it.'

In the morning Jones woke at seven, just before her alarm sounded, and slipped softly out of bed.

Ed was still asleep. In the spare bedroom. He had made it pretty clear that the situation was not going to change, not for a very long time at any rate, even though she was beginning to think she might rather like it if it did. But she knew she mustn't dwell on that.

She left him a note before setting off to Exeter, and arrived just before eight thirty. The university was open on Saturdays and still received an early post. On the way to her office, Jones detoured to the post room to see if anything had arrived for her. She could hardly contain her excitement on finding a jiffy bag addressed to her, with a New Jersey postmark.

Jones ripped it open eagerly. Inside was the USB bearing a scientific paper which could change the world, wrapped by Ed in several layers of kitchen paper for extra protection. It looked so ordinary.

With trembling fingers she unwound the paper, and fed the USB into her laptop, avoiding her desktop computer which was connected to the university's network system.

And there it was. Paul Ruders' Theory of Consciousness. Jones felt the excitement rise within her. A light film of perspiration formed on her forehead, even though her office was cool. She downloaded the document and removed the USB from its slot.

Then she settled herself in her chair, and prepared to go to work.

First she cancelled – by email – the filming for the final part of her current BBC series scheduled for the following day. She was unlikely to be free in time, and in any case would now have little opportunity to prepare. She wouldn't be popular, but she couldn't help it. Her Oxford dinner had been cancelled for her. At that moment

she didn't give a damn about that, nor indeed anything else at all
– except the Ruders Theory.

She switched off her phone and set to work. She had a mammoth
task before her. However, it was the kind of task Sandy Jones
relished.

Almost ten hours later, at around seven o'clock that evening, Jones
rose stiffly from her chair, removed the bottle of malt whisky and
one of the glasses she kept tucked away in her bookcase, behind
a couple of the weightiest tomes. She poured herself a large tot.
Then she walked to the window carrying the glass, and took a
long swallow as she gazed unseeingly at the landscaped gardens
outside.

She felt drained. Empty. She had known that she would discover
something extraordinary. And she'd certainly done that. But Paul
Ruders' Theory of Consciousness was not what she had expected
at all.

Jones had been through the paper in its entirety at least three
times, scrutinizing every paragraph, every clause, every conclusion.
She'd found even the language Paul Ruders had used to be difficult.
It was certainly unlike any other scientific language that she had
encountered. But she remembered the words of another American
pioneer in the field of consciousness, Dean Radin, once a doctor of
psychology at Princeton, who had told Jones that when the breakthrough did come the world would probably not have the language
in current use to explain it properly.

Radin had likened the sheer monumental leap of faith
involved in moving towards an understanding of the meaning of
consciousness to the idea of time-hopping a great brain of the
seventeenth century, such as Benjamin Franklin, bringing him to
the present, then asking him to return to his own time and explain
computer technology, even television and telephones, to the people
of his age.

'He would not have the language,' Radin said. 'He couldn't do it.'

Jones had therefore expected Paul Ruders' paper to be unlike
anything she had ever seen and to involve an enormous leap into
the unknown. In fact she'd found the language used, both in text
and in the mathematics, the equations and the very form of the
arithmetic and the phrasing, an enormously difficult challenge.

Ultimately Jones could barely believe her own assessment of Paul Ruders' Theory of Consciousness. Its implications were more than wide-ranging. They were staggering.

She drained her glass in one. She was not yet satisfied with her efforts. She had to be absolutely sure. She would go through the Ruders Theory at least one more time before leaving her office. And only then would she decide what to do next. If necessary she would stay there all night.

Ed was waiting eagerly for her when she finally arrived home a few minutes before midnight.

'I kept wanting to phone you,' he said. 'But I knew you'd be working.'

'I'm so sorry,' she replied. 'I should have called. I didn't even tell you the package had arrived.'

'I knew it must have.'

'Yes. And I've been studying it ever since. I lost all track of time. There are one or two surprises, Ed.'

'Come into the kitchen. I made some sandwiches. We can talk while you eat. I bet you haven't had anything all day, again.'

Jones nodded absently. She only realized just how hungry she was when she started to eat, and the food, renewing her energy perhaps, somehow made it easier to talk.

Ed sat quietly while she did her best to go through her day's work, and to describe what she had learned and the conclusions she'd come to. Ed wasn't a scientist, but his long-time involvement with RECAP meant that she didn't have to explain in the way she would otherwise have had to. She could take short cuts, throw equations and quite ground-breaking concepts at Ed, and be confident he would understand.

When she'd finished Ed reached across the table and brushed her hand with his fingers. The gesture touched her, even at that moment.

'What are you going to do, Sandy?' he asked.

Jones was still fumbling for a reply when the house phone rang. They both looked at the clock. It was just gone one. A little late for a social call.

The caller turned out to be someone from Sandy Jones's past, an old Oxford acquaintance, whom she knew inhabited a world and moved in circles Jones had never expected to have dealings with. She hadn't heard from him in years.

Ed looked at her enquiringly after she'd replaced the phone in its charger.

'I've been invited to lunch in London tomorrow,' she told him. 'And, trust me, it's not an invitation you turn down.'

Nonetheless, Jones did not really want to make a trip to London. She hadn't satisfactorily sorted out her thoughts on the Ruders Theory and what to do about it. She would have liked the chance to talk it all through more with Ed, who was her only confidante. But at least, she felt, as she boarded the 9.05 Exeter to Paddington express, some vital questions might be answered.

The venue chosen for lunch was a surprise. The Ivy restaurant was, by and large, an in-place for in-people, an established celebrity haunt, and Jones did not consider that her lunchtime host was an Ivy sort of man. She would rather have expected to have been offered lunch at the Savoy Grill, or perhaps even more likely, a dusty Mayfair gentleman's club.

The Honourable Jimmy Cecil, was a man whose background and calling could not have been more different from Jones's own.

Cecil was the nephew of a peer, and a descendant of one of England's oldest aristocratic families. He was also, Jones had been vaguely aware for many years, one of the most important men in Britain in terms of national security. But she did not know exactly what it was that Jimmy Cecil did, and was not even entirely sure which security force or government body Cecil was employed by. When Jimmy Cecil had left Oxford he'd talked vaguely in terms of having been seconded to the Ministry of Defence, Jones recalled. In the university's own corridors of power, which remained considerable, the word had been that he was joining MI5. His name occasionally popped up here and there, usually obliquely, in the columns of the posher papers. And he seemed to hover permanently on the fringes of Government.

Jimmy Cecil was the kind of Englishman whose nature and purpose had not changed in centuries. Even as an Oxford under-graduate, Jones remembered him as a creature apart from the rest.

Cecil was already sitting at a corner table when she arrived, and stood up at once to greet her. He was tall and elegant, with a thick head of prematurely white hair swept back from his forehead in a boyish quiff. He wore a finely tailored, three-piece, pin-striped suit with waistcoat which could only have come from Savile Row, and was of a kind which had been worn by men like him for generations – with barely a button or a cuff altered in deference to whatever might be the current fashion.

'I say, old girl, haven't you put the cat amongst the pigeons,' began Cecil, by way of greeting.

Jones muttered a vague affirmation and sat down.

Cecil poured her a glass of the claret he was already drinking, without asking what she would like, and leaned back in his chair.

'So terribly good of you to come here all the way from Devon,' he drawled. 'I really am so very grateful.'

Jones smiled wryly. As if she would have been able to resist, she thought. Indeed, under the circumstances, as if she would have dared resist.

'So, why don't you just tell me why you wanted to see me, Jimmy?' she asked, being deliberately blunt.

Cecil inclined his head graciously.

'Oh you know, one thing and another. Saw you on the news, of course. Thought maybe you could do with a helping hand. A bit of advice.'

'Really.'

'Really. Well, to tell the truth, old girl, I thought we might be able to help each other out.'

'Did you indeed?'

Cecil smiled wryly and shrugged his shoulders.

'So,' Jones continued, 'I've told the world that I believe the American government, or certainly bodies close to it, might be involved in the explosion at Princeton and all that has followed. By summoning me here today—'

'An invitation, old girl, not a summons,' Cecil interrupted, his voice little more than a murmur.

'By summoning me here today you have already indicated that I'm probably right about that. Am I?'

Cecil didn't answer the question. His face gave nothing away.

'I just wanted to give you the opportunity to share with me anything that you might wish, anything you might think I could assist with,' he remarked obliquely.

He paused and took a sip of wine, then delicately wiped his lips with his napkin.

Jones remained silent.

'The press have also, of course, shown a certain amount of interest in your recent gentleman companion. Ed MacEntee, I believe, is the name?'

'Yes, he's an old friend, that's all,' said Jones.

'Indeed. And I understand there is a suspicion in certain circles, is there not, that he might have a copy of this theory, this theory of consciousness, which seems to have caused so much palaver?'

Jones felt her stomach lurch. How did Cecil know that? She had quite deliberately given no indication of it to the press.

'People have died, Jimmy, because of Paul Ruders' work,' she said quietly. 'People have been murdered. I was nearly murdered.'

'Precisely, my dear. So it occurred to me, should there still be a copy of the Ruders Theory kicking about somewhere, and should you, by any chance have access to it, that you might need a little guidance in what the hell to do next.'

Jones's pulse was racing. It took an enormous effort for her to stay calm, or at least appear to stay calm.

'If I were to need guidance with anything, Jimmy, why on earth would I trust you? I think you know too much, for a start.'

Cecil raised an elegant eyebrow.

'Come, come,' he said.

'I'm not taken in by you, Jimmy. I know this kind of intrigue is right up your street. It's what you do. It's what you deal in.'

'Is it?'

A wicked smile played around Jimmy Cecil's lips.

'C'mon Jimmy. At least tell me this. Who was actually responsible for blowing up RECAP? Who decided to go that far? We know the FBI were involved. They wouldn't have acted alone. So, if the American government really is implicated, then just how high up is the chain of command?'

'Sandy, I'm a mere humble servant of Her Majesty. I abide by certain codes of behaviour. I couldn't possibly put myself in breach of confidence. Even if I did know the answers to your questions.'

Jones sighed. She was still immersed in a highly dangerous game, she realized, and she barely even knew the rules. Jimmy Cecil was

absolutely right. She did need help. She couldn't handle it alone.
But she knew she was going to have to lay some big cards on the
table. She had no choice. She had suspected what lay ahead, and
had actually more or less decided to do so even before arriving at
The Ivy.

She leaned forwards in her chair. Jimmy Cecil, perhaps sensing
the moment, also leaned forwards. Their heads were almost touching
when Jones spoke again. She kept her voice low.

'OK Jimmy, you're right. I actually do have a copy of Paul
Ruders' Theory of Consciousness. I'm not telling you how I got
it. It's enough that I have it. I spent the whole of yesterday studying it and now I have to decide what to do with what I have
learned. I am telling you this because, although I haven't a clue
whether I should trust you or not, I suspect you are extremely well
qualified to advise me. I don't . . .'

Jones paused, thinking not only about Paul, but about Connie,
and Marion, and Ed, and even Ed's idiot brother.

'I don't want to be responsible for the destruction of any more
lives.'

Briefly, Sandy Jones looked down at the table. She was about to
take a quite irrevocable step. She raised her eyes again and fixed
her gaze on Jimmy Cecil.

'You should know that I have a particular reason for no longer
wishing to keep the existence of the paper a secret,' she said, her
voice still low. 'A reason which I may or may not share with you
today.'

Cecil did not respond. His face was absolutely expressionless.
Instead he lifted his wine glass to his lips again, and beckoned to
a passing waiter.

'Shall we order?' he enquired.

Jones could barely conceal her exasperation.

'I'll have whatever you're having,' she said irritably.

'It'll be the steak and kidney pudding then. Though goodness
knows what sort of pud they'll come up with here, accompanied by
sun-dried tomatoes and a rocket salad I shouldn't wonder . . .'

Cecil guffawed. Jones was even more irritated.

'If that's how you feel about The Ivy, what are we doing here?'
she asked.

'You're a celebrity, old girl. Thought you'd fit in rather well.

Stick out like a sore thumb at my club, that's for sure. Particularly after your shenanigans yesterday. Don't want prying ears, do we?'

So that was it, thought Jones.

When he'd completed the ordering, Cecil turned back to Jones with the air of a man who had given the matter in hand quite enough thought and had now made his decision.

'Well, my dear, you have in your hands an extremely hot potato,' he remarked conversationally. 'I know you are aware of that, but I wonder if you have quite grasped the scale of it. In terms of who may perhaps have already taken action concerning the Ruders Theory, well, I think you should widen the list of suspects, as it were. In fact, you should probably think in terms of pretty much the whole United Nations.'

'What?'

'Well, not in name, of course. Not officially. But a number of the member countries have had a degree of involvement. Though they'd all deny it. As indeed I would totally deny that this conversation took place should you ever attempt to repeat it.'

Jones ignored that.

'I can hardly believe what you're saying,' she muttered.

'No? Well, I will tell you this, because I think you need to know a lot more before you make decisions which could have devastatingly far-reaching consequences. Britain is involved—'

'Jesus Christ,' Jones interrupted.

Cecil continued as if she had not spoken. 'So is France, and several other European countries. So is China. So is Russia. So is Israel. Do you think for one second that the Israeli government wants any kind of link of consciousness between its people and those of Palestine?'

'Well no, I suppose not. What are you getting at, Jimmy?'

'Exactly that. Governments are ultimately controlled by individuals. A state like China exists in permanent fear of its people rising up and saying we aren't going to take this anymore. Now, the thing about a link of consciousness is that it is more or less impossible to combat. It doesn't rely on groups of people physically uniting, on being prepared to fight, or actively taking part in terrorism or a conventional revolution. It is quite simply a union of minds. Take one individual thinking a certain way and multiply by, say, 100 million. That is a force no government in the world could cope with.'

'I know that,' said Jones. 'It's one of Connie Pike's sermons, actually. But I didn't think the governments of the world were taking the idea of global consciousness so seriously yet. And certainly not on that scale. I had more in mind that a rogue US Government department was behind the RECAP explosion, and what has followed.'

'My dear Sandy, here in the UK, probably the one thing that all the prime ministers I've personally known, from Tony to Boris, have agreed on is that the power of global consciousness could ultimately be the biggest threat there has ever been to national government as we know it. Think Berlin. The Wall fell in a week. You, of all people, must have asked yourself how that could possibly have happened? After all those years of hardcore communist rule. It was a straightforward example of the power of linked consciousness.'

'Of course,' said Sandy. 'I hadn't thought of it like that. There was no revolutionary army, no Che Guevara. And the worldwide web, with its ability to bring people together, had barely begun. So it's already happened, without most people noticing. I'm not sure even Paul and Connie took their thought process that far. But you are saying that our political leaders did?'

'Indeed. It was regarded as just one of those things, though. Because we have never known how it happened. Not until now, perhaps, and the Ruders Theory. One can only imagine the situation that would arise if we fully understood what consciousness was and, even, heaven forbid, if we understood how to control human consciousness on a global scale. That's the rub, old girl. Control!'

Jones was stunned. She had heard this kind of stuff from Connie and Paul, but Jimmy Cecil was a man at the heart of the UK government.

'You have to realize that we are at a very crucial stage in time,' Cecil continued. 'We have the web now, which, as you implied, gives us a kind of access to global consciousness, in that it provides a regular and constant update on what is happening everywhere. Because of the web alone, governments cannot lie as easily as they once did – which is particularly relevant in countries without even the semblance of a free press. We can be instantly made aware not just of what is happening around the corner, but also on the other side of the world. Now that kind of knowledge can dramatically change the way we behave. Very unusual effects can be achieved by mutual coherence, very fast social and physical change. Thoughts can be swiftly catalysed. They can explode.'

The steak and kidney puddings arrived, together with a selection of perfectly appropriate vegetables. Jones willed the waiter to serve quickly.

Before recent events in America, Jones had always taken much of what Connie had had to say with a large pinch of salt. Connie, by the very nature of what she did, was something of a fantasist. Jimmy Cecil was a different proposition. An international mover and shaker who lived and breathed politics. And Cecil seemed to have explored the possible practical repercussions of the solving of the mystery of consciousness far more extensively than Jones had ever done. Prior to the last few days.

'Do you remember the reason for the 1987 stock market crash?' Jimmy Cecil continued. 'It marked the beginning of computer trading, the mechanics of which turned the economic world on its head. The feedback system was suddenly so much faster. The system, as it was, just could not cope with the volume of deals.'

Cecil placed a large chunk of pud in his mouth and after chewing for a few seconds looked up at Jones in some surprise.

'Delicious,' he murmured. 'Every bit as good as my club's.'

'You were saying, Jimmy,' Jones prompted impatiently.

'Ah yes. Well, it's obvious, isn't it? You're a scientist. You believe the brain is a kind of computer, don't you? A biological computer.'

'Well, up to a point.'

'All right. Up to a point. Well, up to a point, then, imagine any kind of universal method of controlling that biological computer. Global consciousness could be the next great weapon. It leaves nuclear power standing—'

'Connie has always said that.'

'Yes,' Cecil continued. 'But did it occur to either you or her that the governments of the world were also thinking that way?'

'Not on the scale you are suggesting,' said Jones. 'RECAP's problem was always that people with power were sceptical of its work. It's a quantum leap to think in terms of governments actually accepting, fearing even, the power of consciousness.'

'Well, they are. When RECAP was on its own, tucked away in

an obscure corner of Princeton, it's probably true that nobody on the outside gave it much thought. Certainly there was no anxiety about it, nor about the handful of similar institutions scattered around the place. The Global Consciousness Project changed all that. When the RECAP Random Event Generator began to spawn many more of the things, and when, more revolutionary still, they linked them together, via the internet, that was different. Governmental departments across the globe have monitored this project – you must know that, what cloistered academic world do you live in, Sandy? – and have been left in no doubt that something monumental was being illustrated by these REG experiments. It's not just America that has been keeping a close watch on the GCP for decades. In the simplest of terms it's mind over matter, isn't it, Sandy? And the results are fact. Only the questions "how" and "why" have remained unanswered. The possibility that Professor Ruders may have finally answered those two questions is of immense international concern.

'So, you can be assured that whatever course of action has been taken so far regarding the Ruders Theory was' – Cecil broke off and cleared his throat loudly – 'was not taken by the American government alone.'

Jones took a deep breath and let it out slowly.

'It really is even bigger than I'd thought,' she muttered.

'Probably. And you should know that I am only telling you any of this, Sandy, because you have confided in me that you have in your possession a copy of Paul Ruders' theory. You do realize the enormous responsibility of that, and the position that puts you in, don't you?'

'Well, I think I do, yes. I'm well aware that it puts me in further danger, or it would if it came to the attention of the wrong people, anyway. And I therefore certainly realize the risk I have taken in confiding in you today.'

'A calculated risk, I hope. But you really ought to think very carefully about what you should do next, my dear. If we come to fully understand the nature of consciousness, to utilize it in the ways that I have described, then governments worldwide will fall. The established order of things will be destroyed. Life as we know it will be changed beyond recognition. There would be no doubt about that . . .'

'Yes, well, that might not be such a bad thing.'

'If you'll forgive me, those are the words of an idealistic child, Sandy. Whatever might happen eventually, you would in the short term almost certainly be talking about anarchy. Are you an anarchist, as well as an idealist?'

'Of course not.'

'No. Of course not. You suddenly have immense and probably rather unenviable power in your hands, Sandy. The power of whether or not to change the world irrevocably.'

Cecil poured some more claret into Jones's glass.

'Personally I prefer the devil I know. Which is why I do the job that I do . . .'

'And what job is that exactly?' Jones heard himself ask, albeit with little hope of a proper reply.

'Oh, this and that, you know,' murmured her companion, suddenly returning his entire attention to the remains of his steak and kidney pudding.

'I am slightly disturbed by the extent to which you may be personally involved, Jimmy.'

'Really, my dear? You surprise me.'

Cecil helped himself to a second helping of mashed potato. He obviously did not intend to elucidate any further.

Jones put down her knife and fork, picked up her glass of claret and emptied it in one swallow. She was aware of Jimmy Cecil wincing. No doubt the claret was special. Jones hadn't noticed. She had other things on his mind.

'In spite of that, or maybe because of that, I am going to confide in you further,' Jones continued. 'There is something else. Something our government, America and all the other governments apparently so preoccupied with the power of human consciousness should probably know. And, as I was well aware from the moment you called to invite me to lunch, Jimmy, I have little doubt that you are the man to pass on the message.'

Jimmy Cecil speared a particularly succulent looking piece of kidney on his fork and paused with it still a few inches from his mouth.

'I'm all ears, old girl,' he said.

It was almost a couple of hours later before Cecil set off to walk back over Waterloo Bridge to his South Bank base. He hoped the fresh air would help him think.

His American visitor was waiting in his office, as he had expected. He had met Marmaduke Johnson the Second several times before, of course, and trans-Atlantic telephone calls between the two men were not unusual. Indeed, they had become rather frequent over the last few days. Johnson was, after all, the nearest thing there was, for Jimmy Cecil, to an opposite number across the pond. Nonetheless Johnson almost always had the same effect on the Englishman. There was something about Marmaduke Johnson that made the muscles at the back of Jimmy Cecil's neck lock solid, and sent an alert signal to every nerve end in his body.

'How ya doing, Jimbo,' said Johnson, by way of greeting, at the same time grasping Cecil's right hand in a hearty handshake.

Cecil forced a smile of welcome, which he feared was rather more of a grimace.

The tall American was wearing an unnecessarily loud checked suit, Jimmy Cecil thought. But it fitted in well with his good-old-boy personae, or at least the personae he chose to present to the world.

'I'm doing fine, Duke,' responded Cecil, feeling the usual tweak of embarrassment he always felt when addressing the American by the abbreviation he had more or less been ordered to use from the beginning.

Johnson had coat-hanger shoulders, a paunch, no hair, and very white teeth which seemed both too big and too numerous for his mouth. His eyes were small, set rather too far apart for comfort, and were not entirely synchronized. Instead each appeared to be looking in a marginally different direction. And as he came closer, Cecil was reminded again of how difficult it was to focus on both Duke Johnson's eyes at once.

'So what tidings do you bring from the great doctor?'

Johnson's accent was so Deep South it was almost comic book. Jimmy Cecil had always suspected that it could not possibly be genuine. The apparently obligatory black cheroot dangled precariously from the American's lips. A puff of foul-smelling smoke hit Cecil straight in the face. He recoiled. But he knew better than to even attempt to remind Marmaduke Johnson of his building's no smoking rule.

One of Johnson's disconcertingly pale blue eyes was staring intently at Cecil through the unsavoury grey cloud he had created.

The other appeared to be studying the closed door of the Englishman's private bathroom.

Jimmy Cecil lowered himself stiffly onto the chair at his desk and turned slightly away from the American, so that he did not have to deal with the distraction of attempting eye contact.

'I think we may need to put a fairly substantial damage limitation operation into effect, Duke old boy,' he said.

The aircraft had flown across the Atlantic from New York and was about to touch down in South Africa, at Johannesburg. A passenger wearing khaki fatigues with a strongly military flavour and spanking new, almost orange, Timberland boots peered through the window. The cloud was low, and he could see very little. He wondered anxiously what might await him below.

Mikey MacEntee was no longer the Man in Black, as Jones had dubbed him at Princeton police station. That phase had ended. The dark suit, white shirt, and black tie had been consigned to the back of his wardrobe. Only the shades remained in place. Mikey had been told that he was going undercover in Africa. He had therefore done his best to dress in what he considered to be an appropriate manner. As he always did in his perennially futile efforts to fit in. The wide-brimmed bush hat, which he held on his lap, completed his new outfit. This was his Out of Africa look. Or so he thought.

One or two other passengers on the flight glanced at him curiously. Mikey didn't notice.

He wasn't sure what he was going to be asked to do once he arrived in Johannesburg, but he knew that his country was involved in all kinds of undercover activity throughout Africa. Much of it connected with international terrorism. And he realized this new job must be important. He had been told he should travel immediately.

Mikey had been taken by surprise. The FBI ran around fifty attaché offices at US embassies and consulates throughout the world, and FBI operatives were not infrequently dispatched overseas to investigate almost anything that might adversely concern America, but he had never expected to be chosen for such an assignment. The overseas appointments were coveted among agents. To be dispatched on a mission abroad such as this surely indicated that he had finally been accepted as a front-line Fed. And Mikey wasn't used to being accepted by anyone, which is why he always worked so hard at trying to be so.

He had been mightily relieved by the way Mr Johnson had reacted after he'd got shot by that lady cop. Mr Johnson had arranged everything. The damage to Mikey's leg had turned out to be not nearly as bad as he'd feared – the bullet had narrowly missed his thigh bone causing only a nasty flesh wound – and Mr Johnson had arranged for medical treatment straight away, just as Mikey had hoped.

Mikey had expected to be in deep trouble after his part in an operation which had gone so pear-shaped. But Mr Johnson had appeared to be really quite sympathetic.

Mikey had been eating a Chinese – garlic prawns, mixed vegetables with garlic, and fried noodles with garlic – while watching a television news report of Sandy Jones's revelations, when he'd received the call despatching him to Africa.

He'd always boasted within the Bureau about his access to information concerning RECAP, and grossly exaggerated his closeness to the project. It had been purely by chance, really, that he'd found out about the Ruders Theory of Consciousness. He'd put a bug on his brother's phone some months previously, a new device he'd acquired online, more to check it out than anything else. Mikey had never been able to resist experimenting with surveillance gadgets. It was a habit.

But then he'd overheard a conversation between Ed and Professor Ruders which had clearly indicated the existence of an effective theory of consciousness. Mikey had not been greatly excited by this himself, after all he believed that more or less everything about RECAP was nonsense. However he knew how interested his superiors were in the project, even though that had always rather surprised him, and saw an opportunity to increase his standing at the Bureau. So he reported back at once, which led his Agent in Charge to put him in touch with Mr Johnson.

Mikey still didn't know exactly who or what Mr Johnson was, but he knew the man was mighty powerful, that was for sure. And from the moment he'd become aware of the plan to blow up the RECAP lab, Mikey had deeply regretted his rashness, his compulsion to show off and play the big shot. Secretly, because he didn't dare let Mr Johnson know, he had been horrified by such a drastic and murderous turn of events. Particularly as his brother was involved. He'd never expected anything like it.

Mikey was by then in so deep, however, that he could do nothing except continue to play the part he'd created for himself. But the intrigue concerning Connie Pike's survival and the consequent second, and somewhat inept, attempt on her life, resulting in Marion being so grievously injured, had turned him into a complete nervous wreck.

Even as he sat on that aircraft over Johannesburg, he was only just beginning to fully appreciate the scale of what he had so artlessly embroiled himself in. It hadn't occurred to Mikey that anything concerning RECAP, that slightly off-the-wall fringe area of scientific research that Ed and his dotty friends had been rabbiting on to him about since his teenage days, could really be of national importance. Let alone of international importance.

Mikey stretched his injured left leg. It ached constantly and still caused him to walk with a limp, but he realized he'd had a lucky escape from much worse. And he hoped that might be an omen.

All in all, Mikey was glad to have been despatched out of the country, somewhere well away from the furore over the RECAP affair which seemed to have taken hold throughout the United States, and indeed most of the world. He hoped that South Africa might prove to be a backwater in that regard. But on the other hand he realized that this international commotion meant that, almost certainly, any danger his brother may have been in because of him no longer existed. And that was a great relief to Mikey MacEntee.

Mikey didn't realize that his superiors had sent him to South Africa simply because they now regarded him as something of an embarrassment. Why would he? After all, Mr Johnson had been almost kind to him.

He just wished he knew what was in store for him there . . .

At about the same time another aircraft was preparing to land in Honolulu, Hawaii. The Enforcer sat next to the Apprentice in business class. Just like Mikey, they'd been despatched out of New York to do a job, but they had yet to be informed exactly what the job would be.

The Enforcer assumed that there was someone on the tropical island who needed watching and then, perhaps, dealing with, in the way that the Enforcer and his Apprentice specialized in. Someone who was a danger to America.

The Enforcer had no time for anyone who might remotely be a danger to America, and he didn't care at all if the occasional mistake meant that the innocent suffered.

The Enforcer believed in the greater good. He believed in George Washington, Abraham Lincoln and the Statue of Liberty, turkey at Thanksgiving, home-made apple pie, Coca Cola and footballs that weren't round. And Donald Trump.

He also believed in the Apprentice.

They had not made a success of their last job. There could be little dispute about that. They had allowed Connie Pike to escape the Princeton explosion they had arranged, then failed in a second attempt to assassinate her, and instead maimed another woman. All the same, they remained indispensable, surely. Nobody else could, or would, do what they did. The Enforcer was confident of that. In any case, he and the Apprentice knew where far too many bodies were buried. It had been suggested to the Enforcer that, if they wished, they could stay a little while longer in Hawaii than might be strictly necessary. Indeed it had been indicated that it might be a good thing for the pair of them to be away from New York for a bit.

The Enforcer didn't mind that at all. He considered Hawaii to be the most pleasant of places. And neither could he imagine a better companion. He turned towards the younger man.

Then he reached out, took the Apprentice's right hand in his left and squeezed.

The Apprentice blushed.

PART SIX

Truth is incontrovertible. Malice may attack it and ignorance may deride it, but, in the end, there it is.

Winston Churchill

PART SIX

TWENTY

A few days later Sandy Jones flew back to America with Ed, who now knew everything she did. Not only everything about the Ruders Theory, but everything about her meeting with Jimmy Cecil. She could think of no better confidante.

Ed was going home. He needed to return to his teaching job.

'Before it's not there anymore,' he told her.

Jones was travelling with him partly, although she hadn't quite admitted it to herself yet, because she simply wanted to delay their parting, and partly because she needed to see Connie. Marion Jessop's condition had improved enough for her to be released from hospital, and Connie was caring for her at her Princeton home.

Jones and Ed arrived in Princeton late in the afternoon on a blustery Autumn day. They took a taxi to Ed's apartment first. There was a postcard lying on the doormat. From Mikey. It had a South African postmark, and bore a picture of an elephant.

Ed was momentarily elated. He'd received no reply to a series of emails, and had continued to worry about his wayward brother.

'What does he say?' Jones asked.

'"Over here on special assignment. Hope you're well and everything sorted. See you soon. Ciao, Mikey",' Ed read. 'Well that doesn't tell us much, does it?'

'It tells us he's safe,' Jones commented.

'I don't even know if he deserves to be safe. Not after what he did.'

'We're not really sure what he did do.'

'I think we have a fair idea, Sandy.'

'Maybe. But he would only have been a very small cog in the wheel.'

'There's not even any sort of an apology.'

'Well, I suppose that would be an admission of guilt.'

'Umm. I didn't know Feds went abroad on assignments.'

'Neither did I. But, hey, maybe your mad brother was only pretending to be a Fed. Maybe he's really a spook.'

Ed chuckled. Jones was becoming increasingly fond of him. But she didn't dare admit just how fond. Not yet. And certainly not to him. In any case, she was on a mission.

'I'm going to go see Connie straight away,' she said. 'Are you sure you won't come with me?'

'I won't. I need to get Jasper. Anyway, I don't think I'd know what to say . . .'

'It's OK,' said Jones.

'Is it?' Ed enquired rhetorically.

It took Jones about twenty minutes to walk from Ed's apartment to the narrow, white-terraced house, in one of the university town's leafiest streets, which Connie had inherited from her mother.

She opened the front door swiftly. Her hair seemed bigger and redder than ever. She was wearing a lime green top and bright orange trousers with a rip in one knee. In spite of all that had happened, some things didn't change.

'My God, it's good to see you, Sandy Jones. Our saviour!'

She led Jones straight up the stairs to a light airy bedroom where Marion lay propped up in a big lace-covered bed, a cradle over one leg.

'I'm getting to be a dab hand with bedpans.' said Connie cheerfully.

Connie seemed almost unnaturally cheerful. Jones glanced across at Marion. The pain she was suffering was clear in her face, but she greeted Jones with a warm smile.

'How are you doing, Marion?' Jones asked gently.

'Not so badly.'

'I'm glad.'

'She's going to be just fine,' interjected Connie, again with excessive cheeriness, Jones thought. 'We can't wait to get her a new leg, can we, Marion, sweetheart?'

Marion said nothing. She just smiled again. Rather more wanly, Jones thought.

'Anyway, you'd never guess what's gone on here since you hit the newsstands, Sandy,' Connie continued, beaming at Jones. 'They're going to rebuild the RECAP lab. Only it'll be even better than before. New equipment, new everything, and maybe even proper staff again. Certainly a proper budget.'

She glanced fondly towards Marion. 'Thomas is fixing it all. Marion's son, the Dean of Princeton, and now the other saviour of RECAP. After you, Sandy, of course.'

She turned to face Jones.

'Isn't it just great? Thomas says it's the least he can do. He's going to use some foundation money or something. I don't know. Anything to do with finances is a mystery to me, but Thomas says he's pretty sure he can carry the university's governing bodies with him.'

She paused, still beaming at Jones, who made no reply.

'It's marvellous, isn't it?' Connie continued, apparently unaware of, or simply untroubled by, Jones's silence. 'And you won't believe the other marvellous thing. Thomas has actually known about Marion and me for a long time, since even before his father died, we think, though he's never said that, and he's quite happy about it. But he says he's grateful to us for not going public, and grateful to you too, Sandy, for being discreet about our relationship when you revealed what you did to the press.'

Jones again said nothing. Connie carried on regardless.

'And Dom and Gaynor are coming for the weekend. We want to thank them properly for everything.'

Jones spoke then, addressing Connie directly for the first time, quite curtly, with a harsh inflection in her voice.

'Yes, and you'll certainly have a lot to tell them.'

'What?' Connie sounded puzzled, uncertain, as indeed had been Jones's intention.

Jones turned away and walked to the window. Only when she had her back to the other two women did she start to speak again. She couldn't look at Connie. She just couldn't.

'I have a copy of Paul's Theory of Consciousness,' she said quietly.

There was a silence in the room, broken eventually by Marion.

'Why, that's wonderful. Isn't it, Connie? Isn't it?'

Connie said nothing.

'I've studied it thoroughly,' Jones continued. 'I now have a pretty damned good understanding of it.'

Connie still didn't speak. Jones took a deep breath and swung around to face her. Connie had sat down on the chair by the bed and was staring at Jones. Her green eyes wide open.

'And you know what that means, Connie, don't you?'

Connie shrugged, and still did not speak.

'It means I know that Paul's theory makes no sense at all. It's fake. He was no closer to solving the mystery of consciousness than I am! His paper is garbage. A load of drivel. Crap!'

Connie leaned forwards in her chair, her eyes blazing.

'And what exactly makes you so goddamned sure of that, Dr effin' Jones. You're just a TV scientist. You're the fake. Paul was the leader in his field. The number one man. You abandoned the study of consciousness over twenty years ago.'

Jones sighed. 'No Connie. You can't bluff and bluster your way out of this one. I have quite sufficient knowledge. I worked long enough with you both. And, as you've always told me yourself, I have the gift, don't I? No, Connie, no. There is no effective theory of consciousness. Just a garbled inconsequential jumble of—'

'Maybe you've lost the gift, Sandy,' Connie interjected. 'You've certainly forgotten Radin's rule. The mystery of consciousness could only ever be explained in new language.'

'This wasn't language at all. I went over and over it. Paul's theory is rubbish. And you know that. You must have known that all along.'

'Don't be absurd, Sandy.'

Jones laughed grimly. Short and sharp.

'You never give up, do you Connie Pike? You could always talk the hind leg off a donkey. It won't wash any more. You knew the theory was rubbish, and you used that, you played games with it for your own ends. But then the whole thing spiralled out of control, didn't it? Horrendously out of control. And you hadn't bargained for that.'

'I don't know what you're talking about, Sandy.'

'Oh yes, you do.'

Connie stood up abruptly. 'Well, if we really must have this ridiculous conversation, shall we continue it downstairs? I don't want Marion upset.'

'No.' Marion's voice was surprisingly strong. She hauled herself further up onto the pillows. 'No. Stay here. Both of you. Please Sandy, I want to hear this.'

Jones turned to her.

'Oh my God,' she said. 'You don't know anything do you, Marion?

You've even lost a leg because of this fucking mess, and she still hasn't told you, has she?'

'Told me what?' Marion was sitting quite upright now, her eyes firmly focused on her partner. 'What haven't you told me, Connie?'

Connie sat down again.

'I don't know. I have no idea. Sandy seems to have all the answers. Let her tell us both. If she must.'

Jones looked at her. The woman had always had guts. She was still fighting to save the situation. But this time that was impossible. Even for Connie Pike.

'All right,' she said. 'I'll be as brief as I can and then you can ask me any questions you like, Marion. You deserve to know everything. Paul Ruders was a sick man. A very sick man. He had Alzheimer's Disease and his mind was barely functioning at all by the end. I know this because a rather well-connected friend of mine has been doing some investigating. He gained access to Paul's medical records. Apparently the problems began even before Gilda died. But, like many victims of this bloody awful disease, Paul refused to accept that his mind was affected in any way. He thought, or maybe he just kidded himself, who knows with Alzheimer's, that his work was as valid, as considered, and as properly thought-out as ever. His communication skills were so highly developed that he covered up amazingly well, certainly during relatively short periods of time spent with people. You, Connie, were the only person who spent a lot of time with him. Even Ed saw very little of Paul latterly. He told me that. You covered for Paul, Connie. But his mind was in bits. He was convinced that he had solved the mystery of consciousness, and, of course, he shared his thoughts, and his work, such as it was, with you. He always did. And he shared his allegedly ground-breaking theory with you too.

'You, of course, were well aware the work was worthless. But you decided to use it. RECAP was indeed under threat, more than ever before, in spite of the success of the Global Consciousness Project worldwide. My friend also found out that you lost your last major grant over a year ago. You saw a way to use Paul's deluded attempt at a theory of consciousness for your own ends. You thought that if the American government were convinced of the existence and the merit of his theory, RECAP would not only be saved, but its existence would be guaranteed. Certainly for your lifetime.'

Jones paused.

'I don't understand,' said Marion, and her voice sounded very weak.

'Connie knew about Ed's brother, Michael, or Mikey MacEntee, being in the FBI,' continued Jones. 'She was also aware, as we all were, that he wasn't the brightest kid on the block. In fact, God only knows how he got into the Feds. Anyway, Connie decided to exploit him, too. She used Mikey to draw attention to Paul's alleged theory, a theory that she knew would attract enormous interest at the highest level—'

'Oh my God,' Marion interrupted.

Jones moved closer to the bed.

'Yes, Marion. It wasn't Ed, either knowingly or unknowingly, who was feeding his crazy brother information about RECAP. It was Connie. And Mikey, of course, jumped at the opportunity of being able to pass on exclusive, potentially revolutionary, information to his superiors, in order to acquire some self-importance. He always wanted desperately to be at the centre of things.

'But Connie and Mikey were both right out of their depth. Yes, Connie had always talked about the suspicion in which people in high places held RECAP and its work. But she was also quite sure that the American government would not be able to resist the possibility of holding the secret of consciousness in its sticky paws – out of fear as much as anything. Fear of its ultimate power would also make it highly unlikely that the government would attempt to put the theory into use, and if they did, well it was actually rubbish, so it didn't matter anyway.

'It didn't occur to Connie that this fear of the power of global consciousness was so extreme that there were those in government circles who would be prepared to violently destroy not only RECAP and the Global Consciousness Project but also the people who ran them. She believed that by feeding this pack of nonsense to those in power, she would safeguard RECAP's future. Indeed I suspect that was what she asked for in return for keeping silent about the alleged theory for the good of America – a guaranteed future for RECAP, albeit under the tacit control of the US government. And as ever, that was all Connie really cared about.'

Jones glanced towards Connie. Her face was expressionless. Then she heard a little gulp from the bed.

'Oh shit, I'm so sorry, Marion,' said Jones.

'No, go on, please.'

'Right. Well, as we've all said many times, Paul's reputation was such that once it was known that he believed he'd solved this extraordinary mystery, then most outsiders would assume he had indeed done so. His status in the field would ensure—'

'Oh come on, Sandy,' Connie interrupted. 'You don't really think the American government, or any of its agencies, would take the steps they did, steps that led to the sanctioning of murder, without at least being able to authenticate Paul's paper, do you?'

'No I don't. I think you supplied Mikey with a copy of Paul's flawed theory well before the night of the break-in when the bomb was planted in the lab. I think you copied the paper onto a USB and gave it to Mikey. You knew that nobody except a real expert in the field – and there aren't many of those – would be able to make head or tail of it, even if it were genuine. And I have to admit, the paper did look the part. It looked like a genuine and very advanced scientific document, as, of course, it would, coming from Paul, even with a messed-up brain. You knew exactly what would happen after you supplied Mikey with that paper. His bosses came to you to authenticate it. Who else would they go to?

'You supplied it and then you authenticated it, Connie. Brilliantly simple. A full circle. But you totally underestimated the lengths the bastards would go to in order to keep the secret of consciousness just that, didn't you?'

Connie said nothing. Marion was staring at her.

'It's true, Connie, isn't it,' she said.

It was a statement not a question.

Suddenly Connie's face crumpled. She began to cry.

'I'm so sorry,' she said. 'So sorry. It's been awful keeping what I did a secret. After the explosion, well, I knew it was all my fault. Everything had gone horrendously wrong. I just wished I'd died too, along with Paul.'

Jones shrugged.

'You did a bloody good job of carrying on and pulling even more wool over all our eyes,' she said. 'You treated RECAP like a game, Connie, but you had no idea who you were playing it with.'

'I couldn't foresee that they were going to blow up the lab. I didn't know that was going to happen.'

'Are you sure?' Jones rapped the words out.

'What do you mean, am I sure?'

'Well, it was quite convenient wasn't it, to say the least, that you were outside the lab having a smoke when the place was destroyed. Am I supposed to believe that was just a happy coincidence?'

'Sandy, what are you saying? Of course it was a coincidence. Do you think I would ever have done what I did, if I'd thought for one second Paul might be killed? They were after me too. I had an extraordinarily lucky escape, that's all. It never occurred to me that Mikey's people would go that far.'

Jones actually did believe her. Connie had, after all, in her twisted way, been trying to protect RECAP, and maybe Paul as well. But Jones was angry.

'Really?' she queried edgily.

'I can't see into the future, Sandy.'

'But you don't mind manipulating it a bit, eh?'

'Sandy, when I phoned you, before the explosion, I was going to tell you everything. Come clean. Things were happening, like I said. I was beginning to get scared. I realized it was all getting out of control. And the only person I could think of who might be able to sort it out was you. Because of your influence, because of your contacts, because of your knowledge. But it was all too late. I never did get to tell you . . .'

Her voice tailed off. Neither of the other two said anything. After a while Connie continued to speak.

'Anyway, even though I'd been the mole, the deep throat, if you like, I realized, of course, when the bomb went off that I had been a target too, and that my life would still be in danger. I knew too much. So I went into hiding with Marion, as you both know. And I made myself just think about RECAP. I decided it was my mission to see that RECAP was reborn, that the work would continue, and that I survived to make sure of that.'

She paused again, leaning forwards in her chair towards the bed.

'I'm so sorry, Marion. I should have told you. At first I just didn't want to admit what I'd done. I'd got it all so wrong. And then, after you were mown down by the truck, well, I just couldn't bring myself to tell you. You'd been so badly injured, and that was my fault too.'

Connie reached for Marion. Marion turned away. Connie turned back to Jones. She'd stopped crying.

'What will happen now?' she asked.

'Nothing much, probably,' responded Jones. 'It's over, isn't it? You won't be brought to book for what you've done, Connie. The whole thing is too complex, and involves too many people in high places. You were certainly telling the truth about a cover up. That's still going on, I can assure you. No, you could be regarded as having got away with it. In spite of all the death and suffering you caused. Apart from just two points.

'The first is that if RECAP is ever relaunched, I, and the people I know, will make absolutely sure you never have anything to do with it again. And do not think for one moment that I can't do that.

'The second is that you have to live with what you've done, and with the woman you love knowing what you have been responsible for, including the loss of her leg.'

'I didn't drive that truck, Sandy, and I would rather it had been me beneath it than Marion,' said Connie, her voice little more than a whisper.

'You are every bit as guilty as those who did drive that truck, Connie. Possibly more so. It was you who began it all.'

Jones paused. Connie said nothing more.

'You know what,' Jones continued, 'I used to think you were the most unselfish person in the world, Connie. Now I think you might be the most selfish. You have irretrievably harmed the reputation of the very area of science which has always meant so much to you. One way and another the truth about Paul's paper will get out, like these things do, which will be not only a blow to the project but also a tragic slur on the man. Because that man was no longer there when he wrote his flawed paper.'

Connie just stared at Jones, her facial expression undiscernible now.

'Remember the question you used to ask all the time? Can six men in a room change the world?'

Connie nodded.

'Yes, and they're the only ones who can,' she murmured.

'But not if they lie, Connie. Not if they damned well lie.'

Jones didn't want to be in the same place as Connie Pike any more. She hadn't fully realized quite how much Connie had always meant to her. Suddenly it all seemed so meaningless. She headed for the door, turning to look back one last time.

Connie had moved closer to the bed, and was again reaching out towards Marion. Once more Marion pulled away.

Outside Jones half ran down the street. She was in a hurry to get away from Connie. She was also in a hurry to get back to Ed. Ed who knew what she knew. Ed who understood.

He met her at the door, Jasper jumping about at his feet. He must have been watching the street, waiting for her to return. His face was a picture of concern. Jones took one look at him and burst into tears.

She had been totally in control until she'd confronted Connie. She and Ed had been over everything again and again. It had been such a shock for both of them to discover what Connie Pike had done. But Jones had thought they'd each already more or less come to terms with it.

Coming face to face with Connie like that under such horrible twisted circumstances, the woman she had so admired for so long, had been much more traumatic than Jones had expected. She couldn't get over Connie's duplicity. Connie had put almost everyone she was in contact with at risk, including her own partner. Even after the RECAP explosion and Paul's death she'd duped Jones into becoming involved in order to save her own skin – and to protect the future of RECAP, of course.

Jones could still hardly believe it.

Ed took her by the hand and led her into the kitchen, gesturing for her to take a seat at the little table. He made tea, and waited patiently until Jones was calm enough to give an account of her harrowing meeting with the two women.

'You've been very brave, I just couldn't face it,' Ed said, when Jones had finished. 'At least Connie knows now that she hasn't got away with it after all. Not totally, anyway.'

He asked if Jones would like a proper drink. Jones said she would.

'I've got some bourbon somewhere,' said Ed.

He wandered off and started opening and shutting cupboard doors.

The television in one corner of the kitchen was switched on. Jones stared at it out of habit. A news bulletin washed over her. There was a curious item about an FBI agent who had been found dead in bed in Hawaii with his younger male lover, also a Fed. Apparently they'd both been strangled. There seemed to be a suggestion that they may have succeeded in strangling each other. Hawaii State Police reported that they suspected some kind of gay sex ritual.

Jones barely registered that item or any other. She'd done what she'd come to do. She'd needed to confront Connie, painful though that had been. And, Jones had to admit, not entirely satisfactory, either.

There'd been a look in Connie's eye when Jones told her what she had learned and what she thought of her. And it had been a look Jones had not quite been able to fathom. She couldn't help think that there still might be something more, another secret that Connie was keeping.

Jones gave herself a mental shaking. It was over. Really over. She must stop dealing with fantasy and get on with her life. A life she was beginning to hope Ed might one day become part of again. Although she knew that was going to take time.

She also knew that scientific research into the mystery of consciousness would continue all over the world. Without Paul. And without Connie.

TWENTY-ONE

A couple of weeks later in his South Bank office, on the top floor of a very tall building, Jimmy Cecil sat with his chair fully reclined and his feet on his desk. He was reading a confidential report, fresh from Washington, on the RECAP affair.

By and large, the American cousins had glossed over it all quite effectively, he thought. For once. It could have been far more embarrassing, not just for the cousins, but for the UK and a number of the other countries, all UN affiliated, who had been privy to the existence of the Ruders Theory. In America the relevant government departments and the various security forces involved continued to publicly insist that the Princeton explosion had been caused by animal rights protesters, and there was no evidence to the contrary. Or no evidence that anyone was prepared to put forward, at any rate.

All copies of the flawed theory had now allegedly been destroyed. As indeed it had been planned to destroy the theory had it been genuine. Although Cecil had always feared that in reality that would never have happened. At least one copy would have survived in the dusty archives of some secret place somewhere, and ultimately, eventually, would have surfaced. Then the whole kerfuffle would have begun again.

Cecil walked to the window and looked out at the sweeping view it presented of the River Thames, iron grey and threatening on a dull winter's day, snaking along past Westminster, under Waterloo and Blackfriars Bridge, towards St Paul's and beyond.

For a while he stood there mulling things over. The untimely deaths of the Enforcer and his Apprentice had been regrettable. It was also regrettable, if perhaps inevitable, that they'd already been identified as FBI agents. But that had caused only a minor scandal compared with the uproar which would have occurred if certain of their recent activities had ever become public knowledge.

Duke Johnson wasn't saying exactly what fate may or may not have befallen that loose cannon Mikey MacEntee. Johnson, of course, was not a man given to imparting any more information than he had to. It went against his nature. But it seemed that, at the very least, the young man was safely out of the way. And Jimmy Cecil considered it highly unlikely that the MacEntee connection would cause any further problems. Johnson had dealt with the matter rather skilfully, he thought. Any more definite solution concerning the brother of the former man in Sandy Jones's life – or possibly not former any more, Cecil reckoned – may have stirred her up again, which nobody wanted. She had proven to be quite a formidable adversary. For an academic.

A fire boat, on exercise, swept past the riverside building, heading downstream at speed, all its hoses pumping foaming funnels of river water into great arcs which splashed spectacularly back into the Thames. Cecil thought it quite majestic. He watched idly for a few seconds, even though his mind was far away.

All in all, he reflected, the damage limitation exercise had been fairly successfully completed.

It had, of course, been Johnson who had executed the original plan, the bombing of RECAP and all that followed. But Johnson had been operating not only with the off-the-record authority of those in much higher places in America, but also with the tacit approval of the United Nations states involved – something all of them would deny, naturally. Just as Cecil had explained to Sandy Jones.

It was unfortunate that the entire exercise had subsequently proved to have been unnecessary. Jimmy Cecil disapproved of avoidable violence, needless loss of life. But these things happened. And he was pleased that it had ultimately been possible to allow Sandy Jones, a woman he'd always rather liked and admired, to come to no harm. Indeed, not so much possible as obligatory, once the celebrity boffin had so cleverly thrown herself and the whole messed-up operation into the public arena.

It had been a close call though, far closer for both Sandy Jones and Ed MacEntee than either of them would ever know.

Cecil had been left with little choice but to support Marmaduke Johnson when Jones and MacEntee had gone on the run. And he'd then been more or less forced to follow through when the pair of them had managed to get themselves back to the UK – even though they had displayed a level of initiative with which Cecil had been secretly rather impressed.

Individuals were always dispensable. They had to be in the circles Jimmy Cecil moved in. Even individuals you liked and respected. Nonetheless, he had been relieved to have been able to so dramatically rescind, at the eleventh hour, the order to eliminate Jones and MacEntee.

It was, of course, a much greater relief to Cecil that there was actually no effective Theory of Consciousness in existence, and, it seemed, never had been. Neither RECAP, nor any other of the world's scientists, had yet managed to solve humanity's greatest mystery after all.

As far as Cecil was concerned that was good news. The status quo would continue. The people of the world were not going to rise as one against their governments, not for the time being anyway. Cecil had believed for years that one day there would be an almighty sea change. After all, there was little doubt that the vast majority of individuals in the vast majority of countries no longer had much belief or confidence in those who ruled their lives.

Jimmy Cecil was a realist. Jimmy Cecil was a pragmatist. He knew about people, and the way their minds worked. He believed it was absurd to suppose that existence could only be physical. And he had little doubt that the scientific community would one day solve the mystery of consciousness, thus taking a conceptual leap which would be far greater even than the leap from the power of fire to that of nuclear energy.

Meanwhile, Cecil remained devoted to the traditions of conventional government. He remained convinced that any dramatic change in what he regarded to be the natural order of things would lead to a total breakdown in international order, and should be held at bay for as long as possible.

By and large, Jimmy Cecil liked the world just how it was, and intended to continue to do all he could to keep it that way.

Marmaduke Johnson sat alone in his White House office, a small austere room tucked away in an almost forgotten corner. Naturally the president, although highly unlikely ever to publicly recognize his existence, knew where to find him. So did the Secretary of State, the Attorney General, and a number of others, similarly eminent, who would also deny that he existed.

Jimmy Cecil had been absolutely right of course. Johnson had made sure Mikey emailed him a copy of the Ruders Theory right at the very beginning. Just in case. Duke Johnson believed it was his job to ensure that both he and America were always a step ahead.

When he'd heard from Cecil that the paper was not what had been believed, that the Ruders Theory did not stand up, Johnson had decided on a second opinion. After all, Duke Johnson didn't trust anybody. And he certainly didn't trust Jimmy Cecil, even though the two men, and a small group of others like them worldwide, had been supposed to be working as a team over the RECAP affair.

Apart from Connie Pike, there were two, maybe three, scientists in the world who were capable of judging Paul Ruders' work. Johnson had called in the one he thought might be most attracted to the material gain he would be able to put his way, and had presented the paper as if he believed it were genuine. Less than a week later the somewhat bewildered scientist had confirmed that the theory was, to put it bluntly, nonsense.

Ruders, and that mad woman who'd worked with him, had just been crazy eccentrics, it seemed, believing in the impossible, deluding themselves. Paul Ruders had had an excuse, Johnson supposed. He'd been suffering from Alzheimer's. But Johnson still couldn't understand what made the other one tick. It had been Connie Pike who'd supplied the copy of Ruders' work to Mikey. And, as probably the second most foremost figure in the field, nobody had suspected a thing when she'd confirmed its authenticity.

Johnson lit another black cheroot from the stub of the one he had already been smoking. Nobody else smoked in the White House, as far as he knew – and, of course, if they did, he would know. But Marmaduke Johnson's world was a thing apart, a place where he, and only he, made up the rules as he went along.

The little room was hazy with smoke. Johnson liked that, an unsavoury fog providing the illusion of yet another screen behind which he could conceal himself from the prying eyes of democracy.

He leaned back in his chair and inhaled deeply.

With the wonderful benefit of hindsight he wondered how on earth he could have fallen for any of the RECAP mumbo jumbo in the first place.

Unlike Jimmy Cecil, Marmaduke Johnson was not inclined to believe in anything much that he couldn't see with his own eyes, right in front of him, and preferably reach out and touch.

Sandy Jones was at home in Northdown House enjoying an early-evening gin and tonic and a wonderful wintry sunset over the sea, and looking forward to the next day more than she had looked forward to anything in what felt like a very long time.

Three months had passed since the RECAP explosion and all that followed. Life had moved on. In the morning Jones and her twin sons would be flying to New York together to spend Christmas there. She was paying, of course. She didn't mind. She hadn't seen nearly enough of Matt and Lee lately.

She was also hoping to see something of Ed MacEntee. They had been keeping in touch regularly, mostly via Facetime. The old friendship, easy and natural, had definitely been fully restored. Whether or not the old love affair could ever be resurrected still remained to be seen. Jones was beginning to hope quite strongly that it could.

These were comfortable thoughts. But she also couldn't stop thinking about Connie, which was not nearly so comfortable. At first Jones had been so angered by what Connie Pike had done, and had felt so let down by her, that she hadn't been able to be objective.

Since then, as she'd expected would happen, somebody somewhere had leaked to the press that the Ruders Theory didn't stand up. That it was gobbledygook. And eventually sections of the unfortunate piece of work had turned up in various newsrooms. Jones wondered if Jimmy Cecil had been responsible for that. If not, it had been somebody rather like him, she suspected.

Predictably a certain amount of the newspaper flak which followed had been directed at Jones as well as Connie, but most of the thrust in the press still focused on the question of whether or not there had been a major conspiracy and at what level. There was speculation, accurate speculation as it happened, that the security forces and various relevant government departments which may have been involved hadn't known the theory was worthless. However, the American government ignored that, and instead presented the revelation as proof that there had been no conspiracy. The discrediting of the Ruders Theory surely removed any possible reason for there ever having been one, it was argued.

Three months on, the White House spin doctors continued to stick like glue to the original assertion that the Princeton bombing had been instigated by animal rights campaigners, and the RECAP lab destroyed by chance. It was also claimed that Marion Jessop had been accidentally mown down by a hit-and-run driver yet to be traced – which made no sense, of course. Jones had seen the incident. There had been other witnesses. And the lethal Chevy truck had returned for a second go. But this was attributed to its driver panicking, and as Jones was now keeping her head down and neither Connie nor Marion stepped forward to contradict anything, the new official version stood.

Jones had decided that the best thing to do under the circumstances was to step back from it all. The revelation that the Ruders Theory was worthless had not done her reputation any good, because it was she who had first gone public about the theory and claimed that there was a major conspiracy over it.

However, three months was a long time in the world of science. And, fortunately, it seemed that both the media and her colleagues in academia now took the attitude that her earlier outburst had been prompted only by loyalty to old friends – misguided, perhaps, but mildly laudable, all the same.

Jones was still going to be installed as Chancellor of Oxford in the New Year, although she'd heard on the grapevine that there had indeed been those amongst the university's hierarchy who'd made it clear that they would have liked to overturn the vote of the Convocation had they been able to do so.

Her BBC bosses seemed to have taken the attitude that her sudden burst of international fame, albeit tinged with notoriety and linked to a questionable area of science, had added a touch of spice to her image which was not entirely unwelcome. It appeared that they believed her programmes would be all the more popular, and possibly attract a whole new section of the viewing public, in addition to her already established audience.

Her totally out of character behaviour in cancelling filming days at the very last minute was never mentioned again. They had been rescheduled and she was now well into her new series.

But Jones felt that she couldn't take the RECAP affair any further, even if she still wished to, without doing herself irrevocable damage. And she didn't see the point. It was over. Surely it was over?

Connie had been totally discredited. It was leaked to the press that she had more or less co-written the worthless paper with Paul Ruders. The full story of her involvement had yet to be revealed, and quite probably never would be. But her scientific standing had plummeted – along sadly with that of the whole consciousness project worldwide, at least temporarily – and Connie Pike was unlikely to work again, either at Princeton, in the unlikely event of RECAP ever being relaunched, or at any other reputable academic establishment. Somewhat to her surprise, Jones found, as the dust began to settle, that she wished the woman no further harm. And she could only imagine how Connie's relationship with Marion would have suffered.

However, as the days and weeks passed, Jones had also become more and more convinced that she'd missed something. Ultimately it had all been explained in ways that now seemed just a tad too convenient. A little too neat. There was something somewhere that didn't quite add up. And she couldn't get rid of the feeling that Connie Pike had not told her everything.

But this time, there really was nothing in the world Sandy Jones could do about it.

TWENTY-TWO

The previous night the first snow of winter had fallen on Princeton. Connie Pike opened the kitchen door into her little garden at the back and stood for a few moments looking out.

A pale December sun had in places turned the snow the colour of clotted cream, with tinges of blue in the shade. Icicles hanging from the fruit trees shone like white gold. Nobody had yet set foot on the lawn which was covered in a perfect milky white carpet. It was picture book stuff. It was beautiful. It was joyous. But Connie felt no joy. She did not believe she would ever feel joy again.

Her life's work, was no more. Not for her, at any rate, whatever happened ultimately. After the flawed Ruders paper had been made public, discrediting the entire Global Consciousness Project in general, as well as Connie and Paul in particular, Thomas Jessop and the rest of the Princeton supremacy had swiftly reneged on their pledge to rebuild and reinstate RECAP.

Marion, the woman Connie had loved for twenty-five years, was spending more and more time in her own home. Alone. She had told Connie that she'd forgiven her, that she understood. But Connie knew that wasn't true. And as she watched Marion struggling to learn to walk on an artificial leg, while coping with the severe pain which still seemed to be almost continual, Connie could hardly blame her.

She so wanted to tell Marion everything. But she didn't dare. She had unwittingly damaged her partner quite enough. If the whole truth were known it would all begin again. Connie was quite certain of that. And this time the repercussions would surely reverberate worldwide. Many more innocent people could suffer.

Connie took a step outside, walking across the paved area close to her house, the house she was brought up in, and onto the pristine lawn, her rubber boots leaving behind a trail of dark footprints.

She was wearing a shocking pink anorak, lined in orange nylon fur which protruded around the collar and the cuffs, clashing spectacularly with her red hair.

In one green woollen gloved hand she carried a spade. She walked straight to the young apple tree furthest from the house, turned smartly left and took five carefully measured steps towards the now frozen birdbath by the fence. Then she stopped and, quite gently, exploratively, pushed the blade of her spade into the snow.

The snow was still soft, as was the earth beneath it, kept warm by its thick white blanket. But Connie knew that could change any day soon, the snow turn to ice, and the soil beneath it freeze. If she didn't dig now, it might be weeks, or even months, before she would be able to get a spade into the ground again.

She looked up at the cold blue sky and shivered. She was actually warm inside her pink coat, but she shivered because of all that had happened and the quite monumental decision she had made last summer. A decision which had caused terrible death and destruction, but one she had stuck to throughout, because she was quite sure that what had happened already was nothing compared with what would have happened had she taken a different path.

Not only had she so wanted to tell Marion the truth, she'd also been desperate to tell Sandy Jones. She hated knowing that Sandy now thought so badly of her, although believed it likely the English doctor still wouldn't have approved of what Connie had done. Nor accepted her reasoning. Sandy was probably too worldly for that. And, in spite of the risks she had taken in speaking out about RECAP, Connie, the explosion, and so on, Sandy Jones was an ambitious woman who would not have taken kindly to any damage that might have been done to her celebrated career.

Sandy would never have been able to keep the secret. She wouldn't have been able to resist telling the world.

Connie Pike didn't think the world was ready. She hadn't thought the world was ready before the lunatics, who did the dirty work for the other lunatics who dared to sit in government offices, had so horrendously confirmed it. After they had ruthlessly blown up half of Princeton's scientific research block in order to destroy RECAP and murder her and Paul, she'd known that the world wasn't ready.

Connie didn't wish to share the destiny of Carl Oppenheimer. Connie did not wish to be a shatterer of worlds. And neither did she want that to be Paul Ruders' legacy. Paul had been a great humanitarian as well as a genius. And his genius had been such that it had at first risen above the terrible disease of the mind which had so cruelly struck him down.

Indeed the workings of the human mind never failed to amaze Connie, even though she'd spent her entire life studying just that in one way or another. It had been almost as if the early stages of Alzheimer's had opened up certain areas of Paul Ruders' mind, even as they'd closed others, and given him a freedom of thought he would not otherwise have had. All along, of course, he'd confided in Connie, shared his discoveries with her, just as he always had. Although she'd kept that a secret too. But as Paul had become more deluded so he'd proceeded to destroy much of his work, while being convinced that he was improving it. And all the while the interest of the outside agencies which Paul must somehow inadvertently have aroused – and Connie still did not know how – grew more and more sinister.

Mikey had approached Connie and Paul quite aggressively, and told them that he knew Paul had produced an effective theory of consciousness, and that he represented government bodies who insisted upon immediate access. For the good of America.

'If you tell anybody I've made this approach it will be all the worse, for you two and for RECAP,' Mikey had threatened.

Connie hadn't been afraid of Mikey MacEntee, whom she knew vaguely as Ed's rather fanciful brother, but she was afraid of the kind of people she suspected he worked for. So she dismissed at once her first instinct, which was to confide in Ed. She didn't think Mikey MacEntee would harm his own brother. But she feared that his employers might. She feared they might harm almost anyone who got in their way.

Paul, of course, forgot about the confrontation with Mikey almost as it happened, leaving Connie to deal with it. At first Connie stalled.

She knew about Mikey's Walter Mitty tendencies. She told herself he might just be playing one of his games again, even though he had been pretty convincing. But when she and Paul suddenly started being pressurized – and the Internal Revenue investigations and the speeding tickets and all the rest of it began to happen – Connie came to realize that this was no game.

She ultimately decided to appear to comply with Mikey, partly in order to protect Paul himself, but more importantly to protect Paul's work.

It had seemed like such a good idea, at first, to supply Mikey and his employers with one of Paul's later efforts – a completely worthless paper. That way Connie had hoped she would safeguard much more than the future of RECAP.

And as she stood in her back garden on that quite glorious winter's afternoon, Connie Pike still had no intention of allowing the wrong people to get their hands on the real Ruders Theory.

It did exist, of course. Paul Ruders had produced something near miraculous. Something magnificent. And from the beginning Connie Pike had been all too aware of how terribly it could be misused. She remained determined not to let that happen.

Connie didn't know what Jimmy Cecil had told Sandy Jones. Connie didn't even know there was a Jimmy Cecil. But, just like the somewhat mysterious Englishman, she'd always believed that the solution to the secret of consciousness would ultimately prove to be potentially a far more powerful weapon than the splitting of the atom. And that continued to frighten her. Which was partly why she had much preferred the journey of RECAP to the concept of reaching a destination.

Connie Pike tightened her grip on her spade, pushed it more forcefully into the ground, and, using her foot to put extra pressure on the top edge of the blade, began to dig.

She had already played God once, and now she was doing it again. But then, she didn't believe in God. She believed only in the power of the human mind. She believed that, ultimately, human beings held sole responsibility for the future destiny of their race. And that, in the modern world, scientists carried far greater responsibility than anyone in government, because knowledge was so much more powerful than politics. More powerful even than any force, military or otherwise, that governments could exert. She also believed, looking back on the mistakes of the past, that it was not necessarily a straightforward progression for science to meekly hand over to national government a discovery which would have colossal impact on the entire planet.

A metallic clank echoed through the clear air as the cutting edge of Connie Pike's spade hit metal. She dug around, pushing the soil aside, until a steel box, about a foot long, ten inches wide, and six inches deep, was revealed. Then she lifted the box out of the ground and dropped it on to the snow by her feet.

Connie had destroyed every computer file of the original Paul Ruders Theory, and she had done so irrevocably. She'd known the Crime Scenes Investigators would find nothing on the desktop iMac at Paul's house, even though it was true that she had been somehow drawn there after the explosion. Perhaps as a kind of pilgrimage. Or maybe just out of guilt. She wasn't sure. But she'd lied to Sandy Jones about that too. She'd been to the house days earlier, when she had known Paul was at the university, using the key he'd kept hidden in a plant pot in his potting shed. She'd checked out the iMac, and thrown Paul's laptop – which did contain a copy of the theory – into Lake Carnegie, replacing it with another, confident that he was at a stage in his degenerative illness when he was past noticing.

She had half wanted to destroy the theory altogether. And for ever. But the scientist in her, the explorer of the mind, had been congenitally unable to do so.

She'd kept just one copy of the true Ruders Theory of Consciousness. Nobody else in the world knew of its existence. It was a hard copy. It was, in fact, the original. An extraordinary document comprising over 300 pages of A4 paper, covered with words, figures, and equations all in Paul Ruders' neat and meticulous hand. And it lay, wrapped in several layers of plastic, within the steel box at her feet.

Connie did not intend to do anything with the document. Not yet. After all, more than ever before she believed the world wasn't ready. She wanted only to look at it again. To hold it. To study it. To be privy once more to mankind's greatest mystery. Then she would bury it again in her garden.

A bolt of excitement shot through her as she carried the steel box indoors, opened it, and removed the contents. She unravelled the protective plastic and held out, on the upturned palms of both hands, the thick sheaf of handwritten pages.

The real Ruders paper lay before her. Not only Paul's finest achievement, but almost certainly the most remarkable scientific advancement of modern times. Possibly the most remarkable scientific advancement of any time.

She had in her grasp The Secret of Consciousness. Humanity's last great mystery. Her eyes filled with tears.

It was pretty much all that Connie Pike had left now. And, one day, she hoped, perhaps one day, it would be possible to give this great gift of a great man to the world. Without fear.

ACKNOWLEDGEMENTS

The most grateful thanks are due to the late Professor Robert G. Jahn, founder of PEAR, Princeton Engineering Anomalies Research (the inspiration for my fictional RECAP), and to Brenda J. Dunne, MS, twenty-eight years PEAR laboratory manager. They welcomed me to Princeton, invited me to spend time in their unique lab – even taking part in some of their experiments – and shared with me their belief in, and passion for, the extraordinary project that has been a life's work for them both.

Thanks also to New Jersey State Police for permitting me to explore their unusual police station at Princeton (including the cell block!); to my good friend Lucius Barre for his assistance throughout my New York and Princeton research trip; and to the late Ian Robertson, former star of the Kirov Ballet, for his most particular guidance on crossing international borders.

Special thanks to my editor Kate Lyall Grant for allowing me to publish a book which is both dear to my heart and something of a departure from usual.

And finally, a huge thank you to my long-time agent and treasured friend Tony Peake, for his continual support and encouragement through the good times and the not so good. As ever, Mr Peake.